T0265980

'*The Kennedy Moment* is that rare and clever thing—a gentle and moving thriller. Old friends, reunited, are suddenly offered the chance to influence the terrible fate of countless others. Now they face an awful dilemma—whether to act on a once-in-a-lifetime opportunity, or do the much safer thing—nothing. The proposition is outrageous and compelling and the question one of ethics. But is their plan the most unethical thing imaginable? Or might it be their moral duty? In this intelligent, thoughtful work, Peter Adamson artfully persuades us that there might be such a thing as humanitarian terrorism.'

—Staunch Book Prize

'In lucid, persuasive prose Peter Adamson tells a truly gripping story about something profoundly important.'

—*Literary Review*

'This persuasively page-turning political thriller is filled with richly drawn characters and authentic plotting. It's superb.'

—*Saga* Magazine

'This tense political thriller is a marvellously uplifting novel about a group using their friendships to collectively defrag the mental debris accrued in middle age and rediscover the young believers within.'   —*Morning Star*

'Intelligent and thought-provoking, a suspenseful and gripping tale with well-rounded characters and a plot that is outrageous yet plausible.   —*Oxford Times*

'Brilliant, moving, splendidly written, keeps you at the edge of your chair until the very last minute.'

—Marco Vianello-Chiodo

'How ingenious the central conceit, how well-crafted the writing, how alive the characters, the accelerating pace, the shifting scenarios, the building suspense and the surprising denouement. This book screams with relevance in this dark time of Trump and empire's decline.'   —Robert Cohen

'A great story and very moving. It is that rare book which makes you feel sad when you finish it because the process of reading it has been so enjoyable.'   —Fionnuala McCredie QC

Praise for Peter Adamson's previous novels

'A tender and joyous celebration, a book that shows that ordinary lives, half-successful lives, even failed lives, can be lit with glory. At the end I was weeping with happiness. A beautiful, subtle, and very loving book.'   —William Nicholson

'I was captivated by the atmosphere but it was the sheer thoughtfulness of this novel that interested me... one of the most consistently intelligent and fascinating novels about what goes on in people's minds that I've read for a long time. Quite mesmeric in its hold.'   —Margaret Forster

'It took me into a world I knew very little about and opened my eyes to its beauty and interest. What I especially admired was the way the characters were both representative of large ideas and yet also fully human... it's a huge achievement.'
          —Alain de Botton

THE
KENNEDY
MOMENT

PETER ADAMSON

myriad m∞

Myriad Editions
An imprint of New Internationalist Publications
The Old Music Hall, 106–108 Cowley Rd,
Oxford OX4 1JE
www.myriadeditions.com

First published in 2018 by Myriad Editions
This Myriad paperback published in 2019
First printing
1 3 5 7 9 10 8 6 4 2

Copyright © Peter Adamson 2018

The moral right of the author has been asserted

Thanks to Chandos Music for kind permission to quote from
'To Bobby' by Joan Baez. Copyright © Joan Baez, 1972

Every attempt has been made to obtain the necessary
permissions for use of copyright material. If there have been
any omissions, we apologise and will be pleased to make
appropriate acknowledgement in any future edition

All rights reserved. No part of this publication may be
reproduced, stored in a retrieval system, or transmitted in any
form or by any means without the written permission of the
publisher, nor be otherwise circulated in any form of binding
or cover other than that in which it is published and without a
similar condition being imposed on the subsequent purchaser

A CIP catalogue record for this book
is available from the British Library

ISBN: 978-1-912408-26-9
ISBN (ebook): 978-1-912408-08-5

Printed and bound in Great Britain
by Clays Ltd, Elcograf S.p.A.

To the memory of
James P Grant

Author's note
None of the principal characters in this story has
ever admitted to being involved in the events
described here. All names have therefore
been changed.

PART ONE

1 | Don't wear a suit

Oxford, April 28th, 1980

Stephen Walsh frowned down at the keyboard of the *ZX80* computer. Behind it, along with its packaging, stood a fourteen-inch television displaying a steadily blinking cursor. Holding the manual flat in one hand, he pecked at the rubber keyboard with the other, peering up over half-moon spectacles with each expectant prod.

Dear...

We've lost touch, the months drifting into years and the years into decades.

He missed the deep travel and satisfying clack of his typewriter keys but stared, captivated, by the letters appearing as if by magic on the screen.

We're all to blame; the immediate subverting the important, as it ever will. But we said we wouldn't let it happen and so...

He looked in vain for the carriage return as he neared the end of the line.

... I'm inviting you here for a weekend so we can all eat, drink and be miserable, lament how middle-aged we are, and talk about who we were and what we were going to do and what's become of us all.

3

The room was dim in the middle of the afternoon. At either end of the couch, parchment-shaded lamps cast a barely perceptible light on old floorboards. Three of the walls were lined with bookshelves interrupted here and there by niches in which hung faded Soviet posters from the 1920s.

I'm suggesting the first weekend in October…

After typing a few more paragraphs he looked up from the screen and let his eyes travel over the volumes of *History Workshop Journal* and *Radical History Review,* most of them ragged with scraps of paper that had been inserted in their pages. The machine was emitting an audible hum he was not sure he could live with.

He stood and crossed to the window seat from which he could look down on the perfect lawn set in its mellow quadrangle of Cotswold stone. Facing him on the other side of the quad were the stone-mullioned windows of the rooms belonging to the Regius Professor of Modern History. That well-known reactionary having recently decamped for Cambridge, the suite was currently unoccupied. The décor was no doubt in need of updating, but the important thing was whether the appointment would be made before the start of Michaelmas Term. In time for their shabby grandeur to host his little reunion.

Among the many rules and observances in Michael Lowell's life, including being in his office before 7.00am on weekdays and 8.00am on Saturdays, was the stricture that, if possible, no piece of paper should be handled more than once. But the letter he now held in his hand, standing on the little wrought-iron balcony of his apartment in the lakeside town of Nyon in the Canton of Vaud, Switzerland, had already been picked up three times as the bells of St Michel struck the half hour.

We can all lament how middle-aged we are… talk about

4

who we were and what we were going to do and what's become
of us all.

Away to the west he could see the autoroute, already
burdened with traffic glinting in the early-morning sun.
Normally he would have been in advance of the rush. But on
this particular morning, Friday, May 2nd, 1980, his routine
had faltered. Beyond the harbour the mist was beginning to
lift, the lake slowly disrobing on what promised to be another
fine spring day as he read through the second page again.

*Why now? I don't know. The old man died two months ago
and I suppose it stirred up the subliminals (as well as embarrassing me with an immodest inheritance). Anyway that's
probably what started me thinking of lost youth and time
passing, of old ideals and the old friends who once shared them.*

Underneath the signature, in a scrawl of green ink, was a
handwritten postscript:

*'Michael – I already talked to the lovely Seema, who'll
definitely be coming. She's divorced now, as I expect you
know, so don't wear a suit.'*

Below him the roofs of the old town were beginning to
glow in the first of the sun. Later in the day, Mont Blanc and
the Aiguilles would be visible, but for the moment it was only
possible to make out the faint blur of France. He blinked
against the astonishing light. Out on the lake a lateen boat,
motionless in the calm, had already spread its nets.

Seema Mir. Had there been a day in the last twenty years
when he hadn't thought of her?

One of the advantages of being the creative director of
an advertising agency is that you can stare out of the
window for hours on end and people will not only believe
you are working but will quite probably assume you are
doing something brilliant. Toby Jenks, who frequently took

advantage of the scope thus offered, was in fact standing by his window because he was ever so slightly inebriated at four o'clock in the afternoon and had felt himself to be at some risk of nodding off at his desk.

It was the first week of May and the window in question admitted a dull London light into the modern third-floor office on the west side of Berkeley Square. Below, the trees were swaying slightly, much like Toby himself as he locked his hands on top of his balding head and pushed out a fat bottom lip. It had been a bad week. Really, a bad week. Monday had seen his fortieth birthday come and go. Tuesday had brought more hate-mail, including one particularly vituperative letter from a woman in Queensland. Wednesday he had discovered that Sarah had been back to the house and taken away the rest of her clothes and all of her shoes. Worst of all, the day's second post had come and gone, forcing him to face up to the fact that, for the first time in a decade or more, he had not been nominated for a BTA Award.

Over the rooftops a weak sun was attempting to push through the clouds that had covered the Home Counties all week. In the square itself the trees were just coming into bud and a group of young people who might have been students were stretching out on the lawns. That was the thing in this business; you were put out to grass when you stopped being young. As soon as you were no longer a rising star you were a black hole. And probably that's where he was right now, poised at the dread point just past the top of a mixed metaphor. He blinked his eyes into focus. Under his window, a few of the regular dog walkers had gathered by one of the gates to the park.

He thought about pouring himself another Scotch. Ten minutes earlier the bottle had been resolutely put away in the low rosewood cabinet that housed a bank of television screens.

Rubbing both ears hard to wake himself up, he returned to his desk and began looking through his in-tray: product briefs, draft pitches, story-boards, corporate prospectuses, all of which promised nothing but terminal tedium. Coming across a couple of typed letters dictated earlier in the week, he signed them with his initials and transferred them with a flourish to the out-tray. He had cultivated being known by his initials ('friends call me TJ'). And for many years he had also affected silk ties in a different pastel shade for each day of the week. It was an idiosyncrasy that had quickly become famous in the advertising world, as he had known it would, and whenever it elicited comment he would explain that it was the only way most of his colleagues would know what day it was. In retaliation, the thirty or so creative types in the department had taken to referring to the days of the week by their colours ('Thank God its Pinkday'). He might also have been disappointed to know that he was commonly referred not as 'TJ' but as 'Old Tobe', or sometimes 'The Toby Jug', and just occasionally 'High Jenks'.

And, to top it all, the morning post had brought not an invitation to the BTA Awards dinner but a letter from, of all people, Stephen bloody Walsh. *The first weekend in October. Eat, drink and be miserable. Old friends and old ideals.*

He gave up on the in-tray and returned to the window, looking out on a city that was already getting ready for evening. From the far side of the square the row of plate-glass windows that was Jack Barclay's Rolls Royce showroom blazed with the reflected glow of an unexpected sunset. Across the city, lights were going out in shops and offices as hundreds of executives, middle-managers, accountants, designers, copy-writers, film editors, space-buyers, secretaries, shop assistants, hurried through the streets, escaping to evenings of boredom, bliss or argument.

And in front of it all his own reflection confronted him, refusing to go away.

Stephen bloody Walsh.

And underneath the signature, the sly, handwritten postscript with its pretentious Greek 'e's and green ink: *'Tobe, I already heard from Hélène who's definitely coming. So bring a good supply of mints. Ab imo pectore, Stephen.'*

Michael engaged cruise control as the autoroute began to clear. Ahead lay the city of Geneva and a day of meetings, personnel decisions, data-checking, periodic performance reviews, mid-term strategic plans.

... talk about who we were and what we were going to do and what's become of us all.

He took the exit for Pregny and began working his way down to the lake. In twenty years he had never been able even to hear the name 'Stephen' without also hearing the words he had spoken that evening in the small back bar of the Eagle and Child at the end of Trinity Term, 1960: *'You know I believe in speaking truth to power, Michael. But I'm afraid I also believe in speaking truth to friends. And the fact is, of course, she's turned you down because she finds you just a little bit too dull.'*

Stephen had clinked beer glasses with him to show that this had been said in the spirit of honest, straightforward male comradeship. It had been a struggle to receive the words in the same spirit. And it had been a struggle ever since.

He indicated right again and made his way up through the leafy suburbs behind the European headquarters of the United Nations, unable to prevent himself being drawn back to Stephen's words of that evening long ago.

'Pair of them in tears. Couldn't help hearing the odd word. Said if she was looking at the next fifty years she wanted a

little bit more. Something about you being incapable of ever doing anything that would surprise her.'

The blue-and-white flag of the World Health Organization flew at the barrier as he turned in. Was it an exaggeration? Had there been days in the last twenty years when he hadn't thought of her? Last thing at night. Or first thing on waking. Or at odd moments during the day. In a meeting. In the lab. On a plane. It had never needed much – just a passing thought that strayed too near the buried magnet of her and was deflected inwards, making contact with a little metallic click in the mind – and there she was again, as vivid as ever: the calm amusement in eyes that seemed always to be expressing mild surprise; the incipient smile ever at the edges of the mouth; the maddeningly imperturbable composure; the sheer excitement of her; the power to slip effortlessly past any guard he might from time to time have put in place.

Waved through without showing ID, he began patrolling up and down between the strips of lawn, crossing wet patches of blacktop where the early-morning sprinklers had over-reached themselves. But the parking lot was full at this hour and he was forced to take the ramp down into the *souterrain*, pulling off his sunglasses and braking to avoid the scarred curve of the wall.

… old ideals and the old friends who once shared them.

He turned off the engine. The dimness soothed and he let his head fall back, listening to the engine ticking in a crypt of silence. Above him were eight floors of offices, corridors, conference rooms in which three thousand people spent their days, most of them knowing that youthful hopes had long ago run into the sands of bureaucracy. He reached across to the passenger seat for the old Gladstone doctor's bag. Those years in the field had not been like this. Working from dawn 'til dusk on Bhola Island. And later, in Africa, when they were finally closing in on the virus. Had he thought of her even then, in those last days in Merkka and Bardere as they had trudged through the endless rains, driven on by the thought that the greatest of all killer diseases had been narrowed down to just those two villages?

In the gloom the ticking had almost stopped. From somewhere an elevator whined. No, not even then had she been lost to him. Like a paraphrase of Blake – *'there is a moment in each day that Satan cannot find'* – there had always been a moment in his day that Seema Mir could find.

By six o'clock, Toby was perched on a revolving stool in the cellar bar of The Warsaw, just off Soho's Poland Street and wondering if any other member-in-good-standing of London's Australian diaspora might be dropping in. He swivelled round to face the early-evening crowd. Everything too dark or too light. Too much bloody contrast. Too much bloody drama. Is that Gilbert? Grinning all over the place. Sliding round the bar like a fucking oil slick. Grin. Grin. Fucking Gilbert. Fucking Ogilvy's. Taken to greeting his staff with a mock-opera rendition of 'Just one Cornetto' and introducing himself as 'The Man who put a Tiger in your Tank'. Might as well be waving his fucking BTA invitation in my face.

He looked away to avoid a greeting from some agency types descending the stairs. It hadn't always been like this; it was here that he'd had some of his own best ideas. The sensational 'cool girl' ad, with the lovely Silky Mathilde. And the loneliness of the long distance commuter with the Dirk Bogarde lookalike, a man's life set to the rhythm of the train. And the BTA-winning *Mens Sana* campaign for the chain of fitness centres; the only time, he reflected, when his Classics degree had been of the slightest use.

Stephen bloody Walsh.

He spun back to the bar and picked up his drink. Not even half six. Could just pop back to the office, see if it's come in the late bag. Fuck no. Face facts. See that face wobbling in that shallow little circle of Scotch, big and pink and pathetic? That's you, mate, and you're off the screen, wobble, wobble, bye-bye, over the hill and far away. A fresh crowd was descending from the street. Theatre or film types. Or glorious pioneers of the age of videotape. Best of all, yes, best of all, this was the place where he had thought up the first wordless commercial. He saw it now through the gloom of the bar: the tanned, thirty-something Australian descending into the cellar, all laid-back masculinity, listening warily to the voices of effete, upper-class Brits ordering martinis 'with a twist' and peach schnapps with Chambord, followed by a slow, nervous retreat, making his way backwards up the cellar steps and emerging with relief into the last of the evening sunlight which merged into a glowing, overflowing pint of Australian lager.

His reflection confronted him again from between the liquor bottles on theatre-lit glass shelves. He had seen Stephen once or twice over the years: the odd lunch in the West End, and at the college gaudy he had regretted attending. Even back in the day they had had nothing in common. And now they had considerably less than nothing: the adman and the pinko academic, Pauncho and Lefty. No way would he be going. He swung around again to face the mounting din of the cellar. Fucking Stephen. *'Talk about who we were going to be'*. Who am I? Where am I? Same fucking bar. Same fucking sawdust on the floor. Sawdust! It's the West End for Christ's sake! Place stuffed full of Gilberts. Gilberts to the right of him, Gilberts to the left of him, Gilberts to the front of him, trolleyed and plastered. Into the BTA dinner they rode, when can their glory fade, when can that speech be made? But not,

not, Toby Jenks. He frowned into the bottom of the glass. Couldn't stand it all again anyway. All the sham bonhomie. All the cod conviviality. All that pathetic pretence at surprise, all that gushing over people who'd had diddly-squat to do with anything, air-kissing some bimbette from Thames TV who wouldn't know a decent commercial if it ramraided her fucking sweet shop. Ten years of it all, and then suddenly wham-bam-thank-you-Toby and you're not even at one of the round tables with the candlelit place-name, not even one of the also-rans clapping too hard and pretending they don't have a modest little speech tucked away in the inside pocket of the tux, eating their little hearts out with smiles like fucking rigor mortis. No. No way would he go. He had no desire to see Stephen bloody Walsh again. Creep. Marx in Doc Martens. With his aristocratic background and his ludicrous estuary accent. Of course he won't have changed his fucking ideals, he'd never left fucking Oxford, except for a few years on the wild side over at Cambridge.

The bar seemed more crowded now, undifferentiated waves of sound crashing over him, seas of words building and breaking over faces and bodies and the too-bright lights that hurt the backs of his eyes. Jesus, blind as a welder's dog and it's not even seven o'clock. A slim young woman descended the stairs, looking around for her date. It would be good to see Hélène again though. God knows what she'd think of him these days. Didn't think too highly of him back then, as he remembered it. And Seema of course, he'd always loved to gaze on Seema and admire. And Michael. Michael was his friend.

Seema Mir had developed a mild aversion to working in the faculty library with its hushed, cough-inducing atmosphere. Instead, non-teaching days would usually find her in one of the Greenwich Village cafés or, if she needed the exercise, the reading room of the Harvard Club on 68th Street. It was true that some of her favourite haunts were public places and not especially quiet, but she preferred their buzz and vague background sense of connectedness to the self-consciously scholarly ambience of the Bobst or the Cooper Union.

On this particular morning, Tuesday, May 6th, 1980, she had walked the forty blocks uptown to the public reading room of the New York Public Library. There, on one of the vast polished oak tables, she spread the various books and papers from which she was attempting to put together a gene-alogy for the Hemings family. But by eleven o'clock she was forced to admit that mapping the relationships of plantation slaves in nineteenth-century Virginia could not compete with the prospect of coming face to face again with Michael Lowell.

There had been no correspondence. At first, it would have been too painful. And later, perhaps, too awkward. She knew he was living in Geneva, that he was still unmarried, that he had risen rapidly in his chosen career, as they had all known he would. But beyond that, nothing. She leaned back in her chair to look up at the rather absurd *trompe l'œil* ceiling of clouds and cherubs. Probably he would not have changed much; he was not the type to put on weight or let himself get out of condition. Stephen had once said that Michael had contrived to look middle-aged in his early twenties. For a few more minutes she was able to focus on her work, but her thoughts soon drifted back to the question that had frayed her concentration all morning: would it be asking for trouble to accept Stephen's invitation and meet Michael? She stared again at the ceiling. The cherubs offered no help.

Talk about what's become of us all... of old ideals and old friends...

Impatient with herself, she began checking the dates for John Wayles, born Lancaster, England, who had been the first of his line to arrive in Virginia, and for his son, also John, who had fathered six children with an 'Unknown African Woman'. Weren't they all? She bit lightly on the metal ferrule of the pencil. She had, she realized, thought of Michael with increasing wistfulness over the years; drawn to his undemonstrative maturity. But hadn't that been the problem? That he had been *too* mature, too steady? Wasn't that the very reason she had said 'no', as gently as she knew how, when he had proposed to her so very formally in the Botanical Gardens at the end of that long Oxford summer?

For a few minutes more she focused on the web of solid and dotted pencil lines that linked the names, across and down, ending with the twenty or so Fossetts and Hughes who were the direct descendants of her Unknown African Woman. Had she been a housemaid, or a cook, summoned from the kitchen to her master's bed? Had she been Ibo, Yoruba, Ashanti? And what sort of relationship had it been that had created all of the lives spread out before her in the New York Public Library two hundred years later? It had been in a library, far smaller than this and smelling of age and mildew, that she had first met Michael Lowell. She put down the pencil and rested her elbows on the desk. What else had she been seeking when she rejected him? And look where opting for more excitement had got her. The previous week she had run into Howard in Bryant Park. It was only the second time they had met since the divorce and 'unkempt' had been the rather British word that had come to mind. They had chatted amicably enough, but she had refused his rather forlorn invitation to lunch.

For the next half hour she copied on to one page all the notes she had on the Unknown African Woman: the daughter a mulatto, the granddaughter three-quarters white, the great granddaughter seven-eighths white, the descendants merging imperceptibly into the white world, probably without ever knowing that their forebears included both the Unknown African Woman and the six-foot-two-inch 'straight as a gun barrel' Virginia lawyer Thomas Jefferson.

It would be fun to see Toby again as well, though they usually got together on his annual visit to Madison Avenue. Tom, too, though he was apparently in the process of relocating to New York anyway. She would take the weekend to think about it. Inching her chair back, sneakers squeaking on the polished floor, she began gathering up her papers, knowing that at the level of the mind where decisions are really made the question was already settled: she would be in Oxford as the leaves on the trees in St Giles were turning yellow and the streetlamps were haloed with the first tinge of frost.

Abidjan, Côte d'Ivoire, May 14th, 1980

Five thousand miles from the New York Public Library, in a sweltering outpatients' clinic amid the corrugated zinc roofs of Abidjan's slums, Hélène Hevré helped the boy to perch on the edge of the treatment table. He was a Mossi child of perhaps eight or nine years old, wearing only a pair of khaki shorts and a thick swaddling of dusty rags around his right arm. The mother, hardly any bigger than her son, hovered in the doorway, speaking too quickly for Hélène to catch every word.

Fighting against the tiredness washing through her system like some debilitating internal tide, she began unwrapping the layers of progressively less dusty rags. Bared, the boy's elbow was swollen, the skin wrinkled, inelastic. The bones had healed well, but whoever had treated him had splinted the break straight out. Tearfully, the mother began reciting in undulating Mooré rhythms all the things that the boy could no longer do with his useless stick of an arm. Nodding her head in sympathy, Hélène laid a gentle hand on the child's shoulder. The only X-ray machine had been out of commission for over a month.

Two or three more relatives had ventured in, murmuring support: the boy was useless; could not wield a *daba*, could not tie a knot, could not pour water or light a lamp, could not hook a cocoa pod. Once the screen had been tugged into place, Hélène eased the boy into a lying position and asked the assistant to fill the sink with water. Speaking in a calm whisper, she explained what she was about to do. It would hurt. But the pain would not last long. And soon he would have his arm back. The boy set his face in a fierce expression and stared upwards at the ceiling fan. More relatives had now appeared in the consulting room. The tallest of them, peering over the top of the screen, was starting up a running commentary. Unwrapping a roll of dry casting, Hélène handed it to the trainee and nodded again towards the sink. The boy was still staring determinedly at the slowly turning blades.

Steadying herself, she pinned the boy's upper arm to the table while her right hand slipped underneath the forearm. On the other side of the screen the commentary grew more excited, provoking a rhythmic whispering which might have been prayer. Holding her breath, she began to lift the forearm away from the table, steadily applying the pressure until there was a sharp 'crack' and a stifled moan from the boy's compressed lips. Hélène glanced down. The boy's eyes were squeezed tight, the jaws locked, the muscles of legs, stomach, buttocks held rigid so that the thin body had lifted slightly from the table. As the forearm reached the upright position the boy let out a long hiss of breath. Behind the screen, the mother had begun a low moaning.

Nodding to the trainee to hold the boy's arm in place, Hélène formed wet rolls of plaster into a casting around

16

the now-bent elbow. Finishing off with a clean gauze, she placed the arm across his chest while she fitted the sling. '*Courageux, courageux,*' she said, handing him a tissue while the trainee pulled the screen aside. The relatives surged forward, all talking at once as Hélène took a bottle of Fanta from the fridge.

Ten minutes later, she was sipping iced water on the veranda of her quarters, tucked away along with five or six other bungalows in a corner of the compound. It was the hour of relaxation, the outpatients gone and the worst of the day's heat over. On the table beside her, an envelope postmarked Oxford had been slit open with a bamboo paper knife. She removed the straw and raised the glass to her lips, draining the last of the iced water. Even before she had begun to read, the green ink had stirred a faint memory.

We've lost touch, the months drifting into years and the years into decades.

The exhaustion seemed to be washing over her in slow, irresistible waves. Surely this was something more than ordinary fatigue? Or could it be just the accumulated tiredness of years of overwork? Stephen Walsh, by contrast, obviously had leisure to muse over old friends and time passing. And to add a sly, handwritten postscript. *I heard back from the others before I'd even located your whereabouts. They'll all be here, though I have a suspicion Toby's only coming in the hope that you'll be there.*

She sank back into the chair. Perhaps she would feel less tired after the rains had freshened the air. All day the skies had been promising a downpour, and now the first warm drops were beginning to spill over on to the dust of the compound. In Haute-Volta, where she had been all the previous week, the real rains had already begun and had quickly turned the loose, laterite roads into swirling red rivers that had slowed their progress to a crawl. The little girl had died just a few minutes before they pulled in to the village, the tiny body wasted, the legs widest at the knee, the skin grey and stretched across stark ribs. Her name had apparently meant 'Bright Hope'.

... talk about who we were and what we were going to do.

Later, back at the clinic, she had begun filling out the forms: *Cause of death – measles.* Forms that would be used to tick boxes in municipal offices generating more forms in the Ministry of Health and eventually be forwarded to the regional office of the World Health Organization in Brazzaville and thence, in the fullness of time, to WHO headquarters in Geneva where they would one day no doubt appear on the desk of Dr Michael Lowell. It would be good to see Michael again, and he might need to be reminded about the thousands of Bright Hopes.

Her eyelids drooped. On her next home leave, she would get herself checked out at McGill. She might even be able to take in Stephen's little reunion on the way. Why had she ever lost touch? With Seema, who had been her closest friend and had now become an American citizen. And with Toby, her long-lost love, her Australian Lord Byron, her chain-smoking Ginsberg who had howled at every convention and who was now apparently an advertising executive.

She sat up, wanting more water and staring again at the letter: surely she was strong enough to face Toby again with a lighter heart; to push into the attic of childish memories those weeks that had seemed so deeply scarring at the time; to smile at the memory of his wounding loss of interest when she had refused to sleep with him in that long, hot summer at the dawn of the 1960s.

Thanks to an out-of-date address, Tom Keeley received his

invitation a week or two later than the others. When it finally arrived on the morning of Saturday, May 17th, 1980, via his office at the Centers for Disease Control in Atlanta, Georgia, he passed it wordlessly across the breakfast table to his wife.

Caroline scanned it. 'We're on vacation that week.'

'I know. Good excuse.'

'Shouldn't you liked to have gone?'

'Not madly, no.'

She looked at him suspiciously over the top of her reading glasses. 'So-oo, no ex-girlfriends you'd like to spend the weekend with?'

He gave her a saintly smile. 'I spent all my time studying.'

On the Sunday he wrote a brief, handwritten reply, thanking Stephen for the invitation but telling him that, on the dates in question, they would be taking the children on a two-week tour of their own home state of Virginia. He sent his best wishes for the weekend and asked to be remembered to the others.

Tom Keeley never expected to hear anything more about the reunion. He was wrong.

2 | I would know her by heart

Thursday, October 2nd, 1980

Hélène Hevré arrived at Heathrow Airport at a little after seven o'clock in the evening after a six-hour flight from Félix Houphouet-Boigny International Airport, Abidjan. Toby Jenks was there to meet her. It would probably have been more convenient for her to take the coach directly to Oxford, but Toby had written imploring her to stay overnight in London and travel up to Oxford with him on the following afternoon. Rather weakly, she thought afterwards, she had agreed.

Over the two decades since they had last seen each other, it would be fair to say that she had carried with her a vivid mental image of the man who had broken her young heart, and so she had been more than a little shocked to be greeted by the older, larger, sadder figure who had stepped forward, arms outstretched, as she had emerged from the baggage hall. To her own mortification, it had taken her a second or two to recognize him. And she had suffered on his behalf.

Things had been easier once they were seated side-by-side deep in the leather seats of his sports car, a dark red coupé of an exotic make she failed to recognize. 'So unbelievably unfair, Hel. No, I mean really unfair. You just haven't changed one little bit. No, I mean it, not one little bit. Must be your incorruptible virtue.' The comment cut through the years to the time when he had first teased her about her alleged puritanism. Back then, it had been all part of his pride-protecting banter following her rejections of his over-confident sexual advances. But now, twenty years on, it seemed that allusions to her supposed virtuousness were not only to be revived but also routinely contrasted to his own self-confessed decadence.

'Are you cold, sweetheart? I expect it's all a bit of a shock.'

'I'm fine, Toby, really.'

'Damn this traffic. Who are all these people? Where are they all going?'

Hélène Hevré had in fact changed, becoming one of the not inconsiderable number of women who are more attractive at forty than at twenty. She had lost weight when she had first gone to live in Africa, and had lost even more over recent months. The once unformed face had found structure and the pale-blue eyes that had once contributed to an impression of blandness, were harder and more experienced, narrowed by the light of the tropics and, Toby did not fail to observe, startlingly attractive against the warm gold of her skin.

He changed down aggressively and turned off the North Circular. 'Got to lose all this.' Hélène remained silent, absorbed by the striving of the city as they left the stream of traffic and began to thread a way through the narrow streets around Lammas Park.

'Of course I haven't changed much either. You needn't bother to tell me.' He glanced quickly at her with a slight wince, a pained 'what can I do?' facial expression with which she was to become familiar.

'You don't look particularly happy, Toby, if that's what you mean.' The manner, too, had changed. He had not remembered directness among her many qualities.

'Happy? Of course I'm not happy. Nobody's happy. How very Sixties of you, sweetheart.'

Hélène watched a group of young mothers struggling to negotiate pushchairs through the revolving door of a glass-fronted coffee shop. 'But you're happily married, yes?'

'There you go again.' He reached to pat her knee but she intercepted his hand and placed it back on the wheel without changing her expression. He held out his open palm and she gave it a gentle slap, the old games beginning as if the years between had never been. For a second or two he made a pretence of being rebuked and concentrated ostentatiously on driving.

'Okay, I'll confess to being a little bit married. But not the other thing.' He changed up as the traffic thinned a little on South Ealing Road and turned again to glance at her with an exaggerated cheerfulness. 'As a matter of fact I'm rather seriously semi-detached at the moment.'

Hélène smiled and continued to look out of the window, avoiding any examination of her own feelings at meeting the man Toby Jenks had become. Like Ottawa and Montreal, London had also shifted up several gears since she had last looked upon its streets. Every second her eyes seemed to sweep up more wealth, more variety, more clamour for attention than could be seen in all the villages of the Sahel put together. 'So have the others arrived?'

'No idea. I only called you.'

'Very kind of you, Toby. You in touch with any of them?'

'Saw the lovely Seema in New York last year. Very happily divorced. Doing well too, as far as I could see. Writing something called a book.' The wince again. 'And of course I see Michael from time to time. You?'

'Haven't seen any of them. Dreadful really. It's being in such an out-of-the-way place, I suppose. Your mind tends to

22

get cut off, too. Poor excuse, I know.'

'Might be the boonies, but at least you're doing something useful.' The wince again.

'Isn't what you do useful?'

'Christ, no! I think I can say with all due modesty that I haven't done anything remotely useful in the last twenty years.'

She gave him a patient look and turned her attention back to the streets. Cocooned in the car, she felt secure. But the thought of being alone out there filled her with something close to panic.

Toby glanced at her again as they ran into traffic on Ealing Green. She was snuggled low down in the seat, chin lifted in a slight defiance that brought the young Hélène rushing back. She returned his glance. 'That's what the weekend's supposed to be all about isn't it – what we've all done with our lives? Do you imagine Stephen sees himself as judge and jury?'

'Probably. Little creep. It's bound to be absolutely excruciating. Especially for me.'

'So why go?'

'Well, I'll tell you, Hel,' he said, accelerating into a gap in the second lane, 'I'd go through a lot worse to spend the weekend with you. Only I was thinking, why don't we forget Stephen and Oxford. Go to Paris? Or Rome? Or Reykjavik – Reykjavik's nice at this time of year.'

'You have no idea what Reykjavik's like at this time of year. Did you ever think of going back to Australia?'

Toby gave an exaggerated sigh as they reached the north end of the Green. '*Persona non grata*, my dear.'

'You're not serious?'

''Fraid so, sweetheart. Wouldn't have a bar of me. Entirely my own fault of course. Did this little series of spots for a well-known brand of Aussie lager. Or at least it's well known now. Sales through the roof. Alcoholism up fifteen per cent worldwide. Ditto domestic violence and cirrhosis of the liver. Scuds of awards. Fat bonus for TJ. Whole thing a staggering triumph from start to finish.'

Hélène smiled as Toby forced his way out onto Castlebar Road. The Australian accent, she noticed, had all but gone.

'So what went wrong?'

'One or two Aussies marginally underwhelmed. Felt I'd taken *Homo Australopithecus* a bit literally. Wrong image of the Australian male. And the female. Betrayed my own culture, apparently. Bloke in the *Herald* said I'd portrayed Oz to the world as a country where speech was an affectation. Kindly not to darken the Antipodean doorstep again. Seemed to think I was saying the only thing an Aussie female was good for was pulling a pint while some bloke looked down the front of her dress.'

'And were you saying that?'

'Absolutely. You're sure you never saw that ad?'

'It'll all die down. Go back and do some *pro bono* work for the Sydney Opera House.'

'Great idea, Hel.' He raised both hands off the wheel for a moment, spreading his fingers. 'I can see it now. Giant corks dangling all-round the edge of that roof. I could even write them a libretto – "Diggers and Divas: the Opera".' They were turning now into the driveway of a large house at the bottom of Eaton Rise. Hélène looked up at the ground-floor widows as the car came to a halt.

'Will your wife be home?'

'Wife? Home? My dear, what quaint notions you do bring into a man's life.'

That night, Toby Jenks lay in bed congratulating himself on being less inebriated than usual and thinking with full heart and moist eyes of the lean, sun-tanned and still-young woman he had installed, comfortably he hoped, in the third-floor guest suite directly above. It was so obvious. So obvious that he should have dedicated his efforts to winning her respect instead of getting her into his bed. Clear as daylight that she was the one he should have shared his life with, grown old with, possibly even grown up with. The one who could have kept him true to his talents, maybe even allowed him a fleeting glimpse of self-respect from time to time.

He sighed and wondered whether she might be persuaded to come back with him after the reunion. She had been tired and they had decided to eat in: pasta and a jar of some ragu-type sauce was all he had been able to find, and a quite marvellous bottle of Barolo. They had talked of this and that, nothing too strenuous, and yet she had seemed to understand him more in a few short hours than his wife had in five years, or was it six? Her eyes, her look, had somehow seemed to say that she knew what was going on inside while he blustered on with his silly witticisms and world-weary cynicisms and God-knows-what other 'isms' that had become his conver-sational stock-in-trade over all the years of sucking up seven kinds of bullshit in Berkeley Square. There had even been moments of contented silence, and he had persuaded himself that he had felt happy for the first time in years as he sipped the Barolo and their eyes met. He thought of her now lying in the single bed not ten feet above his own, snuggled under a goose-down duvet, probably naked. Almost certainly naked. He closed his eyes. Maybe it was not too late. Maybe he could turn himself around. Make a start this weekend. Once or twice he almost drifted off to sleep thinking of the satisfac-tions of being with a woman such as this, waking up to her, breakfasting with her. Breakfast! Christ, all he had was half a three-day-old loaf and a jar of Vegemite.

Friday, October 3rd, 1980

To an outsider looking in on that afternoon in the autumn of 1980, Stephen Walsh's lot in life might have seemed an enviable one: a fellowship at a prestigious Oxford college with no great weight of teaching responsibilities; comfortable, rent-free rooms with a scout who, if not exactly performing the duties of college servants of old, at least spared him life's more tedious tasks; in the evenings, the excellent if rather rich food taken at High Table and followed, if he so wished, by the conviviality of the Senior Common Room and its well-stocked wine cellar. To our outsider, a commuter, say, shuttling between a 1970s housing development and an office in the city, all this might have seemed the very picture of settled privilege. But Stephen was not settled – not settled at all.

He felt himself drawn again to the window seat and the view across the lawn to the rooms on the other side of the quad. Surely there could be no mistake. Three times this term, in the course of conversation at High Table, the Master had contrived to use the word 'egregious', each time catching Stephen's eye. Given that the Regius Professor was by tradition addressed as 'Regius', it was the kind of Oxford in-joke that Stephen would normally have considered cringe-making. But surely there could have been no mistaking the Master's intention?

With half an hour to spare before heading down to the Turf Tavern, he set about tugging the motley collection of armchairs and the leather Chesterfield sofa into a rough circle ready for the morning. This done, he selected a couple of essays from a pile on the desk and dropped them into the chair nearest to the fireplace. Crossing to the principal bookcase, he checked that his own three books were at eye level, next to works by Paul Mus and Lucien Febvre. After a last look around, he returned to the narrow window seat. Weeks ago he had given up hope of being able to hold the reunion in his grand new rooms, but he had at least expected to be able to make the announcement of his appointment. As an afterthought, he retrieved four or five out-of-date invitation cards from the wastepaper basket and propped them on the mantelpiece next to a bottle of green ink.

Just before 5pm on that Friday, Michael Lowell arrived at Oxford's Gloucester Green coach station carrying the leather Gladstone bag that had once been his father's and that he had for many years used as both briefcase and overnight tote. It was a fine evening and he had decided to walk the mile or so across town to the Cotswold Lodge Hotel. There he took a shower, changed into sweater, jeans and a new pair of sneakers, and by 6.30pm was standing in his navy woollen overcoat outside Blackwell's bookshop on The Broad. He looked at his watch. Half an hour to go. Half an hour in which to collect himself.

To anyone who knew Michael Lowell in his professional capacity, the idea that he might need to collect himself would have seemed a little unlikely. In the jargon of the day, he was a man very much together, at ease in his own skin, respected by friends and colleagues alike for his managerial competence as well as for the professional achievements that had made him one of the world's leading epidemiologists. The prospect of a meeting with any number of heads of state would not have raised his blood pressure a millimetre; but the thought of meeting Seema Mir had his heart pounding as he turned up Parks Road, deciding he had time to walk the three sides of the square that would eventually bring him to the Turf Tavern.

The leaves were falling as he crossed over towards Rhodes House, seat of the Trust that had first brought him to Oxford all those years ago. He slowed his pace, drawing comfort from the solid edifices of science – the Departments of Organic and Inorganic Chemistry, the Radcliffe Science Library, the Schools of Forestry and Zoology – that lined the north side of road. And directly ahead now, through the gathering gloom, the red-brick façade of the School of Pathology, unchanged by all the years. He crossed to the iron gates, looking up at the lights that still burned in the windows of laboratories where Florey and Chain had ushered in the age of antibiotics, where Dreyer had done all the early work on immunology, where Gowans had shown that it was the lymphocyte gene that governed immunological reaction. He took his hands from his coat pockets in what was perhaps an unconscious gesture of respect. Who might be up there this evening? What discoveries were enticing and eluding them as they carried out the tests and checks that could lead to a dead end – or to a Nobel Prize? Two decades ago, all he had wanted was to be part of it all. But the years since had proved his father right a hundred times: breakthroughs in the laboratory were the easier challenge.

He checked his watch and turned down Mansfield Road, directing his thoughts into less well-charted waters. Would he even recognize this stranger of twenty years who had passed her forty-first birthday last week? She might still be slim, or carrying thirty pounds more; the hair still jet and lustrous, or on the brittle road to silver. Her face still angular and elegant, or full and soft? *You might not even know her. But I would know. I would know by the way she walked, by the poise of her, by the something about her that was to be valued above all the ordinary business of the world. I would know her by heart.*

'Michael?'

He turned to his left and saw the slight figure on the other side of the road, half obscured by the shadow of a plane tree. Without looking, he stepped from the kerb to cross towards her and was almost hit by a cyclist who swerved at the last moment and sped off towards Longwall, disappearing into the evening with a mild expletive.

'Hello, Michael.'

'Hello, Seema.'

An awkward kiss on each cheek, holding on to each other's hands as she leaned away, looking up into his face under the light of a college window.

'You look well, Michael.'

'So do you.'

The same subtle, self-possessed smile. The same languid way of speaking. The same inexplicable attraction that had marked him so deeply all those years ago. He looked at her uplifted face, aware of nothing but the astonishing reality of being once more with Seema Mir in the cool of an Oxford night.

She let go of his hands and tilted her head to one side. 'It's very, very good to see you again, Dr Lowell.'

'It's very good to see you, too,' he said, in his best WHO meeting voice. She laughed and took his arm, marching him up Holywell and turning him into the cobbled passageway of Bath Place that leads directly to the Turf Tavern.

In the Middle Ages, the Turf Tavern had been an illegal gambling den. In more recent years, it had become well known to television audiences the world over as the favourite watering hole of the fictional Oxford detective Chief Inspector Morse. It was also within its ancient walls that a future President of the United States famously did not inhale, and that a future Prime Minister of Australia drank himself into the *Guinness Book of Records* by downing a yard of ale in less than twelve seconds.

Despite these convivial traditions, the Turf proved a less-than-ideal meeting place for the five friends who assembled there on the evening of Friday, October 3rd, 1980. Smoke and noise crowded under the low seventeenth-century ceilings and the beer-spilling crush around the two small serving hatches gave the lie to the idea of the British as a nation of orderly queuers. But it was here – to confused shouts of 'Haven't changed a bit', 'So good to see you', 'Can't believe it's twenty years', 'Never thought we'd lose touch' – that Seema Mir, Michael Lowell, Stephen Walsh, Hélène Hevré and Toby Jenks began the weekend that would change their lives.

Over dinner, the noise restricted the conversation to brief, bad-telephone-line exchanges about travel plans or other Oxford pubs they had known and loved. Only afterwards, when the little group carried coffee and drinks out into the garden to brave the cool of the autumn evening, did the reunion really begin.

When the last chair had been scraped over the flagstones and the last coat tugged close, a silence had fallen. On the medieval wall, a caged light bulb illuminated only a vivid green moss. Otherwise darkness hemmed them in. On the table itself, a single candle glowed faintly on cold faces. Stephen was the first to break the spell, looking over the top of his half-moon glasses and enunciating the single word 'Well?'

'This was a great idea, Stephen,' said Hélène, touching his arm. Stephen pulled his mouth down at the edges, implying that this was, of course, like all such assertions, open to challenge. He eventually nodded his head in acknowledgement of the murmured thanks of the others. 'Pity Tom couldn't make it.'

Seema hugged herself against the evening chill. 'Do you realize he's the only one of us with family commitments?'

'Not quite.' Hélène glanced towards Toby who had leaned away from the table and was lighting a cigar.

'Purely financial, my dear. All pain and no gain.'

A little way from the candlelight, Michael sat upright in his overcoat, wondering if it would be ridiculous to stand and place it around Seema's shoulders. Of course she was older. And there was more caution, more sadness even, in the wide eyes. And perhaps less lustre in the hair, now cut short in a modern style to reveal the shape of her neck. Much more startling was what had not changed: the same dreamy, almost ethereal presence; the same readiness to be amused lingering permanently at the edges of her eyes and mouth; the same untouchable serenity. Since their first meeting under the street lights of Holywell she had avoided meeting his eyes, but glanced at him now as she tapped the table. 'So what is programme?' The words were spoken in a light, mock Pakistani-English accent, wagging her head slightly from side to side. The others laughed and looked towards Stephen.

'Oh, take it as it comes, I should think. Meet in my rooms tomorrow, say about ten of the clock? And then I thought perhaps each of us could say something appropriately self-revelatory about what we've all been doing with ourselves these past two decades? More the inner journey than the outer, I thought?'

Toby widened his eyes and buried his nose in a balloon of brandy.

3 | Life and times

Stephen sat astride the bench, the letter open on the long refectory table, the discarded envelope embossed with the three crowns of the University coat of arms. *Dominus illuminatio mea.*

The last of the students had left for their ten o'clocks and he was alone in the Great Hall. Portraits of alumni looked down on him from panelled walls: the great and the good; the gartered and ermined, the begowned and bewigged, the mitred and medalled. All different and all the same. *E pluribus unum.* A single portrait of four hundred years of a self-satisfied establishment.

He took a sip of coffee that had long ago gone cold. The tone of the Estates Bursar's letter had been perfectly polite.

'*As I am sure you are aware... rooms in college at a premium ... normal limit five years... College's firm commitment to accommodating increasing proportion of female tutors.*'

But the bottom line was – he was out. As of the end of Hilary Term. Instead of moving into the grand suite of the Regius Professor, he would be renting accommodation somewhere off the Banbury Road, preparing his own meals, making his own bed, even doing his own laundry. But even dwelling on these details was only a way of pushing away a greater truth: his academic career had come off the rails.

He looked at his watch. Standing to go, he slipped the letter into its envelope and folded it inside the *University Gazette*. When they had last all been together, being a Marxist historian as well as one of Oxford's youngest dons had been about as chic as academic life could get. But the tide had steadily turned, leaving him stranded on a shore that he had expected to be a beachhead. At the top of the Hall stairs he paused for a moment to survey the quad. The truth of the matter was, Karl Marx had let him down. On the other side of the lawn, his fellow tutor in history was swanning towards the library with two female undergraduates in tow. Surely it was not to be Robin Liddell (emphasis on the second syllable, please)? He had been one of those who had turned with the tide, renounced the faith, indulged himself in a grand intellectual *mea culpa* to the delight of the right-wing press. They had not spoken for months, ever since Stephen's review for *The Guardian* had labelled Liddell's television series on the Levellers 'the embourgoisement of history'.

Back in his rooms he turned off the computer. The others would be arriving in a few minutes. And suddenly the whole idea of the weekend seemed contrived, even embarrassing. He had imagined chairing a review of how and why ideas and ideals had changed between gilded youth and tarnished middle age, but he had somehow envisaged presiding over the occasion as someone who, without compromise, had reached the summit of his profession. He checked the room a final time before sitting again in the window seat from which so many hopes had been entertained, unable to lift his eyes to the stone-mullioned windows on the opposite side of the quad.

In what he had called a brief '*tour d'horizon*', Stephen had for some minutes been reviewing the salient features of the two decades since they had all last been together, beginning with the failure of the Bay of Pigs and ending with the rise of the Chicago School and the dissipation of radical energies in identity politics. From one of the armchairs, Michael, who sat through worse than this most weeks, stared at the backs of his hands, the greater part of his attention occupied with finding himself back in this world where nothing seemed to have changed; the surroundings redolent of the long gone, of damp wood and mildewed books, of worn rugs and toast burnt on two-bar electric fires; of centuries of patient study and ticking clocks. And of her faint perfume. That same perfume. He looked down, surprised to see a pair of startlingly white sneakers at the ends of his legs.

The armchair from which Stephen was still holding forth had been positioned at the apex of the little seating arrangement, ensuring that the others were all slightly angled towards it. Toby, who had seen this game played by better practitioners than Stephen Walsh, had broken the pattern by perching on the window seat overlooking the quad. From here he was making a show of darting his eyes around the far corners of the room, implying that he could not be expected to keep a straight face if his eyes met any of the others.

'About myself,' Stephen appeared to be concluding, 'there is little to say except that these are of course the times I have struggled in and with. I needn't mention that it has not always been easy to deny oneself the promotions and preferments enjoyed by those who have seen fit to adjust their ideological sails to the prevailing political winds ... '

Over on the window seat, Toby was watching a female undergraduate approaching the porters' lodge and vaguely remembering that, in his day, the college statutes forbade any woman to enter except laundresses who had to be 'of such an age, condition and reputation as to be above suspicion'. He craned his neck to satisfy himself that the girl below did not meet any of these criteria.

'However...' Stephen gave his little academic cough and seemed about to end. 'I think we might now make a start, and perhaps just go around the room? And as we have all, I'm sure, heard about the rise and rise of Dr Michael Lowell, I think perhaps we might begin with him?'

Toby pointedly returned from the window to his armchair, collecting a couple of biscuits on the way.

Michael reprised his two decades in one minute. Four years at Harvard Medical School, followed by internship and a year's residency before switching to a Master's in Public Health at Hopkins; two years with the US Centers for Disease Control in West Africa in lieu of national service; two years at the International Centre for Diarrhoeal Disease Research in Bangladesh, much of it spent in the field laboratory at Matlab; secondment to the World Health Organization's smallpox-eradication team for most of the 1970s before being appointed to his present post as director of the Global Immunization Programme.

He glanced around to see who might go next, but Hélène intervened, laughing. 'There're just a couple more little things that might have been worth a mention, Michael, like eradicating the biggest killer disease in human history.'

Michael began to say something about the thousands of national vaccination teams and volunteers who had participated in the smallpox-eradication programme only for Hélène to interrupt again. 'I'm very glad to hear you crediting the footsoldiers, Michael. But I'm afraid in this case the generals might deserve some of the credit, too. Everyone knows it was a master class in epidemiology.'

Stephen held up both hands. 'Let's not get bogged down

in detail just yet. We can come back to it all later. Seema, you're up.'

'And we don't just want the CV, sweetheart,' said Toby, clasping his hands behind his head and stretching out his legs.

'I think what we'd really like to know,' Stephen interrupted with exaggerated forbearance, 'is why devote yourself to the topic of Thomas Jefferson's slaves in 19th-century Virginia? What's the connection with *you*, Seema? What's it got to do with who you *are*?'

Michael recognized the warning sign as Seema's eyes widened. She allowed a second to pass, as she had always done, then replied in a voice that was a fraction slower than normal. 'I wasn't aware that one had to have a personal connection in order to specialize in a particular field, Stephen.' Michael watched as she shifted her gaze slowly to the window. There had always been a slow-motion quality about her, an unhurried grace. 'What, for example, is your own personal connection to the Soviet five-year plans of the 1950s?'

Toby chuckled and snuggled further down into his chair.

'Obviously,' said Stephen stiffly, 'it relates directly to my chosen ideological position. Alternatives to free-market ideologies have a political – *ergo* a personal – connection to my own convictions.'

'I see,' said Seema after a beat had passed. Michael watched, entranced by her way of composing her face to a perfect calm before speaking, even while debating a point, sometimes even pausing to think and yet not inviting interruption. 'I see. Then my personal connection with the issue of slavery is a belief that history should be about those who don't have a voice as well as those who make the most noise—'

'That's what Marxist history—'

'And I'm wondering if what you might really be saying here, Stephen' – overruling him without raising her voice –

'your subtext, as you might call it, is that it's quite all right for an American or a Brit to specialize in, say, the history of India or Pakistan, but not for a Pakistani to specialize in the history of the United States?'

Toby could hardly contain his glee as Hélène moved to defuse the tension. 'Tell us how it all happened, Seema. Going to live in America and all.'

She avoided Michael's eyes as she briefly told of the Jefferson Scholarship in Hawaii and the romance that had carried her to the eastern seaboard of the United States. 'A few months later I was married and enrolled in the doctoral programme at Harvard.'

Toby leaned forward with a little intellectual frown that looked dangerously like a parody of Stephen's habitual expression. 'Wasn't there a rumour about Jefferson being quite close to one of his female slaves – I mean, really quite extraordinarily close?'

'You sound like my publisher, Toby. And, yes, he was.'

Stephen's hand rose once again. 'We'll come back to any historiographical issues later, if you don't mind. Toby, you're next.'

Toby looked for a moment as if he might be about to rebel, but eventually reached into the briefcase beside his chair to withdraw a miniature videocassette player. Struggling over outstretched legs, he turned on the TV and attached the cable. He glanced at Seema as he resumed his seat – 'Life and times of the other TJ' – then aimed a small remote control at the device.

The others shifted their positions as the screen came to life, showing rapidly changing close-ups of Toby, starting with the 1960s and ageing him twenty years in a matter of seconds: the hair receding, the face broadening, the flesh loosening, the sequence coming to a halt with a still photo that came disconcertingly to life with Toby addressing the camera. 'Hi there, possums. Well, here we all are at Stephen's little reckoning. Dress rehearsal for the Pearly Gates, what? Hardly worth my showing up. Anyway, here's my very own chronicle of *temps perdu*.' The image of Toby's face dissolved into a rapid series of clips from British and American TV commercials, the real Toby looking pleased at the cries of 'I remember that' and 'You didn't do that, Tobe?' There followed a fast-forwarded sequence of Toby in morning dress leaving a church with a bride who looked like a supermodel, followed after another couple of ads by the same scene in fast reverse, bride and groom rattling back into the darkness of the church. Another commercial break and there was Toby fast-forwarding again from a registry office with a different bride. More ads followed, intercut with a graph showing what might have been a rising salary or career trajectory superimposed on a photo of Toby becoming more and more dispirited until the film shuddered to an end with a distorted close-up seen through what appeared to be the bottom of a dimpled whisky glass that gradually filled and overflowed down his cheeks.

When the television went dead the silence was broken by slightly strained laughter and applause. Stephen continued staring at the screen, nodding slowly.

Hélène was looking troubled. 'Okay, Toby, explain the significance of all that!'

Toby let his arms flop down by the sides of the chair. 'Oh, there's no significance to any of it, sweetie.'

The mood had become noisier, more relaxed as Stephen held up both hands. 'We can deconstruct Toby's artistic little presentation later, but I think we've all got the gist so why don't we break for coffee and then hear what Hélène has to say?'

4 | Spare me the cold chains

It is not the intention here to recount all the conversations of that weekend. But, in touching only on those passages which had a bearing on what was to follow, there is a risk of portraying the discussion as purposeful when in fact most of it was directionless. Only in retrospect were the conversations in the Fellows' Garden on that first morning, and in the University Parks later that day, of any special significance.

The day being fine, there had been a general agreement on continuing the meeting outdoors. Stephen had suggested the Fellows' Garden, which as undergraduates they had been denied. After admitting them with a flourish of his personal key, he caught up with Seema on the gravel path on to which an occasional pine cone had trespassed. He gestured at his surroundings as if to indicate despair. Her smile was a gentle peace offering as she too looked around at the immaculate lawns and shrubberies.

'Certainly a long way from NYU.'

'Actually, I've been thinking of leaving.'

'Quitting Oxford?'

'Of course you'll know that line of Cyril Clemens – "One of the greatest temptations of life is the temptation never to leave Oxford".'

'Wasn't he a complete neurotic?'

'Well, I'm not absolutely certain about that.'

'So where are you going?'

'Oh, nothing fixed. Considering one or two offers. Fact is, Oxbridge palls after a while. Far too pleased with itself. And of course structurally reactionary when you blow off the progressive froth. I assume that New York is not entirely unconducive to academic life?'

After taking a turn around the gravelled perimeter, its herbaceous borders dying back into winter, the five arranged themselves on the grass under the canopy of the ancient copper beech. Stephen held up a hand to still the conversation, summoning attention with a formal little cough.

'Time to hear from Hélène, I think.'

Hélène looked up into the canopy of leaves, fighting back the tiredness beginning to stir in her veins. 'Pretty much the beaten path for a while. Med school at McGill, Royal College Certification, all of it as much to keep my parents happy as anything else. Lord knows they were unhappy enough about my sudden godlessness, for which they blamed Oxford, and for which I blame you. I was a good Catholic girl, you'll remember, before I fell in with present company.'

Toby was about to say something but thought better of it.

'Anyway, licence to practise safely tucked away, I joined up with Canadian University Service Overseas in Liberia, then got myself recruited by CIDA, the Canadian International Development Agency. That kept me in West Africa. Zaire. Mobutu. Terrible. I can't tell you.'

Stephen nodded slowly as Hélène continued. 'Got involved in the Ebola virus thing in '76...'

'More than involved.' Michael, sitting cross-legged on the grass, spoke to the others but raised a hand towards her. 'Hélène and a few dozen others stopped Ebola in its tracks. Stopped it spreading God knows where when we had no real way of coping.'

Hélène looked down at the grass. 'Meant I had to leave, though. We had to move quickly, burn the corpses, stomp all over local ways of reverencing the dead. No way could I work there after that. Got a posting to Côte d'Ivoire with an international NGO out of Ottawa, trying to do primary health care in half a dozen countries. Been with them the last eight years.'

'And doing a wonderful job.' Michael cursed himself, knowing it had sounded patronizing.

Hélène attempted a smile.

'Not wonderful at all, Michael. Not even addressing the real problem which, as you know, is that the poor get to be sick and their kids get to die because nearly all the resources are soaked up by ten per cent of the population trying to imitate the lifestyles they see in the West.'

Stephen continued to nod slowly, staring at her over his spectacles. 'Interesting. Interesting. We'll come back to that.' There was a long pause, during which Toby gazed at her, hands locked behind his head. 'Personal life off limits, darling?'

'No,' said Hélène ruefully. 'But there's not a lot to say. Married to the job, as they say.'

Afterwards the conversation drifted desultorily towards lunch. Toby, eyes closed, face tilted towards the October sun, was listening to Hélène and Michael talking shop. Stephen had been questioning Seema about the history faculty at NYU, but it had soon become apparent that he was no longer listening, his attention drawn to the argument developing between Michael and Hélène, who was in full flow.

'Stupid things we've known how to prevent for years, Michael. Measles, tetanus, whooping cough for God's sake – killing, what, four, five million kids a year? And nobody cares.'

'You know there's a global target...'

Hélène waved a dismissive hand. 'Don't give me your targets and resolutions, Michael. Nothing's going to change. You know who the latest appointee to your Executive Board is?'

Michael lowered his head in resignation, knowing what was coming.

'Thought you might. And you might also know that he's the one who's been spending two-thirds of the country's health budget on building an imitation of Massachusetts General that will serve about two per cent of the population. That's why kids don't get immunized. And that's why ten years from now WHO will just be announcing a new target...'

'But you've also got to recognize the logistical...'

'Oh, spare me the logistics and the cold chains, Michael. You know as well as I do it could all be gotten around if the powers-that-be cared one little bit...'

'Sure, the technical problems could be gotten around, but—'

'And what would it cost? Half a billion dollars a year? A billion? To immunize every kid born into this bloody awful world? For Christ's sake, Michael, it's less than a dozen modern jet fighters. People like Mobutu and his cronies have more than that in their Swiss bank accounts.'

Michael met Hélène's look but said nothing. Toby was picking the heads from a few late daisies. A half smile played at the edges of Stephen's mouth. Around them the lawns were dappled with leaf shadow. Eventually Michael said simply: 'You're right, of course.'

Hélène reached to cover his hand with her own. 'Sorry to rant, Michael. But it's not often I get to address a senior official of the World Health Organization.'

Seema looked on as Michael smiled his slightly twisted,

self-deprecating smile, opening the doors of the past. At their first meeting under the light of the window in Holywell it had seemed easy to look at him with all the delight and pleasure at seeing an old friend after so long, but ever since she had found it difficult.

Stephen was touching his fingertips together in a little steeple. 'Pause there just a moment, if you will. Surely we're just discussing surface phenomena here?' He waved a hand freely as if to say that this could be taken for granted. 'And of course if one focuses on technical fixes, *exempli gratia* antibiotics, vaccines, etcetera, then is it not the case that the oppressed will simply fall victim to some other surface phenomenon because of course the underlying causes remain unaddressed?'

Stephen had fallen into the slightly sing-song tone, lending his arguments a quality of inevitability that his students found intimidating. But Michael Lowell was a different proposition.

'That's partly true, Stephen, but it's not the whole nine yards. First' – he grasped the first finger of his left hand – 'how long do the poor have to wait before progress against the underlying causes means their kids can get immunized? So they can grow up without being malnourished, diseased, blind, paralysed?' He pushed aside Stephen's attempted interruption and grasped the next finger, cursing himself for falling into this old habit in front of Seema. 'Second, the things you say are symptoms also happen to be causes. Do you think poverty isn't made a lot worse when kids' minds and bodies don't develop as they should because of disease? Do you think a family's ability to work and earn a living isn't affected when a son or daughter is crippled for life by polio, or left blind by measles or vitamin deficiency? Do you think it advances economic equality when more or less permanent illness means poor kids drop out of school into a lifetime of illiteracy?'

Seema looked down, shaken, remembering. Michael could be awkward, tongue-tied, unable to find quite the right words. But get him on his home ground…

Stephen took a patient inward breath, implying that there was much he had to say, but this time it was Hélène who interrupted in support. 'You can see it, Stephen, you can see it everywhere. All these symptoms, as you call them – they sap people's lives. They undermine learning at school, getting a job, earning an income, supporting a family, bouncing back from life's setbacks. They *are* symptoms. Of course they are. But they're causes as well.'

'Heraclitus,' said Toby suddenly, as if coming awake. The others looked at him, startled. Toby lifted his chin and looked into the far distance, raising his left hand and placing his right arm solemnly across his chest. 'When health is absent, wisdom cannot become manifest, strength cannot fight, wealth becomes useless and intelligence cannot be applied.' Fifth century BC. Same point really. Said it even better than Michael.'

Hélène gave him a smile. 'Very apt, Tobe. Don't let anyone ever tell you the classics aren't useful.'

Stephen coughed, obviously wanting to get back to the point. 'Nonetheless—' he began, but was stopped by Toby again holding up a hand as if conducting traffic. 'Excuse me, I believe Michael still has some more fingers left?'

'And third, Stephen,' continued Michael, smiling ruefully and enclosing the next finger, 'No one's saying this is an "either or". No one's saying you shouldn't be trying to fight injustice and poverty. All we're saying is you don't have to wait for the arrival of some political utopia before kids can get five cents' worth of vaccine.'

Finally allowed to speak, Stephen began a long account of what had apparently been seminal debates in the Soviet

Politburo about the dangers of short-term fixes distracting from the work of long-term structural change. Toby leaned back on stiff arms, the heels of his hands pressing into the grass, contemplating the contrast with the conversations that filled his days in Berkeley Square as he looked up into the vault of the copper beech, torn through by sunlight like some magnificent stained-glass window. Opposite, Hélène's attention was divided between wanting to support Michael and concern for Toby. She had noticed that at one point, head bowed, he had again seemed close to tears.

All afternoon Michael had entertained a hope of strolling back to the hotel with Seema and perhaps inviting her to join him at the Rose and Crown. Did she still drink Pimm's No.1, 'last remnant of the Raj', as she had called it? But as they left Stephen's college in the late-afternoon light he had failed to make a move and, seeing her deep in conversation with Hélène, had instead fallen in with Toby as he crossed Radcliffe Square.

Between Michael and Toby there had always been a settled bond of friendship that others had sometimes found hard to understand. And it was true that two more different people would be difficult to imagine. Yet they had always made a point of getting together on Michael's visits to London, and more than once over the years Toby had motored down to spend a couple of days in Nyon, often at times when the other relationships in his life had been at their most difficult. The help that Michael had given had never been overt. They had lingered in the cafés by the harbour, done a little fishing out on the lake, talked politics, played chess, and in the evenings explored the restaurants of the old town. But the help had been there nonetheless. For Toby, Michael was one of the few people with whom he could be something close to himself. Michael, for his part, valued the fact that Toby moved in a world different from his own, and knew that, no matter what, he could call on Toby and Toby would be there.

And so it was that Toby, who had hardly spoken since lunch, turned to Michael as they headed up Parks Road towards the Pitt Rivers Museum. 'Can that really be right, mate? Five million kids a year?'

'Give or take a few thousand.'

'And the whatnots are cheap as chips?'

'Vaccines? A few cents a shot. Of course that's not the only cost.'

'No, but, you know...'

Up ahead, Stephen, who had decided to accompany the others back to the hotel, had caught up with Seema and Hélène.

Toby appeared to be working something out, slowing his pace. 'So if I've got this right, it's like we've got this cheap cure for cancer but nobody's bothered to do much about it?'

Hélène had fallen behind to hear what Toby was saying. Michael also slowed his pace as he processed the figures in his head: eight million or so cancer deaths every year worldwide, well over half in the developing world. He had not thought of the comparison, but it was pretty much on the money. 'I guess you could say that. In fact you might want to argue that it's worse. Vaccine-preventable diseases kill similar numbers to cancer, but most of them are kids under five with all their lives in front of them. Plus which, unlike cancer, we know how to prevent it all for next to nothing.'

Hélène was alongside now as the little group approached the ornate Victorian brick of Keble College. Toby puffed out his cheeks and thought for a moment. 'So we've got all this brouhaha about the right to life, all the episcopal head scratching, all these anti-abortionists fire-bombing clinics, all the papal bulls, if you'll forgive the expression, Hel, and all the while we're letting five million kids a year die because nobody's quite got around to giving them five cents' worth of vaccine?'

Michael stopped at the kerb as a group of cyclists pushed off from the traffic lights. 'Well, that's not quite how we express the official WHO position, but that's about the size of it, yes.'

Toby gently took Hélène's arm to steer her across the road. 'Well, far be it from me to take a view, but that can't be right, can it?'

5 | Not really cricket

In 1882, when Benjamin Jowett assumed the vice-chancellor-ship of the university, he drew up what would today be called a 'to-do' list. Number four on his list was the building of a cricket pavilion. The resulting structure, in the Queen Anne revival style, had remained virtually unaltered from the date of its completion to the afternoon, almost exactly one hundred years later, when Seema Mir, Toby Jenks, Hélène Hevré, Michael Lowell and Stephen Walsh stepped up on to its terraces.

The others had by now caught up with the discussion, Stephen having taken over the lead. 'So would I be right in thinking,' he was saying in the manner of one seeking to establish firm foundations before proceeding, 'that *variola major* was selected for eradication because it also posed a threat to the middle class?'

Michael joined the others in seating himself on one of the slatted wooden benches. 'Not at all. It was targeted because it was a major killer that can't survive without a human host. Stop transmission in humans and it's gone. That's not true of most viruses. Polio can survive a good while in the environment—'

'In water, or sewage, for example,' said Hélène, looking out towards the cricket strip that was still immaculate although the season had finished a month ago. Stephen sat, elbows on knees, cheekbones lodged on the heels of his hands, unaware of the late-afternoon sun that was casting long shadows across the park or of the graceful pavilion from which so many famous names had gone out to bat.

'But now it's been eradicated, absolutely eradicated, am I correct?'

'Ye-es,' said Michael. 'By the technical definition.'

Stephen looked up sharply, as if this might do for the lay person but not for him. 'Which is?'

Michael just stopped himself from grasping the first finger of his left hand. 'Interruption of transmission certified worldwide. Zero incidence of the disease. No further need for routine immunization.'

'But the virus itself exists or it does not?' said Stephen, patiently seeking precision.

'Not in the wild, only in the two reference laboratories.'

'Reference laboratories?'

'One at my old stomping ground, the Centers for Disease Control in Atlanta, and one at the Research Institute for Viral Preparations in Moscow. The Porton Down centre here in the UK still has the virus at the moment, and there's one lab in South Africa that has it, but they're both just about to destroy their stocks.'

'Nowhere else?'

Michael hesitated. 'It's been rumoured the North Koreans might have hung on to it, and maybe even the French, the Iraqis, the Israelis.'

Stephen looked surprised. 'Rumoured? No independent verification?'

Michael shook his head. 'The WHO doesn't have that kind of authority. We just have to accept formal declarations from each country that had a smallpox lab.'

'Is there a bigpox?' Toby was sitting astride one of the lower benches, looking up at the swaying trees.

Michael smiled. 'The big pox was syphilis.'

Stephen ignored this exchange and held up a hand. 'But what we do know for certain is that both superpowers have held on to it?'

Michael nodded, resigned to where he knew Stephen was going.

Seema spoke quietly from the top step. 'Wasn't there some big debate about that earlier this year?

'There still is,' said Michael, turning to look up towards her. 'The World Health Assembly debates it every year.'

'You bet it does.'

'And what might the case for keeping it be?' Stephen said, ignoring Hélène's sarcasm.

Michael kept his hands still. 'Research. Vaccine production. A possibility that genetically modified versions might one day be useful as a carrier for something beneficial.'

Toby stretched his arms wide, vaguely recalling that the distance between the pavilion and the wicket had been planned to be exactly the same as at Lords cricket ground. 'Seems to me, possums, the obvious thing to do here is to get hold of a little test tube of the stuff and threaten to blow bubbles with it in Times Square unless the world gets off its butt and immunizes every last kiddie.'

Hélène leaned across the steps to give him a playful kiss on the cheek. 'Great idea, Toby. Beats the hell out of another WHO resolution.' She pulled away before Toby could react, blushing faintly.

'Makes perfect sense to me.' Stephen rose to his feet, attempting to join in the banter.

Toby waited for Michael at the foot of the pavilion steps. When they were both on level ground he placed a hand on his friend's shoulder in mock solemnity. 'Down to you then, mate.'

Michael bumped Toby's ribs gently with his fist. 'Consider it done.'

'Great,' said Toby, doing a little preliminary skip and taking two or three half-running steps onto the grass, swinging his arm over as if bowling an off-break. 'Spot of bio-terrorism never did anybody any harm.'

Seema also stood up from the bird-spattered steps, preparing to go, suppressing a jet-lagged yawn. 'Not really cricket though is it, Tobe?'

Skirting the pitch, the little group set off towards the mansards and multiple brick chimneys of Norham Gardens, just visible above the line of trees that marks the beginning of prosperous North Oxford.

6 | Next year in New York

Seema had switched on the reading lamp in the lounge of the Cotswold Lodge Hotel, hoping that Michael might come down before dinner. A copy of the *University Gazette* lay open on the table, but she found little of interest in the list of appointments and departures, the schedule of *viva voce* examinations, the classified ads for writing retreats in Cornwall and Tuscany. He had hardly spoken a word to her all day.

All summer long she had wondered how she would feel on seeing him again. And all summer too she had resolved, at all costs, to avoid the slightest carelessness with his feelings. She had known he would still be the intelligent, kind, sensitive and slightly awkward man she had shared a year of her life with twenty years ago. But the years had added something. A mellowness. A self-deprecation to his seriousness. A confidence that rounded the edges of awkwardness. And, if she was honest with herself, all the old attractiveness as well.

She looked up from the *Gazette* to the window and the line of trees that screened the hotel from the Banbury Road. This was not the way to go. Twenty years ago she had forfeited any right to spontaneity. It would be unforgivable to risk hurting him a second time.

Stephen arrived before the others came downstairs, taking

the other armchair and immediately picking up the earlier conversation.

'So, you were saying, about New York, Seema. You don't find it uncongenial?'

'Seems to suit me.'

She waited for him to get to the point, feeling sure he was working his way around to something.

'Know Myron Lee?' he asked, with deliberate casualness, looking out of the window.

'Should I?'

'Historian. University of Chicago. *The* man on class structure in the States. Of course I knew him at Cambridge. Just heard he might be going to the New School.'

As no reply seemed required, Seema looked back towards the lobby where Hélène and Michael were at that moment descending the stairs together. She turned away and focused again on the almost bare rose bushes just outside the window.

'What with Hobsbawm popping in and out these days as well,' Stephen was saying, 'it just might be starting to look promising. Thought I might check it out. Pop over to New York after the Michaelmas vac. Chat to Myron. You'll be there?'

'In term time? Yes, I expect so. Are they advertising?'

'Wouldn't know. I imagine they might have something for, err...' He raised a modest hand.

'A much-published Fellow of an Oxford college?'

They exchanged smiles, Seema's amusement having a more inward quality, being less sure that a position at the New School was there for the asking, even for Dr Stephen Walsh.

Toby Jenks sat on the end of his bed in vest and underpants and stared at himself in the full-length wardrobe mirror. He should definitely not have come. There had been no need to expose himself to the slings and arrows of outrageous con-trasts. And now it might be weeks before his cognitive dis-sonance was working properly again, weeks of struggling to regain a false perspective within which to see his life as being remotely acceptable. He wondered about taking a shower. Worst of all, this would be his last evening with Hélène, unless he could somehow persuade her to stay with him in London for a night or two before she left for Canada. He closed his eyes, shutting out the unwelcome visitor in the mirror, only to find his own image replaced by hers. He had always carried a powerful memory of her, occasionally straying into fantasy, and had not in truth hesitated for very long before deciding to accept Stephen's little invitation. But he had anticipated perhaps a little pleasurable flirtation, not being smacked for six, as he put it to himself, opening his eyes again and con-templating the less-than-prepossessing figure that stared back at him.

He had looked in vain for a mini-bar, not wanting to go downstairs too early. Hélène had agreed to a drink before dinner but had immediately turned to include the others in the invitation. He opened the wardrobe, deciding he would defy them all by wearing his usual lightweight black woollen suit and classic white shirt, accessorized with acid green braces and matching silk tie. For a few moments he stood in front of the mirror, pulling in his stomach and drawing himself up to his full six feet. 'Now listen, possums,' he said to the wardrobe, 'you might as well know that what you have here is a fully paid-up member of the *Guardian*-reading, Waitrose-shopping, Mercedes-driving, hesitantly left-wing North Ealing branch of the vaguely discontented middle class.' His shoulders slumped again as he relaxed back to his normal, rather portly five foot ten. Of course she couldn't take him seriously. Who would? He checked his pockets for wallet and credit cards and began hunting around for his room key. Maybe he had time to pop out and find a bottle shop.

'... not much in the way of blood chemistries, and nothing reliable on bacterial cultures...'

Hélène had led Michael to one of the tables set slightly apart. She had intended to ask if he was okay with seeing Seema again, but he had begun asking about her work at the children's hospital. She stopped in mid-stream. 'Sorry I was so hard on you today, Michael. It was the disillusionment talking.'

'You were telling it like it is.'

She gave him a sad smile, wondering whether to mention the strange bouts of tiredness that had become such an unwelcome part of her life these past few months. 'Don't you ever get disillusioned?'

'Can't. I'm paid too much.'

'Well, just so you know what I really think, I think if anyone can achieve anything in that job you can.'

Michael looked unconvinced. 'You know Kabré is on his way out?'

Hélène put the menu down on the table. 'And the guy slated to replace him is likely worse. And I hate to remind you of this, Michael, but he'll love going to Geneva each spring so he can fine-tune his banking arrangements while pontificating about primary health care.'

Michael looked at her steadily over his coffee. 'And his wife will fly to Paris to have her babies...'

Hélène nodded. 'While women in the villages are dying after two days of agony because there's not even basic EOC.'

Michael remained silent. Eventually Hélène reached across the table to cover his hand with her own. 'I know what's going through your mind, Michael. I know you could make excuses. And I love you for not making them.'

Michael smiled and put his cup down, catching sight of Seema sitting in the bay window with Stephen. After thinking for a moment, lips pursed, holding his breath, he looked up again at Hélène. 'I want to invite you to a meeting. In New York.'

'Me?'

'Beginning of February. About three hundred people. Thirty or forty countries. It's a kind of a follow-up to Alma Ata on financing primary health care. Health ministers. Donor governments. A few of the big NGOs. A whole bunch of high-level government people. All the specialized agencies. I want you to speak.'

'They wouldn't want to listen to me.'

His face had taken on a determined look. 'It's you they need to hear.'

Hélène felt a chill spread down her arms to her fingertips. 'What do you want me to speak about?'

'What you've been saying today. Telling it like it is.'

Hélène picked up the menu again. 'Wouldn't that get you into a lot of hot water?'

'I'll survive.'

Hélène's thoughts raced. She had always joined all field workers' chorus of complaint – that the health hierarchy never listened to the front line. She opened the menu. 'It should be an African.'

Michael pulled a face of agreement. 'Yes, but it would be a hell of a lot more difficult for an African to say the kind of things you were saying today. Not to mention all your experience. Not many doing what you're doing stick it out for more than two or three years.'

'I might not be sticking it much longer myself.'

She saw the surprise, the questioning in his eyes, and was

relieved to have the conversation interrupted by the small fuss of accepting drinks and arranging coasters. It had been decided that they would not eat in the hotel, but when the waiter had gone she absorbed herself in the menu.

Eventually Michael reached over and gently pushed the menu down to reveal her eyes. 'Are you really thinking of quitting?'

Again Michael had failed to carry through his plan to walk with Seema as they left the Cotswold Lodge for the restaurant at just after seven o'clock, and it was Toby's arm she took as they crossed the Banbury Road.

'Enjoyed the day, Tobe?'

'No.'

'Well, okay, found it interesting?'

'No.'

'Liar.'

'Okay. I confess it had its moments.'

Toby patted her hand. It was pleasant walking arm in arm with the beautiful Seema Mir, of whom he had always been just the slightest bit afraid.

'There weren't too many moments when you weren't ogling her.'

Toby sighed. 'Can't seem to get her to take me seriously, petal.'

'I wonder why.'

'Oh I know why, sweetheart. Oldest story in the book. La Belle et la Bête, you know. Simple as that, really.'

'I don't think she sees it quite that way. And anyway, doesn't Beauty eventually kiss the Beast and turn him into a handsome Prince?'

'I used that once in a deodorant ad. Flopped, unfortunately. Anyway, they never tell you how the Beast got the

Beauty to kiss him in the first place.'

'I think she felt sorry for him.'

'Really? There's hope yet.'

They had turned into North Parade and were approaching the Luna Caprese, a small Italian restaurant with a stucco façade and grubby red awning that was one of the few Oxford restaurants to have survived from the 1960s.

'Well, it's very obvious to me,' said Seema as they arrived, 'that she's still very fond of you.'

'Oh please, sweetheart, spare me the "fond". I've suffered enough.'

The only significant development over dinner that evening was the discovery that four of the five would be together again in the same city in the New Year. When Hélène had mentioned that Michael had invited her to address a meeting in New York, Seema had been delighted. 'And Stephen's planning to come over as well, I think?'

Stephen blustered, alarmed to see his barely conceived notion born prematurely into the world. He frowned at his napkin. 'That may be in prospect, yes.'

Hélène had protested that they couldn't all get together without Toby. 'No dramas,' Toby had beamed, gratified. 'Got to make the pilgrimage to HQ at least twice a year, drink from the pure fountain of untruth on Madison Avenue. Got a date in mind, Michael?'

'First week in February.'

Toby lifted his glass. 'Right she'll be. We'll make a weekend of it. Celebration even. Hélène and I will probably be married by then.'

'You're married now, Toby.'

Toby conceded the point with a glum look. 'You were always good on the detail, Hel.'

Hélène raised her eyes to the ceiling. Seema covered her glass with her hand as the bottle approached. 'I've a feeling Tom might be in New York by then as well. You know he's going to be chief medical correspondent on the *Times?*'

Michael nodded. 'He wrote me.'

Stephen looked dubious. 'Of all of us I should have thought he was the least likely to earn a living by the pen. Didn't he read chemistry?'

Toby lifted his glass, looking pleased at the turn events had taken. 'Struggle with the idea of a literate scientist do we, sunshine?'

Seema took a small notebook from her bag. 'I'll call him when I get back. See if he can make it.'

With the prospect of getting together again so soon, the mood of the evening changed. There had been no set aim to the reunion weekend, no conclusion envisaged. But it would probably be true to say that each of the five had invested the occasion with vague hopes, perhaps anticipating a possibility of resolving vague, long-deferred concerns of the kind that worry away in the background of all lives. But without the plan to get together again in the New Year, the weekend would have ended with a sense of anti-climax, of some unarticulated opportunity missed. All this was now pre-empted by the promise of New York, though none of the five had any notion of the chain of events that had been set in motion.

7 | Is there someone else?

Body-clock still awry, and wide awake since the early hours, Seema watched from an upstairs window as Michael stood jogging on the spot at the corner of Norham Road. As lean and fit as she had imagined he would be, wearing only shorts and a T-shirt despite the frost that rimed the hedges. A few seconds later he was gone, running lightly and easily towards the Parks. She showered and dressed, refusing to answer her own question as to whether she was applying her make-up any more carefully than usual.

Guessing he would be out for at least half an hour, she called Hélène's room and arranged to meet for breakfast. There had perhaps been a reason for losing touch with Michael, but not with Hélène, with whom all the old warmth and intimacy had returned almost as soon as they had met.

The dining room, converted to a breakfast area by an excess of morning light and the tall jugs of orange juice on the sideboard, was nonetheless redolent of the previous evening's dinner: cigarette smoke lingered on the velvet drapes, and there was more than a tinge of alcohol accompanying the smell of bacon and eggs from the kitchen.

Hélène came straight to the point. 'So, what's the skinny on Michael?'

Seema grimaced. 'Oh God, I don't know. He hardly

said a word to me all day yesterday. It's as if there'd never been … anything. I think he might even dislike me. My head's paining with it all.'

'Nonsense, my dear. The good Dr Lowell is still in love with you.'

'Hélène!'

'He's still in love with you, and so he's afraid.'

'Afraid of what?'

'Now don't be dense, Professor. He's afraid of getting hurt. Not really surprising when you think about it'

A cafetière arrived, and a tray of pastries. There was still no sign of the others.

'I don't think it's that, Hélène.'

'Then you're blind as a bat. Anyway, never mind about his feelings, what about yours?'

'Oh God, don't ask.'

Hélène stared at her, then tilted back in her chair, raising both hands as if to embrace the whole situation. 'Okay, I think I've got the picture. Allow me to summarize, as Stephen might say.' She looked at Seema pityingly. 'Once upon a time there was this beautiful young woman who rejected a young man who loved her to distraction. But as the years went by … ' – she stretched out her voice to emphasize the point – 'and she grow older and wiser, she began to realize she'd made a terrible mistake. Then, twenty years later, chance brought them together again in the city of their youth. But, instead of letting him know, she decided to be especially cool towards him because she didn't want to risk hurting him all over again … '

'Hélène, it would be unforgivable—'

' … and so he was cool towards her because she was being cool to him and making it quite clear she wasn't interested. And so they both lived miserably ever after.' She dropped her hands and reached for the toast.

Seema laughed despite herself. 'Toby doesn't seem to be suffering from any similar inhibitions. He was looking at you like a love-sick puppy the whole day.'

'Don't change the subject.'

'I haven't had a chance to ask you – is there someone else?'

Hélène's smile faded as she steadied the cafetière with one hand. 'There wasn't for a long time. I think African men thought I was too uptight. Maybe even matronly, God forbid. And most others of the unattached tribe were usually just passing through.'

'And then?'

'And then I met Fabrice.'

After a moment or two, Seema reached across the table to take her hand. Hélène bit her lip and looked down at her coffee cup. Eventually she recovered. 'We were two busy, practical, no-nonsense doctors who suddenly found ourselves acting like a couple of kids. We were so much in love I couldn't believe it was happening.'

Another pause. 'And?'

Hélène turned to look out of the window in a determined effort at control.

'He started a group called *Médecins de Réforme*. And he was speaking out. My God, was he speaking out. The kind of things I was mouthing on about yesterday, only not in the garden of an Oxford college.' Hélène had her back to the room and there was no one to see her tears. 'And then, one Thursday night, when we were due to have dinner as usual, he just never turned up. Not that night. Or any other night.'

Seema put her coffee down. 'You never saw him again?'

'Not him nor any of the others.'

'Do you know where he is?'

Hélène shook her head. 'I don't even know if he's alive. Eat your breakfast, Seema – it's a long time ago.'

'How long?'

'Two years and three months. The government denies knowing anything about it, of course.'

'Can't your embassy do anything?'

'If he'd been Canadian, maybe. But they can't do anything about all the Africans who disappear.'

'And you've heard nothing at all? Not even rumours?'

Hélène swallowed hard.

'Oh, there are always people who pretend they're in the know. Mass graves in the forest, some place without roads. Lime pits in an abandoned army camp. An old slaving island just off the coast where no one's allowed to go. Nothing you could ever follow up on.'

'So you've just... waited?'

'Nothing else I could do. I've used up every contact I've got. Got a warning from the embassy and from my own CEO back in Ottawa, would you believe. Jeopardizing the programme, apparently.'

'How awful for you. All this time, Hélène. I wish I'd known. I wish I'd come.'

'Come anyway, I wish you would.'

'I will. I'll come next year. We can plan it all in New York.'

Hélène smiled. 'You know Michael wants me to say all the things I was saying yesterday at his big international meeting?'

'I gathered as much. Will you do it?'

Hélène stared down at the tablecloth. 'I told him it should be an African. He said it would be dangerous for an African to speak out. That's when I knew I had to do it.' She bit back tears again. 'I have to do it for Fabrice.'

Returning from his run, Michael had glanced into the breakfast room to see Seema breakfasting with Hélène.

63

Showered and changed, he set off into town with Toby. 'First rule of travel, Michael. Never eat breakfast in the hotel.'

After bacon and eggs in the Covered Market, he left Toby to go to the bank and headed towards Stephen's rooms. Finding no one in, he crossed the quad to the Buttery. Stephen was sitting alone, looking miserable and staring out over the croquet lawn.

'Good morning, Dr Lowell, ready to do battle with *la formidable Hélène?*'

Michael smiled. 'Morning, Stephen. Hard to do battle when you don't really disagree.'

'I don't remember her being as aggressive as that, do you? Seem to remember her as, you know, bit of a milk-and-water type.'

'Not now.'

'And you mean to say you agree with her take on things? In your position, I mean?'

'Mostly. So, you're moving on?'

Stephen's face performed one of its academic contortions, implying dismissal. 'Nothing decided as we speak. Considering my options, as they say.'

'And the States is one option?'

'Possibly, possibly. Oxford palls after a while, as I told the lovely Seema yesterday.' He scrutinized Michael's features for any reaction.

Michael gave him no satisfaction. 'I imagine these are difficult times for the disciples?'

More facial acrobatics as Stephen made a show of rolling the proposition around in his mind. 'Possibly. If one is focused merely on contemporary events. Intellectually, on the other hand, we live in interesting times. Quite daunting really. Whole sweeps of history that still need re-analysing. And of course we've only just started on the language revolution, subversion of the signified, textual politics of deconstruction and so on and so forth. Lot of intellectual heavy lifting to be done. Just not sure this is the best place to do it. Oxford's never really "got" Marxist historiography – not like the Sorbonne.'

Michael looked at the clock on the Buttery wall. Seema would be on her way down the Parks Road, probably with Hélène. The tension of seeing her again after all the years had ebbed, replaced by a kind of emptiness. She had made it clear she had no special feeling for him. And there was no reason why he should have expected anything else. Nonetheless, the weekend had lost its savour. He had told himself not to hope, but hope had hung on his horizon nonetheless.

Stephen was in full flow, speaking in a manner that made Michael feel redundant. Toby would be arriving soon. Perhaps he should confide in Toby, as Toby had on occasion confided in him.

'I should have thought what Hélène was saying yesterday was quite a virile little example of precisely what we're talking about.' Stephen was clearly veering in a direction to which Michael would have to devote at least part of his attention. 'I mean to say, one can't analyse what she was saying about the African situation by looking at the relationship of the masses to the means of production ... it simply doesn't work. Positively invites analysis by relationships to the power structure ... '

Michael half listened, his thoughts wandering to Hélène. Something was eating away at her, something that might be just the years of commitment and frustration, the daily face-to-face frustrations and confrontations with realities he was now shielded from.

'And apropos of all this,' Stephen was saying, 'there's some- thing I wanted to mention to you, Michael, just between ourselves.' Stephen glanced around the empty Buttery to check that they were alone. 'You remember Toby's little joke in the Parks last evening, about – how did he put it? – blowing bubbles in Times Square?'

Michael smiled. 'Toby being Toby.'

'Very possibly. But one facet of the language revolution is that one knows to examine throwaway lines, even jokes, in the same way as stated propositions. Because sometimes, you see, the humour itself arises out of applying logic to produce a startling result. Startling, that is to say, because it flies in the face of conventional wisdom. Applying an accepted morality, for example, but in a much more rigorous way than society is ready to accept. It's the shock juxtaposition, a kind of dialectic if you like, that gives rise to "the gasp of humour" as it's been called.' He shook his head slowly, staring at Michael. 'That's why Toby's little joke kept me awake last night.' He blinked several times, almost as if coming out of a trance. 'You all sleep well at the Cotswold Lodge by the way?'

'Very comfortable.'

'Ye-es, it has the reputation of being an acceptable temporary abode. Anyway, as I was saying, spent a long time thinking it through. Kept arriving at the same obvious little conclusion. I mean, unless we're talking some sort of hand-me-down, soft-boiled, bed-wetting bourgeois morality here, then you'd have to say that almost any action might be justified if it stood to save five million children's lives a year. Yes?'

Michael remained silent, wondering what was coming. He decided to give Stephen the opportunity either to retreat or to cross a line.

Stephen, leaning forward, peered at him over his spectacles. Failing to read his thoughts, he fell again into his slightly sing-song rhythm. 'I mean to say, if memory serves, the equation we're looking at here puts the deaths of five million children a year against a cost of prevention which is, to all intents and purposes, insignificant. You concur?'

'Yes.'

Stephen, taking the grim tone as encouragement, leaned slightly closer. 'So, one has to ask at this point, what greater crime against humanity could there be, Michael? A crime against humanity of a scale and severity that would surely validate just about any action that stood a reasonable chance of stopping it?'

Michael pushed his chair back onto two legs and folded his arms. 'Where are you going with this, Stephen?'

Stephen made one of his 'isn't it obvious' facial somersaults to which Michael did not respond, instead looking steadily into the other's eyes, inviting him to commit himself. After an uncomfortable moment, Stephen shrugged. 'So, lying awake, as I said, I found myself wondering where someone like yourself, for example, might stand on a thing like that? I mean what your own assessment might be – professional, personal, political.'

Michael turned away to look out across the croquet lawn to the windowless stone wall of the squash courts. The sun was beginning to warm the peaceful, protected space, the morning mist gone and another fine day in the offing. Suddenly he hated Oxford. Stephen had maintained a practised academic tone, as if discussing an abstract problem, but Michael decided not to allow him wriggle room. 'You're asking me what I think about using the threat of releasing the smallpox virus to get the world to immunize children?'

Stephen, looking startled, gave an over-theatrical look around the empty Buttery, as if shocked at the vulgarity. When Michael continued to look him steadily in the eye he shrugged, turning his mouth down at the corners. 'As I said, conventional minds and moralities find it difficult to encompass such a thought but, looked at objectively, it seems to me—'

'It seems to me, Stephen, that it's something that could only be contemplated by someone who'd never been on a smallpox ward.'

The first hour or so of Sunday morning passed inconsequentially, much of it consumed by Stephen's exposition of the theory of false consciousness. The others listened with what Toby, perched once more on the window seat, considered undue attention. On the other hand, he was quite happy for Stephen to take centre stage, hoping that they could reach the landfall of lunch without any discussion of the role of advertising in advancing human well-being.

By eleven o'clock the five had relocated to the Senior Common Room, where a flask of weak coffee and a plate of digestive biscuits passed for college hospitality. The others were examining the portraits on the walls when Seema, mindful of Hélène's breakfast-time fairy tale, carried her cup to stand with Michael in front of the glass-fronted bookcase.

Michael looked up from the brass plaque he had been reading. 'Copy of every book written by a member of the college over the last five hundred years.'

Seema sipped her coffee. 'Are you planning on going straight back, Michael?'

'No, I'm taking tomorrow off.'

She looked at him in the old teasing manner, a poor proxy now for intimacy. 'So it's a myth that Michael Lowell never takes any leave? And where are you off to, may I ask?'

Michael thrilled to the smile playing at the edges of her eyes, but cringed inwardly at having to confess his plan. 'It's just the Monday, then back to Geneva. I've always wanted to see Jenner's place in Gloucestershire.'

'Jenner, as in Edward Jenner? Jenner as in the discoverer of vaccination?'

'It's an important—'

'So let's see what we've got here.' Seema replaced her coffee cup in its saucer. 'You're taking a day off, probably the first in years, and what you're planning to do with it is go on a pilgrimage to the place where vaccination started?'

'I suppose you could call it that,' said Michael, with the rueful look which had always been the counterpart to her teasing.

Hélène was heading towards the door but Seema took her arm as she passed. 'Have you heard where Michael's taking his vacation this year, Hel?'

Hélène joined them, more than willing to join in any teasing that was going. 'He's taking a vacation?'

'It's not exactly a vacation.'

'Tuscany? Vegas? A Caribbean island?' Seema was addressing only Hélène. 'None of the above. After much deliberation and counting the pros and cons on his fingers, he's decided on a day trip to see Dr Edward Jenner's house in, let's see, Gloucestershire, I think he said it was. Where the first child was vaccinated in – when was it Michael?'

Michael knew he was digging himself deeper in. '1796.'

'1796,' Seema repeated the date with satisfaction.

'Jenner's house?' Hélène pretended puzzlement, leading him on. 'What's to see, Michael?'

Michael sighed. 'Well, there's a small museum with the original surgical instruments...'

'Surgical instruments.' Seema spoke in a flat tone. 'And will that be the highlight, then?'

Michael shook his head, smiling. 'Okay, I'm out of here.'

'In Gloucestershire.' Hélène ignored him, as if discussing a patient with Seema, who took her arm as they joined the others filing out into the weak sunlight of the quad.

Back in Stephen's rooms, the talk had appeared to be ambling rather aimlessly towards a lunchtime parting of the ways, until the moment when their host again called them to order. 'To be serious for just a moment or two longer,' he began, 'I think we should perhaps just touch on a topic we all seem to have been at some pains to avoid.' In the silence that followed, Stephen turned in his chair and peered over his spectacles at Toby. 'Not to put too fine a point upon it, Tobe, what the fuck are you doing in advertising?'

The brutality of the question seemed to freeze the atmosphere, and in a few more seconds one or all of the others would no doubt have found a way to come to the defence of the figure slumped on the sofa. But Toby was in need of no such assistance. 'I'm glad you asked me that, sunshine. I had a tiny suspicion you might.'

Stephen peered again as Toby showed no signs of continuing, 'Well?'

'Well, sausage, I'll do my best to provide an answer with the appropriate intellectual depth.'

Michael smiled at Toby's way of emphasizing irony by leaning harder on what was left of his Australian accent. Hélène turned away from frowning at Stephen and spoke in a deliberately affectionate tone. 'But just tell us how you got into it in the first place, Toby.'

'That part's easy enough.' Toby scratched the back of his head, looking round with his habitual, slightly bemused expression. 'After we all split, I thought I'd look for some kind of a temporary job. Pay for a little round-the-world writing trip was the idea, as I remember it. Anyway, I

70

happened to be schmoozing at some weekend house party and happened to be talking to a bloke who happened to be from back in Townsville who happened to be the managing director of a big London ad agency. Turned out we'd both brought our Stuart Sturridge cricket bats over on the boat and never got to use them. Well, that was enough for a little drinkie or two, and when I told him what I was doing he said, "No dramas, mate, come and park your bum with us for a couple of months". First week I was there I had a couple of little ideas for TV spots. Clients happy. Boss tickled. Did I want a permanent job? Thought I might stick it out for six months, grub together enough to go round the world twice. Two years and a couple of promotions later I'd grubbed up enough to go into orbit. Never looked back, really. Or, in my case, never looked forward.'

He settled back in the sofa again, looking up at the ceiling. Hélène was the first to reply. 'Strange how decisions that seem so insignificant at the time can set the course. Do you feel trapped, Toby?'

Toby was forced to recognize her tone as 'fond'. 'Well, haven't helped myself. Made a few little mistakes along the way, as a matter of fact. Cracked on to the lovely Michelle at a photo shoot. Wanted to be kept in a manner to which she'd never before been accustomed. Next thing you know – IMF-size mortgage, plus a little place in the Chilterns for weekends, and certain other aspects of the normal lifestyle in the advertising world also not cheap. Re-mortgage to pay for a little divorce. But, no dramas, job still ripping along, promotions, bonuses, share options, all the things we used to dream about when we were young. Got myself hitched again. Putting in pretty long hours as well by then, believe it or not. Not always easy making sure you get the credit for everything everybody else does in a place as big as that.'

'Be serious for a minute, Toby.' It was Seema now who was sympathizing.

Toby thought for a moment. 'Serious. Well, seriously then, sweetheart, why I'm in advertising is just a combination of whatever little talents I happen to have and whatever little opportunities happened to have wandered my way, plus a double shot of fecklessness and the need to earn a crust, which over the years appears to have become a fairly thick crust.'

Hélène saw her opportunity. 'That's not so different from any one of us. The same things pretty well explain what we've all ended up doing.'

'But it *is* a little different, ta, sweetie. It's different because you all have that other little ingredient in the mix. A *cause*, I think it's called.' He sank back, pushing his legs out again into the centre of the circle. 'And with your gracious permission I'll shut up now – I'd hate you to think I had a serious side.'

Stephen and Michael began to speak at the same time, but it was Michael to whom the others turned. 'Three things to say about that, Toby.' He cringed inwardly as his right hand grasped the first finger. 'Hélène's right. Talents, opportunities, need to earn a living. Explains most of what we're all doing.' Toby was about to protest but Michael had a firm grip on the next finger. 'Second, easy to exaggerate what you're calling "a cause". Remember Florey – guy who got the Nobel Prize for penicillin? Everyone said he'd done it for humanity, but he wasn't having any of it. Said it was the excitement of the chase, the fascination of the science. Said the fact it was of some use to the world was all very gratifying but it wasn't really what pushed him on.'

Toby held up both hands in a gesture of scepticism. 'Don't tell me it's not part of it, Michael. Just listening to you and Hel yesterday ... '

'I'm not saying it's not part of it, but those of us who can earn a living doing something we believe in shouldn't pretend it's the only reason we're doing it.'

Hélène jumped in.

'Absolutely right, Michael. Or that we're more virtuous.' Toby gave her a look which said he was refraining from comment.

'It wouldn't be like you to forget your third point, Michael?' Seema was looking at him in the affectionate, amused way that again brought memories flooding back.

He returned his hands to the arm of his chair. 'Third, it's worth saying that, one way or another, all of us apart from Toby are paid out of the public purse. And there wouldn't be any public purse without commerce, and that includes advertising.'

'And your point?' said Stephen, as if what Michael had said were too obvious to be dwelt on.

'My point is that it would be a particularly unpleasant form of hypocrisy if those of us who are paid out of the public purse to work on "causes" were to hold in contempt the commercial activities that make it possible.'

Toby was surprised to find himself close to tears for the second time that weekend, though he needed no reminding of why Michael was his friend.

8 | A circle completed

Toby unfastened his seat belt, lit a cigarette, and resigned himself to a ten-mile crawl. The reunion had been a mistake, a reminder only of what had been lost. And ahead now stretched only another week of breakfasting alone, knotting up the pastel ties, summoning the energy for the expected bonhomie as he strode into the office, flirting ever more pathetically with the secretaries. To make the prospect even more depressing, tomorrow was what Madison Avenue insisted on calling 'Blue Sky Monday' – a whole morning of meetings that were supposed to encourage 'out of the box' thinking, most of which, in Toby's experience, should have been kept firmly inside whatever box might be available. He drew greedily on the cigarette and thought about switching lanes as the traffic again came to a stop. Was the bored-looking guy in the Ford Cortina also heading back to another soul-sapping week? And the sour-looking girl gripping the wheel of the little yellow Fiat 850 coupé? The city would have been spread out ahead of him by now, but for the fumes of a thousand cars distorting the view.

He flicked on the radio. The US President was apparently fishing in Pennsylvania, something the commentator seemed to think he would soon have a lot more time for. Would she even give him a second thought on her flight across the

Atlantic? He tugged on the handbrake again. She had invited him, perhaps only half-jokingly, to visit her in Africa. He punched another pre-set and began tapping the wheel to a track from *Urban Cowboy*. Well, why not? Fly out for Christmas. No warning. Just appear. Total surprise. Better than pulling crackers on his own in Ealing. He prodded the cigar lighter on the dashboard, deciding to allow himself another cigarette on account of the traffic. Might even stop him making a fool of himself at the office party. Warmer, too. Place was probably fifty clicks south of Woop Woop but there was sure to be an Intercontinental somewhere. Feebly cheered, he released the handbrake and eased towards the North Circular, heading towards a city that crowded in on him under leaden skies.

Stephen sat alone in his college rooms. The idea of leaving Oxford had been a spur-of-the-moment thing, but for the last hour it had been putting down a few tentative roots. Maybe a change was just what he needed. At any rate there would be no harm in going over for a week or two, looking up Myron, checking out the options. Longer, if necessary. After all, he could afford it. And surely in the States a professorship somewhere would be his for the asking.

One or two students were heading towards the Buttery for afternoon tea as he looked down on the college lawns, the peace and calm of it all interrupted only by the slow tolling of the chapel bell, marking the passing of each hour as it had done for four hundred years.

Seema looked at her watch. Still only two hours in. She had refused her dinner tray and had been trying to get to sleep. But the cabin lights were not yet dimmed and no one in the seats around her had settled for the night. She rubbed her wrists. Apart from renewing her friendship with Hélène, the weekend had been a disappointment. She closed her eyes, but shutting out the world seemed only to increase the roar of the engines. What had she been hoping for? Some opening? Some closure? But Michael had been determined to keep his distance. And so it had all been up to her. But how could she have made any move when she was not certain of her own feelings? And how could she know her own feelings if they were not to spend any time together? And then suddenly it was all over, and there was only the tedium of the 747's tireless push toward home.

With an effort she stretched down to wrap the flight blanket round her legs and feet against the icy air from the emergency door. Still more than four hours to go. Plus probably two more getting back into Manhattan on a Sunday night. She bit her lip. New York would be getting ready for Christmas: little white lights on the trees down the Avenue of the Americas; men with fingerless gloves roasting chestnuts in Washington Square; families from Pennsylvania and New Jersey crowding up against the window displays at Macy's; and the usual rather cheerless Christmas tree in the vestibule of the History Faculty. The captain's voice, so deliberately bored, informed them that the cabin lights were about to be dimmed. It would be the third year she had spent Christmas on her own. How had it happened that they had not spent even five minutes together? There had still been something there, she had been sure of it. So why had he made no move to walk with her even once? Was Hélène right? Was he frightened to get closer?

Even through the sleep mask she could still see the jumping light of the film, her head beginning to ache in earnest. She should go to the back of the airplane and drink several of those little paper cups of water. She pushed the mask up to see the light already beginning to fade over the vastness of the Atlantic. Heading in the opposite direction, another jet trailed a disintegrating chalk mark across the darkening blue. It had been great to see Hélène, even if it had brought her guilt closer, made her feel she really wasn't doing all that much with her own life. Most of the time, researching and teaching the history of slavery felt like it was worthwhile. But compared with what Hélène was doing it seemed comfortable, disengaged. Should she have just taken his arm as they left the hotel, as she had that first evening? Could they have dinner together in New York? Keep it light? Stay away from the top of that slope that could lead to so much hurt?

Michael Lowell was neither a self-important nor a fanciful man, but he could not entirely rid himself of the thought that a circle was in some way being completed as he laid a hand on the altar rail. After a moment he raised his head from the most modest of memorials – '*Edward Jenner: the discoverer of vaccination 1749-1823*' – to see the great east window depicting in stained glass the dozen-or-so healing miracles of Christ.

No one knew better that victory over smallpox had been achieved by thousands of immunization managers, technicians, health workers, trainers, vaccination teams. But modesty could not deny him his place near the centre of it all, there on the sixth floor of the World Health Organization headquarters where a small team of nine had co-ordinated the hunting down of the virus in one country after another until the disease that had killed as many as five hundred million people in the twentieth century – many times more than all the wars – was finally gone from the world. Gone, that is, apart from the samples stored in icy stillness in those two bio-safety laboratories on either side of the Cold War. And this greatest of all victories for public health had begun here, in this dark, obscure place that also seemed suspended in a winter stillness. They had been heady days. And if smallpox could be defeated, so the argument had run, then why not polio, measles, tetanus, diphtheria? He did not need to stand here by Edward Jenner's tomb to be reminded how sloppy this line of thinking was.

He left by the ancient lych-gate, his dissatisfactions merging as the light fell over a country churchyard. Back in his rented car, he sat for a while before starting the engine, hands on his lap, listening to the great silence. But it was pointless: pointless to tell himself to forget her when he hadn't come near to doing that in twenty years.

Hélène looked down on her third continent in four days, or at least on what she could see of it through the cloud which covered much of Eastern Canada. Further north there had been the pristine vastness of the Arctic, but as the plane had begun its descent to Montreal her homeland had appeared murky and uninviting. Behind lay images of Africa's endless warmth, and of Oxford's autumnal light, and of the disturbing reappearance of Toby Jenks in her life. And before her... a homeland she hardly knew.

The plane lurched downwards in the heavier air. Should she have been a little bit more open, given his protestations of seriousness more benefit of the doubt, instead of slamming the door in his face? Was it out of a hopeless loyalty to Fabrice? Or a weak, panicky determination to preserve her own equilibrium?

After Les Mille-Isles, the Aérobus from Mirabel began to run into traffic, the crowds pressing ever closer, seeming to threaten her with the promise she had made to Michael. It would have been difficult to refuse. And cowardly not to be prepared to say in public all the things she had spoken about so freely in the safety of a college garden. It was Michael himself who would be taking the bigger risk. Ashamed, as the bus made its stop-and-start way down de La Gauchetière, she told herself to think instead of Fabrice – and of her parents, of how much they would be looking forward to seeing her.

Stephen's request for an interview with the Warden had been granted straight away, his Scout returning almost immediately with a note inviting him to drop by for sherry before Hall.

Now, back in his own rooms, he cringed to think how obvious it must have been that he had been seeking reassurance that he was still appreciated. Pathetic. Infantile. He buried his face in his hands as he heard again the pompous, patronizing tones ushering him towards the door – 'No, no, dear boy, no cause to worry, not at all, not one little bit. Marxism *qua* power in the land may be in what many of us would consider terminal decline, but Marxism *qua* historiography is in extremely rude health, extremely rude health.'

The heat in his brain mounted as he relived the episode. Most of the other dons would already be at High Table, but he could not face Hall tonight. He would eat in town later. But first he would assert himself. Show the old fraud he was not to be patronized. He crossed to his desk and took out a pad of notepaper.

Dear Warden, Thank you for seeing me at such short notice this evening. It is perhaps surprising that college life offers so few opportunities to talk of these things, and I am grateful for ...

With sudden violence, he screwed up the letter and threw it at the scarred leather waste bin by the side of the fireplace.

After twenty minutes' fumbling, Toby threw the Rubik's cube

across the room where it bounced at an unexpected angle from the floorboards and took a chip out of a Royal Doulton vase that had been a present from his mother-in-law. Or his mother in law once-removed, as he now thought of her. He sighed and settled down in front of the TV programme he was supposed to be watching in order to catch a new branding exercise by a rival agency. Hélène would be back in Canada by now. Half a world away. Or maybe it was only a quarter.

His eye was drawn to the accusing chip in the vase. What did he really feel about that chip, he asked himself, tearing open another bag of potato crisps. A great deal of satisfaction, he answered with a small defiance. Sarah, he was pretty sure, was working around to asking for a divorce. God knows they both had grounds. Acres of grounds. A whole country estate of grounds. An entire nation with several overseas possessions of grounds. He waited for the commercial break, fully prepared to be unimpressed. Somewhere in the darker recesses of his mood, he knew, was a lurking fear that redundancy as well as divorce might be pencilled into his diary for the coming year. What he should do was have the courage of his whims and forget it all, go to Africa for Christmas, get himself tucked up somewhere warm with Hélène, instead of sitting here on his own eating Savoury Hoops and watching *Jackanory*. But it was wishful thinking. The girl wouldn't have a bar of him. Not that he couldn't see why. Spending her life feeding the hungry and healing the sick and, for all he knew, visiting the imprisoned, while he devoted his life to achieving a nought point one per cent increase in the market share of barbecue-flavoured crisps. He reached for the remote and, an hour later, awoke to find himself listening to Judi Dench reading from *Tales of Beatrix Potter*.

9 | Look me in the face

Geneva, December 1980

It was the week before the Christmas vacation and the silver Volkswagen stood alone in the parking lot of the World Health Organization. On the sixth floor the usual noises – the light staccato of typewriters, the soft purr of phones, the tired back and forth of photocopiers, the whine of the elevators – had long ago fallen silent.

Michael ran a finger down a column of figures, making a brief margin note requesting the removal of decimal points. Starting again at the top, his eyes scanned the column for measles. And in the silence of the empty building he heard again the voice of Hélène. Her anger and despair in the tranquillity of an Oxford garden had shaken him, perhaps because it had brought back memories of a former self. And because, when all the niceties were stripped away, she was right. And wasn't it reasonable that her anger had been directed partly at an acquiescent health establishment of which he was a part? An establishment that, as soon as you looked at it with anything like fresh eyes, was rotten with complacency? An establishment that allowed millions of children to sicken and die, millions more to be stunted, blinded, crippled, while

81

those who held the power and the purse-strings never gave them more than a second's thought?

He made another effort to focus on the task in hand, proceeding down the totals column, committing to memory the data for the seven or eight countries which between them were home to more than half the world's children. After a moment's thought, he began applying an approximate ratio to convert immunization coverage rates into numbers of deaths from vaccine-preventable disease. A hundred and eighty thousand in Nigeria, two hundred thousand in Pakistan, forty thousand in Zaire. The bottom line, he knew, would still be close to five million. Each an individual child. And for every one who had died, several more now deaf, blind or brain-damaged. Beyond the lights of Geneva, out over the dark expanse of the lake, he saw the measles ward in Bangui, curtained against the brightness of a light that would have tortured the eyes of the twenty or so children in the cots. Where had the hopes of those days gone? Days of working every waking hour to make those early hopes into a reality. And to put behind him the memory of Seema Mir.

He turned the page to the column for polio vaccine, finger again beginning to travel down the list.

'*Bonsoir, monsieur le docteur. Vous travaillez tard.*'

The security guard had paused for a moment in the doorway.

'*Salut*, Marcel.'

'*Un autre café la prochaine fois?*'

'*Non, merci. Trop de café déjà ce soir.*'

The guard continued his rounds as Michael's finger found Ethiopia, translating its six per cent immunization rate into five thousand or more cases of paralytic polio every year. He stared again into the darkness above the lake, seeing huge clouds rolling in from the Ethiopian highlands towards the twenty-a-side football game somewhere on the outskirts of Addis. An advance scud of rain had sent the players running for shelter. All except one: a boy of nine or ten who had been trying to join in, laughing and calling out as he pushed his skateboard through the dirt with his arms. But now he was stuck in the mud of the centre circle, holding his arms over his head to protect himself from the sudden weight of the rains. Michael's finger continued on down the column – Eritrea, Ghana, Haiti, India – hearing the battering on the corrugated iron of the canopy above his head, seeing two of the other boys rush back out to carry the crippled youngster to shelter. The office lights flickered briefly as he reached the bottom line. Four hundred thousand. Four hundred thousand children dragging themselves through life with their arms.

For a moment, something like panic threatened as he stared at the carnage represented by the calm rows of statistics spread out over his desk. Hélène had said it: it could all be prevented for an almost negligible amount. Measles, neonatal tetanus, polio, even whooping cough, for God's sake. It could all be ended within a few years if only the world really gave a damn about all these kids.

Not until after midnight did he turn his attention to his own draft introduction in which, as last year, he had attempted to enumerate the principal roadblocks. But, even as he read it through, he heard again the voice in the college garden: *'spare me the logistics and the cold chains, Michael'*. He looked up from the text. Where in his draft did it say, as Hélène had said, that the real reason was that more than eighty per cent of health budgets were being spent on less than ten per cent of the population? Where, under the subheading of 'Financial implications', did it say *'for Christ's sake, the whole thing could be done for the cost of a couple of F-15 jet fighters.'* And at what point in his own little speech to the World Health Assembly would he look up and say: '*Look me in the face and tell me that it couldn't be done inside five years if the world thought it was important enough.*'

Slowly, he closed the ring binder of spreadsheets and stood in front of his desk, staring down at the blue cover that bore the WHO's serpent-entwined Rod of Asclepius, god of healing. At a quarter to midnight he picked up the phone and checked his watch. It was still only early evening in Atlanta. He punched in the number, without needing to look it up.

10 | *Filer à l'anglaise*

Wednesday, January 28th, 1981

In a sweltering wooden hut three thousand miles away from the headquarters of the World Health Organization, Hélène Hevré was fighting off the waves of tiredness that had been building up all afternoon. Around her, in green-and-white tunics, were gathered the dozen trainees of the cadre *Protection Maternelle et Infantile*. The lesson was supposed to last until five, but her students were already shuffling in the heat, anxious to start the journey back to their villages for the weekend. And she too was anxious to finish packing and leave enough time for her goodbyes. Christmas had come and gone and the speech she had agreed to make in New York was no longer next year but next week.

She checked her topic list: counting red and white blood cells; acute and chronic diarrhoea; urine and stool testing; blood smears for malaria; recognizing respiratory infections... before finally smiling up at them all, her expression acknowledging the heat and bringing the lesson to an end.

When the relief doctor had given her a wave through the window to signal his arrival, she sat for a moment, alone and exhausted at the small desk in the centre of the aisle, heat and tiredness fighting for control of her body. Down both sides of the ward, wooden window flaps were propped open, making little difference to the temperature. Tomorrow she would be in freezing Manhattan, and a few days later in Montreal, where she would check herself into McGill and try to get to the bottom of whatever might be wrong. There were times when the tiredness seemed in remission, only to return in a new onslaught days or weeks later. She had also noticed a slight swelling of the lymph nodes, though that could just be a sign that, like everyone else working in the clinic, she was constantly fighting off some infection or other.

Time was getting short, but she lingered still on the ward, the only sound the unsteady murmuring of the kerosene fridge and the occasional call of a bird from the bank of the river. She had not wanted to go like this; projects half completed, trainees half trained. But it was no use pretending. If she made the speech that lay neatly typed at the bottom of her suitcase, then there was no way she would be able to return to Africa. The government would cancel her visa. And in any case her own organization would just as surely bar her return for fear of repercussions on the programme. Addressing Michael's meeting meant making the break she had dithered over for so long – starting a new life, going home to a place she no longer knew. Above all, abandoning the dream of Fabrice's return, the fantasy of her being there to nurse him back to health and start a new life together.

A few minutes later, back in her own quarters, she took out the bamboo-framed photograph. The handsome, intelligent face looked back at her, delivering the usual shock of contrast between his carefree expression and the thought of what might have become of him. In the dimness she heard his voice, telling her in the liquid cadences of West African French that speaking out was exactly what she should be doing, that charities like her own were doing a good job patching up a few of the thousands of broken bodies at the bottom of the cliff but that the real task was to confront what was pushing them off the top. 'And that, *ma chère Hélène*, is a job for Africans, not expats.' And that was why he had not shown up that night in the garden of L'Eau Vive when she had waited, reading the menu again and again, watching the citron candle burning down, until the nuns had taken off their aprons and gathered to sing their nightly *a capella* prayer. At that moment she had wished that she too could still pray.

She removed a few more photographs from the drawer, along with a bundle of Hallmark 'Thank You' cards. Impatiently, she scraped the tears from her cheeks with one hand and with the other slipped the photos between the folds of her only warm sweater.

Outside the light was already beginning to fade, the air tinged with wood smoke as she stepped out on to the veranda. She stood for a few moments until, on an impulse, she lowered the suitcase to the decking and crossed the few yards of bare earth back to the ward.

She approached the cot in the dim light, her rubber sandals making no sound on the concrete floor. Leaning over, she resisted the temptation to rest a hand on the rail, knowing that the slightest noise might provoke an agony of convulsions. Earlier that day she had quietened the spasms by giving the child as much sedating barbiturate as she dared. One of the trainees had asked about antibiotics. But there was nothing that antibiotics could do now. The infection that had sent the toxins pulsing through the tiny body was long gone. And of anti-toxins there were none. She looked down at the little girl who was momentarily at peace. In an hour or so the mother would return, stealing in apologetically with her plastic shopping bags. Come to sit by the cot for another night. Come, in all probability, to watch her daughter die while Hélène would be high above the Atlantic. The child stirred, but did not wake. Two inflamed cuts marked the upper arm where a *féticheur* had attempted an insufflation of herbs.

She took a last glance around the ward. Between the aisles, the Christmas tree was beginning to drop. How many more mothers were there in the world tonight waiting for their infants to die of simple tetanus? Michael would know. At least to the nearest few thousand.

At half past six she left the compound for the four-mile drive to the airport. On the way she called briefly at the hospital to say goodbye to the *Directeur*, knowing she should have allowed at least an hour if she were not to be accused of the sin of *filer à l'anglaise.* In the event she made her escape after ten minutes, shaking hands in the French African way and raising her hand to her heart. She would miss being one of Les Amis.

On the afternoon of Tuesday, January 20th, 1981, Stephen found himself staring down at the Atlantic through the slightly opaque window of a Pan American 747. The Christmas vacation had been a time of tidying up his affairs, putting his books and belongings into storage, and preparing to leave his rooms. And whether it was the forced inactivity of the seven-hour flight, or the monotonous roar of the great GE engines pushing him towards the New World, or just the distant blue leatherette of the ocean thirty-five thousand feet below, he had also found himself staring into an inner self that was usually far too close to be seen.

What he saw there was a man on the threshold of middle age locked in the youthful embrace of an ideology that had once satisfied so much more than the demands of intellect and conscience. From his teens, the feelings of guilt at the privilege he had been born into had seemed to put him at a psychological disadvantage, as if privilege had somehow invalidated his existence in the new world of the 1960s. And in that world where his social class had seemed to make him an enemy at worst and an irrelevance at best, Marx had offered him a place to stand. Perhaps it was the promise of personal validation, even more than the appeal to youth's raw sense of fairness, that had pushed him to embrace communism; the intellect had merely followed. All this he saw, staring down into the vast confessional of the Atlantic, its blank emptiness so open to metaphor and melancholy.

He ignored the drinks trolley, continuing to gaze down at the ocean, glimpsing for a moment that this probably explained why he had clung on for so long, the fingers of the intellect reaching for every last handhold of justification while all around him others were letting go, conceding the failures and the abuses of the communist dream. All this, he saw from seven miles high, had defined who and what he was as he approached his middle years; and all of it exaggerated by years of joining in the game of leftier-than-thou, leapfrogging over others to positions of ever-greater radicalism, positions which he had the intellectual capacity to defend but which, at moments like this, he could see were surely absurd. And, for a few minutes at least, it was clear to him that it wasn't Oxford he needed to escape; nor was the attraction of New York's New School of Social Research anything to do with its radical traditions. What it offered was a release from the sterile prison he had created for himself over the years, a chance to rethink his position with comparatively little loss of face; leave behind some of the intellectual baggage. Like so many who travel hopefully, he travelled to leave himself behind.

Seema had suspected that something was wrong as soon as the meeting with her editor had been switched from their normal lunch spot to the more formal setting of Gammer & Duce's publishing house in the heart of the Cast Iron District. When she arrived, it was clear that Janie was nervous about something, prevaricating rather than getting down to business.

Soon afterwards she found herself shaking hands with Clyde Robie, a man of about forty who was introduced as the new Director of Publishing. Without preliminaries, he took the opening chapters of Seema's manuscript from his briefcase and tossed them on to the editor's desk. After seating himself casually on the windowsill, he indicated to Jane to start the meeting while he looked down, apparently bored, at whatever might be happening in the street below.

Jane had begun to say something blandly complimentary about the manuscript when Robie, still looking out of the window, interrupted mid-sentence. 'We need to cut to the chase here, Ms Mir. Jane and I agree it needs a little restructuring. Not to put too fine a point on it, the relationship between Jefferson and this Sally girl needs to be front and centre; the rest can follow any which way.'

Seema's eyes widened almost imperceptibly as Clyde Robie turned to look at her, placing the heels of both hands on the windowsill behind him. 'Journalism school day one. Grab line up front. Work in the backstory once they're hooked.'

Seema turned to look at Janie, suspecting a previous conversation in which it had been decided that Clyde Robie's presence was necessary to lay all this on the line. The editor attempted a smile and laid a soothing hand on the manuscript. 'It's just a question of the order, Seema.'

'I'm afraid I have to say it's a little more than that.' Robie had turned to the window again. 'We need to have the thing fleshed out. Pun intended.'

Seema opted not to reply. In the silence, he feigned interest in something going on in the street below. 'Again, not to put too fine a point upon things, we need to be a lot more specific about the sexual relationship. I gather she was sixteen at the time?'

As Robie continued to look out of the window, Seema ignored the question. Behind the desk, Jane was raising a 'what can I do?' eyebrow. Eventually the publishing director turned to face her, eyebrows raised in anticipation of an answer.

Seema gave him a small smile. 'There's a problem with what you're suggesting, Mr Robie. The relationship between Thomas Jefferson and Sally Hemings is not the subject of my book.'

Robie raised both hands in the beginnings of exasperation but something in Seema's look forestalled interruption. 'And so it will be given the place it demands in the perspective of what the book is about, which, as you know, is the lives of individual members of the Hemings family who served as slaves to the Wayles and Jefferson families for the best part of a century.'

Clyde Robie's smile suggested that he intended to be patient, confident in having the whip hand. 'You don't seem to quite grasp the import of what's being said here, Ms Mir. The fact of the matter is you're not the only one working this particular seam. To be absolutely straight with you, I'm not sure Gammer & Duce will still want to publish if you're all round-the-houses on this one while someone from Columbia or Princeton goes for the jugular on Jefferson and this Sally girl. And that's what we feel is very much likely to happen.'

From being a teenager in Karachi, Seema had known herself to be accommodating, malleable even, up to a point. But when the point was reached, mildness was liable to give way to something altogether steelier. She sometimes thought it had been learned from her father, a military man who had been fond of drawing lines in the sand. Lines like the one Clyde Robie had just crossed. She smiled again as she addressed both publishing director and editor, her voice still low. 'I will write the book I set out to write, Mr Brodie. The one outlined in my original proposal and summarized in some detail in our contract, which I'm sure you've read. Whether Gammer & Duce wish to publish or not is of course up to you.'

On the street outside, she slung her bag over her shoulder and headed back up Broadway. The meeting had cleared her mind of one trouble. But the greater indecisiveness remained. Michael had already been in town for several days. And there had been no call.

11 | Can we take a walk?

Washington DC, Monday, January 26th, 1981

On a bitterly cold January day, Michael Lowell checked his coat and found a booth overlooking a bleak Pennsylvania Avenue. Judging by the torn plastic banquette and the tired menu wedged into a condiment set, Paul had not chosen the place for its fine dining.

In normal circumstances there were few things he would have looked forward to more than lunch with the man who had been both colleague and friend since the two of them had graduated together from med school. Paul had been part of the original USAID effort to combat smallpox and measles in West Africa and of the US Centers for Disease Control team working on the global smallpox-eradication campaign. Five years as director of the Epidemic Intelligence Service and two more as head of infectious disease had established him as the country's leading virologist, and it had been no surprise to anybody when he had been appointed principal deputy director of the CDC with responsibility for most aspects of its scientific work.

Always with an eye for the chance to meet if ever their travel plans threatened to intersect, the two of them usually managed to get together three or four times a year either in

Geneva or somewhere on the Eastern seaboard. Both were now what DA, their old boss, would have called 'shiny pants' epidemiologists as opposed to the 'shoe leather' kind of their earlier years, and on more than one occasion their respective institutions had been known to turn a blind eye when the friendship between the two men had led to bureaucratic corners being cut.

But the circumstances on that day in January 1981 were not normal.

He discarded the straw from his glass and took a sip of iced water, adding to the chill in his insides. This was not how it should be. He should have been feeling the usual pleasurable anticipation, not this heavy dread. He looked up from the table to see the snow beginning to drift again, the bunting flapping from the streetlights, the lunchtime crowds starting to hurry. He checked his watch. The flight from Atlanta had probably been delayed by the weather. Either that or there were long lines on the expressway from National. He settled down to wait, occasionally glancing across towards the entrance to the Pennsylvania Avenue Metro.

When he had called before Christmas to ask if Paul might be in DC towards the end of January, he had known that something was wrong. They had arranged the lunch, but Paul – usually a man of few words – had seemed reluctant to end the call. Eventually Michael had tried to sign off by going over the arrangements once again.

'You're sure you'll be in town?'

'Yeah, unlikely there'll be a change now.'

'Good. So, the place on Pennsylvania Avenue around 12.30?'

'Fine.'

But still there had been nothing in Paul's tone to signal a signing off.

'Mike, there's something else I wanted to just let you know beforehand.' The 'Mike' was the clue that something important was coming. 'Checked myself into Hopkins last week. Saw Phil Fossy, remember Phil?'

Michael had felt a chill spread down his arms to his hands. Phil Fossy had also been a contemporary at medical school, but what leapt into Michael's mind was not a face but a fact: Phil Fossy had become a leading oncologist. On the other end of the line, Paul did not wait for an answer. 'Yeah, old Phil. Anyway, tumour. Pancreas. Not good.' The silence had stretched to many seconds.

Now, waiting for Paul to arrive, the snow beginning to settle on the mountains of discoloured ice and slush that lined the sidewalk, Michael wondered again what he could say. And behind the immediate concern another question nagged: could he, should he, still go through with it? Could he still ask Paul what he had planned to ask when he had called before Christmas? He sipped again from the glass of iced water. Paul would probably just tell him that he was out of his mind. If so, he would accept it. Accept that he had lost his balance somewhere along the way. And that would be that. But was it right even to ask? For no reason at all, Seema Mir came flooding into his thoughts. Her self-possession; the way she had of tilting her head almost imperceptibly when asking a question; the lilt of that now barely perceptible accent; the pleasure of listening to that low, gentle voice. He was a rational man, an epidemiologist, a scientist; and his heart ached for her.

A sharp tap at the window startled him. Michael raised a hand, feeling the pleasure instantly inundated by the ice water of concern as Paul Lewis pushed through the revolving door, stamping the snow from his shoes and pulling off his coat.

It was more to find a way of talking about the cancer than in the hope of discovering any unexplored avenue that Michael asked the routine questions and checked all the possibilities, knowing that Paul would not have missed anything. For the first time since his father's death, he found himself experiencing that sickening lurch of the professional suddenly becoming the personal, the opening up of vast depths of impotence under a professional expertise onto which so much power is projected. And at every lurch and churn he was reminded of how much more intensely Paul himself must be experiencing the same journey. He had asked about Anne and the boys, and, though the voice had remained steady, the sadness in his friend's eyes had been immeasurable.

Lunch was consumed almost without being tasted, and when coffee came Paul leaned back in the booth and slapped the palms of both hands gently on the table. 'Okay, Mike, that's it. Just gotta cowboy up here, as my old man would have said. Let's talk about something else. What happened in Oxford? You get to see her?'

Michael looked away. What else could be talked about that would not seem trivial, unreal, irrelevant? One of his own father's relished expressions had been 'apart from that, Mrs Lincoln, how did you enjoy the play?'

'Yes, I saw her.'

'So spill. How did it go?'

'Nothing doing.'

'Why not?'

'She's not interested.'

'In getting together?

Michael nodded.

'Have you asked her?'

'Asked her what?'

Paul clicked his tongue impatiently. 'I don't know, asked her for a date, whatever it is you kids do these days.'

Michael smiled. He and Paul were exactly the same age, though Paul and Anne had married soon after med school and had two teenage boys. He looked out of the window and pointed upwards towards a building on the opposite corner. 'Isn't that where the old Peace Corps office used to be?'

Paul followed his look. 'Sure is. Had my interview with Shriver right there, third floor corner. Those days he interviewed us all personally. Arrived an hour late and apologized with the biggest shot of whisky I'd ever seen. Next thing I knew I was on my way up to Columbia for two weeks' intensive on tropical medicine. Two weeks! Imagine that today.'

'I know. Give us a Kelty pack and a copy of Manson's and we thought we could solve all the problems of the world.'

'Until we got there.'

'You ever think about that time?'

'Yeah, thought about it more just recently.'

Michael hesitated for a moment. 'Hélène's still out there. Gave me a rough time in Oxford.'

'Gave *you* a rough time?'

'Yeah, seems we've become complacent about the millions of kids dying from measles and the rest.'

Paul pushed out his lower lip. 'She's probably not wrong.'

'No. And it got to me when I went back to Geneva. Desk stacked with stats, all the new immunization data for the WHA. All the usual zeroes on the end. Hélène, bless her, sees a kid's face in every one.'

'That way madness lies, as the man said.'

'True, though. Anyway, what's happening in Atlanta?'

Paul again pushed out the lip and put his head to one side in a familiar gesture that brought Michael a new wave of sadness.

'Usual stuff. Except we might have something weird coming down the line. Some very odd PCP clusters popping up in New York and California. Same for Kaposi's. So right off you'd be thinking immuno-suppression, but the really weird thing is it looks like it's targeting homosexual men.'

Michael frowned. 'Targeting how?'

'No idea. Anyway, keep it to yourself. Could cause the mother of all panics. Not to mention offering yet another opportunity for the media to demonstrate its sense of responsibility. And anyway, what we can say about it right now amounts to zilch. Not even going to be in the MMWR for a while yet. Tell you more when I know. Anyway, from the few to the many, how's immunization going?'

'It's not.'

'You got the eighty per cent thing agreed.'

Michael grimaced. 'Yeah, if resolutions were vaccinations I'd be out of a job.'

For another half hour, the two talked about the global immunization programme they had helped set up in the wake of the success against smallpox. There was no need to explain any of the difficulties. Paul had been the one who had warned him when he had first taken the job that expectations for the other vaccine-preventable diseases were wildly unrealistic. No one knew better that there was all the difference in the world between a one-off effort to ring fence a specific outbreak of a viral disease and a permanent system of routine immunization.

Michael finished his coffee and returned the mug to the table. 'Thing is, it always ends up like some late-night college talk about putting the world to rights – the one where everybody ends up saying all we really need is the political will and is there any more wine in that bottle.'

'Yeah, we've all been there.'

The snow in Pennsylvania Avenue had almost stopped, the crowds becoming more leisurely. Outside the window of the diner a maintenance vehicle had stopped to attach one end of a 'Welcome Home' banner across the street, the city preparing for the return of the fifty-two hostages from Iran.

'Yeah, but somehow I can't help hearing DA saying "C'mon guys, let's find a way to end-run this".' Both men smiled at the memory of the man who had been their boss for seven years and who had managed to find a way round, over or through every obstacle that stood in the way of eradicating smallpox. As a badge of honour it could hardly have been more discreet, but both men were wearing the tie-pin in the shape of a bifurcated needle that DA had presented to the members of his team.

'Different proposition, though. There probably isn't any end-run this time.'

'Marathon not a sprint and all that. Thing we're not short of here is sports metaphors. Talking of which, I hear talk of a touchdown on destroying the stocks.'

Paul pulled a sceptical face. 'Don't hold your breath. DA's pushing, but AMRIID will for sure have the final say and they want to play hardball with the Sovs. Obviously we're not going to toss ours in the autoclave unless we're sure they'll do the same. But if there's going to be any trust involved it won't even make first base. It's not just the new guy. Carter was the same at the end. And Defense has also started asking who else out there apart from Koltsovo might be holding a little something back. The French have been suspect from day one, but now they're talking about North Korea and Iraq, for God's sake. And they may have a point. So, no, bottom line is, I'm not expecting to be asked for the pass codes any time soon.'

Michael sat head down, staring at the plastic folder in which they had left the tip. Eventually it was Paul who spoke. 'I'm real sorry you're frustrated with the programme.

Anything I can do at the CDC end?'

Michael raised his head and met his friend's eyes, almost unable to bear the friendship and the bravery he saw there. 'Paul, there is something else I wanted to ask you. Something that came up before I knew about the cancer.'

It was Paul Lewis's turn to realize that something serious was coming. He waited for Michael to go on.

'I don't even know if it's right to mention it.'

'Anything. You know that.'

Michael smiled, hardening the muscles of his jaw, pressing his tongue hard into his palate.

'It's not something we can talk about here.' He knew he was near to tears and looked away from his companion towards the revolving door where a newly arrived couple were brushing snow from coats and jackets.

'Can we take a walk?'

12 | Why this blood-buzzing anxiety?

New York City

Toby Jenks checked in to the Algonquin late in the afternoon of Thursday, January 29th. As soon as he had kicked off his shoes he picked up the phone and requested the number of the Tudor Hotel on 42nd Street. Put through, he asked to be connected to the room of a Dr Hélène Hevré, recently arrived from Abidjan. He waited. London to a brick the mini-bar was in that prissy little reproduction sideboard.

The phone continued to ring as he stared at the framed embroidery map of the world above the bed. It would have been mad to go visit her. Fish out of water. Big fat pink bloke in Africa. Face like a dropped pie. The ringing continued in an obviously empty room. No, New York was more him; the old girl might be a bit down on her luck at the minute but the place still had the old buzz, still made every day feel like it could be a new start. He imagined a well-wrapped-up walk in Central Park, strolling hand-in-hand down Fifth Avenue, stopping in Rockefeller Plaza to watch the skaters strut their stuff, warming up with a cosy hour nibbling blinis in the Russian Tea Rooms, maybe even a candlelit dinner in the Rainbow Room. Or perhaps, who knows, a blissful weekend at an old colonial inn somewhere in the Berkshires, all wainscoting and wood fires. He sighed as the phone continued its empty ringing. None of this was in the slightest bit likely to happen.

What was quite likely to happen was involuntary redundancy, to go with the entirely voluntary divorce he had agreed to with a dismal absence of drama the previous weekend. At least with the agency he had tried, making his big pitch the week before to no avail. The suits had just sat there, not buying it, Chairman grinning like a shot fox, none of them capable of untangling themselves from the old mind-set. Two minutes in, it had been obvious he was on a loser. He had floundered on for another five, arguing for a new kind of agency…integrated with its clients' overall business strategy…building a brand image for the long haul…instantly recognizable corporate identity in the public mind…long-term emotional link with the consumer more important than selling an individual product…an agency of the future. Useless. Fact was, most of them, the lift didn't go to the top floor.

He replaced the receiver and sat down on the bed, head still ringing, heart still longing for Hélène to answer. And somewhere inside the longing, he knew, was a yearning to find something in himself that had been lost along the way. The word 'wholesomeness' came out of nowhere and he immediately began pouring hot scorn on the thought, free-associating to 'wholemeal' and finding himself humming the New World Symphony that had been the brilliant choice of soundtrack for that Hovis ad, Collett Dickenson Pearce's great sepia-style nostalgia commercial.

He reached for the phone and called the Tudor again, even though no time at all had elapsed. Would his divorce make any difference? Probably not.

'*Thank you for inviting an ordinary health worker to this meeting of distinguished international...*'

Standing before the mirror in a tiny room on the 24th floor of the Tudor Hotel, Hélène told herself that nervousness would evaporate once she got going. She had more or less memorized the speech but now she was here in New York, just a few blocks from where it would have to be delivered, her confidence was faltering. She took a deep breath and looked up into the mirror. '*I'd like to take you back for a moment to a children's ward about twelve hours from where we are meeting today...*'

What was wrong with her? Why was her stomach knotted, her heart in her throat? Why this blood-buzzing anxiety, this vague sense of dread about nothing and everything? Could it just be jet lag?

She dropped the speech on the bureau and sat down on the single bed that occupied almost half the room. After a minute with her eyes closed, she picked up the note that had been handed to her with her key. It was typical of Michael to have left it, and to have thought to let her know how he planned to introduce her to the meeting. The handwriting was steady, consistent: *You may not agree. It's possible that some of you may be offended. But those who deal hands-on, day-in, day-out, with the real issues facing this meeting have a right to be heard. And we, all of us, have a need to listen.* This was followed by a paragraph about her medical qualifications, her years of service in some of the most challenging places on earth, the cadres of health workers she had trained, the protocols she had developed and tested, her role in containing the Ebola outbreak four years earlier, the range of her experience across the whole gamut of primary-health-care challenges. Reading it through again, she was almost convinced of her right to address such a meeting. But she knew that all her qualifications would count for very little once she had delivered her message: the callousness of bureaucratic inertia; the wholesale misallocation of funds; the graft and corruption that sapped grand plans; the swallowing-up of health resources by high-tech hospitals for the few at the expense of even the most basic care for the many; the sheer scale of unnecessary illness and death, suffering and loss that continued year after year.

She looked away from the mirror. It would be all right. She had only to think of the children's ward she had left behind for the nervousness to give way to anger. And, if she was going to tell it like it is, then she would also have something to say about the rich countries whose so-called aid was often little more than an export subsidy for all the wrong technologies. And while she was at it – the pharmaceutical companies who encouraged and profited from the whole corrupt and corrupting process.

She stood and crossed the room to stand by the grimy, double-glazed window looking out over the East River to the great sprawl of Queens. In all her view, no leaf or blade of grass existed except by permission of the concrete. It was tempting to think that the contrast was enough to destabilize anyone. But the truth stared back at her: no matter how much her surroundings changed, her inner environment never seemed to vary: always the same mirror of self-observance and criticism, the same doubts and fears, the same seething shames and resolves. It wasn't Fabrice that was stopping her from going either forward or back. It was too many thoughts; too little spontaneity; too much terrified attachment to her own precious equilibrium.

She resigned herself to a new wave of tiredness and lay down on the bed, turning her thoughts to the weekend and her resolve to be kinder to Toby. She had been way too hard on him in Oxford, mostly for reasons to do with the past. How naïve she had been then. And it was surely in proportion to her naïvety that she had been so crushed. For years she had believed she would never recover the personal confidence that had been lost in those innocent days. And it meant that Toby had never quite faded into the past in the way that others had. A part of her could never quite let go of him, and could never quite forgive him either. Was this why she was so afraid to put her equilibrium at any risk? Sleep was closing in. She would forget the past for this weekend. Enjoy his company. Even perhaps a little mild flirtation. It would do no harm. These days she was well in control.

She was awakened by the phone ringing alarmingly on the bedside table. Who knew she was at the Tudor? She decided not to answer.

On that same Thursday afternoon, Stephen Walsh left the New School for Social Research with his mind in turmoil. Myron Lee and the Head of Eastern European Studies had been polite, welcoming even. But they had seemed not to realize why he was there. Unwilling to appear a supplicant, he had mentioned the shock caused in Oxford by his resignation and twice indicated his marked preference for a less tradition-bound intellectual environment. But no encouraging noises had been made. Would he like tea?

Finally he had been forced into saying that, despite a plethora of other offers, he would be open to suggestions from somewhere with a strong progressive tradition. He had even made reference to the New School's origins as a sanctuary for radical European intellectuals and, in what he had thought of as a light touch, had added 'though of course fleeing Oxford is not quite the same thing as fleeing Nazi Germany'. Eventually Myron had rather brusquely announced that unfortunately there were no vacant posts at the New School, and that none seemed likely to arise in the light of the current economic crisis which, as they were sure he would know, had brought New York City itself to the brink of bankruptcy.

He crossed Washington Square, striding purposefully though he had nowhere to go, stopping here and there to read the blue-and-white plaques marking the dwelling places of the famous. At least in Oxford, heading up The Broad or The High, he could count on a good many people knowing who he was.

Back at the Chelsea Hotel the concierge had virtually thrown his room key across the counter and his inquiry about messages had been answered with a terse 'No', as if checking for messages once a day were too much trouble. The elevator cage took an age to ascend, iron bones and joints clanking as it progressed insecurely towards the fourth floor of an establishment that had been a home-from-home for so many misfits over the years; the stairs worn by the feet of Kerouac, the handrail that had steadied the progress of Ginsberg.

He lay on the bed, staring up at the high ceiling and forcing himself to admit the unwelcome callers that had long been waiting in the anteroom of his thoughts. It wasn't just the New School. His letters to friends and colleagues and other scholars in his field, casually mentioning his availability, had produced nothing. And the written applications he had made to Brown and Cornell had not even proceeded as far as an interview. After nearly a month, his only live lead was a letter from a former PhD student encouraging him to apply for a professorship at a university he had never heard of somewhere in the Mid-West. He jumped as the radiator gave one of its occasional chilly shudders. He would leave in a day or so, find himself somewhere less depressing. He closed his eyes. Maybe he was just taking time to get used to the idea that he no longer needed employment. Why not award himself a sabbatical for as long as he liked? Write 'To Hell and Back – the Soviet Union 1945-1955'. He opened his eyes as a faint scratching sound caused him to sit up and examine the pillowcase.

Sinking back again, he wondered whether the others would have already arrived. He had always felt rather sorry for those who had donned the blinkers of compromise, seeing his own vantage point as essentially superior. But here he was lying on his bed and wondering what to do with the rest of his day. The rest of his life. Even the idea of the sabbatical didn't quite cut it, unable to protect him from the fear of being squeezed out of life's sandwich. Perhaps it was envy of their engagement, their sense of purpose, the specificity of their concerns. To feel even the slightest envy for Seema was especially shocking. After all, professorships in America were a dime a dozen.

The man had been meticulous in recording not only the names and duties of his slaves but even the details of the food, clothing and bedding provided for each of them. Seema made another note and looked up from the facsimile of Jefferson's farm book, eyes travelling over the rows of desks, rows of books, rows of journals in their sloping racks, rows of glass and steel floors, rows of windows rising from the great space below. Was this to be it for the next however many years? Living in these rows, depth of field limited to the fifteen inches between her eyes and the page, all imagination confined to the past?

Her work was in one way similar to Hélène's, though the comparison was more troubling than comforting. Both of them were insisting on the individuality of all the victims of racism and injustice who were usually spoken of *en masse*. People with too many noughts on the end, as Hélène had put it. The millions of slaves transported, the millions who had died on the Middle Passage, the millions sold into the New World. The difference was that Hélène was focused on individuals who were alive today, victims of a wrong that could still be righted, while she was reading a facsimile of a two-hundred-year-old book in an attempt somehow to revive the individuality of the dead. With a sudden flurry of activity, she packed up her papers, resolving to walk the streets all afternoon if necessary but not to return to her apartment until she had decided what to do about the presence in New York of Michael Lowell.

Turning into La Guardia Place she welcomed the knife edge of cold on her face, glad of its clean call to the senses. She did not need to stop anywhere for coffee. She did not need to put on gloves or scarf. She did not need to look at her watch or think about what to buy for dinner. She needed to think. Why hadn't he phoned? He had been in New York for two days, nearer three. Hélène had already had lunch with him. Clearly he wasn't interested. Why hadn't she written him in advance? She turned left on Bleecker, pulling her coat collar across her mouth, using her own breath to warm her lips. Hélène had also mentioned that he had put up at the Doral Inn on Lexington, though she had also said something about a side trip to Washington. Should she call him there? Invite him for a drink? Otherwise she would be facing another weekend of … of what? Of nothing. Of the tense limbo-land of a relationship that might be nothing and might be everything without any way of knowing which.

She stopped at a payphone on the corner of Canal Street and Lafayette.

Michael was writing up his notes in a room on the 18th floor of the Doral Inn when the bedside phone rang. The first day of the meeting had come to an end and his own contribution had, he knew, been well below par. For once, he had been unable to maintain focus, get a sense of the meeting's political contours, sort out what was being said from what was meant. The truth was that he had been following the proceedings with only a fraction of his attention, the rest of him back in Washington, thinking of Paul and teasing out every last nuance of the conversation in a freezing Lafayette Park.

The phone continued to ring. He hesitated. One of the participants at the meeting, a Chilean paediatrician, was lobbying for a job at the WHO and had murmured something about a pre-dinner drink. He decided not to answer.

13 | Flies on a summer day

The East Side institution known as Billy's Bar on First Avenue at 52nd Street was not yet crowded when Toby Jenks pushed through the door in the early evening of Friday, January 30th, 1981, and took a stool at one end of the bar.

He looked around with satisfaction. The place had remained aloof from Manhattan's fashionable rush towards stripped pine and exposed brick walls. In fact it was exactly as he remembered it: the same soft gaslight falling on gleaming copper pipes; the same brass, six-handled beer pump; the same red-check tablecloths and waiters in their faded maroon jackets – real waiters who had been there for years and took a pride in the job, unlike those twenty-somethings on the West Side who couldn't wait to let you know they were really resting between parts. And there, at the end of the bar, the same substantial figure of Billy Jr, still operating the antique till, 'playing the piano' as he called it, in his unflappable, 'the-world-may-change' way.

Toby took a swallow of Scotch from the dimpled glass and the satisfaction deepened. There was nothing, absolutely nothing, like that first cold scorch of a good Scotch at the back of the throat. Even the second sip wasn't quite as good. Why couldn't every experience be as good as the first time? He had arrived a half-hour early, planning on putting down a foundation layer before the others arrived, but had scarcely finished his first when he felt the rush of cold air and looked up to see Hélène coming through the door.

After an embrace and a kiss on the cheek, he helped her up to the adjacent barstool and raised an eyebrow to the bartender.

'Mineral water, please.' Hélène tried not to sound prim.

Toby thought he might just as well get another in at the same time.

She looked around appreciatively. 'Nice old place.'

'Been here forever. Started off serving ale to coal carriers right after the Civil War.'

'Not too many coal carriers in tonight.'

Toby looked around, as if checking out Hélène's observation. 'Glad you're a bit early, Hel. Been calling you at the Tudor, as a matter of fact.'

'My, I am in demand tonight. Apparently Stephen called as well.' Toby frowned and stared at his drink.

Hélène put her head on one side to look at him. 'Don't like Stephen much, do we, Toby?'

Toby sighed. 'Got tickets on himself is the problem. Thought I'd given him the flick when I left college. Fella keeps popping up like a prick at a pyjama party.'

'Well, I think you might be being just a little bit hard on him. He's got his beliefs, and after all Marxism—'

'It's not a belief, Hel. It's a pose. Christ, he's the only member of the proletariat who can trace his ancestry back to Norman the Conqueror.'

'Don't you mean William the Conqueror?'

'Not in his case, no.

'I guess advertising and Marxism don't rub along together so well.'

'Main difference is, your Marxists don't know how to get the working classes to behave.'

'And he can't help his background any more than anyone else. And it would have been a lot easier for him to do what was expected of him, take his place in the County set or whatever they call it over there.'

'Yeah, well – he needs to get his ass on a new donkey.'

'At least he's got convictions.'

For a moment Toby looked hurt, but then his expression went into the whimsical 'quote mode' she remembered well. 'Every man, wherever he goes, is encompassed by a cloud of comforting convictions, which move with him like flies on a summer day.'

'Who was that?

'Can't remember.'

'Liar.' Hélène sighed a smile and looked up at him with an expression that he feared might be fondness. 'Do you still write poetry, Toby?'

'Wrote a good jingle the other week.'

'Seriously, do you write anything?

'Christ, no.'

'Why not?'

'Muse done a runner, sweetheart. Somewhere in Africa, I think.'

The look turned reproachful. He raised both hands an inch or two from the bar in apology. 'Anyway, no muse is good news. Dreadful old doggerel. Juvenilia minor I think you might say, if you were being kind.'

'You make it sound like some sort of virus.'

'It was. Is. Still got it, you know. The virus. Never really went away. Just, you know, dormant for a bit.'

She made another face, then softened. 'Your poetry was lovely, Toby.'

He turned his mouth down in dismissal. She leaned forward to meet his eyes. 'It was lovely to me.'

Billy Jr had levered himself from the tall chair behind the till and was lumbering down to refill Toby's glass. Hélène picked up her mineral water, the mood broken. 'So when did you get in?'

'This afternoon. Still feel like I'm flying.'

'You do know that liquor's dehydrating on top of flying?'

'Yeah, well, I drank a lot of water on the plane. Still taste it, as a matter of fact.'

'Good. But you should drink water now as well.'

'You're not serious?'

'Of course I am. Rehydrate yourself. Your body's eighty per cent water.'

Toby looked doubtfully at his glass. 'People are always telling me that, but I've never really been convinced. I mean your head's not eighty per cent water, is it?

'Toby, on average your body tissue is eighty per cent water.'

'Well, I figure if it's that high already, why nudge it up any further? I mean, you don't want to suddenly find yourself in a pool on the floor.' He looked down from the bar stool to the floorboards as if this might be a serious possibility.

'Do you at least drink a glass of water every morning?'

'Christ, no! Bad enough getting out of bed as it is.'

'You don't feel good in the mornings?'

'Does anybody?'

Hélène raised her eyebrows patiently. 'Exercise?'

'Been known to do a few jumping jacks every now and again. Got up to five once.'

She shook her head, smiling.

'Tell me honestly, Toby, do you drink too much?'

'When I've got time.'

'Doctor's orders, Toby. No more than two or three drinks

a day, with some days off every week. You should listen to your body.'

'I do, I do, but a chap can't always be lying down.'

Another cold blast from the door signalled the arrival of the others, who had joined up on First Avenue. As Hélène slipped down from the stool to embrace Seema, Toby leant both elbows on the bar for a moment, frowning into his Scotch. Was this how he should have spent his five minutes alone with her?

Over dinner the conversation had flowed with chit-chat about what everyone had been doing since the meeting in Oxford. At the first pause, Stephen had made his big announcement with a peroration on how rare an event it was for anyone to resign the Fellowship of an Oxford college. The news had not caused quite the sensation he might have hoped for, and to inquiries about his discussions at the New School he had been offhand. Fortunately he was in a position to consider his options.

Toby sighed for no particular reason other than forcing a break in Stephen's monologue. 'So, Tom couldn't make it again?'

Seema shook her head. 'Family moving to New York this very weekend. Said he thought on balance it probably wasn't necessary to ask his wife what she thought about him spending it eating and drinking with his old college buddies while she dealt with U-Haul.'

Toby, smiling over his drink, turned to Hélène. 'How about you, Hel, ready to blow them away with the big speech?'

'I've done nothing but worry about it since Oxford.' The others provided predictable reassurances. Only Michael remained quiet. Stephen asked whether there was to be an agenda for the weekend, to which Toby responded by asking

Seema if there was any news on her book.

'The news is, I probably no longer have a publisher.' Briefly she recounted the story of her meeting at Gammer & Duce.

Toby reached for the wine. 'Picked the wrong gal to bully. On the other hand you can see where the poor chap's coming from. Big story – 'I was the President's under-age sex slave.' Are we talking consensual by the way? Always liked that word. Don't get much chance to use it.'

Seema smiled despite herself.

'I'm under fire on that, too, Tobe. My feminist colleagues insist that a sexual relationship between master and slave is rape by definition.'

'Mmm, that works.' Stephen was holding his wine glass up before the candle flame, examining its colour. 'In fact it's quite a good little illustration of how analysis by power relations gets you straight to the heart of the matter.'

It was when Seema was talking about the surge of interest in slavery among middle-class African-Americans that mention was first made of a senior figure at the United Nations who had hired one of her PhD students to do private research into his own slave ancestry. Unobserved by the others, Michael's focus sharpened as Seema speculated that the researcher, a mature student, 'might be a little bit in love with him, or maybe it's just his gorgeous row-house on Sutton Place.'

After dinner they stopped to pick up ice cream at the Häagen-Dazs on 57th Street before crowding into a chequered cab and heading down to the Village. Toby was up-front chatting to the driver. Michael, crushed in the back with the Gladstone bag on his knees, remained silent all the way downtown. Only as they were crossing 23rd Street did he ask Seema if she happened to know the name of the UN official she had mentioned over dinner

14 | If this is a joke

Following her divorce, Seema Mir had decluttered her life of domestic detritus. To the loft of the four-storey walk-up on Charles Street she had brought very little apart from the two South Asian rugs whose subtle variations of flame and orange found echo in the dark reds and terracottas of the two Kokoschka reproductions on the walls. Another of the decisions she had made at that time was that she would have few clothes or holidays and that her great luxury would be not to cook. Instead she took full advantage of the delis and take-outs that seemed to be springing up on every corner of Greenwich Village and it was for this reason that the tiny Bauhaus-style kitchenette at one end of the loft had maintained its minimalist purity. And it was to this inviting space that Seema, Hélène, Stephen, Toby and Michael climbed that evening after being dropped off around 11.00pm in Sheridan Square.

Seema lit candles and put on coffee while the others unpacked the tubs of ice cream and set out the napkins and plastic spoons. Toby, still a little breathless from the stairs, applied his lighter to twists of newspaper in the stove.

Coffee arrived as the flames began to leap, illuminating floorboards and walls, the Kokoschkas glowing down as a cello sonata played softly in the background and the four of them made themselves comfortable on sofa and chairs, leaving Seema the cane-backed Bikaner planter's chair that was the only antique piece. Soon the talk grew sleepy from wine, warmth and jet lag. A settled comfort reigned as another bottle was opened.

'Before you pour that, Toby, I've got something serious I'd like to bring up, if nobody objects too much.' A few groans were aimed at Michael, who was sitting forward in one of the armchairs, the Gladstone bag on the floor beside him.

Toby continued to pour. 'Gravitas in a bottle this, mate, perfect accompaniment to anything likely to wander down the tedious side.'

Michael smiled patiently and accepted the glass. 'It's a proposal I want to make. Just to get your initial reactions.'

Toby poured for them all. 'Run it up the flagpole and see who salutes. Just heard that today. God, I love America.'

Hélène, fighting sleep, covered her glass with her hand as the bottle neared. 'So let's have it then, Michael.'

Michael took a deep breath. 'It's about what we talked about in Oxford, and I'm afraid it might come as something of a shock.'

Toby, registering something in Michael's voice, returned his glass to the table. Seema and Hélène glanced at each other. Stephen looked bored.

'When I got back' – Michael hesitated for a moment – 'after Oxford, all the new data were waiting on my desk. Latest vaccination coverage from about a hundred countries. Another year, another five million kids killed by measles, tetanus, pertussis.'

He let the silence absorb his words, the mellow mood of the evening already gone. 'Anyway, as I worked through it all, I kept hearing something that Toby said in the Parks that evening: about the obvious thing to do being to "get hold of the smallpox virus and threaten to blow bubbles with it unless the world got off its butt and immunized every last child".'

'Joke, Michael?' Toby had raised his eyebrows patiently.

'Many a true word … as you reminded me the very next day, Stephen.'

Stephen managed to frown and look amused at the same time. 'I said I thought what was happening was a crime against humanity, and that as such it could justify any action taken to avert it. At the time you reacted rather convention-ally, Michael, as I remember it. Though of course—

'Where is this going, Michael?' Hélène was wide awake now, and the first to glimpse what might be coming.

Michael reached down beside his chair for the Gladstone bag from which he had been inseparable all evening. Lifting it to his knees he snapped back the lock, the others watching in silence as he took out a plastic bag containing what looked like a half-pint thermos, the greenish metallic colour clearly visible through the milky polythene. No one spoke as he brought out two more identical bags and set them down on the table.

The cello continued to play softly. Firelight flickered on the walls. But the last of the ice cream on the table was forgotten as Seema, Hélène, Toby and Stephen stared, reactions stuck in neutral, refusing to engage with what they were witnessing. In the silence, the first taps of hail could be heard on the skylight.

Seema spoke first. 'You can't be serious, Michael.'

After a long silence Hélène took Seema's hand. 'Come on, Michael, you're not asking us to believe—'

Michael lifted his eyes. 'I am asking you to believe. But I'm asking you to believe a couple of other things, too.' He grasped the first finger of his left hand. 'First, no one's in the slightest danger from what's inside those jars. It's inert, freeze dried.'

His listeners formed a still-life tableau as he gripped the next finger. 'And second, the threat wouldn't ever be carried out. It'd be just a threat, no more. Just to see if we can't get something moving. It might not work. And if it doesn't then – too bad. We forget about it. These' – he released his fingers and waved a hand at the bags on the table – 'wouldn't ever be used.'

For another twenty seconds not a word was spoken as the others continued to stare from Michael's face to the three plastic bags standing on the table amid the espresso cups and half-empty tubs of melted Häagen-Dazs. More visible now that Michael had leaned back from the firelight, the jars themselves could be seen to be of the kind used to keep soup warm – broad-necked, capped by a black screw-on cup.

It was Hélène who broke the long silence. 'You've gone mad.'

Michael held her eyes. Stephen was staring at the wall, the smallest of smiles on his face. Toby looked suddenly older. Seema took a deliberate sip of wine, compelling Michael to look at her before she spoke. 'If this is a joke, Michael, please tell us all now.'

Occasionally there were outbursts of nervous laughter, and repeated appeals for Michael to confess that this was some kind of nerdish psychological test. But as midnight came and went, disbelief began a slow retreat in the face of Michael's quiet insistence. And when Toby asked him just to go over very slowly what he was proposing, step by step, he did so in a voice that was all the more chilling for its matter-of-factness. They would demonstrate that they were in possession of the virus and announce that they intended to go public with the fact unless the government of the United States made a credible commitment to leading an international effort that would immunize all the world's children within the next five years.

Stephen, attempting to match Michael's matter-of-fact tone, rested his stockinged feet on the coffee table. 'And why wouldn't the response be,' he raised a dismissive hand, 'just vaccinate everybody against smallpox?'

Hélène shook her head. 'That's not what they'd do.'

Michael nodded his agreement. 'Even if there were enough vaccinia in the US – and believe me there isn't – immunizing everybody still wouldn't be the answer. What they'd do is go into surveillance mode: ID suspected cases, quarantine confirmed victims, immunize any and all possible contacts.'

Stephen shrugged, determined not to be impressed. 'Then that's what they'll do.' Seema and Toby were still looking numbed.

Michael looked to Hélène for support. 'They might. But gearing up to do it, organizing coast-to-coast surveillance and preparing quarantine and vaccination protocols would be a risk. A huge risk.'

Hélène nodded, closing her eyes and leaning her head back on the sofa. 'Coast-to-coast panic.'

Seema had been staring at the plastic bags, taking in the full horror of what was happening. Eventually she looked up at Michael. 'Where did those come from?'

Michael raised both palms. 'That's the one thing I can't tell you.'

Stephen picked up one of the bags and examined it with a show of unconcern. 'Forgive my evidence-based bias, Michael, but how do we know this is the real thing?'

'You don't. But I do. And it wouldn't be much of a threat if it weren't. First thing they'd do is test the hell out of it down in Atlanta.'

Toby was staring intently at his friend now. The rain had stopped and the only sound was the faint stirring of logs behind the glass doors. 'Michael, are you sure you're all right, mate?'

Seema added quietly. 'Toby's right. I can't believe … I can't believe we're even talking like this.'

Michael began gathering up the plastic bags, returning them one by one to the Gladstone bag. When he had locked them away he turned to her and spoke with quiet reluctance. 'And can you believe that two thousand more children have died from vaccine-preventable diseases since we met in Billy's Bar tonight?'

It was after 2.30am when Hélène and Toby entered Estelle's late-nite bar on Second Avenue at 38th Street. Michael and Stephen had been dropped off at their hotels after a surreal cab ride through the not-quite-lifeless streets. Not wishing to be alone with her thoughts, and knowing she would be unable to sleep, Hélène had accepted the invitation to a nightcap.

They took stools at the lonely end of the long bar, Toby suggesting a 'cleansing ale'. The bartender, who seemed to know Toby, set up the two beers and left them alone, moving down to the other end of the room to continue watching the hockey game on TV.

They sipped in silence, knowing there was no other topic but not knowing how to begin. Toby eventually waved a hand to attract Hélène's attention in the mirror behind the bar. She smiled weakly and he turned to face her. 'You wouldn't have a bar of this, would you, Hel?'

Her expression was suddenly frightened, and he rested a hand on hers on the brass rail. She left her hand where it was for a moment, but then picked up the beer and bit her lower lip. 'I'd say it was sheer off-the-wall insane if it were anybody else in the world other than Michael Lowell.'

Toby picked up his own beer. 'I know. Not like him to play silly buggers.'

After a long silence their eyes met again in the mirror. 'You wouldn't go along, would you, Toby?'

Toby toyed with a beer mat. The only other occupants of the bar had left their stools and begun a card game at one of the dining tables. 'Love Michael, Hel. Always have. Always will. Not a false note on his keyboard.' The card game was already becoming rowdy and the bartender had turned up the TV. 'Smartish sort of a bloke as well.' He inspected the glass and took a long pull on his beer. 'So if he wants to do this, sweetheart, and for some unimaginable reason he wants TJ's help – he's got it.' He drained his glass in one go then turned to her again. 'My God, Hélène, there's no two people in the world I ... ' He broke off and looked away, hiding his face from her. When he had recovered himself he turned back to give her a cheerful smile via the mirror. 'Glad you're here, Hel. Hate to drink with the flies.'

After a few moments, Hélène placed a hand on his arm and turned him towards her. 'Toby, I've never told you about Fabrice, have I?'

15 | Forget it ever happened

The din of the crowds echoed around the tiled vaults of the great beaux-arts building and the line for a table stretched back as far as the lower concourse, making it obvious to them all that The Oyster Bar in the bowels of Grand Central Terminal was an impossible venue. Toby tried to drum up some enthusiasm for the chowders and pan roasts, and Stephen was saying something about the great age of the railway being an early example of public investment for private profit, but conversation was all but impossible. And what the five of them had to talk about that day did not lend itself to shouting.

Seema and Hélène expressed a strong preference for being outdoors, however cold the day might be, and Seema it was who proposed riding the subway to 86th street from where they could soon be in the lonelier reaches of Central Park.

Twenty minutes later the little group was emerging from the Lexington Avenue subway and heading across town, crossing Park Avenue with its icy flower beds and leafless trees. Hélène walked beside Toby in silence as they continued west on 86th, passing the black doors and raised brass plaques of some of the world's most exclusive paediatric practices.

Picking up coffee and hot dogs from a street vendor outside the entrance to the Guggenheim, they entered the park a little after one o'clock, stopping at the top of the steps to look out over the lake at the skyline of the Upper West Side.

For a while nothing was said as they sipped scalding coffee and bit into mustard-striped frankfurters. Apart from the occasional steam-breathed runner or muffled dog-walker, they were alone on the Bridle Path that circles what was then still known as Central Park Reservoir.

Not until they were approaching the West Drive was the apparent embargo on speech broken. Stephen, breath frosting over the top of a zipped-up parka, gave his little preparatory cough: 'Before we go any further into this thing, I think I should just say a word or two.' There was a pause as a pair of joggers came towards them. When they were once more at a safe distance, Stephen repeated the cough. 'It would not, I think, be entirely fair to allow Michael to bear the whole burden of this enterprise without my acknowledging that it is in fact an idea that, as Michael said, I ventured to put to him on that last morning in Oxford.'

Everything around them was winter dead: the earth frozen, the hollows and dips of the park filled with less-than-pristine snow. Alongside the path the rhododendrons and double-pink cherry trees still had months to wait and at the edges of the lake coveys of mallards, grebes and gadwalls were huddled on the ice. Hélène, walking on the inside nearest the water, spoke quietly into the freezing air, as if warning Stephen to keep his voice down. 'I believe it was Toby's little joke that started it all off.'

Michael stole a glance at Seema, walking by his side. The amusement around the mouth and eyes had gone, the harsh winter daylight exposing the strain and lack of sleep in the lines of her face. He pushed his bare hands into the pockets of his overcoat. 'Thank you, Stephen, and maybe I should also say that it's not entirely fair of me to expect you all to take it on board as suddenly as … as suddenly as last night. I've had months to think about this.'

Several more runners overtook them, flesh glowing pink, breath making brief clouds. When they were a good hundred metres ahead, it was Seema who made the next effort: 'I'm struggling with this, like we all are. My respect for Michael … ' - her voice faltered for the first time and she did not complete the sentence. 'But I think the point is that … in a case such as this … you can't let anyone else make judgements for you. Not even Michael.'

It is easy to get lost in Central Park, or at least to become disoriented among the meandering maze of paths on the north side of the reservoir. Even native New Yorkers, grooved into the regular grid of their city, are known to keep an eye on the skyline of Midtown to be reassured of their whereabouts. On that Saturday they did it the easy way, hugging the lake on the Bridle Path as they fell into a discussion of the unthinkable: its justification, its feasibility, its risks and likely outcomes, pummelling and re-examining scenarios until, tired and cold to their bones, they stopped to take seats around a crude picnic table by the Great Lawn softball fields.

Toby had said nothing since they had entered the park. At times he had even appeared to be letting his attention drift out over the lake towards the comforts of Manhattan. But after straddling a bench seat he rested a hand on Michael's shoulder. 'Probably just me being a little bit obtuse here, mate, but what I can't altogether see is … I mean there are quite a few little things wrong with the world when you start to think about it, which I generally try not to. War, genocide, torture.' He dropped his hand and shuffled slightly away to light a ciga-rette. 'Then there's racism, and the female half of the population not getting a fair crack of the whip, if you'll forgive the expression. Plus apartheid, Abo rights, child marriages. Not to mention trashing the planet, world running out of oil, testing lipstick on monkeys, white rhinos having a tough time of it out there. I mean one could go on for a long time.'

'And your point, Toby?' said Hélène, smiling despite herself.

'My point, sweetie, is who knows where we'd end up with enough laps of this bloody reservoir. I mean why not threaten to release the damn thing if they don't stop clubbing seals or drilling in Alaska, or if the superpowers don't get their ducks in a row for SALT II?'

Stephen's impatience was palpable but Toby forestalled him with a comic policeman's hand. 'Before Stephen is kind enough to enlighten me, I just want to ask' – he exhaled smoke and gestured vaguely towards the trees behind – 'What would we all think if some harmless little group of well-meaning souls freezing their nuts off on the other side of the park were coming up with the idea of blackmailing the world unless they got their own way on something that those of us freezing our nuts off on this side of the park didn't happen to agree with, like, I don't know…'

'Banning abortion,' said Seema.

'…banning abortion,' said Toby with a grateful wave. 'I mean, imagine someone firing them all up with figures about thousands upon thousands of innocent, unborn babies being massacred right, left and centre, then telling them the least they can do is threaten to put anthrax in the mail, firebomb a few clinics, whatever.'

Stephen tried to interrupt again but Toby was in full flow. 'I mean up to this point in my life I can't really say I've seen myself in the front line of defending due process, so to speak…'

Stephen gave a scornful laugh. 'Due process? Due process, Toby? Ossifying of the power structure. Material relationships expressed as ideals. Read your *German Ideology*.'

Toby took out a little notebook from his coat pocket and made a show of preparing to write down the name. 'By?'

Stephen looked away in disgust. Seema suppressed a smile. 'Forgive us, Stephen, but you can't assume we all go along with the idea that due process isn't worth respecting just because Karl Marx didn't have a high opinion of it.'

'Quite right, sweetheart.' Toby had put the notebook away and was drawing on his cigarette, making the tip glow in the cold air. 'And I think it might have been Russell who said "Much that passes as idealism is disguised love of power". Or it might have been my old man. Anyway, we need to watch ourselves here.'

Stephen, parading his look of exaggerated patience, was about to respond when Seema spoke again. 'So do you have an answer, Michael?'

Michael met her eye, cursing himself for his disorientation whenever she addressed him as directly as this, looking into his eyes, speaking his name. He turned away for a moment towards the gritty patches of the softball diamond still visible here and there through the snow. 'I'm not sure there is an answer in principle. But there's the obvious pragmatic point that a lot of progress has come about because people ignored the law and "due process" and went in for some form of direct action.'

Seema, seeing something like pain in Michael's eyes, turned to look away. 'Like the Declaration of Independence, or the Civil Rights Movement.'

Hélène was blowing into her hands. 'Or the ANC and anti-apartheid.'

Toby looked at what was left of his cigarette, as if

wondering where it had all gone. 'Or the FBI break-in. Anybody wish they hadn't done that?'

'Thank you all.' Stephen folded his arms and hunched his shoulders, partly against the cold, partly to suggest that there was nothing more to be said on the point.

Michael frowned. 'Doesn't quite answer Toby's point, though. As I said, I don't think there necessarily is an answer, at least not a neat theoretical one that applies to every situation.'

'*A priori*, as it were,' said Toby, widening his eyes and dipping his chin, as if looking over spectacles.

Hélène refused to let herself smile. Michael placed both hands on the table with a small slap. 'It seems to me in the end we just have to make the call on the basis of what's in front of us, the opportunity we've got, the likelihood of success, the consequences of failure, the risks – to ourselves and others.'

Toby exhaled smoke and shook his head. 'Not good enough, mate. With the exception of my honourable friend to the left, I think we'd all be willing to salute "due process" and all who sail in her. But as we also seem to have agreed, sometimes a little *extra-mural* action seems justified. *Ergo* the real question is – under what circumstances is it right to flush due process down the dunny? And even if there isn't a neat little theoretical answer, Michael, sure as hell there's an obligation to show not just that something is very wrong but that normal means, due process if you like, isn't going to put it right. And on top of that, you've got to demonstrate that the likely outcome, *ceteris paribus*, is pretty well overwhelmingly in favour of the greater good, as commonly understood by all sane and reasonable people as represented by the five of us sitting here freezing our etc etc...'

Michael could now not help smiling – needing no reminding that Toby was no fool. 'Challenge accepted. And here's the thing, Toby – if you think my answer's not up to it then I suggest we forget all about it and go sit ourselves by a radiator somewhere.'

'Now you're talking.' Toby bent with an effort and pushed the cigarette into the icy grass at his feet.

Helped by the cold, Michael managed to keep his hands in his pockets. 'First off, we're not imposing our own cause on anybody. We're demanding that governments do what they've already agreed to do. Virtually every country has signed up to a formal resolution on immunizing the world's kids. What I'm saying here is that the "cause", if you like, is something that *has* been decided by due process.'

Toby held up both hands in a shorthand acknowledgement of the point, then pushed them back into the pockets of his parka. Hélène stared at him for a long moment, and turned her attention to what Michael was saying. 'Second, I think we can safely say that due process isn't cutting it. Nothing's happening. As I said, the data are all sitting there on my desk.'

Toby again held up his hands while Stephen looked away across the park with the patient air of a man waiting for the obvious conclusion to be reached. Michael continued to address Toby. 'Next, people who fire-bomb abortion clinics or hijack planes are inflicting harm on others for the sake of advancing their own beliefs. That's not what we'd be doing here. We've no intention of releasing the virus. We're not going to get anybody hurt. We're not even going to carry out the threat to go public, because that in itself might do a lot of harm. Like I said, if it doesn't work we just…forget it ever happened. Milk-and-water stuff, isn't it, Stephen?'

Stephen made his patient 'told you this all along' face as Toby again gestured assent. The temperature was dropping further, the light beginning to fade, the first purple of evening gathering its weight over the park.

Hélène was shaking her head. 'You really, honestly, seriously, think there's a chance they'd give in to it?'

Michael bit his lip in thought. 'I believe there's a chance. Sure, they'll do everything they can to find out where the threat's coming from. But if they don't get anywhere then sooner or later they're going to start weighing up the pros and cons. And what they'll likely focus on is the political fallout of a panic. Government totally unprepared. Loss of public confidence. That's what'll get weighed against what it would cost to go along – a few billion dollars plus twisting a few arms and spending some political capital around the world.'

Stephen had wrapped his arms around his body and was staring up at a flight of Canada geese passing over the lake. 'What we may safely assume is that they'll follow the path of least political resistance.'

Seema was searching Michael's face. 'And no one would get hurt?'

'No one would get hurt.'

'Except very possibly us.' Toby was lighting another cigarette, stamping his feet in the pile of white-rimed leaves under the table. It was Michael's turn to raise his hands in acknowledgement of the point. 'No denying that, Toby. Trace it to any of us and we pretty much know what to expect.'

A silence fell as the thought of the personal risk, long held in the background, came out into the open.

Toby eventually broke the spell, cigarette smoke mingling with the frost of his breath. 'Can't be a consideration though, can it? Doesn't count for a lot in the scales of what we're talking about. Seems to me we could cheerfully leave it right out of the paddock.'

Hélène looked at Toby, and then down at the worn earth and frozen snow. Only Michael did not seem surprised.

'We should go,' said Seema, rising to her feet as the sun made a feeble attempt to break through a low band of cloud.

'Preferably somewhere warm.' Toby looked at his half-smoked cigarette and dropped it in a drift of snow.

As they crossed Fifth Avenue, Hélène waited for Toby, who had decided he could probably manage another hot dog, and now the two of them walked together, some little way behind the others. Toby sighed with a mixture of satisfaction and regret as he swallowed the last of the frankfurter, wiping a touch of mustard from his lips before pulling his parka up over the lower half of his face. 'How do you stand this after Africa?'

'I quite like it, to tell the truth. Probably be colder in Montreal.' She took his arm as they crossed Park Avenue. 'You were good today, Toby.' He squeezed her arm happily in the crook of his own. 'But maybe you could cut down just a little bit on the Latin. Resist the temptation to wind Stephen up at every possible opportunity?'

Toby smiled under the zip of the parka, accepting the rebuke as a small intimacy. 'Can't help it, Hel. Fella thinks he can sit me in a high chair and feed me shit off a spoon just because he's a don at some poxy Oxford college.'

'Was a don. And it was your college, too, in case you'd forgotten.'

'Yeah, well, we all make mistakes.'

Fifty yards ahead, the others were disappearing down the steps into the subway. 'Do you really mean that, about Oxford being a mistake?'

'Do as a matter of fact. Should have stayed in Oz. Apart from meeting you, of course.'

At the time Michael, Hélène, Seema, Stephen and Toby

were leaving Central Park that afternoon, Tom Keeley was bypassing New York on Interstate 95, surrounded by his family and discussing nothing more strenuous than how much further there was to go to their new home in New Canaan, Connecticut. Thirty years would go by before he had occasion to wonder again about that day. And to speculate about what might have happened if the dice had taken one more roll and placed him with the others on the path circling what is today known as the Jacqueline Kennedy-Onassis Reservoir.

16 | Too much reality

Further talk was impossible as the Lexington Avenue train battled its way under Manhattan. Hélène and Seema were seated opposite each other, Michael in one corner, Toby and Stephen strap-hanging. Occasionally eyes met, connecting for a moment their inner silences across the relentless, ricocheting noise. For each of them, half a lifetime of experience was being brought to bear on what they had to decide that day, but common to them all was the dawning sense that circumstance had somehow stripped away the carapace of heart and mind that makes it possible for most of us, most of the time, to ignore the larger realities of the world.

It was Hélène who had scraped away the first layer by insisting that those millions of children were all individual boys and girls, each as loved and precious as any child in Europe or North America. That such an obvious truth needed acknowledgment was in itself testimony to the power of the carapace; but with that truth out in the open a layer of protection was gone. Michael had peeled off the next layer; the comforting assumption that the tragedy of millions of deaths was something that could only be righted by the long, slow struggle against poverty. He had said that it could all be prevented now, by means that were available and affordable today. All of them knew that no one in the world was better

133

qualified to make such a call. And another piece of the carapace was gone.

Perhaps even this would not have been enough if the last layer of protection – the layer that says 'there's nothing I can do' – had not also been ripped away by what Michael had produced from his Gladstone bag the previous evening.

All this is not to deny the usefulness of the carapace. Humankind cannot, indeed, bear very much reality, and for ordinary human beings to function there have to be limits on what they are prepared to face up to, empathize with. And so the carapace ensures that few are called upon to make a decision like the one that faced the two women and three men riding the Lexington Avenue subway that Saturday afternoon on the last day of January, 1980.

Each was also aware, as the long, hollow melancholy roar of the train carried them ever closer to Union Square, that the journey of decision making they were embarked upon was not a journey of reason alone. In the inner silence beneath the swaying bedlam, each knew that they were wandering the labyrinths of the mind where reason is curdled with instinct and emotion, where cowardice and inhibition tangle with courage and the yearnings of conscience, and where fathomless genetic predispositions interact with all that life has taught and brought.

For Hélène, facing Toby but screened from him by bodies in windbreakers and overcoats, the process was freighted with all the accumulated frustrations of the years, the anger undischarged, the shame at past avoidances, the fierce desire to break through the callous crust of inertia and corruption. She glanced up at Michael. She had provoked him to this, she knew. And there was no way she would abandon him now. Nor could she shrink from the only opportunity there might ever be to stand shoulder to shoulder with that other man whose ghost was riding the subway with her that day. The yearning to honour his memory, to be worthy of the love they had had, to live up to the ideals they had shared, was already making up her mind.

For Stephen, hanging from a strap in the centre of the carriage, the confusion was perhaps greatest. He had attempted to make reason and objectivity the hallmarks of his sheltered life. But beneath his brittle determinations, he too was aware that reason was ensnared by pettier concerns: by the self-image that he clung to as a life-raft in the seas of not knowing who he was; by some unarticulated need to redeem himself, to be somebody in the world's overwhelming anonymity. It was easier to think of other things, and for a time he was able to tame any inner shame by translating such thoughts onto a more abstract plain, reminding himself of Althusser's argument that even philosophers do not live in the realm of pure reason but are combatants in 'the only war without memoirs or memorials, the war humanity pretends it has never declared, the war it always thinks it has won in advance, simply because being human is nothing but surviving this war'.

Seema, sitting cold and troubled, struggled to stop her eyes from straying to Michael, the man she thought she had known. Instead, she looked across the carriage at Hélène and knew that her friend's decision was already made. Toby's too. And Stephen's, of course. Her eyes finally found Michael. And the look that passed between them was so disturbed and confused, so full of history and hurt and hope, as to defy any steady interpretation. She had so firmly resolved not to risk hurting him again, and so had not allowed herself the smallest transparency. And now this. Which made any other preoccupation seem trivial, even shameful. The tiled blur of 28th Street flashed by and she closed her eyes, allowing herself to believe in a moment of weakness that this was not really happening, that they would emerge into Union Square and she would take his arm and the world would be normal again. Eyes closed against the roar of the train, she tried once more to get back on track, think objectively, but was soon derailed by the thought that this might be the one chance she would ever have to address the vague, long-standing tensions of her own life: her subcurrent of guilt; her nagging sense of a lack of any real engagement outside of a library or a lecture theatre. She opened her eyes as she sensed the train beginning to slow, ashamed that the processes of reason had been so easily suborned. Toby was right. Their own individual concerns should be weightless in the scales of what was now before them.

Not even for Michael, who had given up his seat after 59th Street, was there to be immunity. Of the five, he was the only one who had had time to consider at length. Yet he too knew that illegitimate considerations had entered the mix. Knew, too, that those considerations were centred on the slight figure who was at this moment seated only a few feet away amid all the noise and the charged, dirty, electric smell of the New York subway. It was for this reason that he decided if he could not persuade her then he would retreat. And that was the strap that he clung to now as he tried to avoid looking too often at Seema Mir. He turned instead towards Toby, who was reading a leaflet about transcendental meditation that someone had handed to him as they had boarded the train.

It was Toby who was perhaps the least confounded as they climbed the subway steps and emerged into Union Square. Of all of them, he was the least attached to the world as it had been twenty-four hours before; the least wedded to who he was, to the life that had been, and the life that might be to come. He would have been the first to admit that, up to this point in his life, he had not devoted excessive thought to

any of the wider sufferings of the world; only since meeting
Hélène again had he been confronted by that other reality.
And, without knowing how to express it, he had been moved
by it. Knew, too, that emotion was always in the driving
seat, that everything is about something else, and that in his
own case his decision was somehow tinged with the vague
hope of regilding a tarnished life. Even, perhaps, of placing
himself on a different footing with Hélène Hevré. But the
previous evening, in Estelle's bar, he had committed to doing
his best to be swayed only by what good might be done, and
if this also helped him salvage something of himself then he
would consider it a bonus. And, having so determined, he
shouldered aside irrelevance as best he could, trusting all else
to the man by whose side he walked as the five of them made
their way to the West Village.

All of this mental and emotional luggage and more was
carried up the four flights of stairs to Seema's apartment at the
end of that long, cold afternoon. And, at one time or another
during the course of the evening that followed, there was not
one of them who did not think of the warmth and ease that
could have been theirs, lounging companionably on the couch
or on one of the gorgeous coloured rugs, watching the fire
blaze behind the glass doors and enjoying all the conviviality
of good wine and the gathering of friends.

No one was in any hurry to return to the subject, and for
a few minutes something like an ordinary conversation struggled bravely on: Seema was asked about how she had found
the apartment, and about getting the wood for the stove up
the four flights of stairs. Stephen said something about creep-
ing gentrification. Hélène wanted to know about the rugs.
Even Michael said something about trying to find time to play
chess in Washington Square. But it could not last. And it was

Toby, sitting warming his hands at the stove, who led them all back: 'Small suggestion. Why don't we drop the abstract stuff for a bit and talk about the nitty-gritty? Might help?'

The others, either welcoming the proposal or too exhausted to challenge it, acquiesced. And so it was that details began to be worked out before any decision in principle had been made.

Toby, cupping both hands round a mug of tea, turned away from the stove. 'So, maestro, shall we take it from the top?'

Michael looked up into the loft space above, ordering his thoughts. The skylight was dark now except for a few stars in the bitterly cold night.

'The opening gambit would be pretty straightforward. One of the samples goes into a left-luggage locker, say in Grand Central. The key then gets delivered to the target with a letter setting out the demand and a statement that we're saying will go to the *New York Times* and the *Washington Post*, along with a second sample, if the demand isn't met.'

'Specifics, mate.' Toby was also staring up at the skylight. 'Delivered to whom?'

'We'd have to make that call.' Michael grasped a finger. 'But, first off, it has to be someone who can be predicted to go more or less straight to the top without going through a whole bunch of intermediaries.'

'Cut the risk of panic.' Hélène glanced at Seema as she spoke.

'Right.' Michael had already moved on to the next finger. 'Second, the circumstances of delivering the letter have to be such as to exclude any possibility of it being opened by anyone else. And third, it has to be someone we can get it to without any possibility of it being traced back to us.' The general assent needed no voice.

Toby had begun to play with a cigarette. 'So, some big

enchilada who lives alone, whose private address we know, and who doesn't know any of us. Does it have to be New York?'

'No, but it would be favourite.'

Stephen was brisk, impatient. 'I think you may already have a candidate in mind, Michael?'

Michael glanced at Seema. 'I was interested in the UN guy you mentioned last night, Seema. The one that student of yours is doing research for? You said something about a house in Sutton Place?'

'A few blocks up from the UN.' Seema's voice was dead, suggesting that contributing this information in no way constituted acquiescence.

Michael continued to look at her, pained by the trouble in her face. 'I looked him up in the UN staff book. There's only one Assistant Secretary General with US nationality based in New York. His name is Camden Hughes.'

'That's the guy,' said Seema, still reluctant to participate.

'Appointed by the Secretary General six months ago. Washington nominee. Career civil servant. Also happens to serve on the Federal Advisory Committee at the Centers for Disease Control, which might be handy. And you think he lives alone?'

Seema hesitated, but eventually responded as if the question had been asked in some ordinary context. 'Yes. Apparently his wife died a while back. It was after that he moved to New York.'

'Know the number in Sutton Place?'

'No, but I know which house.'

'Okay, let's check him against the criteria again—'

'Excuse me, Michael.' Seema had spoken very softly, but she had quietened the room. 'I'm not comfortable with this. I don't agree with Toby that getting down to the specifics will help us come to a decision. I think it helps us drift into it.'

Toby raised a guilty hand. 'Quite right, sweetie. Sorry. Cart pulling the horse along nicely there for a minute.'

Stephen looked at Seema dubiously over his spectacles. 'And may we take it you are voting against?'

Seema held his eyes. 'It's not going to be a vote, Stephen. If any one of us can't go along with this thing in principle then the same principle demands putting a stop to it.'

Stephen addressed his question to the wall. 'And how would you propose to effect such a unilateral decision?'

Michael replied for her. 'By exposure. And Seema's right. If any one of us can't go along, we'd all be bound to do the same.'

Stephen wagged his head from side to side as if analysing the issue at some more complex level. 'I suppose that works. The truly illogical position would be abstention.'

'So we've each got ourselves a veto?' Toby looked towards Michael.

'Each has a veto.'

When Seema realized that the others were all still looking at her, she glanced at each in turn, ending with Michael. 'My doubts come down to one thing. I'm not sure we're not taking too much on ourselves.' She ignored Stephen's facial contortions, expressing infinite patience, and stared instead at the flames. 'I'm wary about people who put too much faith in their own rightness – moral, political, religious, ideological. Wary of certainty, I suppose. It too often leads to misjudgement and imposition, quite often with an ugly outcome. A fine line, I think, between certainty and Fascism. Being uncertain, a little hesitant about one's own judgements, isn't always a sign of weakness.'

Stephen eventually spoke. 'And how much time do you think you might need?'

Seema replied immediately, but quite calmly. 'I don't know, Stephen. And I won't accept any deadlines.'

Soon afterwards, by unspoken agreement, the evening ended in a subdued shuffling of coats and gloves.

On the landing Seema detained Michael for a moment, placing a hand on his arm as the others descended towards the street. Michael turned towards her, not knowing what to make of the look in her eyes.

'Michael, are you sure? Are you serious?'

After a moment he leaned forward to kiss her cheek. 'You know me, Seema. I'm always serious.'

17 | The young master

No one even really knew where the man lived. Some said it was a shelter for the homeless in the Bowery, others that he belonged to a commune living in a cellar on the Lower East Side. All that was known for sure about Bilbao Benny was that every morning he set up shop by one of the stone chessboards in Washington Square, unpacking a vintage Russian chess clock, a quart bottle of some cloudy fruit juice and a pack of Marlboro Lights. Where the name came from was also a mystery. He was of African origin, but equally clearly had Arab blood. There was a rumour that, despite the soubriquet, his first language was Portuguese. In the summer months, if the days were hot and business slack, he would bring an old Spanish guitar and play haunting, lyrical, compositions under a huge, dirty umbrella that had obviously once belonged to a hot-dog stall. The music – 'played on the heartstrings' was how Benny described it – reminded some of the *norma* tradition of Cape Verde. His playing tended to draw crowds, but there was no upturned fedora or propped-open guitar case. Benny was just passing time until another client took the chair on the opposite side of the chessboard. Nor was he a hustler. His rules were simple: you put your five dollars under the clock to sit down and play. What happened to your five dollars when you won, if legend was to be believed, no one had ever found out.

Michael Lowell had been just fourteen years old when he had first sat down opposite Bilbao Benny. Although not a prodigy, he had been a fine high-school chess player and in his sophomore year one of his teachers had suggested lessons with a US Chess Federation Master. Michael had put the idea to his father and not long afterwards Dr Lowell Senior had taken Michael with him on a business trip to New York where, on a fine spring morning, he had sat him down at one of the boards under the trees in Washington Square.

It would be fair to say that, up to that point in his young life, Michael Lowell had known very little outside the white, privileged world of the Berkshires and he had been a little alarmed to find himself playing chess with a six-foot-four-inch rake-thin African with bloodshot eyes who was shod in filthy sneakers with a hole cut in one side to accommodate a misshapen toe. The first seven or eight moves had been played in silence. After that, Benny had begun to murmur morsels of advice in an argot that Michael could scarcely follow. But it hadn't taken long to figure out that his father had brought him to Washington Square to learn about more than chess.

Thereafter, he had sought out Benny whenever he had accompanied his father to the city. And, more than twenty-five years later, he still tried to fit Washington Square into the busy itinerary of his visits to New York.

On the morning of Sunday, February 1st, 1981, he arrived in the southwest corner of the square at around ten o'clock. He had intended to call on Seema and invite her for breakfast. But before he reached Charles Street he had changed his mind. She might still be asleep, or sleepless and exhausted. Instead he headed first for Washington Square. At least with Benny you knew what kind of problems you would be facing.

'Well, if it ain't the young master.'

Michael sat down and unfastened the Gladstone bag. As always in the winter months, Benny was wearing a black woollen beanie pulled over his brow and a down-filled vest over the top of an old raincoat fastened with a schoolboy's snake belt. Michael took out a cellophane-wrapped pack of 200 Marlboro Lights and placed it on Benny's table next to the Zippo lighter. 'Duty frees.'

'Duty frees,' said Benny. 'Due-to-freeze. Always did like the sound of that.' The board was already set up and a wave of the hand invited Michael to take white and start the clock. There was no small talk. Chess was the only game in Benny's town.

For the next twenty minutes, Michael pushed aside tiredness and summoned concentration, not in the hope of beating his man but out of a determination to make him concentrate. Putting aside other concerns as best he could, he brought to the table all that Benny had tried to teach over the years. 'The moment' had always been Benny's mantra. The moment to take the game to the opponent. The moment to do the unexpected, always discriminating between what was soundly unconventional and what was just 'eee-rratic'. The 'berserker', as Benny termed it.

After thirteen moves his opponent's clock had crossed the five-minute mark and, though his own dial was already showing seventeen minutes, Michael knew he had Benny thinking. He tipped his head back to stare up at the bare trees breaking into the winter sunlight. He would call by the apartment. Maybe invite her to brunch. A fingerless gloved hand pushed a pawn forward and then Benny leaned back, scratching the side of his neck and lifting his face to the morning sun, letting Michael know that if there had been any cause for concern it was now over. After four more moves,

Michael found himself up against his own flag and settled for a pawn sacrifice that he knew represented a failure to resolve. He felt Benny's eyes flicker upwards.

'College-boy move, huh?'

Benny closed and opened his eyes in slow, sarcastic assent. Two minutes later, he was taking Michael's five-dollar note from under the clock and pushing it into the lining of his coat.

'If I ever got my five bucks back I think I'd have it framed.'

'I estimate I'll most likely spend this one.'

For a few moments the two of them sat in silence, Michael also lifting his face towards the sun. Above the square, silhouetted squirrels were making their stop-start progress along impossibly fine branches. On the corner, a chestnut vendor had set up stall. Sighing with apparent content, Benny unstopped the bottle on his table and took a deep swig of the cloudy liquid. The benefit of a quart of fruit juice every day was one of the few things he would enthuse about.

'The young master wanna go again?' he said eventually.

Michael had never been sure whether it was an ironic reference to his abilities at chess or to the contrast in their situations in life, but from the day when his father had first sat him down here a quarter of a century ago Benny had addressed him as 'the young master'. Whatever the reason, the forty-two-year-old Michael found it as disconcerting as the fourteen-year-old schoolboy had done.

'Catch you later. Got some errands to do.'

18 | Better than anyone I know

Toby had taken a cab and picked up Hélène on the way. Stephen had walked the mile from 23rd Street. By the time Michael arrived, Seema was handing round coffee and bagels.

For the first minutes the conversation was sustained by short-lived exchanges about all the different kinds of bagel, about the cold, and about the down-and-outs spending the night in the cardboard cities under the bridges. But when these topics had run their course and the last bagel had been politely left by them all, a silence had fallen.

It was Seema who took the plunge. 'Okay, before we go on – or back – there's something I want to ask Michael.' She was rocking slightly in the planter's chair. 'Yesterday you said there'd only be one roll of the dice. So why the three containers?'

'To give us the option ... ' Michael hesitated for a moment and started over. 'If it succeeded, if we got the commitment, the danger is it wouldn't be sustained. It has to be for the long haul ... '

Seema stopped the rocking movement of the chair. 'I want all the cards face up, Michael. What you're saying is we might have to do it all over again.'

'Maybe. It would be down to us to make the call at the time.'

146

'So it's not just "one roll of the dice". It might have to be twice, even thrice?'

Michael shook his head. 'Let me back up aways. What I meant is ... we stop at first base. If it doesn't work, if we don't get the commitment, then that's it. We tried. We failed.'

Seema nodded, acknowledging that there had been no intention to deceive.

Stephen's face had assumed its thoughtful position. 'How long is it viable for?'

Michael sipped his coffee. 'Freeze dried, it's pretty stable as viruses go, even outside of a fridge. A few months, even a few years. Truth is, we don't know.'

Toby spoke with his eyes closed, resting his head on the back of the sofa. 'I've got a little question as well. I'd like to ask why we're proposing to put the squeeze only on the US of A?' He opened his eyes and looked around at the group. 'I mean, why not all those other governments that Hel's been talking about. It's their kids, after all. And most of them seem to have cash to splash on fancy hospitals, like Hel said, not to mention a lot of very unpleasant weapons, plus scraping a few bucks together for some pricey real estate not a million miles from where we sit. I'm thinking of the place Seema pointed out last night.'

Seema nodded. 'Nigeria House on 42nd.'

Stephen's mouth turned down as Toby returned his cup to the table and warmed to his argument. 'There's a bloke I know, client actually, merchant banker, nice chap, told me a dozen families in Nigeria could pay off the national debt twice over just with what they've got sitting in their Swiss piggy banks. So I'm just asking – why only the poor old US of A?'

Michael could not help smiling. 'Because, Toby, only the poor old US of A has what it takes to twist enough arms up enough backs in enough countries to get the job done. We're talking dollars, sure, but we're also talking leverage, commercial clout, defence deals, aid programmes, trade treaties, diplomatic recognition, and a whole bunch of other stuff.'

'Point taken, so long as we're clear it's not because all the ills of the world are down to Uncle Sam.'

'Oh, that's just so naïve!' Stephen was unable to sustain his air of patient forbearance. 'Don't you get it yet, Toby? It's "poor old Uncle Sam" that props up all these venal little regimes, gives them all the moral and material support they want. We're talking protection for US investments. We're talking access to cheap raw materials. We're talking making the world safe for capitalism. We're talking markets for US exports and weapons. Weapons, we might add, that are always sold for "defence" but always end up being used against internal movements that might show the slightest leaning towards any kind of progress for the masses…'

Toby held up both hands in a forestalling apology. 'Sorry, sunshine, forgot about all that. And about the Russkies being passionate about Ethiopia, Libya, Syria, and – what's that other place? – Angola out of pure unadulterated concern for the suffering masses. Pig's bum, mate.'

Stephen made a very visible effort to remain patient. 'The Soviet Union shows solidarity with those few socialist governments struggling to free themselves from the grip of a neocolonial world economy. And, yes, it helps progressive resistance movements that try to do something for the mass of the people. Helps them toward some sort of national liberation in the face of—'

Toby assumed a look of exaggerated enlightenment. 'I see. National liberation like in Poland, Hungary, Bulgaria, Czechoslovakia – not forgetting Afghanistan, of course, just the other week. Anybody want to share that last bagel?'

Hélène fought a sudden onset of tiredness, her thoughts wandering out of control. Fabrice would have agreed with so much that Stephen had to say. But it was much easier to imagine him getting on with Toby.

The others let Stephen finish his speech on the Soviet Union's need to buffer itself after years of wartime suffering, no one wanting to prolong this particular argument.

At the first pause, Hélène put the day back on track. 'I still want to know how this thing would work in practice and what each of us would have to do.'

Stephen turned away, picking up a copy of Saturday's *New York Times* as Michael began a reply.

'The heart of it all is the statement, the one we threaten to go public with. It has to be something so special that the administration would go to almost any lengths to avoid seeing it in the *Times* or the *Post*. My hope is it will be written by someone who could do that job better than anyone I know.'

The others followed Michael's look. Toby was sitting on the floor, staring intently at the glass doors of the stove. For a few moments the silence was broken only by the quiet roar of the flames. Hélène finished her coffee, hoping the caffeine would soon kick in. 'And the rest of us?'

Stephen lowered the newspaper. 'I should have thought it was obvious that I should make the drop. Grand Central, or wherever. I don't want to be in the position of having suggested something I'm not prepared to put my own neck on the line for. Besides, I'll be here. The rest of you, I assume, will be going back whence you came?'

Michael looked around at the others. 'Okay, Stephen, but before that there's something else we'd need to consider. I can't take the samples with me through airport security. If we decide to call the whole thing off then I'll destroy them.

That isn't a problem. But, if we're going ahead, they have to stay here in New York.'

'They can stay in my fridge at the Chelsea.' Realizing that he might have sounded over-eager, Stephen attempted to make light of the offer. 'Probably less lethal than some of the bugs already in there.'

Seema looked at Michael in a fleeting glance of alarm. Michael shook his head. 'What about chambermaids, cleaners? Then there's the package to deliver. Key, letter, statement.' He looked around at the faces of the others, each stage in the process seeming to make the plan more real. 'I can do that myself. I'll be back in New York before too long.'

Hélène clicked her tongue. 'That's crazy, Michael. Hundreds of people at the UN know who you are and a lot of them live in Midtown. You're the last person who should do it.'

Toby looked up, frowning. 'So have we decided on this Hughes character?'

Stephen dropped the newspaper on the floorboards. 'Seems to me he ticks all the boxes. And if it is to be Hughes, then it'd better be me again. No one knows me around the UN, I'm pleased to say.'

'I will do it.'

The voice was still quiet, but seemed to fill the whole space of the loft. Stephen pulled a sceptical face. Michael looked alarmed for the first time. 'Seema…'

'If we decide to do this, I will keep the vials here. And I will deliver the package.' Though quiet, there was something about the statement that defied challenge.

It was Toby who broke the tension. 'What chance of forgetting all about it for a couple of hours while we go out for brunch?'

'Not good, but we could give it a try.' Hélène was looking

round for her shoulder bag as the others, relieved at the suggestion of escape, began to stir.

As they crossed the Avenue of the Americas, huddled against the wind, Seema took Michael's arm, slowing her pace so that they fell some way behind. For two blocks they walked without words until, waiting for the lights at the corner of Bleecker, he turned to face her. 'You know you just have to say the word and all this will be over?'

'I know that, even if I don't know why.'

'I think you probably do know why.'

The lights changed and they walked another block in silence, hardly noticing their surroundings as they passed by Pei's brutalist Silver Towers. The cold bit deep as they turned in to the wind on La Guardia Place.

'We've never really talked, have we, Michael? Not in Oxford. Not here.'

When Michael made no reply she glanced up at him. 'And now this. Which makes it impossible to talk about anything else.'

Another block went by in silence.

'The others are all with you, Michael, you know that?'

'And you?'

Years later, Michael would remember the exact place, waiting under the bare trees halfway across Houston. They ignored the stop light changing to green, allowing others to cross towards the softer street lights and welcoming restaurants of Soho. And he remembered, too, the complete conviction that he should not be the one to speak.

'And so am I.'

'Seema … you can take all the time you need … '

The brunch at Florio's was a failure. As if by osmosis, each was aware that the decision had been made and that talk of anything else was irrelevant. In the event, they could not wait to get back to the apartment.

When the fire had been revived and silence had fallen, all of them knew that the time had come. It was Michael who formalized it: sitting upright and resting both hands on his knees, he looked at each in turn. 'Stephen?'

Stephen pulled an extraordinary face, waving a casual hand, implying it had been a no-brainer all along.

'Hélène?'

'I won't be here. But for what it's worth, yes, I'm in.'

'Seema?'

'Yes.'

Toby?'

'Consensual.'

Another silence followed, each aware that the chasm they had looked into all weekend was now being stared at from the other side.

The discussion that day continued long after there was anything more to be said. By three o'clock, Hélène was drifting in and out of sleep. On the sofa, Toby had long ago fallen silent. Michael stared into the flames, wondering at his capacity to be at one and the same time permuting possible outcomes of the plan and absorbed, heartstruck, by the woman sitting almost opposite him in the firelight. Eventually, seeing strain and tiredness all around him, he suggested going back to their hotels. 'But before we go, there's something I want to just mention.'

'It's not another of your little suggestions is it?' Toby had opened his eyes.

Michael looked at the skylight above. The day had grown dark, but no lamps had been switched on and only the flames from the stove lit the faces around him. 'Toby said yesterday we shouldn't take into account the risk to ourselves. And I guess that's right. But the point is, if we're identified, the plan fails. So no risks. And as I see it there really is only one risk.' He looked at each of the others. Hélène was still fighting sleep. Seema and Toby had both guessed what might be coming. Stephen was folding up the newspaper, apparently unconcerned. Above their heads, the wind battled with the chimney stacks.

Michael shuffled forward to the edge of his chair. 'Let me back up aways. None of us has any kind of record, or any kind of connection to any group that's likely to come under any suspicion. We all belong to establishment institutions. We're not going to be on NSA databases or FBI wiretaps. The only way we could ever be traced would be via witnesses or forensics. And there won't be any.'

Toby rubbed his eyes. 'Forensically, in Michael we trust.'

'The only risk is that one of us lets something slip.' The expressions of the others suggested that no warning was needed, but Michael was shaking his head. 'I know what we'll all say. But it could happen. Secrets create pressures. And this secret would have to be for the rest of our lives. Nothing could ever be said. Not in a moment of anger, or under stress, or in some kind of life crisis, or because we don't want to keep anything from someone we love, or because one night years from now one or other of us has a glass of wine too many.' Toby winced, though none of the others had looked at him. 'There are five of us. And a lot of years to come. Something like this comes with psychological pressures that we've none of us any experience of.' He looked from one to the other. 'Okay, that's it, I'm through.'

The rain on the skylight above became more insistent as they each imagined possibilities, circumstances, consequences. After a few moments, Hélène stood up from the sofa with a shake of her head, as if to stop her eyes from closing again. 'It's really weatherin' out there.'

19 | For the rest of our lives

Hélène had known what was coming as soon as Michael had invited her to lunch.

They had arranged to meet at the Swiss Inn where they were able to find a corner well away from the more popular window tables overlooking First Avenue. They ordered quickly.

When they were alone Hélène began with a deep sigh and a long, dubious look at her companion. Michael gave her an apologetic smile. 'Get much sleep?'

'Not much. I went off okay, then woke with a start about two o'clock thinking "Holy Mary Mother of God, what are we doing?"'

Michael's smile faded. 'I think I'm going to change my mind and have a glass of wine.'

'Okay, I'll join you. Better make it just one, though. Oh God, I wonder if we're going to be saying that for the rest of our lives?'

Michael looked around. The restaurant was almost empty, the only other diners being a couple who had taken a table by the window. 'Not too long on atmosphere.'

'It's terrifyingly ordinary.'

They were silent as the waiter placed two glasses of white wine before them, along with a small plate of olives. From outside came the deep foghorn of a truck bruising its way up First Avenue. When the waiter had gone, they raised their glasses and lightly touched rims, Hélène taking only a token sip. 'Let me save you some trouble here, Michael. I can't make the speech, can I?'

Michael also returned his glass to the table. 'No.'

'It's okay, I'd already worked it out. "Telling it like it is" right here in New York so close to … you know … I'd be in the frame right off.'

Michael lowered his voice, though there was no one within fifty feet. 'It would trigger an investigation like you wouldn't believe. They'd be going through every single one of your contacts as far back as kindergarten. Wouldn't take long to get to me. And that would be too much of a coincidence.'

'I know. I realized as soon as I saw the speech on my bedside table when I got back last night. It's one or the other.'

Food arrived and for a while they ate in silence. The tables by the windows were filling up, the background hubbub beginning to rise. 'Fish is good.'

Michael looked as if he were noticing what they were eating for the first time. 'I can imagine how much you've put into it, how good it would have been.'

Hélène shrugged and took a more determined sip of the wine. 'I must admit, I'd worked myself up to it. I did want to make the speech.'

Michael put down his knife and fork. 'You already made it, Hel. You're the one who woke us all up, including me.'

Hélène surprised herself by being suddenly close to tears as she poked around in the salad with her fork. 'Remind me to leave you asleep next time.'

The waiter arrived to refill the glasses from a jug of iced water. By the time he had gone, Hélène had composed herself again. 'So what do you want me to do?'

'I don't want you to do anything. I want you to go back and do your best to forget about it.'

'It's not something that's likely to slip my mind.'

'What I meant to say is… you've already done your bit. In every possible way. The only thing you can do now is—'

'Give you my blessing?'

Michael took another glance around the restaurant before speaking again. 'Yes. I do want your blessing, Hel. It's partly what Seema said. You can put too much faith in your own judgement, too much trust in your own… mental balance – sanity, I suppose. People can get bent out of shape without realizing it.'

'I don't think it's insane, Michael, if that's what you mean. You know what I think is insane.'

He nodded, thinking of all that Hélène had witnessed over the years.

She leaned towards him. 'Anyway, as I see it, no one stands to get hurt.'

Michael had given up the pretence of eating his lunch. 'That's what Seema wanted to know. But we can't be absolutely sure of that. It's possible they'll decide to tough it out and start vaccinating first responders, health personnel, emergency services. That would probably cause some kind of a panic and maybe a whole bunch of people won't believe that it can be contained and start demanding vaccines.'

'And some people might get a bad reaction to the vaccine? Tell me, Michael, what's the fatality rate for vaccinia?'

'Slightly under 0.0001 per cent.'

'Thought you might have a rough idea.'

Hélène thought for a moment. 'So, okay, let's talk about balance. The chances of a fatal reaction from the vaccine are less than one in a million. But the very least we could expect is that immunizing kids gets kicked way up the agenda, accompanied by publicity like you'd never get in your wildest dreams, however many reports you published. And if that happens it's going to save hundreds of thousands of young lives.'

Michael thought for a moment. 'I guess I'm trying to keep some kind of a toehold on "first do no harm".'

Hélène made her impatient clicking noise. 'If physicians were puritans about that, we'd never have risked vaccinating anybody, never have risked giving anyone a blood transfusion, never have risked performing a caesarean ... '

Michael held up his hands in submission but Hélène was in full cry. 'And in this particular case I'd have thought the balance of likely harm and likely good is what I believe they call over here a no-brainer. So, yes, Michael, you have my blessing, for what it's worth.'

Michael looked steadily at her, hoping his eyes were conveying something of the depth of his respect. 'You don't need to do anything. I'll say you took sick. You going on to Montreal?'

'Yes. And, as it happens, it won't altogether be a lie. First thing I'm going to do is check myself into McGill.'

Michael looked up in concern, thoughts instantly leaping to Paul. Hélène smiled, 'Probably nothing. Been feeling tired these last few months, that's all. Not your normal tiredness, I don't think.'

'Anything else?'

'Lymph nodes a bit swollen a lot of the time. Probably just means I'm fighting off some infection, which I probably always am. Still ... whatever it is, it's knocked me for a loop.'

'Any suspicions yourself?'

'Not really. You know how it is. People like to think we always have a name for everything. And a drug of course. But, as you well know, it's not like that, especially in Africa.

Anyway, I'll get myself thoroughly checked out. Take advantage of the insurance for once. I'll go tomorrow, have an extra couple of days with Mom and Dad.'

'And you've lost weight.'

'And I've lost weight.'

'Diarrhoea too?'

Hélène hesitated. 'Yes. For a few months now, I guess. Again not unusual in Africa, as you may know.'

'Keeping yourself hydrated?'

'Drink ORS like Toby drinks Scotch. Stephen's a bit worried about that, by the way. You?'

'Not really. Thing like this, he'd get a grip. Actually *he's* a bit worried about Stephen. Thinks there might be a few kangaroos loose in the top paddock, as he put it. By the way, can you make time to brief Toby before you go?'

'Nothing I can tell him that you can't.'

'Not so. We already had breakfast. I talked him through my side of things. Now he needs to talk to you.'

Hélène looked at him suspiciously. Michael decided not to smile. 'He needs to talk to you.'

'Okay.' She was about to stand up to look for a payphone. 'I'll give him a call now.'

'He's at some lunch meeting up on Madison.'

Hélène sat back again. 'Difficult to imagine Toby's other world, eh?'

Michael nodded. 'He's been doing a pretty good job imagining ours.'

'Yes. Yes he has.'

'When does he leave?'

'Tomorrow morning. On Concorde.'

'I don't believe you.'

'Apparently the agency's been invited to pitch for the Concorde account. Seemed like a good idea if he flew back on it. Got to do his research.'

Hélène shook her head in bemusement. 'Don't really think of Toby all sleek and supersonic, do you? And that reminds me of something.' She paused for a moment before looking up. 'I want to repay my airfare.'

'Let me take care of it.'

'I can't let you do that.'

'I couldn't live with myself if I didn't.'

Hélène sipped her wine and turned to look across the rapidly filling restaurant towards the crowds now in full flow out on First Avenue. 'Isn't it nice to be arguing about something ordinary?'

Seema was aware of her reputation for serenity. One of her colleagues, an Italian-American, was in the habit of referring to her as La Serenissima and had gone so far as to ask her whether this was a particularly Asian quality, or whether it was just … Seema. La Serenissima herself, amused, tended to see it as just a lack of the normal New York angst, that almost palpable agitation of many of her colleagues who could disturb the peace of a room just by walking through the door. Whatever the quality was, it seemed to have abandoned her now as she sat at her desk in the Bobst Library.

Tracing references in a nineteenth-century farm book was mostly tedious work, and demanded patience: patience and peace of mind. And to be finding it difficult was perhaps not surprising, given that an hour ago she had buzzed Michael up to the apartment where he had again removed the three containers in plastic bags from his briefcase and placed them in a row on the bottom shelf of her fridge. She had no trouble believing his reassurances that they were perfectly safe. But she had already decided that she couldn't face seeing them every time she took out a carton of half-and-half. She would buy a mini-fridge like the ones the students often had in their rooms. It would go in the cupboard under the spiral stairs. Stephen would carry it up to the apartment for her. Anybody else might ask questions.

She picked up her pencil and again tried to focus; Jefferson had owned three slaves named Sally and it was not always clear which one was being referred to. Nor was the task made easier by the tendency of Southern slave owners to call every older black woman 'auntie' and every older black man 'uncle'. She turned the page. Michael had been dashing between his breakfast briefing with Toby and his first official meeting of the day at the UN. Their goodbyes had been embarrassed and unsatisfactory, and it was clear that whatever there might be between them it was on hold, suspended, impossible to access except through the portal of the astonishing thing that had happened; the thing that now held them both together and apart.

She opened her file and began running a finger down the page, putting a cross by the names of Sarah Hemings' descendants who had names associated in some way with Thomas Jefferson: Madison, Wayles, Mary, Eston, Munroe...

Marble Hill, Yonkers, Hastings, Dobbs Ferry, Tarrytown, Ossining – the townships of the Hudson Valley flew smoothly by, the miles succumbing to the lulling rhythm of the train, the great river appearing and disappearing from view as Hélène headed north, tiredness a warm flood in her brain.

She had hesitated before agreeing to meet in Toby's room at the Algonquin. But it had to be somewhere private and in the event Toby had been business-like, getting straight down to the briefing, asking questions and scribbling rapid notes. Even their goodbyes had been almost formal, and she had known that he had been determined not to fall back on his usual jocular advances. When the time had come to depart, he had kissed her cheek and wished her *bon voyage*. And that was all. Though his eyes had held a different message.

She had tried reading, but her novel seemed to belong to another world; a more real world. In the distance she recognized the great span of the Tappan Zee Bridge, the thousands of red tail-lights heading home to the suburbs, the stream of headlights making for an evening in the city. And then it was back to the sprawl of shopping malls and gas stations and the scattering of homes from whose chimneys smoke faded into the evening sky. Ordinary homes. Ordinary lives. Or maybe not.

The great river reappeared, wider now, as she tried to focus on the future. The speech had not been made. There was nothing now to stop her going back to Africa. Darkness had begun to fall. And, as the view faded, it was to Grethe Rask that her thoughts turned, the rhythm of the train carrying her towards the appointment she had already made at McGill. She had served alongside the Danish surgeon in those scary Ebola days on the Zaire-Sudan border, and they had stayed in touch. Greta, too, had complained of tiredness in the months that followed, though she had continued working long days in the Red Cross Hospital in Kinshasa. Eventually, so she had confided, the weariness had come to weigh down every hour and, what with the weight loss and the repeated infections, she had decided to return home, suspecting a lymph cancer. No cancer had been found. But within a few weeks she had been unable to breathe without oxygen. On December 12th, 1977, at Copenhagen's *Rigshospitalet*, Margrethe Rask had died. She had been just forty-seven years old.

Hélène shook herself free from the thought. There were a hundred possible causes for tiredness and weight loss, even for lymph swelling, especially if you lived and worked with patients in a poorly equipped hospital surrounded by every kind of infection, known and unknown. McGill would have the answer. Except that for Greta no answer had ever been found; she had appeared to die of pneumocystis, but since when was pneumocystis a fatal condition? The darkness was almost complete as the countryside began to open out again. It was a shame to be taking the night train.

Stephen lay flat on the hotel bed hoping that the pain in his lower back would be temporary. Through the thin wall behind his bedhead came the strains of a protest song accompanied by the noise of several sets of footsteps. The whole place, it seemed, creaked and groaned with every movement on floors, landings, corridors. In a day or two, he would get his act together and move.

In the meantime, the pieces of his weekend needed to be rearranged into some more acceptable picture. Michael was obviously going to be in the driving seat when it came to the medical detail, but the essential concept had been very much his own. The song about Steve Biko came to an end as he struggled to open the French windows, one of which had to be lifted slightly over a warped floorboard. Somehow the room managed to be both cold and stuffy at the same time. He pressed a hand into the small of his back, wondering whether to go out and read his book at one of the neighbourhood coffee bars.

He sat down again on the bed. If by any chance the balloon did go up then he would also be needed to provide the counter-narrative, probably written from a prison cell. Tell the story from a perspective that valued the lives of the poor and the oppressed as much as those of the rich and powerful. His role, in that eventuality, would be as a kind of embedded historian: in fact precisely the historian as 'conscious tool of history' that Marx had envisaged.

He crossed to the kitchen area and opened the fridge. It had been right of course to allow the samples to be kept at Seema's. Somewhat squeamishly, she had bought a mini-fridge especially for the purpose and carrying it up the four flights of stairs had done something to his back. If he was going to stay, he should probably join a gym. After they had transferred the containers, still in their plastic bags, to the little Frigidaire, she had rushed back to NYU, where she had been due to lecture on the quaint topic of Slaves and Smallholdings.

Carrying a Coke, he returned to the open window. Not that his own academic career could any longer be described as mainstream. In fact the pieces of his weekend that he was having most difficulty in accommodating were the two letters that had been handed to him at the desk that morning. The first brought news that the *History Workshop Journal* would not be publishing his article on 'The Social Production of News' on the grounds that they would soon be bringing out a piece on a similar topic by Stuart Hall. The second enclosed details of final salary payments and pension rights.

Looking down on the noise and traffic that Monday morning, he could not help thinking of the peaceful quadrangle he had left behind. Even if his star had been fading, he had belonged there in a way that he could never belong on 23rd Street. In fact exactly where, now, did he belong? The street below was thronged with people hurrying to and fro as he lifted his head to the fire escape and the narrow strip of day above. He belonged, he decided, to what they were now embarked upon. He and the others whom he had summoned together. He held on tight to the handrail and looked down again to the street.

If only all these people knew.

20 | The curvature of the earth

What Toby wrote that day, travelling eight miles above the Atlantic at approximately twice the speed of sound, had nothing to do with 'capturing the in-flight experience' or 'slapping down some initial thoughts'. Instead he was focused on what Hélène had told him at The Algonquin, struggling to edit her words, phrases, half-finished sentences, into a coherent message while trying to preserve something of the pain and the anger – and the tears when he had pressed her to describe in more detail what he had never seen and could not imagine.

> To see a mother cradling her child's head for hour after hour; to see the little head turn suddenly on a body that is unnaturally still; to want to stop even that small movement because it's so obvious there's no energy left in the child's life. To see the pink inside the mouth and the wrinkled grey of the skin, the colours of its life and death; to see the uncomprehending panic in eyes which are still the clear and lucid eyes of a child. And then to know – in one endless moment – that life is gone.

He crossed it all out and turned back several pages to the list of facts and figures he had extracted from his breakfast meeting with Michael, beginning to write quickly in a pencil scrawl unintelligible to anyone but himself.

The drinks cart passed by unnoticed as he read through the paragraphs he had written. Something in the back of his mind told him to pause and re-imagine the reader, not the Hughes guy but whoever might see it next, probably someone in Washington. It was an odd brief – write something that will convince a handful of people that what they are reading must never be allowed to be seen by anyone else. He rested the notebook on the food tray and began to read again, making deletions, remembering his Faulkner, killing his darlings. The essential thing was to hit the right tone. It didn't need extravagance or too much in the way of rhetorical flourish. It needed to be spare, serious, sane; it needed to be so normal and responsible that there was no way it could be dismissed as the work of crazies, hotheads, fanatics, zealots of any stripe. In the end, it had to make a case with which reasonable people might feel moved to agree.

He placed the notebook on the empty seat beside him and stretched his arms and legs as best he could, blinking and looking around at the discreet cream and grey-blue décor of the cabin. Two rows in front of him, the pale lemon lights on the bulkhead tracked speed and altitude. Writing his initial pitch wouldn't be difficult. There was only one reason why anybody would pay eight thousand dollars for a one-way trip across the Atlantic. And it wasn't the 'in-flight experience', which was cramped in the extreme, the kerosene-like smell of the re-heaters lingering in the cabin, the windows the size of a stunted grapefruit, the headroom a contradiction in terms, the Connolly leather seats tighter on the bum than normal business class. He reclined the seat again, feeling it tilt all in one piece, pressing his thighs up under the tray. It was all embarrassingly obvious. A Concorde ticket came with its own sonic status boom. All that was required was some sort of a figleaf to cover the nakedness of the 'ego-libido' as Toby himself had christened it. And there it was in those pale lemon lights on the forward bulkhead. Mach 2.2, proclaiming how exceptionally important one's time was. Unlike the aircraft itself, its appeal was not rocket science.

He glanced at his watch. Damnation. Halfway there already. He turned back through his pages and began again to read.

These children die with the rash of measles (2 million a year), with the convulsions of tetanus (1.2 million children a year), with the paroxysms of whooping cough (1.5 million children a year).

He consulted his notes of the morning, copying out more legibly the epitaph on twentieth-century medicine that Michael had quoted to him: 'Brilliant in its scientific breakthroughs, ingenious in its technological invention, and woefully inept in its application to those most in need.'

He read on, scribbling in the margin at points when anything snagged in his brain, nagged by the feeling that something was falling short, some intangible element that would give the pitch more bite, more purchase on mind and memory. It was not an unfamiliar feeling, this realization that a piece of work was almost there but not quite, the edge still slightly rounded instead of being cut-to-the-touch. He had even experienced something similar when playing chess, knowing that he was missing some advantage that lay just out of the mind's reach. He thought for a few minutes more and began to write again.

Ten minutes later he closed the notebook and flexed his fingers, pushing his feet out under the seat in front. In another hour or so he could have had the piece finished, ready to send as soon as he got to the office. But there wasn't time. Raising a hand to the window he could feel the heat of the plane's friction through the air, though the plane itself was so steady as to seem locked in ice.

Half-crouching, he made his way back down the plane. 'Like the inside of a covered wagon,' was how a Braniff executive had described it. He smiled at one or two of the passengers who met his eye. How many of them would also have valued a little more of this precious, uninterruptable time? Even before he had returned to his seat, he had clinched the centrepiece of the pitch. The stewardess, elegant, gorgeous, leans towards the distinguished-looking, mature businessman working on his papers as he returns home in the hushed luxury of Concorde, the panel showing Mach 2.2, the curvature of the earth just visible (cheat a little bit, use a shot from space). Cut for a couple of frames from her lips to the label on the vintage Champagne, then back to the businessman, glancing up briefly, appreciatively, but refusing the champagne with a polite, distracted smile, before returning to his work. The figleaf. The moment of refusal. A Savile Row figleaf. Guaranteed to put supersonic bums on supersonic seats.

He returned to his seat and opened the notebook. 'Hélène' was written at the top of the page. He had been so intent on his task that they had not spoken of anything else. She had wished him luck with the writing, then lingered just for a moment in the doorway. But he had merely muttered a *bon voyage* and let her go. He had known that it might be a long time before he saw her again. But nothing he could think of to acknowledge the fact had seemed in any way appropriate. He had merely raised the notebook in salutation, and held her eyes as the elevator doors had closed between their lives.

He looked again at his watch. He would do the polishing tonight. There would be no one at home. And it was not something he wanted to carry forward into his week at the office. He glanced up at the flight information on the forward bulkhead. Mach 2.0, whatever it meant, was far too fast to be returning to his world. From the undersized window it was indeed just possible to see the dazzling blue-and-white curvature of the earth, way too far below. But above was a blackness that was odd on a daytime flight. The answer came to him only slowly. The darkness was not sky. It was the darkness of space. And for the first time the wonder of it came to him, the terrible unfamiliarity of being poised on the margin, suspended between the familiar atmosphere of the world he knew and the inhospitable beyond.

PART TWO

21 | All over nervous

One of the pluses of Tom Keeley's mid-career change from the Centers for Disease Control to the *New York Times* was not having to be in the office by nine. Often he worked late into the evening, but not having to leave early meant a leisurely breakfast with Caroline, after the boys had left for school, and it had quickly become a cherished part of the day – sitting at the kitchen table with a second cup of coffee, or going back to bed for an hour and making love in the light, airy room that looked out directly on to the Connecticut countryside, or just talking over the joys and worries of bringing up two teenage boys.

'Everything was fine until I asked if I'd missed anything at the reunion. And then suddenly she's all over nervous.' Caroline interrupted his account of the previous day's lunch with Seema Mir by offering to make more toast. He followed her into the kitchen. 'Said it had been good to see the others but couldn't wait to get off the subject.'

'Maybe it was to do with that other guy, Michael. Don't they have history?'

'They were an item that year in Oxford, for sure.'

'So maybe it was a big deal and all, seeing each other again?'

'Could be. But she seemed more scared than anything. And the thing about Seema is, she's usually so ... I don't know ... composed.'

22 | We wish to make it clear...

Nyon, Switzerland, Friday, February 6th, 1981

Michael poured himself a glass of wine and carried it through to the dining table. It was not quite dark, but a winter mist had descended on the town and all that was visible were a few milky street lights and, here and there, a window already lit in the mansards of the Rue Delafléchère.

He turned on the lamp and opened the package delivered by special courier earlier in the day and marked 'Personal' in three different places.

This is to inform you that the senders of this letter are in possession of lyophilized smallpox virus. As evidence of this, a sample in a sealed vial has been left in a rented locker on the lower level of Grand Central Terminal, New York. Key enclosed.

Failure to respond to the demands set out below by midnight Eastern Standard Time on March 6th, 1981 will result in the statement accompanying this letter being released to the media, along with a second sample of the virus.

In order to avoid this, it will be necessary for the President of the United States to make a public commitment to the goal of universal child immunization by the end of the current decade.

Michael paused a moment. No matter how many times the plan had played out in his mind over the weeks, seeing Toby's words on the page sent a chill crawling over his skin.

This goal has already been endorsed by the government of the United States, along with the governments of almost every other nation in the world. It is defined as achieving routine immunization coverage of at least eighty per cent of children aged between twelve and twenty-four months against measles, tetanus, diptheria, whooping cough and poliomyelitis.

In addition, we wish to make it clear that no public response by the President will be accepted as adequate if it does not also contain the precise text given below:

Michael, surprised, read the last lines again. This had been no part of the plan. He turned the page.

Twenty years ago, President John F Kennedy committed the United States to the goal of putting a man on the moon within a decade. Today, the United States commits itself to another great goal: a goal for our times; a goal to be achieved here on earth; the goal of immunizing all of the world's children against the major killer diseases of childhood …

This goal, too, can and will be achieved within a decade. And it too will be a giant step for mankind.

Michael closed his eyes for a few moments, then read through the text of the letter again. Toby had seen the weakness.

Seen that it would have been too easy to make some weasel-worded commitment, an opening gambit in a game of wait-and-see. But after such a statement, invoking the sainted name of Kennedy and carrying unmistakable echoes of that famous inaugural, it would be almost impossible to go back on.

> *It will be achieved not by the United States acting alone but in partnership with all nations …*

Good, Toby, good …

> *… to those countries across the globe struggling to break the bonds of disease … we pledge our support.*

After thinking for a few more moments, he returned the letter to the table and opened the accompanying press release. He had assumed it would need work, and probably some toning down. But again he had underestimated his man. Instead of opening with a dramatic threat, the statement began with a sober announcement of possession of the virus and a warning that 'further action would be considered' in the event of an inadequate response. The threatened press release went on to detail the demand and justify the action being taken, spelling out what the world was allowing to happen to millions of its most vulnerable citizens. Michael took a sip of wine as he read on, his excitement mounting.

> *No earthquake, no famine, no flood, has ever killed thirteen thousand children in a single day. Yet diseases that vaccines can prevent are killing that number of children every day; yesterday, today, and tomorrow. Every single one of those millions was an individual child with a name and a nationality, a family and a future …*

He rapidly checked the figure. No exaggeration was involved.

The cost of preventing this tragedy would be approximately five hundred million dollars a year. It is an enormous sum. About as much as the world spends on its military capacity every eight hours.

Another check for gross error. Military spending currently over five hundred billion a year. Near enough.

Allowing this tragedy to continue when the means to prevent it are available and affordable is unconscionable. Nothing can justify it. And it shames and diminishes us all.

Finally, we wish to point out that this action is being taken not in order to impose the will of a minority but to ensure that the governments of the world make good on promises they have already made on behalf of all the world's people.

Texts for Michael's approval were a five- or six-times-a-week occurrence, and he was aware of a reputation for being difficult to satisfy. But there was nothing in Toby's statement that he wanted to change. Night closed in as he remained in his chair, imagining the statement being read by those who would themselves have to imagine it appearing all over the media. As best he could, he worked through the likely actors in the scenes that lay ahead, on what each might say or do, on the risks and dangers, the contingencies and likelihoods, coming to dwell finally on the likely reactions of the others under the pressure he knew was in store, ending with Stephen Walsh.

Eventually he went to his desk and took up a pen. Toby

had made only one tiny error: a spelling mistake that most non-medical people might make. After another moment's thought, he returned the pen to the desk.

23 | Nothing could be simpler

Entering Grand Central by the Vanderbilt Avenue entrance, Stephen was suddenly aware of how difficult it was to walk normally. He had chosen the busiest time of day, when commuters were concentrating on getting home. Passing the information booth, he speeded up – partly to avoid being jostled by those around him and partly because walking at a leisurely stroll through the main concourse of Grand Central Station at a quarter to six on a Friday evening would in itself have been conspicuous.

He had entertained no doubts about nominating himself to make the drop, but had not anticipated the fear that he might bungle it, that something might go wrong, something silly like not being able to operate the left-luggage locker, or not having the right coins, or losing the key. In any case, a dummy run would do no harm.

Asking where the left-luggage lockers were located might be a bad move. But on the other hand, walking around in circles might also attract attention. Descending the broad stone stairs to the lower concourse, he cut his way across the stream of commuters towards a Ho-Jo's counter where he hoisted himself onto a stool and ordered a black coffee. There was no hurry, and it was fascinating watching the human tide ebbing out of Manhattan. Was it any wonder that false consciousness held sway, when this was what people's lives were like?

He swivelled around on the stool and there, on his left directly under a stone arch, were the lockers. Coffee in hand, he watched as a Hispanic woman hurried towards them, a backpack hanging from one shoulder. Without hesitating, she twisted the handle, pulled open the door, pushed the backpack inside, closed the door again, dropped a quarter into the slot, and turned the handle again – clockwise this time – allowing her to extract the key. A few seconds later she had disappeared into the crowd, unnoticed by anybody but himself.

Nothing could be simpler.

24 | The sender of this letter

The opening moves were made more quickly than Michael had anticipated. Early on the Saturday morning, he was called with a request to stand in for the Director-General at a meeting in New York on inter-agency co-operation. Normally he would have groaned at the prospect of two days of discussions with similarly high-level representatives from the World Bank, UNDP, UNICEF, FAO, WFP, UNESCO and one or two of the smaller agencies, all discussing the need for co-operation while in country offices all over the world the turf wars continued much as before. But on this particular Saturday, the last-minute request to travel to New York was received with different emotions.

Packing never took Michael more than a few minutes. Into the Gladstone went a no-crease business suit, one tie, two pairs of socks, two drip-dry, non-iron shirts, and two sets of underwear. Washing out shirt, socks and underwear in his hotel room ready for the next day was as much a part of his routine as brushing his teeth. But on this occasion there was something else he had to pack. Something that would take most of his Saturday morning.

The shrink-wrapped pack of quarto paper, bought from a drug store near The Doral Inn on Lexington Avenue, was waiting in his desk drawer. Had it been purchased in Switzerland the size would have been A4, identifiably European. As he had explained to the others, fingerprints cannot be entirely removed from paper, and it was only after pulling on a pair of surgical gloves that he opened the pack and took out the old but almost unused Olivetti portable typewriter, bought as a present for his father just a month before his death. The open suitcase at his side, he slid the first sheet between the rollers and began typing a fair copy of Toby's drafts.

The sender of this letter is in possession…

Each step was unalarming in itself. Memorize the next few words, hit the right keys, check each word as it appears, don't think too far ahead.

… will result in the statement accompanying this letter being released to the media…

But he could not long resist imagining the reaction of others reading this text. He knew the name of the next person who would see it. But not the person after that.

… make a public commitment to head up a global effort…

He finished typing both letter and attachment and read them through. Still wearing the surgical gloves, he unwrapped the pack of six manila envelopes bought from the same store and, selecting one, slid the typed sheets inside. After thinking for a moment he went to the kitchen for a sponge and a small bottle of Evian water. With these, he sealed the gummed flap.

The last item of stationery, also brought back from New York, was the sheet of peel-off labels that he now fed into the Olivetti. Line up the label. Type the single line - *'Personal – to be opened only by Camden Hughes.'* Peel the label. Place it in the centre of the envelope. All very mundane. He carried the package into the kitchen and wiped the surfaces and edges with surgical ethanol, just as he had done with the flasks and the inner plastic bags sitting in Seema's apartment. Tearing off two more clear plastic bags from an unused roll, also bought in a New York drug store, he slipped the envelope inside one of the bags. He then wiped the outside of the bag and, with a little more difficulty, fitted it inside the second bag. Finally he laid the package flat between the two shirts at the bottom of the Gladstone bag. Only then did he remove the gloves.

Toby's original manuscript still lay on the table, waiting to be fed into the stove. He crossed to his bookcase. After a moment's thought, he pulled out an early draft of the report to the 34th World Health Assembly – a version that had since moved on through several more iterations. From the Gladstone bag, he took out the pocket-book used for recording travel expenses.

It took several hours to take each word of Toby's text, find the same word in the draft report, and write out the numbers of the page, the line, and the position of the word in the line. It was a simple Arnold Cipher, unbreakable by anyone not in possession of the text on which it was based. When he was finished he returned the pocket book to the bag and sat for a moment wondering what he might say if he was asked why he was carrying a pocket-book with several hundred apparently random numbers scribbled over a dozen or so pages. The answer came to him with the memory of his old boss. They had been standing together in the departure lounge of Geneva airport, looking at a glass case in which was displayed a range of Swiss Army knives. DA had joked that he would consider buying one if there was an epidemiologist's version. Waiting to board, they had discussed what special tools such a knife might have, eventually deciding on a pivot for spinning the knife in order to select a random direction, and a pull-out list of random numbers.

Later that day, he fed Toby's manuscript to the flames. The draft report to the World Health Assembly had been replaced on his bookshelf between two small statuettes from his collection: the first a wooden figure of Sopona, the smallpox deity of the Yoruba; the second a ceramic figurine of Sitata Mata, seated on a white donkey, to whom Hindus throughout the subcontinent had appealed over the centuries for protection against the disease.

On the Sunday morning, with a few hours to go before leaving for the airport, he packed the work he had brought home for the weekend, intending to stop by the office to drop off several tapes of dictation. Just before lunchtime he placed the Olivetti typewriter on top of the Gladstone bag along with the rest of the bottle of Evian and a few tomatoes from the bottom of the fridge. On the corner of the Rue Delafléchère he bought a baguette and a small wedge of Vacherin, then descended the stone stairway to the marina where he rented a motor boat for the afternoon. By two o'clock he was out on the lake, well wrapped up in ski jacket, hat and gloves, engine cut, fishing for the local whitefish just off Prangins-Yvoire.

The harbour wall was visible as a faint blur, more a disturbance than a shape, hovering between the misty lake and the almost indistinguishable sky. For a while he allowed himself to be mesmerized by the slow slapping of the lake on the boat, the ripples spreading out from his line and disappearing gently into the mist. The silence mocked his closeness to the town. New York a universe away. He would call as soon as he got in, perhaps even tonight. He was sure she would accept his invitation to dinner. But only because of what they had embarked upon. And he was not sure that they would be able to talk of anything else without it seeming trivial, irrelevant. Had he built a trap for himself? Was the relationship, whatever it might have become, now constrained, frozen inside the icy intimacy of their secret? He rested the rod on the bow of the boat, trapping the end under his foot, and began tearing off chunks of the baguette, breaking the cheese in his freezing hands, biting into the tomato, wishing he had brought coffee and a thermos.

The sharp taste of the cheese and the sudden roughening of the water seemed to be telling him things did not stay the same, that it was impossible to look ahead envisaging every move. For a long period after that year in Oxford, his life had held few joys. But satisfaction had eventually been found again, in work, in colleagues, in challenges. And Seema Mir had slowly retreated to a safer distance, though many were the reminders that would bring her flooding back. He had supposed it was like an infection that was dormant, though he was sceptical of scientific concepts being used in loose, analogous ways. Just as he had been sceptical of the theory that he had sublimated his feelings into his sixteen-hour days. The float bobbed a few metres from the boat, the line pulling gently at the rod. There had been one or two other brief relationships, entered into with a view to seeing if it were true, as Toby had insisted, that he would be capable of loving someone else. But they had matured not into love but into steady friendships as he had realized that greater intimacy, instead of banishing Seema from his thoughts, brought her distressingly nearer.

He threw the heel of the baguette into the lake and stared,

mind in neutral for a few moments, as the ripples disappeared in the choppier waters of the afternoon. And in that moment he saw clearly that what he wanted was to shake that famed serenity, reach her at some level that was at least close to the way she disturbed his every waking moment. She had said she was with him. And that should be enough. If he had been unable to persuade this strange, often dreamy, even passive-seeming woman whose humanity and sensitivity of spirit would always be his touchstone, then he would not be doing this.

He returned to harbour just after four o'clock on the afternoon of Sunday, February 8th, minus the Olivetti. By five o'clock he was on his way to the airport, the Gladstone bag on the seat beside him.

25 | The presence in the shadows

The murals of the New York Public Library Catalog Room offer fine opportunities for distraction to the uncommitted reader. Seema's favourite, directly opposite her this Monday morning, depicted the Ottmar Mergenthaler linotype machine that was perhaps America's first great contribution to the technology of publishing. She had not expected things to happen so fast. Michael had said it would probably be a month or more before he could return, and after Hélène and Toby had gone she had gradually allowed herself to pretend, sometimes for hours at a time, that things were normal. But not this morning. Small wonder that the papers on the desk stared back at her unread.

She had been out picking up a late supper when Michael had called from the Doral to say that he was unexpectedly back in New York. Had in fact just got in, and would she like to have dinner this evening? The message on the answering machine had also mentioned, after a pause, that he had brought her a letter from Toby. Would he want her to deliver the letter now, this week? She stared again at the mural. In the background, over Merganthaler's left shoulder, a newsboy shouted a headline under the Brooklyn Bridge, another of the wonders of the age. She had not called him back at the hotel. It had been three o'clock in the morning,

Geneva time, and she imagined he would have gone straight to sleep. And by now he would probably be in a meeting. She had never invited anyone to dinner in the apartment before. She would make an exception for Michael. But any prospect of intimacy was quickly dispelled by the thought of the letter he would be bringing. The rules of the game between them, complicated enough before, were now so distorted that there was no working out of the right moves, no way of resolving whatever feelings they might have for each other. There would no doubt be practical matters to discuss, though the thought again filled her with an all-drenching dread that was new in her life.

At a quarter past twelve she packed her papers and joined the other readers who had begun drifting out of the Catalog Room to make their way down the steps towards the various lunch spots around Bryant Park. She turned right and quickened her pace, intending to walk the thirty or so blocks back to the Village, stopping at a payphone on the way.

Michael's meeting had been switched at the last moment from UN headquarters to the conference room of UNICEF's headquarters in the old ALCOA building on the corner of Mitchell Place and First Avenue. Here he had spent the morning sitting behind a laminated place-card bearing his name, title and agency, occasionally looking up at one of the giant barges slowly butting its way up the East River. As lunchtime approached and sandwiches were sent for, the meeting had become tired, even a little tetchy. Michael himself had contributed little, apart from having to defend WHO's interest in what he had known was an essentially petty squabble with the UN Development Programme over 'lead agency' status in countries where the WHO had a regional office. He had been hoping to take a walk outside over the lunch hour, partly to wake himself up in the cold air, partly so he could stop at a payphone and call Seema. Probably he would have been more awake if he had known that, at that moment, Seema Mir was passing by the ALCOA building, having diverted via First Avenue on her way back downtown.

Walking to the West Village via Sutton Place was a long way round. But it was at a time of day when First Avenue was at its pedestrian busiest, as the thousands who work at the UN and the various banks and offices of Midtown headed out to lunch.

She turned east by the 59th Street bridge, making towards the FDR Drive, slowing her pace slightly as the crowds thinned in the sidestreets. A minute later she turned right and crossed to the row of four-storey townhouses on the tree-lined east side of Sutton Place. Without pausing, she glanced at the recessed entranceway to Number 13. At Sutton Park she turned right again on 53rd and rejoined First Avenue five blocks north of the building where Michael was sitting in a 6th-floor conference room eating a tuna salad from a plastic tray.

The brass letter box had been approximately fourteen inches wide.

The conversation between the two of them for the rest of that day was conducted via answering machine. During an afternoon break, Michael left a message suggesting dinner at Angelo's on Mulberry Street. An hour later, Seema left a message at the Doral confirming the arrangement. The thought that Michael might also have invited Stephen crossed her mind for a moment; long enough for her to register disappointment.

But Stephen had not been invited. And in the event the dinner at the long-established restaurant in the heart of Little

Italy had gone well. The conversation had at first been stilted, subdued. Most of the tables were occupied and the 'big thing' was off the conversational menu. Yet it loomed over them, making any other topic seem forced, as if it were merely trying to fill the void. Michael had persisted in asking about her research, and his interest had led her into explaining some of the problems. The big thing was still there in the shadows, but a kind of intimacy, an enjoyment of one another's company independent of what was being said, had grown between them as the evening lengthened, as if the presence in the shadows were being kept at bay by the plucky light of the candle.

After dinner, she had moved the candle slightly to one side so that they could see each other more clearly. 'My hope, in the first place—'

They were interrupted by the arrival of espresso and Sambuca. When the waiter had left, she began again. 'I wanted to write a book that would be about slaves as people, try and find a way to restore that dimension of individual humanity. And I thought in the case of the Hemings family I might just be able to glean enough information to do that.'

'And is there enough?'

'If I fill in some of the detail of what their lives were like from a much wider literature, then, yes, I think there is.'

'Because they were Jefferson's slaves?'

'Yes. They were owned by Martha's family – Martha Wayles, Jefferson's wife. They came to him when he married her.'

'So it's a biography of a family.'

'Exactly.'

'But your publisher wants it to be more about Jefferson?'

'Not only that. They want it to be about the relationship between Jefferson and Sally Hemings.'

'And you think that would undermine what the book's trying to do?'

'It would carry a kind of subtext that says the only reason she's important or worth knowing about is because she was Jefferson's mistress. And I wanted the Hemings to be important and interesting in their own right.'

Michael sipped the wonderful, viscous espresso and thought for a moment. 'You could say that it's the danger inherent in the whole concept, though.'

Seema picked up the spoon and removed the coffee beans from the Sambuca, alive to the fact of how much she was enjoying telling Michael about her concerns, despite the threat from just beyond their little circle of light. 'I know. We only have any information about their lives because they belonged to Monticello, and a lot of the people who might read it will really only be interested because of Jefferson. But, Michael, there's a difference, isn't there? The fact that they were Jefferson's slaves is the reason we know about them, but that doesn't mean it's the only thing that makes them interesting, which is how my publisher sees it.'

'Do it the publisher's way and you undermine your purpose.'

'Exactly. But do it my way, and apparently I undermine the sales.'

To her own surprise, Seema suggested they have a second round of espresso and Sambuca, not quite knowing whether this was to prolong what was, or to postpone what was to come.

'Of course it's so frustrating not to know more. I've never worked on anything that made me wish so desperately that we could reach back into the past and really *know*. But there is enough, I think. She was obviously a remarkable woman. And sometimes just knowing about the context brings her alive.

I mean, imagine a seventeen-year-old girl who'd never left a plantation in rural Virginia suddenly being transported to the most glamorous city in the world, accompanying Jefferson's daughter to balls at Versailles on the eve of the French Revolution. I think it could be wonderful. But the truth is I really need a sabbatical to finish it. Six months. A year would be better.'

And so the evening had passed more enjoyably than either could have anticipated. But the presence in the shadows could not be banished indefinitely, and when they left the restaurant at midnight it followed them out into the streets, closing in on them as they headed towards Washington Square. Seema attempted to keep it at bay for a while longer by telling him how the square had been the first soil in America to be owned by Africans, slaves who had been given the land as a buffer between their Dutch masters of New Amsterdam and the Native Americans. After that the talk died away as they cut the corner of the square, avoiding the addicts and the broken bottles and needles.

Just as she was wondering whether to invite him to come in, he unfastened the brass clasp of the bag. 'I've got something for you.'

She looked at him in the darkness of the doorway. He set the bag down on the tiled floor and took out the envelope inside its two plastic bags. He paused before handing it to her. 'Are you sure you're still all right with this?'

'Do you want to come up and we'll go over what I have to do?'

He picked up the bag again and his voice faltered. 'No, it's been ... too nice an evening to spoil with this' – he handed her the envelope – 'for me, I mean. Can we talk about it tomorrow?'

'We could meet here at the end of the day.'

'Seven o'clock?'

'Fine. Shall Stephen come too?'

'No need. I'm seeing him for breakfast. I'll brief him then.' He leaned forward to kiss her cheek. 'Goodnight, Seema.'

'Goodnight, Michael.'

He was stepping back into the street when she spoke again, from halfway through the inner door of the building. 'Michael.'

He turned on the sidewalk.

'I had a nice evening, too.'

26 | Let's do it

Stephen's meeting with Michael had left a slightly sour taste. They had been unable to talk about the plan in Zum-Zum's, the German-style deli where they had eaten a hurried breakfast. So the conversation afterwards, as he walked with Michael to his meeting, had been necessarily condensed. And it had felt a little too much like taking instructions.

Back in the lobby of the Chelsea, he poured himself more coffee and put the *Times* aside, his mood not improved by an article about a Unitarian clergyman who had apparently lost his faith but carried on pretending. According to the story, he had felt that who and what he was – to his wife and family, to his friends, his congregation and his community – had been entirely built on the foundation of being a Christian minister. To abandon the foundation, he had feared, would be to bring the whole edifice tumbling down. And so he had remained silent, going through the motions of being a priest for more than ten years until the inner conflict had led to a breakdown. It had been a moving story, ending with a description of the love and support shown by those whose repudiation he had feared. In the last few paragraphs, the writer had speculated that no one could know how many other members of the clergy were in a similar position, offering as an aside a chilling if not entirely relevant reference to Edgar Allen Poe's famous comment that 'no one will ever know how many coffin lids are scratched on the inside'.

The piece had sharpened the sour taste and he ordered a second bagel, eventually leaving the Chelsea Hotel soon after half past nine to walk downtown to Seema's apartment.

They had lunched together twice in the time since the others had left New York, and visited an exhibition at the New York Historical Society one bitterly cold weekend, but Seema had deliberately not invited Stephen to the apartment. Now, as she buzzed him up, she was still thinking about the previous evening.

He refused the offer of coffee and seemed anxious to be on his way. 'So, they're still in the little fridge?' he asked, determinedly offhand.

'I've never even opened it.'

Stephen was forced to kneel under the spiral staircase to take out the first of the plastic bags, its contents almost invisible through a crusting of frost. He closed the door and shuffled backwards on his knees until there was room to stand.

Resting the canvas shoulder bag on the table, he stowed the container inside and took an age fastening the straps. This done, he turned towards her and took a deep breath. 'Point of no return, I guess.'

'I guess so.'

'You've got the letter?'

'Yes.'

'Michael show you it?'

'No, it's all sealed up. Clean of any prints or anything. It's just to be taken out of the bag and pushed through the mailbox.'

'With gloves.'

'Of course.'

'Quite right.'

He pushed an arm through the strap of the bag and paused at the open door to the landing. 'Okay, let's do it.'

No one needs an excuse to wear gloves on a February day in New York, and Stephen attracted no attention as he crossed the main concourse of Grand Central. He had delayed his arrival until the evening rush hour and the steps were crowded with Amtrak commuters streaming towards the platforms. From a point halfway down the staircase he had already identified a partly open locker.

At the last moment, without knowing why, he veered towards one of the coffee counters. There he surveyed the concourse, just one of thousands of rush-hour commuters waiting for a train. He sipped from the plastic cup, the world running past him as time stood still. So far, his involvement had been driven by Stephen the radical historian. The other Stephen had not been consulted. Until now.

For twenty minutes more he remained on the revolving stool, accepting a refill and slowly admitting that it was in any case too late. Not to go through with the plan now would be to sustain a blow which no version of himself could survive. Feeling slightly numbed, he paid his bill and unfastened the straps of the shoulder bag. The locker he had first identified still stood half open as he rounded the foot of the stairs. It was twenty minutes to six.

Glancing up to see if anyone might be watching, he opened the door all the way, took out the still-cold plastic bag and pushed it deep inside the locker. Letting his shoulder bag fall to the floor, he felt in his jeans pocket for the quarter and inserted it into the slot, turning the handle clockwise until the coin dropped. He was about to turn away when he remembered the key. Quickly he tugged it from the lock and, telling himself that there was no need to hurry, walked towards the foot of the stairs. On the bottom step, he rested the bag on the stone balustrade and took out a leather coin purse. Gloved hands struggling with the zip, he placed the key inside the purse and returned it to the bag, fastening it with both buckles and ducking his head inside the loop of the strap so that it sat diagonally across his chest.

By a quarter to six he was crossing 42nd Street to the lobby of the Chrysler building. After walking in one entrance and out of another, he spent the next hour walking haphazardly around Midtown, ending up near the Port Authority Bus Terminal where he stood in line for a yellow cab. Progress was slow in the evening traffic and it was after 7.00pm when he finally arrived in his room at the Chelsea Hotel. He locked the door. Still wearing the gloves, he removed the key from the purse and polished it for a full minute using a soft cloth and a small bottle of lens cleaner. He then transferred it to the clear plastic bag waiting on top of the mini-bar. Finally he placed the bag and key inside an identical second bag, torn from a roll bought earlier that day. Only then did he take off the gloves and open the half pint of Jack Daniels he had picked up at the liquor store on the corner of 23rd.

27 | The heart of a perfectionist

Montreal, February 10th, 1981

Hélène sat in her father's study reading job advertisements in the *Journal of the Canadian Medical Association*. Her parents had gone to bed hours before, having failed to extract any information about the sender of the hand-addressed letter that had arrived for her that morning, postmarked London.

What they would have made of Toby Jenks in person she could only imagine. She had opened the envelope with trepidation, but in fact the letter had been sensible, chatty, humorous on the subject of supersonic travel and inquiring whether she had made any progress with her decision about making a new life for herself in Canada.

The weekend in New York had been altogether too overwhelming for any sorting out of her feelings. When she had told him about Fabrice, in that late-nite bar in the small hours of the Saturday morning, she had seen how disturbed he had been. For her. For himself. And she had all but heard his inner thoughts as she had spoken of the commitment and courage of the man she had loved and who was now almost certainly dead. At one point, after he had drunk two more beers, she had heard him say, almost under his breath, 'Ah my dear, I cannot look on thee'. It had always been his habit to come out with lines, often quotations or fragments of poems, that were enigmatic, wistful, meaning more to the speaker than the listener. Remembering now, she walked through to the kitchen and took a beer from the two-four in the fridge, the floorboards of the old house creaking at every step as she carried it back to the study.

The letter had mentioned, seemingly in passing, that he had also written to Michael. But of course there had been nothing about the content. She sipped the beer, imagining him drafting and redrafting, knowing that under all the bluster beat the heart of a perfectionist. And she did not entirely believe his line that he had abandoned poetry for jingles.

It was now nearly eleven. She had drunk only a third of the beer, but could already feel the first slight disorientation. The house was in darkness, apart from the reading lamp by her father's chair. Best of all, the letter had made no absurd declarations, placed her under no pressure. Perhaps Toby might be capable of growing up. Fine. But she would not be the prop to his vine. Not that she was capable of being anybody's prop at the moment. To her relief, the tests at McGill had shown up nothing, and the consensus had been that her symptoms were the result of fighting off the constant threat of infection. Her parents had agreed and prescribed a return home to Canada.

She closed the journal and replaced the beer on the coaster. In any case, there was no point in thinking about the future, with or without Toby Jenks, until the weeks to come had told their story.

28 | *Iacta alea est*

Shortly after seven o'clock on the evening of Tuesday, February 10th, Assistant Secretary-General Camden Hughes left the headquarters of the United Nations by the main gate, pausing only to unfurl an umbrella. Turning right on to First Avenue, he set off to walk the seventeen blocks to Sutton Place, almost keeping pace with the red tail-lights crawling uptown towards the 59th Street bridge. Most of the commuters would already be home, but there were still hundreds of pedestrians on First Avenue, mostly heading for the restaurants and bars on Second and Third.

As he cleared UN Plaza, a slight figure wearing a raincoat and carrying an A&P shopping bag watched from under the awning of the Metropolitan Café on the opposite side of First Avenue. After waiting at the lights to cross 49th Street, Hughes set off again up the slight incline, causing the figure in the raincoat to step out from the doorway and begin keeping pace with him, separated by a jostle of pedestrians and three lanes of traffic.

Hughes was a tall man and in a hurry to get home, and Seema had to stride out to stay half a block behind, hand at her throat to secure the plastic rain hood around her face. The evening was as wet and moonless as forecast.

On the corner of 52nd Street, he stopped by a neighbourhood supermarket and came out a few minutes later carrying a plastic bag in the same gloved hand as his briefcase. At the next corner he turned off and headed east on 53rd. Seema crossed First and followed, staying well behind. When he turned left into Sutton Place South she hurried to the corner to keep him in sight.

For four blocks she kept her distance as Hughes passed under the awnings of the expensive apartment buildings of Sutton Place, crossing eventually to the block of narrow-fronted townhouses between 57th and 58th Streets. Reaching one of the doorways, he removed his gloves and began struggling one-handed with the key. A lamp, suspended from the small second-floor balcony, illuminated the number '13' carved in elegant Gothic script into the stone of the lintel.

As Hughes disappeared inside, Seema continued on uptown. The rain was becoming heavier. Turning left under the massive girders of the 59th Street bridge, she rejoined First Avenue and turned south again, heading against the traffic. A few minutes later she re-entered Sutton Place at 56th Street.

Approaching the two steps to the door of Number 13, she pushed a gloved hand inside the A&P bag and removed the brown envelope from inside its plastic cover. It slid easily into the brass letterbox. As she had known it would.

The Kokoschkas looked down on the scene as Seema poured wine and raised her glass to the two men. *So, I guess we've crossed the Rubicon.* The breezy tone fooled no one, least of all herself. Stephen turned his mouth down, as if to say 'no big deal', but in the end he could not resist raising his glass. '*Iacta alea est.*'

Michael turned an inquiring look at Seema, who sighed patiently. 'The die is cast. It's what Caesar is supposed to have said when he crossed the Rubicon.'

'According to Suetonius,' said Stephen, 'Who of course was mistranslating Menander's Greek.'

Seema screwed up an empty packet of potato chips and threw it at him. The stove was burning normally again after the black smoke made by Stephen's gloves.

For a few minutes they discussed how to let Toby and Hélène know and then the conversation turned to travel plans: when Michael would be going back to Geneva; how long Stephen planned to stay in New York; would Hélène already be back in Africa. But it was impossible, finally, not to speculate on what might be happening in Sutton Place.

Stephen refilled their glasses. 'I imagine the FBI will be the first port of call.'

Seema frowned. 'What will they do, send an agent with the key?'

Michael shook his head. 'They can't just go along there and open it. They'll have no idea what they're dealing with. It could be a door-operated detonator, or some kind of aerosolized device. It could be anything.'

Seema was making an effort to remain calm. 'So how will they pick it up?'

Michael summoned up the scenario he had already envisaged many times. 'My guess is they'll go for a bomb scare. Seal off the area. Blast screens. Maybe a robot. Then announce it was a hoax. By that time the vial will probably be in a bio-safety containment lab down in Atlanta.'

29 | Take this cup from me

By eight o'clock Camden Hughes had warmed and eaten the dinner left for him by his housekeeper and was sitting in his study wishing it had been possible for him to leave the office at five o'clock instead of seven. As usual, he would probably have no more than an hour or two before tiredness took over, and it was on this account that his biography of Marcus Garvey was proceeding more slowly than he had anticipated. But now, as he sipped his favourite blend of coffee and savoured the quiet of his study, he reflected that, although these hours were too short, they were still there to look forward to.

Youthful impatience had perhaps prevented Camden Hughes from recognizing an academic calling. After Howard University, he had been steered towards the law by a father who had been the grandson of a slave. But Camden had found himself unsuited to life at the bar and when the chance had arisen he had been glad to join the Civil Service Commission and to move his wife and young family to the nation's capital. There, over three decades, he had steadily moved up the ladder, eventually becoming head of the Federal Labor Relations Authority. But, following the death of his wife, a certain restlessness had descended and it had not been too difficult to persuade him to accept an offer to run the United

Nations Office of Human Resources Management in New York with the rank of an Assistant Secretary General. Now within touching distance of retirement, the move had meant a useful boost to his pension. But he was already a wealthy man, thanks to his late wife's estate, and the greater attraction of the move had been New York City itself. Despite a conventional appearance, and a conservative, almost courtly, manner, he had retained an attachment to the Civil Rights struggle of his youth and in middle years this had mellowed into an abiding interest in African-American history in general and the Harlem Renaissance in particular. While his wife was alive, he would not have dismayed her by contemplating a move to New York. But as a widower the prospect of being closer to where it had all happened had proved compelling. True, he had been disappointed when the job at the UN had turned out to be more demanding than he had thought and, as the months went by, the Garvey biography had begun to look more and more like a retirement project. But the day when he could devote all his time to it was now not too far off and, unlike many of his colleagues, Camden was not unhappy to think of himself as the retiring type.

He had heard the clank of the brass letter box soon after he had switched on his reading lamp, but decided to ignore it. Probably it would be junk mail, or his copy of the Sutton Place Newsletter, or a memo from the office that some zealous P5 had thought he should read before tomorrow's round of budget meetings. But this was his own time, and he forgot about whatever might be waiting on the doormat as he sank into his chair with an early volume of *The Negro World* and a half-finished cup of coffee on the table by his side.

Twenty minutes later, on his way back from the bathroom, he stooped to pick up the manila envelope from the mat, carrying it with him into the study. Leaving it on the desk, he replaced his reading glasses. He had just placed another record on the turntable when he caught sight of the label – '*Personal – to be opened only by Camden Hughes*'.

The Cab Calloway number was still playing softly on the turntable, though the book-lined room seemed strangely silent. The three sheets of paper lay on the side table with his coffee cup. Draped over the arm of the chair was a plastic bag containing a single key.

Eventually he reached up to switch off the reading lamp, closing his eyes and sinking back into the chair. A long delay might have to be accounted for. Yet his first move was likely to be critical. For a few moments his mind seemed unable to engage, as if the long anticipation of his quiet time had made it more difficult to turn himself around into day-time mode. It might of course be a hoax. There had been others, though all before his own time at the UN. In any case, the thought had little to offer in the way of comfort. And there was something about the message that suggested it was far from being a hoax; something that he would have to go back to once he had decided what to do in the here and now.

After a few minutes he crossed the hall to the kitchenette and made a second cup of coffee. Clearly, the most important thing at this stage was to do nothing that might trigger a panic. Which meant involving as few people as possible. The second requirement was to kick this thing upstairs as quickly as possible; he thought briefly of his old boss at the Office of Management and the framed quotation on his desk: *Take this cup from my lips, O Lord*.

He returned to his chair, still not switching on the light. The question was – which of his two hats to wear? He glanced up, as if expecting advice from the bronze bust of Duke Ellington that occupied the only free space on the shelves. As an Assistant Secretary-General of the United Nations, his duty was to put on his overcoat and outdoor shoes, retrieve his umbrella from the stand, and walk back to the UN where he knew his current boss, the recently installed Under-Secretary General, would still be at work. Then, after an hour or two at most, he could be back in his study and breathing freely again. The evening would have gone, but so would the responsibility. He looked again at his watch; fifteen minutes had passed.

The problem with this course of action was that the idea of anything being kept secret in the glass house of UN headquarters was risible. The USG would doubtless also kick the matter upstairs to the Secretary General who, although a charming dinner guest, was known for near-terminal indecisiveness combined with a finely-honed talent for covering his ass with layers of bureaucratic padding. For sure, his first instinct would be to share the responsibility as quickly and widely as possible, which would mean emergency committees, task forces, special advisers, with discussions transcribed, minuted, and very possibly translated into Swahili. It would be all over the Delegates' Lounge by tomorrow lunchtime. Probably the Soviets would have to be informed, and the French, and the British.

He walked over to his desk and stood for a moment, slowly turning the illuminated globe under his fingers. Africa came by, five or six times bigger than the United States, soon followed by India, with more people than both put together. The leather-inlaid surface of the desk glowed as he revolved through the emptiness of the Pacific. His only other option was to act not as an international civil servant but as a high-level appointee of the United States government, which is what he was in fact if not in name. That would have the advantage of bypassing the UN and dealing direct with – with whom? Someone at the

State Department? Defense? The Department of Health? The FBI? To make any of these his first contact, even supposing he could identify the right individual to call, would no doubt be a betrayal of his position at the UN. But the message that had been delivered was a message for the government of the United States. And going that route, if he handled it right, would involve a much smaller number of people. A much tighter response altogether.

He perched on the edge of the desk, sipping the second coffee. Underneath the concern with what to do next was a strong urge to sit in the armchair to work out his personal reaction to the contents of the envelope that had been put through his mailbox by someone who would by now have disappeared into the New York night. But at this moment he did not have the leisure.

Just under twenty minutes had passed by the time he flipped the hood of the Rolodex, located a card under 'B', and punched in area code 404.

The flames behind the scorched-glass doors had died down an hour ago. On the table, a bottle of wine stood beside a stereo softly playing *The Dark Side of the Moon*. Seema, Michael and Stephen sat around in the light of the two remaining candles, only occasionally exchanging a few words. There was nothing left to say, but no one wanted to go out into the emptiness of the night.

They had attempted to talk of other things: the launch of the International Year of the Disabled that had been featured on the ten o'clock news, and the fire that had apparently destroyed the Las Vegas Hilton. But there was only one reality that meant anything as the candles guttered and the music played on like the soundtrack of an earlier life. Four months ago they had been five friends at an insignificant college reunion. Ten days ago they had been having a quiet dinner together in Billy's Bar. Even four hours ago, they had still had some sense of being in touch with normality.

'Anybody want more wine?' Seema turned the bottle in her slim fingers, reflecting the candlelight. When Michael and Stephen both shook their heads she set the bottle on the table, controlling the waves of anxiety that were throwing themselves at the walls of her composure. 'So, how long did you say it would take them?'

Michael, coming out of his own reverie, looked as if the question had taken him by surprise. 'To get it into a laboratory? I don't know. A day. Maybe two. They'll move fast, but there'll be a whole bunch of precautions.'

Stephen had gradually left behind the pretence of being blasé and had been quiet, introverted all evening. Now he too stirred himself towards some semblance of normality. 'I assume anyone working in one of those labs is fully protected.'

Michael nodded, relieved to be on firmer ground. 'They'll all have had their annual smallpox jabs. And everything'll be done in the containment lab. Things have gotten a lot tighter down there since Lassa and Marburg. Class III biosafety cabinets, decontamination chambers, double-door autoclaves, glove boxes, HEPA filters.'

Stephen, too, took refuge in the specific. 'And I guess they'll know what they're looking at more or less straight away?'

'Not right off, no. They'll probably split it into two or three parts and fix one with a pigment, probably crystal violet. Then it'll go under the lab scope for a first look. Only a thousand times magnification, but enough to tell them they're looking at a virus.'

Stephen was frowning in concentration, though nothing in

what Michael had said was at all difficult to follow. 'But not what kind of virus, I take it?'

'They won't have much of an idea until they get it under the electron scope.'

Seema sank back into the Bikaner, afraid of what Michael was saying, feeling the pain of anxiety beating against her brain with each new stage described.

'Smallpox is one of the ugliest diseases imaginable, but the structure of the virus itself ... ' Michael paused, looking up at the other two, the candles casting an inconstant light on hands and faces, '... is beautiful, awe-inspiring.'

Seema, too, stared into the unreal halo of the candle flame and pushed herself further back in her chair, feeling the lattice work of fine cane through the silk of her shirt, her hands tight-clasped in her lap.

Stephen assumed his world-weary smile. '*Nature with a beauteous wall doth oft close in pollution.* And that's when they'll know?'

'They'll know it's a pox virus. To be certain it's smallpox they'll have to culture it. Take two or three days.'

Stephen twirled his empty wine glass and held it in line with the candle flame, as if the viscous runs might be able to tell the future. 'And that's when the fun begins.'

'The fun will begin long before then.' Michael looked up with concern at Seema, now leaning far back into the shadows.

Camden Hughes had almost given up when the phone ringing softly in an Atlanta suburb was answered by the tired voice of Becket Bradie.

'Beck? It's Camden, from New York.'

'Camden. Good to hear you. How's it going?'

'Okay. At least it was until a half hour ago. Listen,

Beck, truly sorry to raise you at home of an evening, but something's come up you prob'ly should know about. May I ask, this line is likely to be secure?'

The Director of the US Centers for Disease Control had listened in silence to the soft, almost lulling tones of Camden Hughes reading the contents of the envelope that had been delivered to his home. Then he had asked for two or three of the paragraphs to be read over again. Even before replacing the receiver, Becket Bradie had known he would be cancelling his vacation.

Returning the phone to the desk, Camden Hughes looked back with regret at his armchair. There was nothing more he could do now. The cup had been taken from him. But neither was there any possibility of rescuing his evening. He strolled over to his bookshelves and stood for a few moments, looking with something like nostalgia along the sets of magazines: DuBois' *Crisis*, Charles Johnson's *Opportunity*, and his treasured collection of Garvey's *The Negro World* with every issue from 1918 to 1933. In all his fifty-eight years he had had little exposure to the world outside the United States. Long ago, his personal interests had settled on the Civil Rights struggle. Yet he knew he would not have to think very hard to bring connections to the fore. Eventually he returned to his chair and picked up the three sheets of paper. Switching on the lamp, he read them through again more slowly, troubled now in a different way. He breathed in deeply. One of the connections stared at him even now as his eyes came to rest on the framed photograph on the bookshelf. It was too far away to make out the four lines that had been scrawled on the ivory mount, but he had long known them by heart.

I weep for the sufferings time forgot,
the lives not lived, the injustice borne,
I weep for the laughter that died at birth
and the waste, the waste of it all.

Underneath, the only one of the Harlem poets he had known had scribbled: '*To Camden* – Freedom is never given; it is won.'

30 | The girl next door

Eight hundred miles southwest of Sutton Place, Becket Bradie stared up at the ceiling of his basement den. On the radiogram, a Brahms symphony was playing as if the phone call had never happened. His glass stood empty on the small swivel-table attached to the stem of the lamp. After a few moments he pressed the lever to bring the recliner upright and struggled to his feet, deciding he could afford to pour himself a small bourbon. Not bothering with the ice, he carried his drink back to the chair.

Like his caller, Becket had been looking forward to a quiet hour or so before bed, listening to music and perhaps reading a chapter of the book on the Lewis and Clarke expedition that he had been trying to finish for weeks. Since his divorce, his working day had gotten longer, and the decision to book himself on to a singles cruise out of Miami had been a rather forced attempt to break out from a binary pattern of work and sleep. The cruise had taken some working up to and, under the surface annoyance, he acknowledged a distant feeling of relief.

For a moment or two longer he listened to the music as though the evening were still his own, sipping the bourbon, regretting not bothering with the ice, closing his eyes without reclining the chair. He could allow himself a few more minutes.

Like at least half a dozen others in the upper echelons of the world's leading public-health institutions, Becket Bradie had risen via the Peace Corps, the CDC's Epidemic Intelligence Service, and the USAID-funded public health campaigns in Africa in the 1960s. In other words, he was part of that can-do generation of global public-health pioneers that has become legendary.

Now, eyes still closed but brain back in work mode, he faced up to the problem that had been dropped into his lap, wisely he had to admit, by Camden Hughes. For the moment he was in space. The question was – how and where to throw the pass that would get this thing into the end-zone without a hundred other people having to handle the ball. He pushed his fingers under his cheekbones and rested the weight of his head on his hands. If maximum air-yards was what he needed, then what it came down to was deciding who, these days, was his highest-level contact in the Administration. And it had better be the right call. He took another sip. Goddamn it, there should have been a protocol in place for something like this. He opened his eyes again as the Chicago Symphony Orchestra brought the piece to a close. On the wall of the den were the familiar ranks of photos: a faded black-and-white shot of himself with Tom Weller at Harvard; a truck being winched out of the mud on a rubber plantation in Eastern Nigeria; a younger version of himself waving a jet-injector outside the medical centre in Yahe; the staff posed on the steps of the Holy Family Hospital in New Delhi; a group shot from Bihar taken after they had identified eleven thousand cases of smallpox in a single week. For a moment or two he felt the outrage, the contempt for anyone who could even consider releasing this most dreadful of all diseases into the world again. But underneath the anger he also knew that there had been something that was troubling in a different

213

way about the words that Camden Hughes had just called through.

But for now all he had to decide was what his own first move was going to be. He dwelt for a moment on the largest of the photographs, an already slightly faded black-and-white picture of his parents taken at his graduation ceremony more than thirty years ago. And suddenly the answer to his problem was so obvious it almost brought a smile to his face. That he had not thought of it immediately was entirely down to the fact that, to him, Toni Restelle was still the little girl growing up next door in Vaughan Street, Portland. Far too little in fact for him to have taken much notice of her at the time. But in the last six months it had been almost impossible not to notice her, so often had she appeared on the networks. It had been obvious she was going places on the ticket but, despite the speculation, the news of her appointment as White House Chief of Staff had still come as something of a shock.

At this moment, it was a welcome shock. They had kept in touch, meeting up at least once a year at Thanksgiving and sometimes at New Year's when her parents traditionally invited the neighbours in to drink fruit cup and enjoy themselves for a couple of hours embarrassing their children with their reminiscences. He was pretty sure he had her home number in DC.

He thought for a few minutes more, dismissing alternatives, then pulled the phone to his lap. It was ten minutes past ten on the evening of Tuesday, February 10th.

So cheerless was the loft when Michael and Stephen had left that Seema had even thought of rekindling the fire. If Stephen had been the first to leave, there might have been a chance to talk of other things. But when the conversation had finally died and Stephen had shown no signs of leaving, it had been Michael who, seeing the tiredness in her face, had brought the evening to an end. Sleep was unthinkable, and all that was left was this exhausted, wide-awake loneliness. She lit two new candles in a small show of defiance and resolved to make herself a hot drink. But for the moment she remained where she was in the chair, wondering if she was also in Michael's thoughts as he walked the forty or so blocks, as she knew he would, back to the Doral Inn.

Becket Bradie found himself having to strain to hear her voice against what sounded like a party in the background.

'Good evening Ma'am. This here is Dr Becket C Bradie of the Centers for Disease Control via Vaughan Street, Portland, Maine.'

'Beck! *Quelle surprise*! Listen, sweetheart, if by any chance you've very sweetly called to congratulate me, can I call you back later and we'll have a proper chat? It's crazy here.'

'Many congratulations, Toni, but I'm afraid things might be about to get a whole lot crazier. Can we meet first thing in the morning?'

'You're in DC?'

'Atlanta. But I can be with you by nine.'

'Beck, I don't want to come all over self-important on you, sweetheart, but I'm the new kid on the block and my schedule tomorrow is unbelievable.'

'Believe me, Toni, this call is strictly business and whatever else is on your agenda this will go straight to the top.'

31 | That can't happen

Camden Hughes was woken at six o'clock on the morning of Wednesday, February 11th, by a telephone call from Atlanta. He made sure his long inner sigh was unheard, as Becket Bradie asked him to take the first shuttle to Washington, bringing the envelope and all its contents and handling everything as little as possible.

He made himself a quick coffee and left a message at the UN asking his deputy to stand in for him at the morning's budget meetings. Within fifteen minutes of taking the call, he was out on First Avenue, flagging down a cab for La Guardia.

Seema and Michael were unable to summon much enthusiasm for talk of ordinary things as they ate breakfast at a greasy spoon on the Avenue of the Americas where toasted bagels were accompanied by long silences and much abstracted staring out at the crowds emerging from the 14th Street subway. Both wondered if an ordinary conversation would ever be possible again.

Seema held her coffee halfway to her lips, blanketed in a kind of stupefaction in which everything outside the window was as it was before. Except that there was now a chasm between herself and this New York morning, a stranding of the person who is me, sitting here with this man, my hands wrapped around the ridges of a cardboard cup. I am a forty-one-year-old Professor of American History at the University of New York. I am writing a book about a family of slaves on a Virginia plantation in the nineteenth century. I am divorced and living an independent life in Greenwich Village. And this morning I am breakfasting with an old friend from college days who is now a high-ranking official of the World Health Organization in Geneva, Switzerland. Except that...

The weather all down the east coast was unrelenting that winter and the skies over Washington were bleak and cold as the Lincoln Continental left National and turned north on the Expressway. The back of the cab, by contrast, was way too warm and rivers of condensation obscured what view there might have been of the waterfowl sanctuary. Normally, a car would have been sent by the Washington office of the Centers for Disease Control, but that morning the office had no knowledge of Director Becket Bradie being in town and the car now heading towards the Potomac was a regular District of Columbia licensed cab. In the back seat, Camden Hughes handed over the Gristedes supermarket bag without a word as the nose of the cab tipped up towards the 14th Street Bridge.

Becket had donned a pair of surgical gloves many times in his life, but never in the back of a cab on his way to an appointment at the White House. On the ten-minute ride he read the letter and statement through, glancing only briefly at the metal key in its sealed plastic bag. There was no partition in the cab, and talk was impossible. Returning the envelope to its bag and peeling off the gloves, Becket's murmur was almost inaudible. 'You could wish they sounded a little bit more like cranks.'

Camden Hughes nodded his head slowly before wiping

away some of the condensation from the window to reveal the blurry skyline of the nation's capital.

Three thousand five hundred miles away, Toby sat alone in the drawing room of his home in Ealing. Since getting in from work, he had been sitting by the fire burning pages torn from his notebook. He stared into the flames, thinking of Hélène, as another page curled into a dark bruise and suddenly ignited. He wished he could send her what he had sent to Michael and reflected with a sigh and another sip of Scotch that the best thing he had penned in years would, he sincerely hoped, never see the light of day.

Michael had called the previous evening. They had conducted an absurd conversation with Michael attempting a kind of impromptu code. Congratulations on the latest ad. Great grab line. Bound to boost the response rate, give the product more traction. Mail shot already under way. Let you know when we have first sales figures. It had taken Toby a while to realize that the call was from New York and he had struggled for a response. 'Well, you know what they say in the States, Michael, "send it out local, see if it comes back express".'

Alighting from the cab on Pennsylvania Avenue, the two men in overcoats were name-checked by a young armed marine and invited to proceed on foot to the east entrance of the White House. There, a waiting secretary introduced herself and led them down a long corridor, passing the office of the Vice-President, to a small reception room.

Becket Bradie was still struggling with the idea of waiting for an audience with Toni Restelle when she appeared, greeting him with a hug and a kiss. After shaking hands with Camden Hughes, she took Becket's arm and steered them through to an elegantly furnished office where they seated themselves at a small conference table. Camden had been surprised to find that Toni Restelle knew who he was.

'So, it's good to see you, Beck, but what's with the big mystery?'

Checking that the door was closed, Becket Bradie took a deep breath and lifted the supermarket bag to the polished table top, not quite knowing how to relate to this version of Toni Restelle. He had seen her in a trick-or-treat costume with a witch's hooked nose, in a pink tutu with bleeding knees, stuck halfway up a tree with the seat hanging out of her jeans, in a graduation gown with sash and mortarboard, and in a sen- sational, figure-hugging cashmere one-piece last Thanksgiving. But he had never before seen her in a slate-grey business suit and ivory silk shirt, wearing a choker of small pearls and light, day-time make-up, her hair scraped back and held by a tortoise-shell comb. She frowned now as he drew the surgical gloves from his briefcase and pulled out the manila envelope, still in its plastic, from the supermarket bag. 'This was pushed through the mailbox of Camden's home in Midtown Manhattan sometime between eight and nine o'clock last night.'

Toni Restelle accepted the offered gloves, pushing back the slit sleeves of her suit jacket. Frowning at the envelope, she snugged the gloves and took out the three sheets of paper and the plastic bag containing a single key.

There was silence for two minutes as she read, the two men looking patiently around the room. The Regency-style drapes were sashed back so that, despite the greyness of the day, the corner office was not in need of artificial light. There were framed photographs of political figures, past and present and, over the fireplace, a Thomas Eakins oil of two rowers on the Schuylkill.

'Who else knows about this?'

Toni moved her hands below the arms of the chair as the secretary entered with a tray of cups and a thermos of coffee.

When they were alone again, Becket glanced at Camden Hughes. 'On our side of the fence, just the three of us.'

'And you think it's genuine?'

Becket shrugged. 'We can't afford to think anything else until we can get a look at whatever's in that locker.'

'It hasn't been collected?'

Becket shook his head. 'We can't just send a couple of guys along with the key. We have no idea what's in there. If it's the virus and if it's freeze-dried and if it's in some kind of airtight container it'll be pretty safe, but we can't know that. We'll need a HazMat team and they'll want to have Grand Central evacuated, couple of blocks cordoned off.'

'Prob'ly someone might notice that.' Camden Hughes watched as Toni Restelle calmly poured coffee from the insulated jug.

'Okay, let's assume we find a way to get it into a lab and it turns out it's what they say it is. Most people have had their shots, right?'

Becket accepted the cup. 'Most people who lived in the US through 1972, when we called a halt on routine smallpox jabs. But single-shot immunity fades with time. So a lot of people are going to be susceptible, as well as every kid under the age of eight. Which means their moms and dads are not going to be immune from panic.'

Toni Restelle looked again at the letter. 'They're not threatening to release it. Or at least not yet. They're only threatening to go public. What do we say if that happens?'

Becket shook his head. 'Better it didn't happen. Instant demand for vaccination, especially for kids. And not enough supplies, all hell breaking loose – be hard to avoid a coast-to-coast panic.'

The Chief of Staff looked up from the letter. 'That can't happen.'

Neither man said anything as she tugged off one of the gloves. 'So, how do we stop them going to the press with this?' She dropped the envelope on the table, letting the glove fall with it.

Camden Hughes returned his cup to the saucer. 'Favourite would be making the acquaintance of whoever wrote it.'

'And second favourite?'

Becket shook his head again. 'If we don't find out who's behind it then it looks like we all have just over two weeks to get ready for it going public. I suppose you could try for an injunction, but...'

'Wouldn't hold five minutes.' Toni Restelle was thinking hard. 'Just so I know what we're talking about here, go ahead and give me your worst-case if the virus got itself released someplace.'

Becket had anticipated the question. 'A lot depends on whether we know where and when. It takes ten or twelve days to develop symptoms, so we'd have that time to surround the release site – immunize all possible victims and their contacts. The vaccine stops the disease developing even after someone's been infected, or at least stops it becoming lethal. If it's a covert attack – meaning we don't know the when or the where – then we're in a lot deeper. We wouldn't know anything about it until we got symptoms showing up. And most physicians aren't going to think smallpox when they get presented with back pain, headaches, muscle pain, nausea, fever – could be any viral infection. The rash comes a couple of days later, but even then it might get itself mis-diagnosed as chickenpox or EM. And by that time it can be passed on by person-to-person contact. So you've got a real small window between the first case being identified and the second wave of infection starting. In practice those infected could be both symptomatic and all over the place before we knew anything about it. We might still be able to cope, given that most people are probably still immune, but it would be a whole lot more difficult.

'And what would "coping" involve?'

'ID all possible cases, quarantine victims, immunize anyone and everyone they might have been in contact with. But the critical thing at that point is speed, speed and more speed. So we'd need to be super-ready.'

'There's no plan in place for anything like this?'

'Every State and County Health Officer has a CASE manual.'

Toni Restelle frowned.

'Comprehensive Action for a Smallpox Emergency.'

'They've all read it?'

'Don't have to. Every copy's got a wallchart in the front. Take it out. Stick it up. Follow it step by step. Tells you exactly what to do if you think you're looking at smallpox. Each step keyed to the relevant page in the manual. But it would still mean alerting all – and I mean all – clinical staff and front-line health personnel so they know what they're looking for. Fact is, Toni, hardly any of the front-line people today have ever seen a real case. Even physicians. Most of them probably wouldn't know it from chickenpox without sending scrapings to a lab. So I'm not saying the thing would be a breeze, but if we got things up and running fast enough there's a chance we could get it back in the bottle.'

'But people would still die.'

Becket nodded. 'But like I said, how many depends on how fast on our feet we are.'

'But with most people still being immune, it would be hundreds not thousands?'

'Hard to say. If we're lucky. And ready. If it's not a covert attack. If it's a small outbreak in a limited number of places. If cases get picked up in super-quick time. If the quarantine plans work and isolation wards can cope. If we have vaccination teams good to go immediately. If no one gets on a plane or decides to go kiss all his relatives in the Mid-West. And, Toni, above all – if there's no panic.'

'That's a heck of a lot of ifs, Beck – why couldn't we just vaccinate everybody again now, say it's purely a precaution?'

Becket Bradie shook his head. 'We'd want to avoid that, Toni. For one thing, we don't have enough vaccine, not even for the kids. And even if we did, there'd be a tiny percentage of people who'd get a real bad reaction. We've just spent years backing up WHO to persuade countries they don't need to carry on vaccinating. Same goes for those tatty certificates of smallpox vaccination we've all still got in our passports. It'd be a huge setback. But all that's by the by. The main reason is – it just isn't the best way of coping. Mass immunization's not nearly as effective as ring vaccination, like I said.'

Toni slowly tugged off the other glove and readjusted her sleeves, thinking for a few seconds before turning to Camden Hughes. 'Any idea why this was delivered to you, Mr Hughes?'

'I've been pondering that one pretty much since this thing all blew in. No reason I can hit on. Leastways no reason that's got to do with me personally, far as I can see. Went through all the people I know who know where I hang my hat, scratching around for any kind of a hook-up with a thing like this' – he gestured at the envelope on the table – 'but nothing came to mind even in the early hours when these things tend to float up, leastways for me. Best guess is – they were out looking for someone in New York City who's at a certain height up the pole, with contacts a lot higher up the pole. Even that leaves a big field in New York. Seems to me my principal qualification was – someone who lives alone and has themselves a street-level mailbox.'

Toni nodded and began replacing the contents in the envelope, holding it with the empty glove in her left hand. 'I'm sure you're right about that. Unfortunately it doesn't narrow down the search a whole lot.'

'No, Ma'am.'

The two men remained silent as Toni Restelle studied the envelope on the table. After a few seconds she stood up abruptly, smoothed her skirt and used the other glove to pick up the envelope. 'Okay, gentlemen, can I ask you to wait here for a few minutes? Help yourselves to more coffee.'

Camden Hughes pulled his chair closer to the table and poured for them both. 'Whip-smart young lady.'

Becket accepted the cup pushed towards him. 'Yeah. Weird thing is I've known her since she was an annoying little kid in a velvet jumpsuit.'

Camden looked up from his cup, a smile dawning. 'So that's how we got ourselves a hole in one.'

Becket nodded. 'And it's why I'm struggling just a little bit to imagine her in the Oval Office right now telling the President of the United States what he should do.'

Camden tore open a tube of sugar and poured it into his cup. 'You know they've christened her "Manapo"?'

'Manapo?'

'Seems some celebrity magazine nominated her Most Attractive New Arrival on the Potomac.'

'How do you know these things, Camden?'

'Man likes to keep his ear to the ground.'

Becket smiled and watched Camden stir coffee. The man had no medical background, and there were those who considered him to be a token African-American on the Federal Advisory Committee. Becket knew better. Over the last few years, Camden Hughes had steered the agency through the kind of legal, personnel and admin issues that had left other rapidly expanding federal institutions with reputations in rags.

Toni Restelle took a seat outside the Oval Office, the leather slip case on the carpet at her feet, and began putting in order what she had absorbed in the last half hour. Inside, the meeting was obviously coming to an end, the casual loudness of it all indicating that it was probably an all-male gathering.

The girl who had grown up next door to Becket Bradie had come a long way from Vaughan Street, Portland. Armed with an MBA, another Masters in International Studies and a few years on the *Christian Science Monitor*, but with very little in the way of political background, she had been invited to join the Presidential campaign team after stepping in to rescue the Maine Primary from a potential public-relations disaster. From this foothold she had made herself indispensable both as organizer and increasingly as strategist, gradually becoming one of the Candidate's closest advisers. Always ahead of the game, able to go against the flow without making too many enemies, and seeming not to need sleep, she had ended up managing the core campaign team, including running the Candidate's schedule. According to some insiders, she was also responsible for the changes in emphasis and presentation that had helped turn the polls around and secured victory the previous November. There had been others, better qualified and more experienced, who had coveted the office of Chief of Staff, but Toni Restelle was the one the President wanted to have around and in the end that had been all that counted. Now, as the door to the

Oval Office opened and she reached for the slip case, she had a clear sequence ready to present. One thing she had learned along the way was that you went to the boss with solutions, not problems.

'Okay, here's what happens.'

Toni had gone straight back to her desk, sliding the envelope in its plastic bag into a drawer. The two men heard the fall of a lock as she straightened. 'An NYPD HazMat team will pick up whatever's in the locker, using a bomb scare as cover. What I need you to do, Beck, is to get whatever you need up there to take delivery and get it back to a lab.'

Becket nodded. 'We can get a bio-containment transport there by tonight.'

The Chief of Staff came around from the desk and took a seat at the table. 'Let me have the licence plate. What about the pick-up team, drivers, lab guys? They have to know?'

Becket shook his head. 'That's no problem. Things turn up from time to time – unlabelled ampoules from the back of a freezer in some lab somewhere, or maybe a package marked "anthrax" turns up in a mail room. Stuff happens. The guys know how to bring it in.'

'What about the lab people who do the ID. They have to know what it is?'

'Even then it could just be something that's been found late in the day in one of the research labs. Some of these places were a bit careless about clearing out the freezers when they were all asked to certify destruction. Like I said, it's happened before. Just the checking isn't going to set off any smoke alarms.'

'Okay. But if you get a positive ID, can you make sure only one more person knows what it is?'

'Yes, though, as I've said, there's no real need.'

'Humour me on this one, Beck. How long before we know?'

'Once we get it back to the lab? We'll know if it's a virus more or less straight away. Probably another couple of days or so to know if it's smallpox.'

The Chief of Staff stood to bring the meeting to an end. 'I'd like you both to be on standby. No need to stay in DC, but be on the end of a line, and be ready to get yourselves back here, okay?'

Camden Hughes could not help smiling as they were escorted back to the east entrance and out on to Pennsylvania Avenue.

32 | Ours not to reason why

Becket Bradie's first act on getting back in his office that afternoon, was to despatch a bio-safety vehicle on the seventeen-hundred-mile round trip to a location near Basking Ridge, New Jersey. Working in shifts, the two CDC drivers were under orders to pick up a potentially hazardous substance from an NYPD compound and head straight back to Atlanta. Depending on exactly when the bomb squad were given the order to go in, there might be a delay of a few hours in New Jersey. At best, whatever had been left in the locker at Grand Central would not be in Atlanta until the early hours of Friday morning. This confirmed, Bradie called through the licence plate on Toni Restelle's private line. Then he put his head round the door and asked his secretary to call his deputy. The next few minutes were spent cancelling his travel plans for the following week. The holiday was already history. He left his desk and sat down to wait in one of the two armchairs overlooking the CDC campus.

Paul Lewis, he knew, could not long continue to shoulder the workload of principal deputy. After a talk in the middle of January, the two men had agreed that no announcement of Paul's illness would be made until the spring. Without attracting too much attention, the top end of the organizational chart had been rejigged to ease the burden of some of the committee work, but otherwise things would carry on much as normal until the end of March. More immediately troubling to Becket Bradie was that it felt entirely wrong not to be levelling with a man who held all of his trust and respect.

When Paul arrived, closing the door behind him and taking the second chair, it was obvious that the illness was beginning to take its toll. His suit jacket was tent-like around the middle, his face was showing signs of becoming gaunt, and there was a brittle brightness in his eyes that pierced Becket Bradie's heart.

After a few preliminary inquiries, Becket came to the point. 'Paul, odd thing to ask, but there's a lab job coming up tomorrow that I want to ask you to handle yourself.'

Paul Lewis looked up at him in surprise, prepared to be amused. 'Sure. If I can remember where the labs are.'

'And I'm afraid you might have to go looking for them at an unsociable hour, like the early hours of Friday morning.'

The smile left Paul's face. 'What's up, Beck?'

'Can't give you the whole story. Don't know the half of it myself. But there's a possibility that a small quantity of variola has liberated itself from one of the labs that wasn't properly checked. As we've said, national certification was a farce.'

'So where is it?'

'It'll be here late Thursday or in the small hours Friday, all being well. Sorry I can't level with you on this one, Paul. Orders coming from Washington, which is where I was all day yesterday by the way. Probably turn out to be a lot of fuss over nothing, but anyway all we're required to do is take delivery and tell them asap if it's variola.'

Paul's face was still registering surprise. 'Okay, but why not the regular lab guys and why the middle of the night?'

Becket Bradie raised both hands from the arms of the chair in a gesture that implied Washington moved in mysterious ways. 'Because apparently it's come from some unusual source, that's all I know, and we need an immediate ID without anyone other than you and me knowing about it. They even asked me if I could do the lab work myself, but I'm no virologist and anyway there's no way I could find the lab.'

Paul shrugged. 'Obviously we can't be certain without going to culture.'

'How much will the scope tell you?'

Paul pushed out his lower lip. 'Whether variola is in the frame.'

'Okay, and how certain can we be at that point?'

'If it's negative, a hundred per cent. If it's not we'll just have to wait two or three days for the culture.'

'And then?'

'Then we'll know if it's an orthopox virus. But if it is, we'll only be looking at smallpox or a white pox. And at that point you'd have to say that the variola would be favourite.'

'Okay, that's it. You all right for a late night?'

'Sure, but I'm still thinking why the cloak-and-dagger stuff. It's not the first time something without a label has turned up in the corner of a freezer in some badly run lab in the wilds of God knows where. Usually turns out to be some lab assistant's little stash of Friday-night fun.'

Becket shook his head. 'Don't ask. Whole thing's probably a Level 4 waste of time.' He raised his hands again from the chair. 'But we ain't got the option.'

Paul stood up to go. 'No problem, I'll be here. Got plenty to catch up on.'

'Why don't you take off home now? Get some rest before the circus hits town.'

'Nah, I'm okay. By the way, if the scope doesn't rule anything out do we go straight to culture?

'I'm hoping we won't need to but, yes, get right on to it.'

'You want me to let the biosafety people know?'

'No. And, by the way, if this thing gets past first base we'll need to get someone from Detrick to take a look at it and maybe someone from NIH as well. You set that up?'

Paul paused, his hand on the door handle. 'From Detrick?'

'Yeah. Can you do that?'

'Sure, but they're going to think something very odd is happening if the CDC calls them in to ID a virus.'

Becket gave him a 'my hands are tied' look. Paul rose, shaking his head. 'Ours not to reason why.'

33 | Lounge lizards

Late on the morning of Thursday, February 12th, Michael Lowell showed his pass at the delegates' entrance to the United Nations HQ on First Avenue and rode the cantilevered escalator to the mezzanine floor. Turning left in front of the tapestry of the Great Wall, a recent gift from the People's Republic, he headed for the murmur of a thousand voices coming through the open double doors of the Delegates' Lounge.

The vast carpeted area with the view overlooking the East River was packed with UN staffers, ambassadors, diplomats and second and third secretaries from a hundred countries as he slowed his pace to a stroll and made his way into the crowd. Ten years earlier, when he had first joined the UN, he had thrilled to the sight of so many nationalities, languages and cultures gathered under one roof. But he had soon come to think that the really striking thing about a scene like the one before him now was not its diversity but its uniformity: almost all of the three or four hundred people gathered here lived in the same style, read the same newspapers, wore the same kind of clothes, attended the same shows and galleries, talked about the same topics in the same languages, and in many cases sent their children to the same schools. Stephen would doubtless have said that what homogenized these representatives of so many nations was that they were all members of the same class. The irritating thing about Stephen, as Toby had sometimes remarked, was that he wasn't always wrong.

Under normal circumstances the Delegates Lounge would have been the last place Michael would have chosen to spend his lunch time. But the place was well known as a swamp of gossip and rumour and, steeling himself, he began to make progress towards the bar, stopping here and there to exchange a few words with colleagues or acquaintances, mostly those he had met at inter-agency meetings or on one of the joint ventures that are a feature of life in the specialized agencies. More than once he was stopped by a complete stranger, of the species known as lounge lizards, whose main area of professional expertise lay in knowing not only everyone's name but exactly where he or she stood in the hierarchy.

He never reached the bar, but then he had never intended to. What he had reached was the conclusion that no hint of what had happened in Sutton Place the previous evening had been leaked. After less than an hour, he was heading back up First Avenue, satisfied that Camden Hughes had made the right call.

34 | To satisfy our masters

Thursday, February 12th, 1981 was an unremarkable day in
the offices of the *New York Times*. Recently installed chief
medical correspondent Tom Keeley had spent the morning
looking into rumours about a virus that appeared to be
circulating among the gay community up on Fire Island.
Picking up the threads again after lunch, he was interrupted
by a call from the news desk: someone had apparently
broken a record by climbing all one thousand five hundred
and fifty-seven steps of the Empire State building in eleven
minutes; could he quickly pull together a five-hundred-word
sidebar on the risks of stroke and cardiac failure associated
with sudden, violent exercise?

By the time the piece was finished and checked, it had
been too late to do much else and he had decided to call it a
day. Walking the few blocks to Grand Central, his attention
was drawn to a wall of flashing blue lights on the opposite
side of Bryant Park. At 42nd Street he saw that the area was
being sealed off by police barriers and incident tape stretching
uptown as far as The Roosevelt. On the corner of Madison
he stopped for a word with an NYPD officer staffing one of
the barricades; a bomb scare had shut down Grand Central
Terminal and half a dozen blocks of Midtown Manhattan. He
wondered whether to repair to a bar and wait the incident out

but, having spent the afternoon writing about the benefits of moderate exercise, he decided instead to walk to his brother's place on the Upper East Side, thinking that he might relieve him of his car keys until the following morning.

Reaching the apartment in time to catch the seven o'clock CBS news, he learned that an NYPD team had recovered a suspected bomb from a luggage locker in the lower concourse of Grand Central and that on examination the device had been found to be harmless. The main focus of the bulletin was on the disruption to commuters who had piled into buses and cabs, leaving thousands more hanging around Madison and Lexington Avenues hoping that the terminal might reopen in time for them to get home while there was something left of the evening. By the end of the week the story had died down; just another crazy moment in the life of a crazy city.

At seven o'clock on the evening of Thursday, February 12th, an unmarked van left a razor-wire compound in Basking Ridge, New Jersey, to begin the eight-hundred-and-fifty-mile return drive south, staying with I81 deep into Virginia then picking up I85 for the final stretch to arrive in the early hours of Friday morning at the headquarters of the Centers for Disease Control near the Druid Hills Golf Club in the suburbs of Atlanta, Georgia.

A little under an hour and a half later, Deputy Director Paul Lewis was in Becket Bradie's office informing him that a DVE under an electron microscope had identified the substance brought in from New Jersey in the middle of the night as an orthopox virus. Variola was therefore a distinct possibility, and culturing had begun.

Becket absorbed the news and indicated the two chairs by the window. Nothing else was said until they were both seated and coffee had been poured. 'So, what are we looking at? Two more days?'

'Yeah, maybe three.'

'And then it's a hundred per cent?'

'Almost. There'll still be a remote possibility of a white pox.'

'Wouldn't that be just as bad?'

Paul Lewis shook his head. 'Nasty piece of work, but not good at getting itself from one body to another.'

The two men sat in silence for a few seconds, looking out at the grey skies and the lightly drifting snow. On the parkway below hundreds of CDC staffers were arriving for the day, the double line of cars stretching back from the checkpoint to the Clifton Road.

Becket finally stirred himself. 'Sorry to have you go through the motions with this, Paul, but when you're ready we should get someone down from Detrick to look at it. Bethesda as well, just to satisfy our masters.'

Paul Lewis raised his eyebrows in exaggerated forbearance. 'Okay, I'll set it up.'

'Good, now go get some sleep.'

As soon as the door had closed, Becket Bradie reached for the phone.

The following Monday morning, NYT city editor Bob Delius stopped by Tom Keeley's office to mention that there might have been something strange about the bomb scare that had shut down Grand Central on the previous Thursday. One of his beat reporters was married to someone whose brother had been on duty with the NYPD HazMat team that afternoon, and from this source word had filtered back that the device retrieved from Grand Central had been driven to a compound in New Jersey where, rather than being detonated, it had been transferred to an unmarked vehicle whose licence plates carried the peach symbol of the State of Georgia. With an eye for detail that would have done a reporter credit, the officer had also noticed that the words embossed under the licence number had read 'Dekalb County'.

'Mean anything?' Delius remained in the doorway, eyebrows raised.

'Spent the last five years there.'

'Thought so. Think you could make a couple of calls?'

That afternoon, Tom Keeley called three former colleagues in the Epidemic Intelligence Service of the Centers for Disease Control in Dekalb County, Atlanta. All were keen to hear about how the new job was going. Eventually, he had worked the conversations around to the incident at Grand Central and the unmarked van with the Dekalb County plates. The first two calls drew a complete blank. The third, a notorious aficionado of agency gossip, produced enough rumour to fill an edition of the staff news. The only item that interested Tom Keeley concerned an unconfirmed report that one of the CDC's bio-safety vehicles had made an unlogged overnight trip on the previous Thursday, plus a suggestion that something strange had been going on in the early hours of Friday morning when the lights had apparently burned most of the night in the bio-containment labs and the Deputy Director's car had remained in the parking lot all night. He also learned that the CDC had begun to take seriously the idea that an unrecognized virus of some kind appeared to be targeting the gay community, though the investigation was being focused not on New York's Fire Island but on San Francisco's Castro Street.

At this phase in his life, Tom Keeley was struggling to get to grips with a wider range of medical issues than he would ever have been asked to grasp as a research scientist and the incident at Grand Central quickly dropped below his radar – mentally filed away as just another of those unexplained loose ends that regularly trail behind a correspondent's life.

It was to be almost thirty years before he thought of it again.

35 | Common ground

At the last moment, Michael had switched to the evening flight and called Seema to invite her for lunch before returning to Geneva. They had arranged to meet at the Brazilian Pavilion on 52nd Street, just off Second Avenue. The weather was still bitterly cold, though the heavy clouds of the previous week had given way to flawless blue skies.

The restaurant had been almost empty, and for fifteen minutes the atmosphere had been strained, a rendezvous in limbo, every topic of conversation artificial. Neither of them interested in the food, they both took an age over the menu. And when Michael said he would have the salt cod with smoke-flavoured black beans, Seema ordered the same. Both were struggling, and each saw the struggle in the other's eyes.

Michael managed a sympathetic smile as the waiter brought water and left. 'Well, this is an improvement on yesterday lunchtime.' Seema widened her eyes, enquiring. Michael hesitated for a long moment, absorbing her look, then turned to face the street. 'I spent nearly an hour in the Delegates Lounge over at the UN. It was an odd feeling. Place was crowded, but I still felt conspicuous.'

'I know, I felt just the same even walking the streets this morning, even sitting in the library. What were you doing in the Delegates' Lounge? I never figured you for schmoozing.'

'Can't abide the place. But as a rumour mill … I got treated to several current whispers, including one about a Chinese DF-5 ICBM test launch that apparently only just missed some place in Papua New Guinea, and another about some Russian who's been drawing a salary at the UN for the last three years and has only been seen in the office twice.'

'Nothing else?'

Michael's eyes held hers for a long moment. 'Nothing else.'

'That's good, isn't it?'

'I think so. We can be pretty sure Hughes went for the end-run.'

After that the conversation had begun to flow a little more easily, with talk about how dull Michael's earlier meeting had been without Hélène's speech and how long Stephen was planning to remain in New York. Seema picked up the menu again for no particular reason. The words 'Brazilian Pavilion' were embossed in gold letters on the cover. 'It was in a pavilion that it all started, wasn't it?'

Over coffee, in search of a safe topic, the talk had drifted to the missing years, Seema telling him in more detail the story of her return to Karachi. 'I hated it. And I hated myself for hating it. Everybody assuming I'd marry straight away, have children, evenings at the Gymkhana Club, perhaps a little light academic work two afternoons a week at the University.'

Michael tried to picture her living such a life, but failed completely. 'Your parents wanted to arrange a marriage?'

Seema nodded, as unable as he to imagine herself in this alternative universe. 'Being a "modern miss", as they put it, they knew I'd want to have a say in choosing a husband, so they started drawing up a shortlist. When the offer of the Jefferson Fellowship came out of the blue I didn't know a thing about it. All that mattered was – it was a ticket out of Karachi.'

'Hence the interest in Jefferson?'

'Initially, yes. It seemed only right to know something about my rescuer.'

Neither had any inclination to bring the lunch to a close. And as the talk stretched on into the afternoon, almost without them noticing there stole upon them again that pleasure of communication that was independent of what was being said, that enjoyment in getting to know the mundane details of each other's lives, that gentle dissolving of time and place and self that was unfamiliar to them both, allowing them to escape for a time from the iron cage whose bars were forged of secrecy, and of the still-stunned awareness of what they had done.

Seema eventually had to interrupt with some determination in order to turn the conversation away from her own life. 'What about you, Michael? Has there been anyone?'

'No, not really.' Michael looked down the fold lines in the tablecloth, resisting an impulse to tell her about all the times he had thought about her, all the places in the world he had carried her with him, all the occasions when he had been subject to an irrational certainty that she had been somewhere nearby. Seeing the unease in his eyes, his reluctance to say out loud the things he might be thinking, she eased him on to safer ground, asking about life in Geneva and whether he got to travel much in Europe. He talked for a while of Nyon, but his fear of boring her was tangible and despite her best efforts he soon found a way to turn the conversation back to her own interests. He talked first about life in those parts of Africa from which most of the slaves had been taken, eventually hitting upon the story of the slave, Onesimus, who had introduced variolation against smallpox into North America. And from here it was but a short step to telling her about Thomas Jefferson's letters to Jenner and his enthusiasm for vaccinating slaves, until at a certain point Seema could not stop herself from laughing at the earnestness of his search for common ground between his world and hers. In a moment both were laughing and, just for a second, touching fingers across the table.

36 | It's Harvey

Paul Lewis entered the director's office to find Becket Bradie sitting at his desk surrounded by papers.

'It's Harvey.'

Becket absorbed the news for a moment. 'Isn't that the one all the labs had?'

'The very same. WHO insisted on all registered smallpox research teams having the same strain of the virus to work on. Could have come from any one of them.'

Becket came round to join Paul in front of the window facing out over the campus.

'And how many were there in the end?'

Paul clicked his tongue. There were dark hollows in his cheeks and the skin of his hands and face looked worn and thin. 'Must have been sixty or seventy labs that had that particular flavour in the freezer, in maybe a couple of dozen countries.'

Becket sighed and turned to look out at the beginning of another Atlanta day. 'And you're getting the others in?'

'Ferguson coming down from Detrick this afternoon, and Herrick as well, though that might not be until tomorrow morning. They're going to think it's awful strange, Beck. No real co-operation with DoD for years and then suddenly we call them in to ID a virus. CAM results clear as day. Like

I'm calling in a couple of the world's leading zoologists to confirm a horse is a horse.'

Becket again responded with the 'ours not to reason why' gesture. 'So what have you told them?'

'What we agreed. It's come in from Iraq. One of the labs that was supposed to have certified. And for some reason best known to themselves, State's insisting on three independent verifications.'

Becket nodded. 'Leave it at that, would you? When they get here, I mean.'

Paul Lewis nodded with an exaggerated expression of bafflement, then got to his feet. 'Anything else?'

Becket also stood. 'I suppose there's no chance of narrowing it down any further, where it might have come from?'

'None at all. Common-or-garden variety.'

'And now it's back in the freezers?'

Paul nodded, pushing out his bottom lip. 'Everything back to normal down there. Not hard to find, by the way, just follow the signs.'

'Go on with you, and let me know when they've confirmed your horse is a horse will you? And Paul, how are you feeling?'

'Curious.'

'That's not what I meant.'

Late that afternoon Becket Bradie was back in the nation's capital. After a short wait he was once more ushered into the office of the Chief of Staff. Toni Restelle was seated at the small conference table. Opposite her was a heavy-set man in his fifties.

'Beck, this is Bill Marriot. Bill's representing the FBI and the CIA both.' The two men shook hands, Marriot's grim expression making it clear that he was up to speed. When they had taken seats, Toni locked her fingers on the table. 'Okay, tell us the worst.'

'It's smallpox.'

After a few seconds of absolute silence, Marriot stood up and walked round behind his chair, resting his hands on the pierced back. 'Okay. First off. At this moment in time, who knows about this thing?' The suit fitted perfectly across the massive chest and shoulders. The necktie, hanging down in front of the chair back, displayed the blue, gold and white stripes of the US Navy.

There was the faintest of smiles on Toni Restelle's face as she answered, not turning to look at him. 'The President. The three of us here. Camden Hughes, the guy who took delivery of the package in New York. That's it. Plus, of course, whoever shelled out the quarter for the locker in Grand Central.'

'What about the pick-up team, drivers, porters, the lab guys and their aunts and uncles?' Marriot exuded assertiveness with a none-too-subtle undertone of 'I'm dealing with a bunch of amateurs here.' Becket again spelt out that it had not been difficult to pass off the pick-up and ID as routine.

'You mean you've got stuff like this coming in all the time?'

Becket decided to put the aggression in the man's voice down to an unfortunate manner. 'No, I wouldn't say all the time. About once a year, maybe, we get something in. There were a lot of labs around the world doing research on smallpox.'

'Labs where?'

Becket shrugged. 'Belgium, Chile, Poland, the UK. Bilthoven in The Netherlands, Japan, South Africa, Iran, Iraq. Maybe seventy labs in total around the world. And they weren't all as meticulous as they might have been when they were asked to certify destruction of stocks.'

'When was that?'

'Most had certified by the end of last year.'

'Most?'

'I believe Porton Down still has to certify, and one lab in South Africa.'

'Inspections?'

'No. The WHO just has to take each country's word for it. But the problem's more that the freezers in most laboratories aren't regularly cleaned out. Once in a while someone finds something they're not sure about, maybe a vial without a label. Happened a couple of times just recently. An unmarked ampoule turned up in a lab in Tanzania that turned out to be variola. Batch of a dozen came in from California about a year ago. So just the checking process isn't going to set off any alarms.'

Bill Marriot's expression left little room for doubt that he considered all this lax beyond belief. 'Something "turns up" – it comes to you, right?'

'Either to us or the Research Institute for Viral Preparations in Moscow. Depends where it's found.'

Bill Marriot returned to his chair, feeling that he had probably established his grip on the proceedings. 'Okay, we're gonna need a team.'

Becket looked sharply at Toni. 'I take it you've discussed the need—'

Marriot waved a hand. 'We have. And I'm not the one who needs to be told about keeping this under wraps.'

Becket recoiled at the man's tone but Toni Restelle appeared unruffled, even favouring him with a small smile as she reached for the coffee pot. 'What you might need to be told, Bill, is what the President has to say about it.'

Marriot put whatever he had been about to say on hold as Toni poured for the three of them, taking her time. Eventually she leaned back from the table, cup in one hand, saucer in the other. 'The President thinks that a leak would likely cause a panic, and that a panic is not what he wants right now.' She smiled again. 'His exact words were that it might be best if we ran this show on a real tight "need to know" basis that didn't include "any Joe Blow with CIA clearance". And I think there might also have been something about heads rolling and keeping on rolling?'

Bill Marriot made a long show of lighting a cigarette, realizing that any attempt to put down Toni Restelle at this point would look like he was challenging the President. In the pause, Toni returned the cup to the table and raised both hands, palms facing the two men. 'Two response paths. First – find whoever's responsible, preferably before they release that persuasive little statement to the *Times* or the *Post*. Bill, you'll obviously lead there and we'll come back to that in a moment. Second – prepare for this going public, which we pray to God doesn't happen. As I said, the President has quite a strong preference for never hearing about this again. But we have to be ready. Beck, you'll obviously lead on that.'

Becket smiled inwardly as Toni continued and Bill Marriot held in a lungful of smoke.

'You'll both be reporting to the President, via his Chief of Staff in the first instance. Now, on the manhunt, Bill, I'm going to need an answer for when the boss asks whether you can get a search up and running without breaking any china – in other words, he's going to ask how you can hunt for "who" without word getting out about "what" and "why"?'

Marriot again waved a dismissive hand, leaving a wraith of smoke over the table. 'We're always pushing out the word to listen out for this and that, dealing out keywords to the NSA guys, that kind of thing. There'll be rumours but there are always rumours. No one's going to get too spooked.'

Toni nodded thoughtfully. 'And I can take it there's no news yet on the package?'

Bill Marriot sighed out smoke. 'Only just got it in.'

'So, nothing else for the moment on the search side of things?'

'We could use more help from you guys,' said Marriot, turning to Becket Bradie. 'You're sure your people can't tell us anything more about where it might have come from?'

'I'm afraid not, Bill. Most sources of smallpox virus you could think of would be likely to have that particular strain.'

For a second Marriot showed his disbelief at this state of things, then snapped back into practical mode. 'Okay, we'll need a list of all the labs that might have held it, personnel details, any known leaks in the last ten years, everything you've got on them, names of foreigners employed...' – he waved the cigarette again.

Becket thought for a moment. 'Give me twenty-four hours.'

Marriot looked unimpressed. 'Then we've got the language analysts going over it. We'll see what they come up with.'

Toni Restelle turned to him slowly. 'You've given it to language analysts?' Bill Marriot paused, enjoying the moment, giving the Chief of Staff a patient look. 'Different analysts got different blocks of text. Sensitive stuff excised. By me.'

Toni gave him a long look, then relaxed. 'Okay, so let's move on to the response side of things. Bill, I don't think we need keep you but you're welcome to stay.'

Marriot pointedly remained where he was as the secretary entered and handed her boss a note. When the door had closed again, Toni looked up from the single sheet of paper and turned to Becket Bradie. 'So, response oversight team: ourselves, plus the boss wants Warren Taylor. So four. Anybody else?'

'Camden Hughes is an obvious point man in New York.'

'I don't think so.' Bill Marriot's tone was contemptuous. 'You know what our number one lead is at this point in time?' He looked at the other two. 'It's your friend Camden Hughes. First question: why him? And I gotta tell you there are question marks all over that guy's CV.'

Becket was coming to the conclusion that giving in to an instant dislike for Bill Marriot would probably have saved time. Taking his lead from Toni Restelle, his voice remained calm. 'Camden Hughes has nearly four decades of fine public service behind him. May we know what the question marks are?'

'You may not. But it's no secret he has, or had, contacts that bat deep in the Civil Rights movement.'

'The Civil Rights movement?' Becket was losing the struggle to remain patient. 'Being part of the Civil Rights movement gets you a suspicious persons docket over at the Bureau these days?'

'Look after the security of your labs, Dr Bradie, and leave us to tend our business. This guy's also writing a book about Marcus Garvey – that's Garvey as in "blacks of the world unite" Garvey.'

'I knew that. Very interesting life, I'm told. And, by the way, I hear some professor over at Princeton's writing a new biography of Luther King. Why not put him under suspicion, too?'

'Let's get things back on track here.' Toni Restelle had assumed a look of forbearance. 'We don't absolutely need Hughes at this point, so let's go along with Bill for the moment. Who else?'

She was looking at Becket, who hesitated for a moment, wary of the reaction to his next suggestion.

'You're probably not gonna like this either, but we more or less have to bring in the World Health Organization. They're the ones who ran the global smallpox-eradication campaign – know everybody who's anybody in smallpox, every lab, every researcher practically. Plus for the last couple of years they've had the IRR up and running – International Rumour Register – to investigate anything that comes up anywhere in the world that just might be smallpox making a comeback. If anyone knows which labs were most likely to leak the stuff – which researchers went where when it was all over – then it's them. And in any case, if the shit does hit the fan in a few weeks' time we'll have no choice. This thing doesn't stay behind the yellow line at the immigration desk.'

Toni Restelle assimilated this for a moment. 'Okay, but principals only at this point. What's the top guy's name?'

Becket Bradie grimaced slightly. 'Director General? Almasi. Egyptian. Bureaucrat's bureaucrat. Lifetime guaranteed one hundred per cent ineffective. Got the job on Buggins' turn, as the Brits say.'

'I thought you wanted them in?'

'I do. But I think we oughta sideline the protocol here. The relevant guy over there is an American. Top man. Key figure in the global smallpox campaign for the best part of a decade. Also happens to be ex-CDC and someone quite a few of us have worked with. Completely sound.'

'So we bring him in instead?'

'That way we could involve WHO but still keep it in the family.'

'Name?

'Michael Lowell. Dr Michael Lowell.'

37 | This is from the top

Michael's ability to compartmentalize, a facility that had served him well over the years, seemed to have abandoned him as he sat, twisted sideways, at the tiny desk in his room on the fortieth floor of the Doral Inn. A moment ago he had even found himself speculating about whether Stephen might have been foolish enough to join the crowds watching the NYPD operation at Grand Central. Not that it was really a worry. Even if the FBI had been photographing the crowds it would only signify if they could manage to match faces with anything they had on file.

For the last hour he had been dictating letters onto tape. Tedious work, but he had made it a rule to deal with the fall-out of meetings before flying back to face the backlog in the office. He pulled another set of papers towards him, knowing he was not cutting through the paperwork with his usual bow speed. He clicked 'record' on the miniature dictaphone but eventually hit the 'pause' button. Toby's texts would almost certainly be being read in Washington by now. But by whom? He stared at the blank wall, re-running scenarios. But the possible paths divided too early and too often to lead him to any strong probabilities. Eventually, one of those paths would have to end at the White House. But who knew how many steps there might be between Sutton

251

Place and Pennsylvania Avenue?

All that remained now was to annotate the draft communiqué of the inter-agency co-operation agreement, adding his own glossary for the benefit of senior staff. He stared at the title: 'Operational definition of lead-agency status in Regional and Country offices of the Member Organizations of the United Nations Family.' By now the search would be well under way. But no matter how many times he traversed the ground he could not find a way that would lead anyone back to himself or any of the others. There were no fingerprints, hair, fibres, saliva. And none of the usual search parameters could possibly flag any of the five. Don't imagine these guys have any magic powers, is what he had told Seema as they had walked back from lunch. They'll need something to go on. And they've got nothing at all. For a few minutes he wrote in the margins of the meeting papers on the desk, explaining the ambiguous or meaningless phrases that compromise had thrown up, knowing that significance was likely to be attached to them in the disputes that would rumble on in the months to come. Seema had not in fact pressed him for reassurance, but he had sensed the need. And in the end the lunch that had started so awkwardly had been the highlight of his week, his year, except for the anxieties that had surged to greet them as soon as they had stepped back out into the normal world. He signed off on the draft communiqué and added it to his impromptu out-tray on the bed. Would there be other such times? Or was it just wishful thinking to believe that, without the shadow of their enterprise, the lunch would have been perfect, that she had enjoyed the time together as much as he, that it might be the first of many such times? Had what seemed to exist between them for those few hours been only the binding of the secret they shared? He did not know. And he dared not hope.

By half past four he was ready to go, Gladstone bag packed, passport, wallet and Swissair ticket laid out on the bed with overcoat, scarf and gloves. He still had a few minutes to kill and wondered whether to set an alarm and lie on the bed for fifteen minutes. He might get some sleep on the flight, but would go straight to the office from the airport. He decided against it and instead made a last check of the closets and drawers in the room he had occupied for the past week.

Satisfied, he collected up his travel documents and overcoat. The room was anonymous again, the walls and drapes an anodyne beige, the pictures inoffensive. Nothing at all to dislike, and yet vaguely terrifying. He stood for a moment longer, unable to stop himself bringing to mind the candlelit loft in Greenwich Village with all its warmth and personality, its sense of possibility. He was on his way out when the phone rang on the bedside table. He left the bag propping open the door. Probably the front desk wanting to know what time he planned to vacate the room.

'Michael Lowell.'

'Michael. Becket Bradie here. How's tricks?'

'Beck, good to hear you. You in Atlanta?'

'DC, Mike – something's come up. Ever heard of a place called Poughkeepsie?'

'Some place on the Hudson?'

'Can you get yourself there mid-morning tomorrow?'

'I'm just about to leave for Geneva. One more minute I'm out of here.'

'Glad I caught you. Saved you a trip back from Europe. Listen, can't talk on the phone but something real big's coming down the line that needs you and me both. Can you get yourself up to this Poughkeepsie place first thing tomorrow?'

'I guess…'

'Great. Call this number and let me have your schedule. Metro North from Grand Central. Sorry, Mike, this is from the top. And as I said, it's big.'

Michael scribbled the number on the telephone pad.

'Got that?'

'What happens when I get there?'

'You'll be picked up at the station. Some hideaway place up in the Shawangunks, about a half-hour drive. Be good to see you.'

'You too… No clues at all?'

'See you in the morning.'

38 | If only they knew

The dog-eared postcard was scrawled in Stephen's habitual green ink:

> *Toby,*
>   *Just wanted to confirm that Michael and I received your letter. We will of course let you know as soon as we hear anything.*
>   *My own future remains uncertain, but I find myself enjoying the change from dreaming spires to shining skyscrapers...*

Creep. Be surprised if Michael had even shown him the drafts. He flipped the card over to reveal an aerial view of the southern tip of Manhattan, the twin towers dominating the foreground with Greenwich Village spread out behind. He had been updated by Michael's call, but the postcard had still brought a shiver as he slipped it back into his jacket pocket and reached for his glass.

For a day or two, drafting those texts had given him a good feeling. But now that was in the past, leaving him to face weeks at the office that were more and more difficult to get through. He swivelled around on the bar stool, turning his face away from the Friday-night schmoozing. All in all, he wished they would remove that illuminated mirror in which he had rather too often seen his own visage staring back at him from between bottles of obscure liquors that, as far as he could see, nobody ever ordered. Behind his reflection he recognized the usual crowd in the bar: the would-bes and might-bes and has-beens and never-had-a-hope-of-beings from the worlds of show business, advertising and other professions for which his respect knew no beginning. He looked down at the beaten copper of the bar to escape the sight of his own face. This was not how the others were spending their Friday evenings, or their lives. Twenty years ago the five of them had all started off together; all of them young, gifted and white; except for Seema, of course, who was young, gifted and brown. The world at our feet. 'There was nothing before us, there was everything before us.' He looked up at himself between the perky little optics, his face larger and his eyes smaller than he had ever imagined they would be. And through his reflection he contemplated the week past and the week to come, the already-forgotten product briefings and script conferences, the client lunches and the video presentations, the blue-sky Mondays and the TGIFs, the empty home and the empty bottles. His image blinked back at him. Yes, you mate. All things dobbed in you'd have to say it's pretty impressive: what you might call putting something back into society; pushing a comprehensive range of planet-destroying aspirations; making remarkable new discoveries in the field of human needs; putting new width into the generation gap; touching new heights of supersonic snobbery.

Hélène looked around at the familiar quarters that she had thought never to see again. She had yet to unpack but found herself lying on the bed listening to the already nostalgic sounds of the African evening. The ceiling fan rotated in the dimness. She dozed miserably.

When she awoke again the light had fallen and the movement of the fan was more felt than seen. Sleep had brought no relief. The tiredness that had followed her over the Atlantic was more powerful than anything jetlag could explain. And it would be there tomorrow, and the day after that. On top of it all she recognized the malady which always struck on her return to Africa. In New York or Montreal she was anonymous, unremarkable; back here she was shadowed by a certain consequence, a sense of others' awareness of her own presence that related solely to the fact of being white. Partly, she supposed, it was the interest aroused by any foreigner. But partly, also, it was the residual body language of colonialism, in word and look and gesture. Being Canadian did not matter. Being white was all that counted. Sometimes she thought it was just her, that the malady was whatever the opposite of paranoia might be – seeing the symptoms of what she had come to think of as 'unmerited status syndrome' in ordinary, everyday politeness. But that was not it. She could observe the differences in the same way as any woman can observe the ways in which she is treated differently from a man. And she cringed to think of it.

Outside, the evening cicadas had started up and the heat was beginning to abate. She should turn the fan off. Drink some water. Shower. Change. Bestir herself and go out to dinner. She had not been back to *L'Eau Vive* in two years, not wishing to invite remembrance of the night she had waited there so long. Waited for the lover she would never see again.

On the bedside table, just at the edge of her vision, she could make out the blue air-mail envelope; the envelope that contained the proof that all that had happened in the last few weeks was real. She reached for it again, switching on the lamp.

Dear Hélène,

Great to see you in NY. I hope the rest of your trip went well and that you found your parents in good health. I have rarely known NY so cold, but I guess it must have been worse in Montreal.

There were several more lines with bits and pieces of news. Finally, at the very end of the letter, just above Seema's signature, the paragraph whose meaning had taken a second or two to register.

I also wanted to let you know that I've posted the letter and proposal we discussed. I'm not sure I'll hear anything back, but will let you know if I do.

Stephen had used the words 'Wall Street' so often in his lectures as to have made of it an almost mythical place. But, setting foot in the real street for the first time, it was the ordinariness that astonished him. In offices way above, new schemes for rent-seeking were doubtless being concocted, but down here at street level the scene was distinctly sublunary: a sprawl of scaffolding and traffic violation signs, fire hydrants and ATMs, shop awnings and steam vents. Like the rest of the city, an unfinished chaos of energy and greed. Ahead stood the hopelessly belittled spire of Trinity Church, pointing a forlorn finger towards a less material world. Breakfasting at the Chelsea that morning, he had found himself descending deeper into the quicksands of morbid introspection from which it seemed there could never be any escape. He knew no one in the city, apart from Seema, and he had nothing to do but absorb himself in the nuances of his own circumstance. He bought a coffee from a street vendor and carried it across to the bench in front of the church.

With the life of Wall Street flowing all around him, he acknowledged to himself that he was at a low ebb. He had even diagnosed the problem. He had Gramsci's pessimism of the intellect without his optimism of the spirit. And, comforted in some small way by this formulation, his mind strayed as always to the one 'big thing' that offered consolation.

If only all these people knew.

Setting the coffee down on the bench beside him, he opened his shoulder bag and pulled out the *New York Times*. There was Tom, of course. Why hadn't he thought of that? They had never had much in common, but it would be someone to talk to, share a lunch with. And he was presumably contactable through the paper.

After a few more minutes he looked up from the *Times*, irked by a vague dissatisfaction that prevented him from concentrating. Surely, seated here at the beating heart of capitalism, he ought to be experiencing something more than this almost comical sense of its banality, this acute awareness of its complete indifference to his own presence. But, reduced from the global engine of exploitation to a shabby street-corner hot-dog stand, from the Camelot of capitalistic hegemony to the rather grubby stars and stripes hanging unenthusiastically from a pole above an office entrance, he was finding it difficult to relate to it all in any very satisfactory way. And surely there ought not to be so many pigeons?

Seema was standing, distracted, by the kitchen window looking out on the fire escapes and the February drabness of Lower Manhattan, when the phone rang, echoing round the loft.

'Michael! Has anything happened?'

'I called to let you know I'm still here.'

'In the city? What happened?'

'Last-minute change of plan. Another meeting. Upstate.'

'How long for?'

'No idea. I'll be through Manhattan again on my way back.'

'You've no idea when?'

'No. I'll call you.'

For a few more minutes they talked of something and nothing, Seema biting back the questions.

'Michael, I don't have anything on this week. Call me when you come back through town. We could get together. Even if it's only for a coffee on your way to the airport.'

The man holding up the card with the words 'Dr Michael Lowell' in red felt-tip looked as if he might be a survivor of the hippie community for which the college town of New Paltz had once been famous. Red check shirt, jeans, Budweiser belt buckle, tooled leather boots, thin hair drawn into a less-than-luxurious ponytail, he extended a hand as Michael approached. It was not clear whether the station wagon boasting a half acre of wood-effect panelling was a regular cab or a private vehicle. The driver had simply given his name as Ken. Michael threw the Gladstone bag on the back seat and slid himself into the front.

Leaving the town line, they headed west across the Mid-Hudson Bridge towards New Paltz and the Catskills. Only two hours away from New York, as Ken pointed out, but a different world. Michael agreed, watching the last few clapboard homes of Poughkeepsie pass by and thinking this might just be a conversation Ken had enjoyed many times before.

After twenty minutes or so, the station wagon turned off the Minnewaska Road by a sign that read 'Mohonk

Mountain House', where they were flagged down by two armed and uniformed marines. The pair obviously knew Ken, but asked Michael to step out of the car and show ID. After checking the Gladstone bag and consulting a list, they were waved through on to an unsealed road, broadening here and there into passing places as it curved gracefully through the landscaped grounds of a country estate. In another quarter mile, as they were rounding a long downward bend, there appeared before them a Victorian fantasy castle sitting on the edge of a half mile of frozen lake.

'Ain't got nothin' like that in New York City, Mike.'

39 | No one wants to talk

Tom Keeley bent to kiss his wife on the top of her head as he came back to the breakfast table, carrying toast. She caught his arm and lifted her face towards him. 'Don't kiss me on my head, it makes me feel old.'

He kissed her, lingeringly, on the lips. 'You still look sixteen.'

'Go put your glasses on.'

The boys had left for school. It was warm enough to have the windows open, a pale February sun streaming in as Caroline poured more coffee. 'So I thought you didn't get on too great with this guy?'

'He's okay. Can't say I ever really took to him. First time I met him he stopped me on the landing outside my room and asked what I was "reading". When I said Chemistry he looked at me over his glasses and said "how amusing".'

'Oh God, an Oxford type. And you had to share a room?'

'God no! Same staircase is all. Got to know him a bit. Bad case of adolescent Marxism. Doesn't seem to have cleared up.'

'He's not still a Marxist?'

'Yeah. Going down with the ship.'

'He call you at the *Times*?'

'Yeah. Lonesome, I expect. Doesn't know anybody in the city. Doesn't even really seem to know what he's doing here.

Resigned from his college apparently. Made a big deal of it. No one's ever done it before, if you can believe that. Bottom line is he inherited a fortune, so I guess he can do what he likes.'

'And what he likes is hanging around the Chelsea Hotel?'

'I guess that's some sort of a left-wing, Bohemian, thing. He was always a bit strange. Seemed awfully tense, though.'

'Sounds unbalanced to me.'

'Yeah, funny how some people can use their intelligence to find the most complicated route up their own ass.'

They sat for a while longer in silence, the sun on their faces, holding hands as they looked out over the frozen pond, the tall reeds in its grip, ivy strangling one of the white oaks on the bank. Dead leaves, edged in white, had settled in drifts over the lawn.

'More coffee?'

'Better go.'

'Did he tell you what happened with Seema and that guy Michael?'

'No, not really. Funny thing was, it was just the same as that lunch with Seema. Soon as I mentioned the reunion he changed the subject.'

Caroline began collecting up the breakfast things. 'So you think something happened no one wants to talk about?'

'Dunno. Thing is, he also acted more than a tad strange when I said something about not being able to get home the other night on account of the bomb scare.'

'Was he there?'

'Not as far as I know. And then, when I mentioned about whatever it was being taken to the CDC instead of being blown up or whatever, I swear to God he went pale. Like he'd had some kind of a narrow escape.'

'New York's probably got him wired. Must be a shock

after living in an Oxford college all your life.'

'Yeah, Oxford it's not.'

'Anyway, good thing for you that Grand Central thing was on the news or I might not have believed you spent the night at your own dear brother's.'

'Thanks for that.'

'Go to work.'

40 | The words he knew by heart

Tradition as well as tranquillity lay behind the choice of Mohonk Mountain House for the first Presidential retreat of the new administration. The hotel, built in the nineteenth century by the Quaker twins Albert and Alfred Smiley, had in its time welcomed Presidents Theodore Roosevelt, William Howard Taft and Rutherford B Hayes. Come the turn of the twentieth century it had held conferences on the living standards of Native Americans and the possibilities for international arbitration of conflict. Run by the descendants of the Smiley twins, the two-hundred-room wood-and-granite hotel still prided itself on making a contribution to public life.

The resort had not been closed to the public. All entrance roads were guarded and the two-thousand-acre estate was regularly patrolled, but a few vacationers were still to be seen ice-skating out on the lake, sitting out on the glassed-in decks with blankets around their knees or reading in armchairs by the great open fireplaces. The President and his staff, with perhaps a half a dozen Cabinet members and advisers, had taken over only the twenty-eight-room central tower block, along with its separate lounge and meeting rooms.

Becket Bradie, reading a newspaper by the fire in a corner of the main lobby, looked up to see Michael Lowell getting out of a station wagon that had come to a halt under the massive pine-built loggia. When the two had shaken hands, he led the way through the parlour to the wooden veranda that curved around the front of the hotel twelve feet above the frozen lake.

Michael lowered his bag to the floor. 'Okay, Beck, let's have it. What's this all about, marines and all?'

Becket glanced back to make sure they were alone. Though the frozen lake was beginning to steam in the strengthening sun, it was still too cold for anyone to be occupying the half dozen rocking chairs. He was about to answer when the door to the parlour swung outwards again and an attractive woman in her mid-thirties wearing jeans and a sweater headed down the veranda towards them, 'May I take it this is Dr Lowell?' After being introduced she turned again to Becket Bradie. 'Unless Dr Lowell would like to freshen up first, I think we should begin straight away.'

Becket held up a forestalling hand. 'Toni, Michael just got here and I think I can safely say he hasn't the faintest idea of what this is all about.'

'I'm sorry, Dr Lowell hasn't been briefed?'

'No, and I should probably tell you right off, Michael, the President is here. That's the extra security you were asking about.'

Toni Restelle smiled at Michael's confusion. 'I'm sorry, Dr Lowell. But, if you don't mind, we'll go through and start. We can brief you in there.'

The Chief of Staff led the way back through the warmth of the lobby with its granite fire surrounds and red plush seating, making for an unmarked door. After passing through a second, smaller anteroom, they entered an oak-panelled study where two others were already seated at an antique table. The two half-stood as Toni Restelle made the introductions. 'Dr Michael Lowell of the World Health Organization, this is US National Security Adviser Warren Taylor... and can I also introduce Bill Marriot, who is representing both the FBI and the CIA today. Becket of course you know.' She gestured for them all to sit, leaving the head of the table to Warren Taylor and taking the chair on his right. The National Security Adviser gave a nod to her questioning look and she turned to face the little group.

'Okay. Welcome everybody. And thanks for changing your plans to be with us, Dr Lowell. You're obviously wondering what this is all about. Best I just give you these. She drew several sheets of paper from a folder and slid them over the table. 'Pushed through the home mailbox of a senior UN official in New York City on Tuesday night last. These are the only copies. The others have all seen them. Take your time.'

Michael took the sheets and read through the texts he knew almost by heart. The others occupied themselves with murmured conversations or looked round at the Hudson River School paintings and the fading photographs of the hotel's famous guests.

Michael maintained his expression as his eyes came to rest on Toby's final paragraph:

> ... we believe that the demands we make reflect the deep longing of ordinary people everywhere for a world in which children no longer suffer and die in numbers which are beyond the emotional embrace of the individual but which haunt the conscience of mankind.

He made a show of going back over certain points in the text as the others returned their attention to the table, gradually falling silent and looking at him expectantly. He squared the sheets up and placed them in front of him. 'I take it that whatever was in the locker has been recovered?'

The Chief of Staff looked towards Becket Bradie, inviting him to take up the story. 'It's our old friend Harvey, Michael.'

'It's been cultured?'

Becket nodded. Michael turned again to face the Chief of Staff. 'Who else knows about this at this point?'

'Right question. The five of us in this room, plus the UN guy who took delivery, name of Hughes, Camden Hughes. And of course the President. So seven. If we're talking our side of the fence. And I'm sure I don't need to tell you about the need for us to keep it that way.'

'Any indications where it might have come from?'

'None.' Bill Marriot's tone was defensive.

Michael looked down again at the papers, leaving others to lead. After a few seconds, Toni Restelle crossed to the sideboard and filled a coffee cup from a pewter urn, placing the cup in front of Michael before returning to her seat. 'I know this is all a bit sudden, Dr Lowell, but we have a couple of hours to set up a range of options for the President. Bill here's in charge of the search for whoever's behind this thing. We'll begin there. Bill?'

Marriot turned to address himself directly to Warren Taylor. 'Well, first thing is, we've been given precisely zip to go on. Stationery all standard office supplies stuff. Typewriter an almost unused Olivetti Lettera 32 portable, of which there are only about a zillion out there. Forensics, we ain't got diddly. Locker key, envelope, paperwork, all either clean or wiped down with surgical spirit. Envelope sealed with some kind of mineral water, not spittle. Dr Bradie here tells me the container, ampoule, vial, whatever, is also clean. And, according to those who are supposed to know, the thing itself also gives us a big fat zero. I understand there might have been seventy or more labs that the WHO let have that particular strain, Harvey or whatever dumb name it's called, in maybe a few dozen countries, some of them dubious. And if you don't mind my saying so, Dr Lowell, the system for checking and certifying what happened to those stocks looks, shall we say, lax, from where I'm sitting.'

Michael said nothing. With a slight movement of the hand, Toni Restelle managed to convey the irrelevance of this comment to current proceedings. 'Anything else?'

Marriot continued to address himself to Warren Taylor. 'We had our analysts go over the text. Broken up into extracts, like I said, so nobody got to see the whole shebang. Some suggestion the writer might be a Brit rather than an American. Quite Latinate apparently, whatever the fuck that means. These guys are all smoke and mirrors anyway.' He tapped out a cigarette from a pack of Marlboro and rolled it for a moment between his fingers, aware of being in the presence of senior representatives of the health establishment. 'So where's that leave us? Well, I have to tell you folks, nine times out of ten it's human intelligence that breaks these things. Something like this, it usually comes through informants. Everybody out there knows it's "first squeal, best deal". And for sure humint's the only way we ever got anyplace on biological weapons, where what we're looking for is handily tucked away in bona fide institutions running apparently legit research programmes. And what we're dealing with here' – he pointed with the still-unlit cigarette at the papers on the table – 'probably isn't all that different. Problem is, humint generally only works with some kind of a reward attached. We've put the word out in the usual places. But, without saying what the deal is, our hands are tied. And so far there hasn't been as much as a whisper on any of the grapevines. And believe me we have quite a vineyard.' He looked around the table, as if these last words were a challenge, then lit the cigarette with a

Zippo lighter. 'The only leads we got here are where the thing might have come from, and where the drop was made. Even if security at the World Health Organization isn't all it might be, you still don't get to pick this kind of thing up at the drug store on the way home. And why the hell the UN guy? Our friend Mr Hughes? Didn't just pick him out of the Manhattan phone book with a pin either. We're all over his contacts and his contacts' contacts and believe me it's quite a list. Hop and a step from Hughes puts you in three-in-a-bed with the likes of Seale and Carmichael. Throw in a jump and you've got Malcolm X in there as well, and quite a few others of the same stripe. Though I got to say there's nothin' that specifically connects up with anything like this' – he waved the cigarette again in the direction of the papers, leaving another wraith of smoke over the table.

Becket Bradie raised a dispersing hand. 'Well, if you don't mind my saying so, Mr Marriot, a hop, step and a jump could probably connect any one of us here with anybody from Dick Nixon to Mickey Mouse. Camden's thinking was that they probably set about finding someone who lived alone in New York City with high-level contacts and a low-level mailbox, and as far as I'm concerned that makes a whole lot more sense.'

Toni Restelle intervened. 'Clock's running. Anything else on the search side of things?'

Marriot straightened in his chair and let his gaze travel from Becket Bradie to the others. 'Yes, there is something else, as a matter of fact. The other fact we gotta throw in the mixer is – you only have to read that stuff to get it, Dr Lowell – this is quite a ways from your typical half-assed, semi-literate terrorist threat. These guys aren't your usual boil-in-the-bag fanatics. We're talking guys who know what they're about. And this vaccines thing they're so all fired up about isn't something they got into the day before yesterday. Seems to me our most significant lead is what's being threatened here. Seems to me this is some guy, or a whole bunch of guys, who've been involved in this thing in one way or another for quite a while and have gotten themselves frustrated. They're not on the same page as the networks we're looking at – they're not connected with known terrorist groups, religious fanatics, organized crime syndicates or any other form of low-life that our people are likely to stir up in the mud flats. That's why the grapevine's silent as the grave. Suggests to me we're probably just futzing around with the usual stuff and we might get a whole lot more traction if our medical colleagues here could see their way to setting aside their professional loyalties or whatever and give us something to go on. I'm talking scientists, researchers, health professionals, lab guys, activists, non-profit types, Peace Corps veterans, anybody else in your line of country, gentlemen, who might just take it into their heads to get out of bed one morning and pull a stunt like this.'

Toni Restelle appealed to Becket Bradie with a look and invited the FBI man to finish.

Marriot reached into the centre of the table for the glass ashtray, enjoying his moment. 'Taking yourself for example, Dr Lowell. You're here because we're told you know as much as anyone about the who's who of this thing, no pun intended. All the labs that held the stocks, all the scientists involved around the world, all the rumours that no doubt come to the ears of your organization, which I understand sits on the banks of Lake Geneva. We'd like to hear your thoughts, Dr Lowell – and I'm talking people, places, any little incidents in the past, any little suspicions you might have had, any little things you might have heard, people you might have had your own private little doubts about.' He waved the cigarette again at the papers on the table. 'Anything at all occur to you as you read through that thing?

And the same goes for you, Dr Bradie. Seems to me you're the guys best placed to give us the steer on this. Whoever these guys are, chances are they're in your world, not mine. All the rest is probably just fucking flies.'

Becket Bradie held the FBI man's glare. 'Tell me, Mr Marriot, did your language people pick up the spelling mistake?'

Caught off guard, Marriot could offer only an uncertain frown. Becket let the pause continue for a beat longer than necessary, then reached for the sheets from the table. 'Diphtheria is missing its first "h". It's a mistake a lot of people might make. But not something anyone in "our line of country", as you put it, would be likely to get wrong.'

Bill Marriot breathed in dismissively through his nose. 'Okay, so we're not talking some Ivy League Medical School. Fine. That still leaves us a little scope here. I still say we need to ask you to read that thing again and again until it starts to bubble up names, organizations, connections, anyone who comes to mind for any reason at all. Everyone and anyone you've ever heard of who might have … it's like a homicide … we're talking motive, means, opportunity. Doesn't matter if it's a long shot.' He raised one arm over his head as if holding up the torch of liberty, the powerful chest pulling at the buttons of his shirt. 'Feed me your long shots.'

Becket Bradie looked across at his WHO colleague. Michael met his glance then turned again to Marriot. 'I can give you a list right now of the countries that are rumoured to have hung on to stocks, Mr Marriott – France, North Korea, China, Cuba, India, Iraq, Iran, Israel, Pakistan, Yugoslavia. But if you want a list of people working in global public health who've gotten frustrated by the lack of progress then it would probably be quicker to give you a list of those who haven't.'

'I don't find that one little bit helpful, Dr Lowell.'

In response to another look from the Chief of Staff,

Becket Bradie raised a hand in conciliation. 'We'll do as you ask, Mr Marriot. But I should tell you Michael here hasn't known anyone who can't spell diphtheria since he was in grade school.'

Toni Restelle glanced again at the half grandfather clock standing in the corner of the room. 'Warren, do you want to say anything at this point?'

The National Security Adviser shook his head, making it clear he was happy for the Chief of Staff to continue leading the discussion.

'Okay. We need to keep in mind that the immediate threat here isn't the release of the virus. It's the threat to go public with the fact that persons unknown have the virus in their possession and are making demands of the Government of the United States. You've all read this little beauty' – nodding towards the pages that Becket had returned to the table – 'and I don't need to tell you what having this all over the *Times* or the *Post* would mean. First thing the President's going to want to know is how we propose to stop that happening. Seems to me we have to tell him it's likely to hit the media unless Bill's people can locate whoever's behind it, which from what we've heard you wouldn't want to bet the farm on.'

'Court order wouldn't keep the wraps on a thing like this.' It was the first time Warren Taylor had spoken. 'And, with that in mind, I'd suggest our recommendations have to be based on both threats. First, what do we need to do to get ready for this thing going public? Second, what do we need to do to prepare for the virus itself being released at some point further down the line?' He turned again to face the Chief of Staff, making it clear he was handing the meeting back to her charge.

'Okay, gentlemen, following our first meeting in the White House, Wednesday, the President has been briefed as follows.' She looked up at Becket Bradie and Michael Lowell – 'Please jump in, gentlemen, if you have any issues.'

'The President's first response was, in his own words, "We sure as hell can't have that all over the goddamn papers". Second, he expressed quite a strong preference for locating whoever's behind this' – a glance at Bill Marriot. 'That said, the President asked what the medical guys had to say and in particular he wanted to know why we couldn't just "immunize the hell out of this thing" by restarting vaccination. I informed the President that this was not what was being advised by the CDC and outlined the surveillance and ring immunization approach, as explained to me by Becket here. I also informed the President that most people over the age of eight would likely have some degree of immunity and that an outbreak could probably be contained, possibly without major loss of life – if we were ready, if we acted fast enough, and if we could avoid a panic. I further passed on concerns about the dangers of public panic undermining a controlled response.'

She looked up for a moment, giving Becket and Michael the opportunity to comment. Both remained silent. 'Okay, the President had the following questions. One, why aren't we carrying enough vaccine stock and why don't we at least start up mass production right now so as to be ready for a worst-case scenario. Gentlemen?'

Michael indicated that the CDC Director should go ahead. Becket took a deep breath. 'Suddenly starting up vaccine production all over again would be a disaster, Toni. First off, far too many people would need to know about it. More important, I come back to the point that the way to deal with this thing isn't vaccinating everybody and his dog. It's identifying any cases real quick, quarantining patients, and vaccinating everybody who's likely been in any kind of close-up contact. The one thing we have going for us is that smallpox isn't like in the movies – it really isn't easy to pass on. You've more or less got to be up close and personal for some time. We're talking face to face. And it isn't infectious at all until it becomes pustular, twelve days or so after being contracted. So we might be able to contain it if we're really ready and on full alert. Problem is, the more you do to get ready for something like this, the more likely you are to trigger a panic.'

Warren Taylor raised a slow hand. 'And I have to tell you there's probably another reason we might not want to go down that route.' He paused for a long moment. 'Having consulted with Defense on this, with great discretion I assure you, it appears there's very little doubt the Soviets would see starting up vaccine production as a hostile act.' Seeing the lack of comprehension in the eyes of Toni Restelle and Bill Marriot, he looked for support to the two medical men across the table. 'If I have this thing right, gentlemen, the biology of vaccination can be turned right around to make modified viruses that one side would be protected against but an enemy would be vulnerable to. In other words, biological weapons.' He waited for the confirmation nods from Becket Bradie and Michael Lowell, then continued: 'The Soviets would likely assume we'd been lying about bio-weaponry all along, just like they have. Might even tempt them to start getting ready what they deny they've got but we know they're sitting on. And that includes several tons of some kind of smallpox virus stockpiled at Zagorsk. Maybe even a vaccine-resistant strain. We don't know. At the very least, I think we can safely say it would blow all agreements out of the water. And of course we'd lose any chance we might have of getting them to agree on mutually verified destruction of stocks.'

There was silence around the table for a few seconds before Toni Restelle restarted the discussion.

'I'll refer the President to you on that if necessary, Warren, but for both reasons let's agree to exclude that option. Becket, do we have enough vaccine to do this ring-immunization thing without restarting mass production?'

Becket again glanced at Michael. 'We have about fifteen million doses in stock at the CDC, so, yes, I'd say we ought to have enough in the short term.'

The Chief of Staff looked across the table, searching his face for any sign of uncertainty. 'And if the President asks what happens if there's an outbreak in New York or San Francisco?'

'Same answer. ID every case within a few days and get the cavalry in place.'

'And we can be ready to do that?'

'In theory. As I said, every health department official already has access to a CASE manual. But it's been a few years since the plans were put in place and we'd need to think about running some kind of refresher course. We might be able to do that while still saying it's just a routine readiness exercise, but we'd have to go carefully.'

Toni Restelle absorbed the information. 'Seems to me there'd be no harm in getting that particular ball rolling right now, but we'll come back to it. Next, the President wants to know if the US armed forces are immunized.'

Becket Bradie indulged in a grim smile. 'The armed forces and everybody else likely to be in the firing line are still getting their shots. And they'll continue to do so as long as Moscow refuses to stop vaccinating the Soviet military.'

The Chief of Staff turned to Michael. 'The President also asked about international implications. Dr Lowell?'

Michael looked up at the woman who was preparing to brief the President and who still had not taken a single note. 'What happens if the virus gets released from some kind of atomizer at JFK, or on a 747 headed for Paris?' He paused to let the implications sink in. Then answered his own question. 'What Becket says about the US would still apply. The answer would still be ID and surround. But it would be way more difficult. Most places have shut down routine smallpox vaccination and there are only twenty-or-so countries that still have vaccine in stock. So maybe about a hundred million shots worldwide with no way of knowing if they're still potent. Plus which the WHO has sixty-eight million shots stored in Geneva and another six million in Delhi. Not enough to cope if anything went seriously wrong. And then you have to think about the increase in international travel and a new generation of public-health officials who mostly wouldn't recognize a case of smallpox if they saw one. Just to remind you, it has to be ID'd within a very few days. So the short answer is, we'd be in big, big trouble. Most countries don't have anything like the public-health infrastructure of the US, and most of them would probably be reluctant to restart expensive nationwide surveillance programmes unless there was a compelling reason. If we were to suggest a compelling reason, it would likely trigger panic. And a panic would most likely result in a wrong deployment of limited vaccine stocks, making things a whole lot worse. It would also be a big setback when we've persuaded just about every country that smallpox has gone and they can stop vaccination.'

'Beck?'

'I agree. Nothing to add.'

Toni Restelle leaned back in her chair. 'Anybody got any good news I can give the President, or shall we all just put our hands together and say a short prayer for the messenger?'

41 | The cards face up

Over the next half-hour, the Chief of Staff struggled to keep the discussion from sinking axle-deep in technicalities. And, when fresh coffee arrived, she collected up the papers still lying on the table and suggested they take five minutes to stretch their legs before entering the final hour of the morning.

Michael opened the French windows and stepped out on to the balcony, blinking at the sudden glare from the lake. Directly below, a young couple were ice-dancing under a perfect blue sky. Captivated for a moment by the perfection of the scene, he eventually forced himself to raise his eyes to the Shawangunk hills, planning the intervention he had hoped somebody else would make.

Toni Restelle was tapping her spoon on the side of her cup. 'Okay, gentlemen.'

When they were all seated again the Chief of Staff returned the spoon to the saucer. 'Okay, we have three-quarters of an hour. Let's back up aways, get some kind of an overview. Broad outlines of options. Dr Bradie?'

Becket stared out of the window for a moment, collecting his thoughts. 'Tough it out. President hits the networks. Tells it like it is. Stay calm and co-operate with the health authorities. Government has this thing in hand. Health services prepared. Give 'em the facts. Smallpox can't be passed on by casual contact. Vaccination can protect even after the event. Need for everybody to be alert to symptoms. Respect any quarantine arrangements. US won't give in to blackmail. Terrorists got it wrong if they think they can intimidate the administration. American people not easily panicked.'

Toni Restelle absorbed the line of argument, then turned to Michael. 'Dr Lowell?'

'It's an option. For the US. But is every health authority really prepared, Beck? Every first responder, every walk-in clinic? They've probably all got the manual on a shelf somewhere, but when's the last time they looked at it? Plus which, you brief hundreds of thousands of health personnel to look out for signs of variola and you're going to have tens of thousands of paediatricians, physicians, clinic staff, auxiliaries, nurses, ambulance crews, all of them calling in the cavalry for every case of chickenpox. So getting ready to ID any case anywhere within a day or two is going to have to be some remarkable effort. And, like we said, the more intensive it is, the greater the likelihood of provoking a panic.'

The Chief of Staff kept her eyes on Michael. 'And globally?'

Michael sighed. 'We could attempt the same, like we did in the Seventies. But it'd be a whole different ball game. International travel's been increasing at a rate. Same goes for domestic travel, commuting, people working in large air-conditioned buildings. And I should also point out that the whole surveillance infrastructure's been wound down since eradication – routine immunization stopped, sentinel sites decommissioned. Most front-line health personnel wouldn't recognize smallpox. From a global perspective, we'd have to hope it was just the US.'

Bill Marriot was about to protest this when the Chief of Staff interrupted with another glance at the clock. 'Other options?'

There was silence around the table. 'Warren?'

Warren Taylor, who had hardly spoken all morning, stared thoughtfully at the polished surface of the table, allowing a few more seconds to elapse. 'There are maybe a couple of other options we haven't considered. First is – do nothing at all.' The others looked up to see if the suggestion was serious. The National Security Adviser looked at each in turn. 'Like Mr Marriot here says, these people aren't deranged.' He gestured towards the papers on the table. 'They don't come across like loony-tunes. And what they're about is protecting kids, not killing people. Chances are, they're not contemplating releasing the virus. They're hoping the threat will be enough. Wanna take the risk, we could just sit on our fannies, call their bluff.'

Toni Restelle considered the suggestion in silence for a moment or two. 'It's an option, Warren, but it's a pretty big call. Even if they don't intend to go all the way they might well be prepared to carry out what they're threatening right now, which is to go public. And from the Administration's point of view...'

Warren Taylor shrugged. 'Yeah, they might go for second base.'

Toni Restelle looked slowly around the table, inviting other contributions.

Michael breathed in deeply, staring at the papers on the table. The moment had come. The silence seemed suspended in time, the world stilled, save for the maddeningly slow back and forth of the pendulum in the grandfather clock. But as he was about to look up and catch Toni Restelle's eye, Warren Taylor intervened again.

'There is of course one other option.'

In the long moment that followed it dawned on all around the table what that option might be. Several more seconds passed. Michael relaxed his shoulders just a little.

'I realize it's an unwelcome thought.' Warren Taylor allowed time for another pause, taking his time. 'A heretical thought to some, I would imagine. But it seems to me we should set out the full deck and leave it to the President to make the call.' The National Security Adviser paused, offering an opportunity for anybody else to come in. Becket Bradie leaned his elbows on the table. 'I must admit I was working around thataways, too. So long as we're running through options.'

Bill Marriot could contain himself no longer. 'Let's have the cards face up here. You guys want the Government of the United States to consider giving in to blackmail?'

Warren Taylor chose to reply in the same slow, quiet voice. 'I'm proposing we take just a moment to look at the practical consequences of such an alternative, Mr Marriot.'

Michael stared up at the portraits of the Smiley family on the wall. To the right, through the closed French windows, the skaters were still making fleeting appearances out on the lake.

'Just to give this a little context' – Becket also ignored Marriot's attempted interruption – 'let me point out that these people, whoever they are, are not trying to force the US into anything it's opposed to. There isn't a thing in that' – he waved a hand at the papers lying in front of the Chief of Staff – 'that the Government of the United States doesn't already support. Matter of fact, there isn't a thing in it that it's not already signed up to.'

Bill Marriot glared his incredulity. 'What's that supposed to mean?'

Becket's expression implied that the answer ought to have been obvious. 'It means that what's being demanded here is actioning a commitment the US made when we voted in favour of UCI at the World Health Assembly.' Seeing the frowns around the table, he glanced across the table at Michael.

Michael spoke quietly. 'Universal Childhood Immunization. The World Health Assembly adopted it as a target to be reached by the end of the 1980s. The US voted for it, along with 'most every other government.'

Bill Marriot slapped the table. 'So what? These resolutions don't mean diddly. But now we suddenly think we might get around to doing something about it?' He turned to Toni Restelle, looking for support. When none was forthcoming he held up both hands, as if to stop proceedings. 'Let me ask this again. You wanna recommend to the President that the Government of the United States gives in to blackmail?'

Warren Taylor looked up from the table. 'I repeat, we're talking about setting out options, Mr Marriot. And, while you could of course call it giving in to blackmail, you could also call it doing what we said we'd do. You could call it doing something in practice that we're committed to in principle. And I guess if you were really having a good day you could also call it doing what's right—'

'So what?' Marriot's anger now spilled over the rim of pro-tocol. 'These guys can wear as many white hats as they like, they're still a bunch of terrorists trying to blackmail the US—'

Warren Taylor carried on in an even voice as if there had been no interruption. '…And I guess if you happened to be so disposed you could also call it the United States of America leading the way towards what many might see as a great humanitarian achievement. As someone said, we're quite aways here from your usual kind of terrorist threat…'

Marriot ignored a warning look from the Chief of Staff. 'What you're forgetting, if I might say so, sir, is what all appeasers forget' – ignored also the slight narrowing of the National Security Adviser's eyes – 'You give in to these kind of threats and the bastards come back for more. Always. Always. Anyone who'd pull a stunt like this isn't going to stop here. And the next time they have an even tighter grip on your balls because you can't 'fess up that you caved in the last time around.'

Toni Restelle looked at her watch. 'I hear what you're saying, Warren, but Bill has a point. White hats or not, there's a big principle in the pot here.'

Warren Taylor gave her a look that might have been taken as fatherly but was also respectful. 'I wouldn't argue with that, Toni. Whether it's an absolute, now, is for the President to say. Thing like this – in my experience we're usually looking for the least bad way to get ourselves out the other side, not some principle that sets a shining example for all time.'

Toni Restelle conceded the point and turned to the others. 'Let's run with it two more minutes. Anybody else? Dr Lowell?'

Michael tried not to let his face show the speed his mind was moving at as he decided to address Marriot. 'Not really a medical point, but I don't think we need necessarily see it as giving in, or at least not all the way.' Bill Marriot looked up with some suspicion as Michael continued. 'Mr Marriot's people seem to have been given nothing at all to go on. And I'm not sure how much more help Beck and I can give. Even so, I'd back his people to find whoever's behind this thing if the time scale was two years instead of two weeks.'

Bill Marriot, mollified without wishing to be, said nothing. Becket Bradie eventually broke the silence. 'I think maybe I'd like to add something here. Seems to me there's got to be at least a possibility that, if we go with this, it just might be the last we hear of it. At least for the rest of the decade. And even supposing they do come back for more, like Mr Marriot here says, we wouldn't be in any worse position than we are now.'

'What would it cost?'

It took a moment or two for Toni Restelle's sudden change of tack to register, and Michael became aware that both the Chief of Staff and the National Security Adviser were looking to him for an answer. He paused only for a moment. 'The bottom line here isn't dollars and cents. What'll make the difference is the muscle the US can put behind it. Anything like eighty per cent vaccination coverage means governments getting serious, not just making speeches and buying in a few more air-conditioned Jeeps. And not just today's governments. Incoming administrations as well, at least for the next few years. Some of them are going to want to get on with the job of their own accord and they'll welcome all the help they can get, and others are going to need pushing every step of the way. You can always get a minister of health or a provincial governor to say he's on board, but nothing really happens unless their political masters make it clear it's for real – that it's more than just another paper priority. It's when the funds are there waiting to be drawn down, when the logistical difficulties are made to disappear, when the Cabinet insists on a monthly progress report, when it's spelled out that jobs are on the line – that's when you get action. It isn't only or even mostly about the money, it's just as much about keeping feet to the fire.'

Toni Restelle glanced first at Warren Taylor then back to Michael. 'I hear you, Dr Lowell, but for present purposes I still need a figure. Bottom line for Uncle Sam.'

Michael met her eyes. 'Whoever these people are, they've

done their homework. The figure in that statement is in the right ballpark. Five or six hundred million a year for the rest of the decade. For the US, I don't know. Depends on how much other countries could be persuaded to chip in at some kind of pledging conference. But' – and Michael at this point looked deliberately from one to the other of the officials around the table – 'I'm not going to apologize for coming back to this. In the end it would come down to political leverage, and very probably some heavyweight leaning on governments that were all talk and no action.'

Toni Restelle held Michael's eyes for a moment then turned to the CDC Director. 'Becket?'

'I agree with everything Michael's just said. It's not about commitments on paper. And on the cost – I'd defer to Michael if we're talking worldwide. But I should tell you it might well cost the US more than that to restart routine smallpox immunization at home, not to mention what we'd probably have to pony up to help other countries do the same. Just to give you some idea, we're estimating that not having to give a shot of smallpox vaccine to every citizen of the US is saving the Treasury around a hundred million dollars a year right now.'

Michael held himself in check, but the Chief of Staff had noticed the hesitation. 'Dr Lowell?'

Michael raised his fingertips from the table just a fraction to indicate that what he was about to say wasn't a major consideration. 'Might be worth adding – there can be a whole lot of kudos in a thing like this. The Soviets know all about it. They got a lot out of smallpox, especially in India.'

Warren Taylor looked up, surprised. 'I thought that was us?'

'It pretty well was, in the end, especially in the toughest spots. But it was Zhdanov who proposed eradication back in '59 and it was the Soviets who kicked the whole thing off, donated hundreds of millions of vaccine shots. Got a lot of political mileage out of it, especially in South Asia.'

The clock stood at half past twelve when Toni Restelle, after a glance at the National Security Adviser, placed both hands face down on the table. 'Okay, gentlemen, unless there's anything else I think that's a wrap. Lunch is right down the hall. By all means take a walk outside, explore the place or whatever, but remember this is a public place. Can I ask you all to be back here at, say, 2.30?

Michael Lowell and Becket Bradie, wearing neither coats nor gloves, walked the lakeside path, enjoying the startling exposure to the elements after the closeted intensity of the morning. The day was becoming colder, a wind springing up, a dullness of cloud descending on the Shawangunks. By unspoken consent, the first part of the walk was accomplished in silence, the path climbing steadily away from the lake towards the outline of a gazebo on the clifftop.

Becket stepped inside and leant on the rail, looking down on the quarter-mile stretch of ice and the unlikely edifice of Mohonk Mountain House. 'Be good to come back here some day with nothing to worry about.'

'When did you first get to hear about this thing, Beck?'

'Tuesday night. Hughes, the UN guy, found the envelope on his doormat about nine o'clock. Called me at home. He's on the Centers' Federal Advisory Committee.'

'Smart move.'

'Yeah, didn't do a whole lot for my weekend. Sorry you had to get dragged in. Glad I caught you in New York, though.'

'And the Chief of Staff was the one you called?'

'Yeah. Toni. Stroke of luck there. Known her since she was a kid. Grew up in the same street back in Portland. Parents been friends for years. It meant Tuesday night's little communication got through to the President in what our Mr Marriot would no doubt call a hop, step and a jump. Took just a little while to get my head around the girl next door being Chief of Staff, but after a couple of meetings with the grown-up version I have to say it doesn't seem so strange anymore.'

'Powerful position.'

'You betcha. And a lot of it comes right out of controlling the information flow. President's right to use her as cut-out of course, preserve deniability and all. Result is, she gets to decide what he hears as well as who he sees, not to mention relaying the decisions back in whatever way seems best. The way Edith Wilson ran the country right after World War One.'

'And you don't approve?'

'I do if it's Toni Restelle, adult edition thereof. Somebody else in there I might be more worried.'

'Beck, I've been waiting to ask you – how's Paul doing?'

Both men looked down on the stillness of the frozen lake a hundred feet below where two or three fallen pines were frozen into the ice. The silence said that there was nothing of good cheer to be relayed. Eventually Becket turned away from the view. 'Brave. As you'd expect. Fact is, he doesn't have long.'

Michael looked down at the beaten earth floor of the gazebo. 'Anne and the boys?'

'Can't imagine what they're going through.'

'He still at work?'

'We're battling with him, telling him to take off, spend time with the family. It's the obvious cliché, Mike, but, when you think about it, it's not necessarily the easy option.'

The breeze was now being forced up from the lake at an eye-watering rush and they were about to turn and head back when the figure of Warren Taylor appeared at the top of the climb, treading warily in his business shoes. Slightly out of breath, he sank on to one of the rough wooden benches. 'You fellas didn't get yourselves lunch?'

'We thought we'd clear our heads first. Maybe grab a sandwich at that coffee counter place.'

'Give me a couple minutes and I'll walk down with you. Plenty of time. I imagine Toni is still briefing the President on this morning's little discussion.'

Becket Bradie took the bench opposite. 'She didn't appear to be taking notes.'

Warren Taylor smiled. 'Not a single one, but I'd bet any money the President has a succinct account of everything germane by the time I sit down with him at two o'clock. Fact I'd go a whole lot further. I'd say Toni will have gotten him facing the right way before he's finished his Key Lime pie.'

As Becket frowned his surprise, Michael seated himself on one of the benches, pulling his jacket closed. Warren Taylor took a few more moments to recover, then turned away from his two companions to begin addressing an imaginary fourth occupant of the gazebo. 'While the Bureau's spinning its wheels, Mr President, you got a difficult choice to make here. On the one hand you give the order to alert a few hundred thousand public-health officials to keep an eye out for an outbreak of smallpox, with a real strong possibility of the mother and father of a panic, clamour for vaccines, shortages everyplace, honeymoon over, history of the first hundred days already written, administration's not up to the job of protecting the American people.' The National Security Adviser paused and held up a hand, glancing at his companions but then turning again to the imaginary occupant of the gazebo. 'On the other hand, sir, you get to make a historic speech, a Kennedy moment you might call it, committing your administration to an enterprise that boosts the prestige of the United States all around the known world, lets everybody know the heart of a great humanitarian beats inside the tough welfare reformer, gives you a legacy to die for and puts you in with a shout for a Nobel Prize. Plus, by the way, sir, we're talking nickel-and-dime stuff. Price of a couple of aircraft carriers.' Again he glanced back to check the reaction, but once more held up a hand. 'And what's more, Mr President, this way we get the precious gift of time for the Bureau to hunt down whoever's behind this thing. And if they don't, and the bastards come back for more, why, I don't rightly like to say this, sir, but by that time it'll likely be somebody else's problem.'

The National Security Adviser finally turned to face the other two. 'Now how difficult do you fellas think that decision's gonna be?'

Becket blew on his hands. 'That's the way you think he'll go?'

Warren Taylor got to his feet and turned for a last look at the view. 'I dare say there'll be a little interlude of chin music about the principle of the thing, and of course he'll want a day or so to think about it. But in my opinion the toughest problem he's going to face is how to make the rest of the speech as good as those passages somebody out there has very kindly drafted for him.'

At half past two that afternoon, Becket Bradie, Bill Marriot and Michael Lowell were informed by Toni Restelle that the President was taking the rest of the weekend to make the call. Drs Lowell and Bradie were asked to hold themselves available in case further consultation might be needed. Both were assigned suites in the central tower block and again warned that Mohonk Mountain House was a semi-public place.

Afterwards, the two spent an hour sketching the outline of a provisional plan for coping with the news of the threat becoming public. At four o'clock, when afternoon tea was served, they took a time out on the veranda, breathing in the pine-scented air and taking a last look at the lake. Michael wrapped both hands around his tea cup and leaned his elbows on the balustrade. 'What do we know about Bill Marriot?'

'Only what Toni's told me. Ex-US Navy SEAL. Came up through military intelligence. No title. No listed public profile. Sits at the top table at both the Bureau and the CIA apparently. Go-to guy whenever they have to be coerced into co-operating.'

Michael had been hoping to discuss Marriot's request for names before meeting with the man again, but at that moment Marriot himself appeared on the veranda, his body language making it clear that this was no time to be drinking tea and taking in the view.

For the next hour, Michael dredged up a dozen names of researchers and laboratories, many of them laboratories in the Soviet Union or the Middle East, some of the researchers dead or retired or moved on, and all of them likely to lead Bill Marriot's people precisely nowhere. It was distasteful work and he could not wait for the meeting to finish, unable to dismiss from his mind a picture of himself standing atop a ladder with a bucketful of fish as Marriot rose repeatedly from the water to take one red herring after another from his outstretched hand. Pressed, he had agreed to provide the WHO's list of the eight hundred or so institutions around the world known to be carrying out research on viruses. There was nothing secret about the list, and he had also suggested that Marriot's people scan the *Index Medicus* for the last few years to identify the laboratories that had published papers on smallpox or been cited in the references. Again, this was no secret; it was how the WHO had compiled its own lists in the first place. By the evening, he was suffering from a rare headache and opted out of dinner, picking up his key at the desk and retreating to his room on the third floor of the tower block.

There he opened a window and propped himself against a pillow on the canopied bed, surrendering to silence, allowing his surroundings to ease the tensions of the day.

The Mountain House eschewed obvious luxury. The charm of the place resided in its settled quality, the quietness of old floorboards, the weight of brocade drapes framing the leaded windows, the polished nineteenth-century furniture, and the tranquillity of an establishment that had been receiving guests for a century and a half and knew how to do the job without trying too hard. For a few minutes he allowed himself to imagine staying here with Seema; sitting side by side in the steamer chairs on the veranda, or skating out on the lake, or setting off for the day on one of the trails into the hills, or chatting comfortably beside a Victorian fireplace. Or here, in this room, this quiet, this bed. It was now twenty-four hours since he had taken the call.

He stared up at the elaborate moulding of the ceiling light, enjoying the smell of beeswaxed wood mixed with the piney tang of the mountain air. He closed his eyes, waiting for the headache to lift into the silence. On the edge of the lake, Bill Marriot appeared in a Homburg, skating unsteadily with the help of a tubular chair. On the deserted jetty, Becket stood watching as Marriot neared the hole at the edge of the ice, doing nothing to warn him, speaking quietly of Paul Lewis's recovery, which seemed to be an established fact. He and Michael turned back together, but instead of the Mountain House there was now only a dilapidated gazebo, and when he stepped inside it was not Becket but his father by his side,

carrying the Gladstone bag. And it was his father who was
inserting the little fingers of both hands in the corners of his
mouth to perform the famous piercing whistle that would
warn Marriot of the danger. But the man out on the ice now
was not Marriot but Toby, who turned the chair around
and gave them a cheery wave. When he turned around the
Mountain House was there after all, and in the lobby a stone
chessboard before a blazing fire. There was no sign of the
slow, sarcastic smile as Benny rose to shake hands.

42 | A kiss is still a kiss

Michael breakfasted alone in the windowless ground-floor area that served coffee and croissants to early risers before the Mohonk dining room began serving its full breakfast menu. Just after seven o'clock he was joined by Toni Restelle. She declined coffee and informed him he was free to leave. Communication was to be kept to a minimum, so she would like to thank him now for his input; a car was available to take him to the station at Poughkeepsie whenever he was ready. All this in a manner that, though efficient, also left Michael wondering why the young Becket Bradie had not taken more notice of the girl next door.

Deciding that the Mountain House was better than a Manhattan hotel for the few hours more planning that were needed, Michael and Becket spent the morning fleshing out the previous day's preparedness plan, including agreeing a list of the individuals and institutions who would need to be brought in if the threat were made public. After lunch they were driven to the rail station at Poughkeepsie, from where Michael called Seema to ask if she could meet him at the East Side Airlines Terminal on 38th Street. He had already had himself rebooked on the overnight flight to Geneva.

The Metro North train that left Poughkeepsie some time

before four o'clock that afternoon was almost empty, being on its way to bring commuters home to the suburbs, and the two men had no trouble finding themselves seats in the centre of a deserted non-smoking carriage as the train began its long rumble down the Hudson Valley.

Becket took a last glance around the carriage. 'I'm going to be a busy man, Michael. My guess is you will be too.'

Michael shook his head. 'I can't see it happening.'

'No? You think the President wouldn't do 'most anything to stop that statement getting out? And any which way this thing breaks, the immunization thing's going right up the agenda. Right now nobody's even heard of the eighty-per-cent goal outside of our own charmed circle. Couple of weeks, that could change. Millions might know about it – what it could do, what it would take. And an awful lot of them might be persuaded. You guys ready for that?'

Michael watched the wealthy townships of upstate New York passing by in a blur. 'Be nice to be pushing on an open door, but we'd need an awful lot of help. Particularly from Atlanta.'

'While I'm there, you've got it.'

Michael nodded. 'I know. You back there tonight?'

'I wish. Last flight's already gone. Planning to call Camden Hughes, see if he's free for dinner.'

'You got clearance from your friend Marriot?'

Becket scowled at the thought. 'Camden Hughes is solid gold.'

Michael looked out of the window to the broad expanse of the river. The sun was low now, setting the Hudson on fire and casting the distant Catskills in purple. 'Seriously, Beck, you'd better assume Hughes is being watched. And his place will probably be bugged by now as well.'

'Maybe, but I'm not about to start avoiding the guy on

account of him being involved in the Civil Rights Movement.'

'Don't underestimate these guys. Could cause a lot of trouble.'

'Coming from someone who spent 'most all of yesterday afternoon blowin' smoke up Marriot's ass, I'll take that as seriously as it deserves.'

In the end they had less than half an hour together before Michael boarded the Carey's bus to Kennedy. Failing to find a bar or coffee shop, they walked the jogging path beside FDR Drive towards Riverside Plaza. For an instant, as they strolled these bleak surroundings, he thought about taking her hand in the cold, but was immediately deterred by how inappropriate it might seem. The only reason she had wanted to see him, even for a few minutes, was because she would be desperate to hear if there had been any developments. As they turned away from the wind screaming up the East River past the great residential tower blocks, their upper storeys lost in swirling cloud, he told her that the hunt for whoever had delivered the letter was going nowhere. He also told her that a response oversight team called the 'Mohonk Committee' had been set up, that it had been deliberating with the President and his Chief of Staff at a resort hotel in upstate New York for the last two days, and that as yet no decision on the response had yet been made.

As they turned to walk back towards the hangar-like structure of the East Side Airlines Terminal, Seema stopped, letting her hood fall back. She took both his gloved hands in hers and looked into his eyes for almost the first time since they had met that day. 'Michael, how do you know about this committee?'

'Because I'm on it.'

The last few passengers were about to board the silver

Carey's bus as he lowered his head and kissed her lips, gently, for the first time in twenty years. It was an awkward kiss, uncertain and brief, somewhere between a goodbye and a declaration. But a kiss.

43 | A little bit of your heart

Camden Hughes and Becket Bradie met at La Petite Marmite in Mitchell Place, an upscale restaurant popular for expense-account lunches but generally quiet in the evenings. The service was as starched as the white tablecloths and as uptight as the cut-glass goblets, but it was one of the few restaurants in Midtown with enough space between tables to allow of a private conversation.

When their order had been taken, Camden looked around to make sure that they were alone. 'Mohonk Mountain House. No, can't say I ever heard of it. And you say the President was there?'

'And half the Cabinet. Secretary of State. Defense. National Security Adviser. Some foreign-policy thing. We were just the sideshow.'

Camden, dressed as always in dark suit, white shirt and Fifties-vintage striped repp necktie, could not keep the curiosity out of his eyes. 'I'd like to hear about it, but no need at all to tell me anything I don't need to know.'

'Nothing much to tell anyway. No decision yet. I'd rather hear some more about the book. How's it coming along?'

'Well, thank you. Slowly, I think is the answer. But before that there's something I think I ought to tell you. I would surely have asked you back to Sutton Place this evening

297

to share a one-pot dinner and drink a little wine, but I thought maybe we'd be more comfortable in this uncomfortable setting seeing as how my home has been entered and searched, and I'm assuming it's now wired for sound.'

Becket frowned, returning the glass of iced water to the table, condensation making a damp ring on the cloth. 'I don't believe they did that.'

'I'll allow they were discreet.'

'How do you know they were there?'

Camden sighed. 'Man lives alone, he knows when a stranger's passed through. Little things. Hood on the Rolodex closed all the way when you're pretty sure you left it half open just where it sticks. Magazines your memory tells you were leaning the other way on the shelves. Papers maybe a tad too squared-up. More than that. Something in the air, not the smell exactly, just something a little bit different from all the other nights. Like I said, you live alone, someone passing through your life, man knows.'

'This is Marriot. Bill Marriot. FBI *and* CIA. He was up at this Mohonk place too. Kept on asking why they picked you.'

'Suppose the man's just doing his job.'

'To use his own words, the man's fucking flies. McCarthy mentality, only it's the Civil Rights Movement he seems to think is some kind of unAmerican activity.'

'Well, I guess there's no harm done, and certainly the unfortunate functionary at 935 Pennsylvania Avenue who drew the task of listening to the tapes is going to find the long winter evenings just flying by.'

Food arrived with a flourish and the two men remained silent as the wine bucket was placed on its stand. None of the adjacent tables was occupied but Becket glanced again around the restaurant. 'I'm really sorry that happened, Camden. Be just temporary. But I know it's not what you want in your own home.'

Camden frowned, thinking of the special importance that the privacy of his study and the few quiet hours of each day played in his life. 'I'll take it for a while. Then I've got some contacts of my own to call in. And of course a certain knowledge of the federal law in such matters that could make things awkward for your Mr Marriot if he pushes too hard or too long. Days are gone when the Bureau was a law unto itself. And, if I'm not mistaken, I seem to remember that little change came about after a group of citizens decided to employ distinctly illegal means.'

'Where are you headed, Camden?'

'Just sayin'. Those papers so inconveniently pushed through my door that night. I read them a second time. And a third. As I suspect you did. And I was wondering if just a little bit of your own heart wasn't singing from the same hymn sheet?'

'I asked Michael Lowell pretty much the same question this weekend. The WHO guy.'

'And?'

'And he was about as evasive as you and I are being. Good thing we're not in your apartment, by the way. But as we're not, what went through your own mind?'

Camden Hughes put down his knife and fork and leaned forward, elbows on the table, fingers locked. 'Is it true, Becket? Five million youngsters every year? Vaccines sitting there costing a dime a time? No one bothering to get out there and do it?'

Becket Bradie also rested his knife and fork. 'We generally dress it up a little differently, but the answer's yes, it's true.'

Camden stared, frowning his incredulity. 'And it could be done, like they say, if anyone cared?'

'The answer is yes.'

After a long pause, Camden pushed his half-eaten dinner to one side. 'Most of my life's been spent insisting on what you might want to call correct procedure. Due process. Letter of the law. Even when sometimes it seemed a little stuffy. And that was because there was always something bigger behind the little things. Something bigger than the petty details I found myself insisting on. Due process was a long time coming. It's what's replaced might is right, power growing out of the barrel of the gun, or the stock of a whip. But when I read that statement… the thought of those kids. And, I have to tell you, though I try not to have any kind of a chip on my old shoulder, I could not entirely help but recall that these are 'most all black and brown kids.'

'So a piece of you sang with what they were saying.'

'Bigger piece than I'd've thought. You?'

Becket met his companion's eyes. 'Camden, best years of my own life were spent with a fine bunch of colleagues trying our damnedest to rid the world of a disease that brought more death and distress to this world than any other. And I'm telling you smallpox doesn't have any competition for that title. Not even the plague gets close. And the thought that anyone might threaten to release it into the world again should fill me with anger. Does fill me with anger. But when I read that thing… I'm not going to tell you I couldn't understand where they were coming from. I thought about that statement saying it's like we've found a cheap cure for cancer but decided not to bother with it because it only kills the poor. First off, I saw it as just hyperbole. But I kept coming back to it, playing with the figures, and I have to admit it's pretty much on the money.'

After a long silence, Camden Hughes poured more wine and again checked the restaurant. 'So what's going to happen.

You have any idea?'

'I don't know. There's a theory that we're dealing with sane, intelligent people who wouldn't dream of using the virus, people who are hoping just the threat to go public will be enough. If the President buys that, he could decide to do nothing. Call their bluff. But the risk there is that they'll go to second and hit the media with that persuasive little statement. And if the President thought that was likely to happen he could take pre-emptive action. Hang tough on TV. US won't give in to threats. This thing can be handled. But one or two people over the weekend were distinctly of the mind that he might not want to risk a public panic.'

Camden Hughes sipped wine, not taking his eyes off his companion. 'You mean he might even go with it?'

'It's one possibility.'

A minute elapsed as Camden absorbed the thought. 'Well, I guess all I can say is, worse things have happened.'

'I guess.'

'What does your childhood sweetheart think?'

Becket smiled. 'I don't know. She plays the part of the *rapporteuse*, the go-between, only you can't quite escape the feeling...'

'That she might be running the show?'

'She for sure directs the traffic.'

Camden chewed for a while, amused. 'And your friend from the World Health Organization?'

'We might just be able to get it back in the bottle as far as the US is concerned, but globally it's a whole different ball game.'

Camden nodded. 'And your man Marriot?'

'Marriot thought the whole thing must be coming from someone in "our line of country" as he kept on saying. Some individual or maybe a group working in public health who've gotten themselves frustrated.'

'Not entirely unreasonable.'

'No. It's not. Have to admit something about the guy made me think everything he said was unreasonable even when it wasn't. We pointed out the spelling mistake – no one in "our line of country" likely to flunk "diphtheria" in a spelling bee.'

Camden looked dubious. 'Mmm. Just might be. But… statement like that – fair standard of literacy in the English language, I think you'd have to say – could be said to be the kind of error that smells of the lamp, if you catch my drift.' He looked up at his companion, a smile brimming in his eyes. 'Come to think of it, could even be someone at the WHO or the CDC wanting to deflect a little attention.'

'You're a suspicious man, Camden.'

'Easy. Not a suspicion I'm about to pass on to your Mr Marriot any time soon.'

'Marriot's going to love your book by the way. Mentioned it several times up at Mohonk. Big fan of Marcus Garvey.' Becket paused for a moment. 'I'm ashamed to ask, but who was he?'

Camden's voice relaxed, rising from a half whisper to its normal quiet. 'Black leader in the years right in front of World War Two. Born in Jamaica. Spent his life in the US. Believed in uniting the black race wherever they were in the world, wresting economic independence from whites. Bit like Fanon – "liberty has to be taken, not given". Ahead of his time in preaching the mind has to be freed as well as the body. Started *The Negro World*, of which I am the proud owner of one of the very few complete sets in existence. Also founded the Black Star Shipping Line that got him into a whole lot of trouble. Predecessor of the Panthers in a way – "For over three hundred years the white man has been our oppressor, and he naturally is not going to liberate us… We have to liberate ourselves".'

'I can see why Marriot is a fan. What was it that drew you?'

'Oh, I don't know. More the fact that his life pulls in so many strands from such interesting times. As a man, I have to say I prefer Langston Hughes. No relation as far as I know. Met him once or twice. But there's a whole slew of books on Hughes. You know *Freedom's Plow*?'

'No.'

'Never yet met anyone who did. In my book it gets a shot at the great American poem. *First in the heart is the dream – then the mind starts seeking a way.*

'So how long before the book's finished?'

'Oh, I should think I'll have to retire before I can really get to work.'

'How long is that?'

'No set retirement age for those of my exalted rank, but the option arises 'bout two years seven months from now.'

Becket smiled. 'And, when the time comes, what would you say about playing a bigger role at the CDC?'

Camden Hughes looked over his wine glass. 'Down there among the swamps and the medical mafia? No sir, I'll be staying right here in the land of the free. Besides, a man's about a foot shorter down there if he doesn't have an MD to his handle.'

'Think about it. Still leave you time for Garvey.'

Camden Hughes smiled and shook his head. 'Time comes when it's right to take your hand off of the plow. Poet never thought of that. Too young, I expect. So, what happens next? You out of this thing?'

Becket shook his head. 'If the President decides to hang tough I guess I'll be heading up the response team. Try to get us in shape. Assuming Marriot's people are still chasing their tails.'

Camden's expression became stern for a moment at the

mention of Marriot, gradually softening into an amused inquiry. 'And if your friend Ms Restelle calls it the other way? If the Chief, in his infinite wisdom, hits the airwaves with that little speech someone has very thoughtfully drafted for him?'

'I guess I'd be called in anyway. Start planning how best to help get the ball rolling on immunization.'

Camden leaned forward slightly over the table as the wine waiter threatened. 'Now maybe you'd like to tell me, Dr Bradie, which would you rather be doing?'

44 | Competing with James Dean

Hélène unbuttoned the man's striped shirt in which the little girl had been wrapped and saw what she expected: wrinkled grey skin being sucked in between the ribs with each shallow breath. For a moment there had been no movement at all save for the liquid fear swimming in the eyes. And then from somewhere the tiny body found the energy for a harsh, paroxysmal cough. And then another. She rested a hand on the bones of the shoulder, noticing the dry, cracked skin around the lips as she placed the stethoscope on the chest, listening to the unmistakable cracking, snapping and whistling of advanced TB.

Half an hour later she was back in her own room, lying on the bed under the steady motion of the ceiling fan and weeping for what she had done. The injection she had given wouldn't do a damn thing. Its only purpose had been to help protect herself from the mother's grief. There was nothing else she could have done for the child. But still she wept tears of pity and shame.

She dozed miserably for a while, then forced herself to get up and carry the week's mail out to the veranda. The sun was slanting under the eaves, still fierce enough to burn, and she shuffled the wicker chair back into the shade. The tiredness in her limbs was still there, but the swelling in the lymph nodes had calmed down over the last few days.

Seema's letter was chatty and inconsequential until the last paragraph.

> *No word yet on our application. Apparently Toby wrote us a marvellous letter of recommendation, though I haven't seen it myself. Otherwise all well here. Stephen still around, though getting fidgety I think. Michael had to delay his return at the last moment on account of some meeting, so I was able to see him again, just briefly, when he came through town again on his way to JFK. He said to send you his love and say he'd be in touch soon.*

And the postscript that came as no surprise at all:

> *I don't know why I didn't tell him this, but I'll tell you – I'm living in hope.*

Hélène looked up from the flimsy air-mail paper towards the glow of the setting sun. The night *gardien* had arrived and was installing himself by the gate, setting his machete beside him on the earth.

Becket Bradie called Michael at home late in the day, Geneva time, on Tuesday, February 24th. Figures were guardedly exchanged about vaccine stocks and Michael was able to confirm that the CASE manual had been received and checked. Other than that the conversation amounted to little more than a courtesy call: a week had passed since the meeting at Mohonk Mountain House. No word had come down from Washington.

Michael inquired after Paul. The news was not good.

Seema sat at the window table of a favourite coffee shop on West 8th Street. Out on the Avenue of the Americas, two black teenagers wearing only T-shirts against the February cold were rollerblading through the traffic. On the corner of Greenwich Avenue, a wino was shouting abuse at people buying newspapers from a street vendor and an elderly woman was cleaning up after her dog. An ordinary New York morning.

The absurdity was that she had found herself able to work again, making progress with the book in a way that had not been possible for weeks. It had happened without any great resolution on her own part. Perversely, it seemed to have something to do with what they were embarked upon. And something to do with Michael. Again today she had turned down Stephen's offer of lunch in order to spend the day in the library. But whenever she emerged from her work she was aware of being suspended over a bottomless abyss. The search would surely be in full cry by now, and she had almost made a mantra of Michael's words about the impossibility of their being traced. Ashamed of her self-concern, she tried to recall the conversations that had led up to it all, in an Oxford garden, in the cold of Central Park, in the comfort of her own apartment. And always she came back to the heart-in-mouth consideration of what might be happening in response, each line of speculation running into the sands of the unknowable, her thoughts ending up, as always, with the man she had thought she had known.

When Stephen awoke from his afternoon doze it was as if he were opening his eyes to the Chelsea Hotel for the first time. Surely a strange choice for someone who could afford a suite at the Waldorf. He went to the bathroom and splashed water on his face. The lock had no key and the curtain was a bed sheet loosely tacked across the window. Was this all that the Bohemian ambience really came down to? One or two battered pieces of period furniture. An ancient copy of the *SCUM Manifesto* on the nightstand. A mawkish poem half-written, half-scratched, in biro on the inside of one of the drawers. Hallways that stank of stale weed. And a few original but bad paintings with which unrecognized geniuses might be supposed to have paid their bills.

He returned to the bedroom, vaguely wondering if his inability to decide between the Chelsea and the Waldorf was in some way emblematic of who he was; a man whose sense of himself seemed to have no fixed abode. And for a terrifying moment the wiring of his brain seemed to fuse in an intense burst of nothingness, as though who he was had somehow emptied itself of any capacity to control itself, burning out thought, memory, personality, self. When it was over he stepped out on to the wrought-iron balcony, still carrying the towel, breathing heavily and glad to exchange the smell of stale ganja for the fresh diesel and petrol fumes arising from 23rd Street sixty feet below.

The trouble was he could not decide from one day to the next whether he loved or hated this city, finding its anonymity elating one moment and depressing the next. Below him a yellow cab had come to a stop under the awning. On the corner of 7th Avenue a group of old men were stamping their feet in the cold and drinking from bottles wrapped in brown paper bags. He stepped back into the room and looked at his watch. It was too early to go out to dinner. Maybe tomorrow he would make the move. Maybe to the Plaza. Swap Bob Dylan for Jay Gatsby.

Toby's lethargy had not been lifted by the announcement that they had been awarded the Concorde contract on the basis of no more than his outline pitch. It had been a fillip to his own position but had failed to stir any of the old excitement. Only the mention of more or less unlimited free tickets for Concorde had sparked any interest. At least whenever there were empty seats, which apparently was virtually every flight and probably explained the haste to appoint a new agency. He sipped his drink. Why didn't the damn thing fly somewhere useful? Abidjan, for example. Not that he'd go. Making a pathetic pink pest of himself. No chance of competing with whatsisname – Saint Fabrice of Boggley Wollah. Or was that India? Courage and idealism a cut above the average, apparently. No doubt handsome as hell. Plus he had the over-whelming advantage of being dead. Like trying to compete with … James Dean seemed somehow inappropriate but it was all he could think of at the moment.

He waved to a group of fellow Australians beckoning him to join them in one of the booths at the far side of the bar, no doubt to continue their week-long argument over that underarm delivery at the MCG. Personally, he was quite grateful to the brothers Chappell for demonstrating that it was possible for an Australian to sink even lower in his own estimation than Toby Jenks. He shook his head in response, indicating his intention to leave, feeling strangely out of it all, itching to talk to one of the others who now inhabited the same lonely universe as his own. He didn't bother to hide a yawn. Time to go home. Not that there'll be anybody there. God knows where she might be. Away with the pixies probably. He eased himself down from the bar stool. Time to cut and run, mate. Bail out. While there's still time to spin it like you quit at the top. Done it all. Bored. Fresh fields and pastures new. Little place in Provence. Grow a few vines. Learn to cook. Or paint. Up at dawn. Walk six hours a day. Get back down to 180 pounds. Write the slim book of verse.

45 | Happy hour

Friday, March 6th, 1981

Hélène sank back in the wicker chair, more tired than she could ever remember. Tired and remote. Just over two weeks had passed and nothing had been heard. Maybe nothing would be heard. Maybe the unbelievable thing they had done would just fade away eventually to be forgotten like a vivid dream. And, if one or more of them should happen to meet again some time, perhaps they would be too embarrassed even to mention it.

By the gate, the *gardien* was emptying a bag of charcoal into the brazier. She looked at her watch. It would be getting near six o'clock in London, too, and Toby would already be well launched on 'happy hour', a term she had learned in New York and thought of often since. She settled back in the shade, realizing that the thought of Toby's happy hour made her sad, knowing that there was something about him she could still love.

With an effort, she fetched a glass of water and the portable radio out onto the veranda, turning the dial to push the red line along to the first of five or six possible wavelengths. The last of the sun had disappeared but the warmth lingered on, and for a moment she allowed herself to think of beginning a new life in Canada, indulging in a fantasy of getting Toby into shape with hours of the cross-country skiing she had so missed over the years. Hard to imagine, in the still-warm African evening, those vast and glistening slopes, the serrations of snow-laden pines, the taste of damp wool over her mouth.

After poking the aerial this way and that, the BBC World Service found a way through and she balanced the set on the top rail of the balcony. Sinking down again into the wicker chair, she tried to concentrate on a discussion about the South African government's Group Areas Amendment Bill. She would treat herself to a more modern shortwave when next she passed through an airport. Or maybe soon she wouldn't be needing one. Her thoughts strayed this way and that, following the gentle promptings of association and memory, as if guided by nothing more than the faint breeze that stirred the sand in the compound. The child with TB wasn't the worst of it. All week the children's ward had been filling up with a measles outbreak. Probably half of those now lying in the extra cots would die.

The signal had improved slightly and a government spokesperson was making great play of the decision to exclude sports from the Bill. Normally she would have been interested. But there was now only one real interest. She sipped her drink. There were no regrets. And if she occasionally felt fear or panic then she had only to think of the two or three mothers who would be quietly sobbing on the steps of the clinic when she went back on shift in the morning. In any case, it was only a selfish fear. Fear, and something else. A something else that had taken a long time to bring to the surface: a desperate desire for Fabrice to know what she had tried to do.

From outside the gate came the sound of a motorbike hammering down the road, making her tense her muscles to think of the children on the ward. Tonight they would be in her dreams. Despite all the years, she had failed to cultivate that necessary degree of detachment that all health professionals need to acquire. And perhaps that, too, was part of the impossibility of going on.

She was awakened by the jaunty signature tune of the BBC World Service News, redolent of Empire, as if Queen Victoria herself had come prancing on to the veranda holding up her skirts. The sun was losing some if its ardour as she listened to a report about the highjacking of a Continental Airlines flight. Eventually she sat back again and rested her head on the cushion. Was she really going to go back home after all these years? Abandon what she had done with her life? Had she never really been committed, deep down? Had she come to Africa because she was scared she wouldn't be able to succeed in her own world? And had she stayed out of pride, or not knowing what else to do?

... the goal of immunizing all the world's children against the major killer diseases of childhood.

She sat upright, unsure if the words had been in a dream.

That goal, too, can and will be achieved by the end of the current decade. And it too will be a giant step for mankind.

She covered her face with her hands and dropped to her knees by the balustrade before gripping the bars of the balcony rail and pushing her ear close to the tiny radio.

To those countries across the globe struggling to break the bonds of disease, we pledge our support. In the face of the difficulties to be confronted, which will be many and great, we say – ask what America can do for you.

A minute later she lay on her bed, sobbing uncontrollably into her pillow.

Perhaps it was the loneliness of living in a hotel, but there was no doubt that Stephen had developed a kind of compulsion for walking the streets of New York. And so it was that on the bitterly cold afternoon of Friday, March 6th, he found himself sitting at a metal table outside a Dunkin' Donuts outlet just off Times Square. He had been there for the best part of an hour, sipping coffee and reading through the notes he had made, looking up from time to time to wonder anew at the late twentieth-century madness that was arrayed before him like some surreal stage set. Here was false consciousness made flesh. Capitalism's *reductio ad absurdum.* Here was the maelstrom of excess, cheek by jowl with poverty and degradation. Here was the sensational unashamedness of commercialism gone mad. Here was an overwhelmingly senseless crusade against the senses under the banners of greed, envy and lust. And here was every flashy temptation, every soulless joy, every base appetite titillated and promoted in ever-changing patterns of artificial light while in the streets below the huddled, broken lives shuffled along, heads bowed, seizing on a food wrapper left in a trash can or a half-smoked cigarette in the gutter. And here, too, stretching down 42nd Street, was the scarcely less obvious prostitution of the dead-eyed girls of indeterminate age posing in the entrances of strip joints offering 'continuous shows', 'no waiting,' 'ten different girls' and 'as much as you can see for $1.00'. And, in the centre of it all, running under that famous, ever-changing Coca-Cola commercial, a ribbon of electronic figures recorded the latest changes in the Dow and the Nikkei, interrupted occasionally by snippets of news about the death of a movie star or a nuclear test on some atoll in the South Pacific.

He returned to his notes, scribbling another line on the concept of alienation, dashing off the words he would look up later – 'human beings cannot be free if they are subject to forces that determine their thoughts, their ideas, their very nature of human beings'. A shadow fell across the table and he lifted his head to see a figure standing before him, oppressively close, the smell of sour clothes pushing up against his face as a cup of coins was thrust towards him. He dug in his jeans pocket and found two quarters, glancing up only briefly at the man, the scarred mind visible in the eyes. The man moved on and in the space where he had been the giant advertising screen was mindlessly changing the pattern of lights ... *Coca-Cola – It's the Best* and, running underneath it in two-foot-high pixellated letters, the words '*US to immunize world's children ...*'

Toby Jenks was still at the office, though the rest of the department had gone home hours ago. So far, he had restricted himself to two Scotch-and-sodas and was managing to maintain himself in that state of mellow, sunlit well-being that fell well short of the darker shadowlands of inebriation. Opposite him the bank of television screens were tuned to different channels, all with the sound turned down. The letter of resignation sitting before him on the desk had taken just a few minutes to write. And the decision itself hardly any longer to make. Why his path should suddenly have become clear was, he thought, just one of life's little mysteries. Probably it had been foolish to think that there had to be a plan in place. Just do it.

He glanced up at the bank of screens, two of them showing the same picture of Leonid Brezhnev while the others paid tribute to Walter Cronkite. The thing to do now, just before he headed off to Soho, was to write to Hélène. Nothing fancy. No stupid witticisms. Just tell her you've resigned. 'No intention of pressing for an answer ... just thought I'd let you know ... fresh start ... offer still open ... always assuming still at liberty.'

He was beginning the letter when a simultaneous change on all of the screens caught his eye and he glanced up to see a mugshot of the President of the United States addressing a microphone. He returned to his letter but, after a second or two, picked up the remote from the desk and brought up the sound.

Twenty years ago, President John F Kennedy committed the United States to the goal of putting a man on the moon within a decade.

He held down the volume rocker on the remote.

Today, the United States commits itself to another great goal, a goal for our times, a goal here on earth…

When his secretary came in to see what the commotion was about, she found her boss standing on the desk yelling, 'You little ripper!'

Stephen remained for several minutes on the southwest corner of 42nd Street, fixed there by the ribbon of news carrying its telegraphese over the heads of the tourists and the street vendors, the prostitutes and the drug dealers, the down-and-outs and the millionaires, the traffic lights changing ineffectually over the gridlocked chaos of Times Square. Fazed by the riot of frenzied advertising competing for his attention on all sides, he waited for the message to come around again, thinking for a moment he might have projected his inner imaginings onto this most external of worlds. But no, there it was again, chasing along after *Walter Cronkite signs-off from CBS News… US to immunize world's children… President pledges…*

He closed his eyes against the mayhem, wondering which world was real.

At first he looked frantically for a cab, then abandoned the idea in favour of running all the way downtown, only to stop and wave at any cab whether showing a light or not. Even to himself it was the strangest of reactions, this surging through his veins, this quality of lightness, as if some great and permanent weight had been lifted from his spine, his breathing becoming easier and deeper even as he became out of breath, as if he were standing on a rarefied mountain top rather than in one of the most polluted places on earth, as if the frustrations of the years, the poisonous clouds of angst and resentment, were blowing away in a cleansing breeze. 'Live with significance' – he had never been without its sharp spur and chafing bridle – and there it had been in red electronic letters scrolling across the world.

On the corner of Macy's a chequered cab slid into the kerb and fifteen minutes later he was pressing the intercom in the lobby of Seema's building. He forced himself to take the stairs at a steadier pace so as not to be out of breath. On the top landing, the door was already open.

'Turn on the TV.'

The loft had become too small to contain all that was happening in Seema's brain. Stephen, in any case, was slumped on the couch completely lost in his own thoughts. She made an excuse, not knowing if he had heard, and slipped out of the door, intending to buy wine and something to eat.

She turned right on West 4th. Where was Michael now? She had tried a dozen times to reach him, but he was not answering. And there was no way to contact Hélène, except by leaving a message. She turned onto the Avenue of the Americas, glad of the crowds and the lights and the bars and the fact that no one was taking any notice of the tears that were stinging her face in the freezing air. She stopped by a mini-mart and took a basket from the rack, not able to think beyond wine and cheese and crackers. With the bag in her arms, she hurried on to nowhere, unwilling to stop walking, as if to stop would be to change to a different reality. In the window of the TV store C-Span was reshowing the scene that they had watched half an hour earlier, a fixed-camera view of the White House press room, the President silently miming the words she was certain that Toby had composed.

It was the time of day when the surface of the lake appears brighter than the sky and the first pink touches the distant majesty of Mont Blanc. Michael had left the office earlier than usual on a fine spring evening and headed home along the lakeshore road. Arriving on the Quai des Alpes, he managed to find a space on the waterfront and strolled through the streets of the old town, picking up a few things for his evening meal. It was unseasonably warm, and he sat for twenty minutes by the lake enjoying a cold beer and the soft breeze. He could not look at the lake now without also seeing the typewriter sitting in the silt two hundred metres down.

Back in the apartment, he ate spaghetti with fresh tomatoes and basil, the *International Herald Tribune* propped against the bottle of olive oil beside his plate. At eight o'clock he washed up and went to sit by the window, switching on the reading light over his chair and intending to spend the time before bed reading a colleague's report on the field trials of a new protocol on Integrated Management of Childhood Illness.

After a few pages he put down the report and reached up to switch off the lamp. Darkness had fallen, dividing the view from his window into the nearby lights of the town and the far distant lights of Yvoire and the French shore. Would she also be eating alone tonight, reading in the cane-backed chair, perhaps with the wood-stove lit and the candles burning? Or was she out to dinner with friends or colleagues? Or might she have a date? He thought of calling, but dismissed the idea. He had already called twice since getting back. On the second occasion the conversation had been stilted, strained. She had obviously thought he was calling with news and had waited for some cautious, coded word that might give her a clue as to what might be happening. Once it had become clear there had been no special reason for the call, she had tried to help him out, keeping the conversation going with what little news she had of work, of a lunch with Tom Keeley, and of a city showing signs of beginning to emerge from winter.

At work all day, he had been conscious of looking for an excuse to schedule another trip, and of hoping for a fax or a call from Atlanta. In June he would be required at the inter-agency UCI consultation. Until then he would have to bide his time.

When the telephone rang he wondered for a wild moment if it might be New York, or Washington, but heard instead the heavily accented tones of the Director-General asking him, without preliminaries, if he had heard the news.

He listened for two minutes, then said goodnight and turned on the lamp. For a few moments more he sat calmly at his desk, unable to digest what he had heard, yet thinking that his boss might have sounded a little bit more excited. Eventually he picked up a pen to draft the response that the DG had asked for. But he could not begin. Could not conceive of a response. Could not dare to believe.

After a minute he reached for the portable radio on his desk. Willis Conover's jazz programme was in full swing as he tuned in to Voice of America to await the next bulletin.

A few minutes later he walked out on to the balcony. He had been given the bottle of Champagne years before, but it had remained at the back of his fridge. It had always seemed a waste to open it alone. Fighting back unaccustomed tears, he watched the cork fly out into the night. Then raised his glass in the general direction of America.

Stephen stirred on the couch. The bottle of wine stood empty on the coffee table. He opened his eyes, his world reassembling itself, and found himself alone in the apartment. He thought he remembered Seema saying something about going out to buy food.

He sat up, feeling sick and empty, his head swirling unpleasantly. He needed coffee, but sank back into the couch, the taste in his mind as stale as the wine on his parched palate. Motionless, he stared at the white slope above, watching the spidery nebula of the junk in his eyes swimming around the ceiling. The television had been turned off. Euphoria had gone. In its place, some portion of bitterness had returned. Michael was the one who had done it all, run the whole show. And in any case nothing fundamental had changed, though no doubt the others would be running around congratulating themselves.

From out of nowhere he experienced again that instant, frightening fusing of the brain's wiring, a momentary suspension of all conscious capacities. When the moment had passed, his world returned to him, though under what seemed like a deep shadow. He reached out an arm to see if there might be anything left in the bottle. Above, a sudden rain had begun to tap at the skylight. Breathing more quickly, he turned to face the spiral staircase in the corner. He was alone with the virus not two metres away in the little fridge he had carried up the stairs only two weeks ago.

So many the world's injustices. So uneven the struggle. What was it Lenin had said? 'Away with softness.' And surely it would be soft to abandon the only truly powerful lever that had ever come within reach of his hand or was ever likely to again? Literally within reach of his hand. He stared up again at the ceiling. Michael had carried it in an ordinary briefcase, sat with it in Billy's Bar, stood it there on the table in front of them all. You didn't need Harvard Medical School for a pair of latex gloves and a bottle of meths.

He crossed the loft and unlatched the door to the landing. Peering over the iron balustrade he could see all the way down to the lobby. There was no sound of anyone on the stairs.

46 | Smelling a rat

'So, wasn't that amazing?'

Tom Keeley sighed with satisfaction and pulled the sheet up to cover them both before sinking back on the pillow. 'It quite often is.'

Caroline slapped his hand. 'I'm talking about the President's speech.'

'That was yesterday.'

'I know when it was. But weren't you just thrilled?'

Tom rearranged the pillows and sat up in the bed. The house had been a great choice, every room with floor-to-ceiling windows, making it light and cheerful even in winter. 'It's more than you could have hoped from any administration, let alone this one.'

'But?'

'No, I'm all for it. It's fantastic. And doable, too. In fact in some ways I wish I was still at CDC. I could get involved in helping to make it all happen.'

'You could help by writing about it, keeping feet to the fire?'

'Yeah, that's going to be needed too down the line, and I'm your man.'

Caroline felt for his hand under the sheets. 'I can still hear a "but" in there somewhere.'

'Well, okay then, I can't help thinking there's something odd there. Ringing speech from a cracked bell. I mean, isn't this the same guy who said "the government is not the solution to the problem; the government is the problem"?'

'In other words, you've become a cynical journalist inside of a month. I blame that Delius guy.'

'Yeah, Bob seems to have taken on my journalistic education. After we all finished up listening to the announcement on C-Span, I was all fired up about it and Bob leans over and says: "Remember, Tom, when a leopard changes its spots a good reporter smells a rat".'

'Pleased with himself, was he?'

47 | When shall we five...

There was of course no absolute need for the five to meet
again. The dice had been rolled, the gods of the game
had smiled, and there was nothing more to be done. Yet
Michael Lowell, Hélène Hevré, Seema Mir, Toby Jenks and
Stephen Walsh were eventually drawn together again by some
magnetic field of emotional necessity, each of the five wanting
to be with the others if for no better purpose than that of
collectively pinching themselves and raising a glass in each
other's company.

Despite being inundated by the demands being made on
his Division, it was Michael who brought them together
again. On the evening of 11 March, he called Seema to say
he was returning to New York. The following morning he
faxed Toby asking if he needed to refresh his memory of the
in-flight experience. In his lunch break, he went down to the
WHO travel office on the main concourse and arranged an
open return ticket from Abidjan to New York in the name of
Hélène Hevré, at the same time booking a return ticket for
himself and charging both to his personal account. Back at
his desk, he wrote a brief note to Stephen, care of the Chelsea
Hotel.

This time there was to be no dinner at Billy's, no meeting in a bar or restaurant where the collective pinching might be inhibited. On the evening of the first day of spring the five came together again in Seema Mir's loft apartment on West 4th Street. It was one hundred and sixty-nine days after the reunion in Oxford.

Toby, Stephen and Michael arrived within minutes of each other, embracing and gathering round the stove as Seema handed round wine, a Joan Baez record playing quietly in the background. For a strange first few minutes nothing much of consequence was said, as if it would have been wrong to begin before their number was complete. But, just as further small talk was becoming impossible, the buzzer sounded and the little group crowded out on to the landing to cheer Hélène's slow progress up the four flights of stairs.

Once she had taken off her coat the atmosphere of pseudo-normality collapsed, leaving a suspended moment of silence in which Hélène raised her glass towards Michael. But still no one spoke. And then suddenly Toby was turning away in tears and Hélène had taken his hand and was sitting him down on the couch. Seema too had buried her face in her hands, Michael looking at her in consternation. Only Stephen stood apart, frowning up at the prints on the walls, more affected by the edgy wistfulness of Joan Baez who, in one of those maudlin coincidences that popular music seems to throw up, was embarked on *Bobby's Song*. But he, too, eventually raised a glass, staring up into the white space of the loft.

Like these flowers at your door, and scribbled notes about the war, we're only saying the time is short and there is work to do...

He drank deep of the wine, feeling the buzz almost immediately.

And we're still marching in the streets, with little victories and big defeats…

When they had all recovered, Hélène sank back on the couch, still holding Toby's hand. 'So, for God's sake, tell us what's happening, Michael.'

'Well, I guess it would take the whole weekend. My deputy passed me a note in the middle of a meeting yesterday. "It's like the whole world's gone suddenly sane".'

Toby looked up with red eyes and would have reached for his glass if Hélène had not still been holding his hand.

For the next two hours, the talk was of what was happening around the world, Michael retailing the news coming in to the WHO of initiatives being approved and funded, along with requests for training and technical assistance, country missions being hurriedly put together and reports of independent national initiatives. Hélène chipped in with stories from half a dozen West African countries: commitments by heads of state, resolutions approved in parliaments and national assemblies, funds being made available where no funds had been before. Both told of the surge of enthusiasm among the NGOs and grassroots health workers who for so long had staffed the front lines of frustration. To everyone's surprise, Toby had as much to recount as anybody, having been monitoring the wire services and clipping agencies. Stephen at one point mentioned the dissenting voices raised in the Eastern bloc and by left-wing sources in the West, all of them pointing out that the Third World was again being made to dance to America's tune, its priorities decided in Washington, its governments bribed and bullied into falling in line. All this was greeted with sober looks, but it had not stopped the wine from flowing or the tensions of the past few weeks from evaporating.

Towards eleven o'clock, Michael, with what he hoped was mock formality, asked for the floor. 'I just want to say something a little bit more sobering before it's too late.'

''S'already too late, mate.' On the sofa Toby still had not let go of Hélène's hand.

'I just want to point out that nothing ever goes perfectly according to plan. There's a lot of momentum out there right now, and plenty of people wanting to ride the wave as long and as far as it goes. And it's true that the US would find it next to impossible to go back on this thing any time soon. All thanks to Toby, we should say…' From the cane chair, Seema looked at Michael: there was something heartbreaking in his earnestness at times like this and she acknowledged that her own feelings were of an infinite tenderness towards his attempts at lightness of touch, his wish not to sound as if he were making a speech. '… But I just wanted to make sure you know the momentum will falter eventually. It always does. Hélène knows this better than anybody… All health interventions face an ever-steepening slope. It just gets harder and harder to reach those you haven't reached. Plus which this isn't a one-off effort. We're talking about getting vaccines to hundreds of millions of kids a year, every year. A lot of them in places that aren't too easy to get to.' He paused, realizing he had indeed fallen into a speech. 'Just so long as we all know we won't see a steady, uninterrupted rise to eighty per cent. If I had to make a guess, I'd say it might get up to sixty or seventy per cent, and then after that we'll be in difficulties.'

'Isn't that why we have a couple of jars in reserve?' Toby's question opened a chasm under the sudden seriousness of the proceedings.

'That was what I thought at first, Toby. Or at least I thought we ought to have the option. But I have to say I don't think it's on. We'd have to give it two or three years before we could say the US was backsliding on the deal, and by that time we'll be facing a possible change of administration. We couldn't be sure it would work again. We couldn't even be sure that the virus would still be viable, though we can probably be reasonably confident that Seema won't want it in her fridge for the next three or four years. So I think we need to accept that this is the end of the line.'

'So we get rid of the other vials?'

In the silence that followed Seema's question, all of them except Stephen turned their attention back to Michael.

'I'll take care of that this weekend. But there's something else. Last serious word – I promise. We have to remember that one careless word could still bring the world down around our heads. The hunt hasn't been called off. Just the opposite. Every network the FBI and CIA can plug into is listening and looking for the slightest whisper of this thing. And I should tell you the guy who's directing the operation is mad as all hell that the administration "caved in", as he sees it. I'm pretty sure he could only bring himself to accept it at all because now he's got all the time in the world to hunt down what he calls "the bastards behind this thing".'

Toby's look of gentle happiness had changed to one of amused suspicion. 'How do you know all this, brother?'

'I talked to the guy about it.'

Toby turned to Seema. 'What's he talking about?'

Seema smiled. 'You didn't know Michael was hunting with the hounds as well as running with the hare?'

'No. I'm afraid you're quite wrong there, sweetheart. Straight as they come, Michael, always has been.'

For the next few minutes Michael briefly told the story of his recruitment and the meetings at Mohonk Mountain House. Hélène lay back against Toby's arm on the sofa, looking stunned. 'You were there? For the whole thing?'

Michael lowered his head. 'Said as little as possible. Becket Bradie was there. CDC Director. He and I advised on what would need to be done if Toby's statement hit the media. And of course we had to review the plans for if the virus ever got itself released.'

Stephen leaned forward from the armchair, frowning. 'How very interesting. So you can tell us what calculus was made?'

'Political cost-benefit analysis, just as you predicted, Stephen. Ignoring it or toughing it out was on the table. But in the end I think they thought the potential downside was just so much bigger than anything there was to be gained. I also got a distinct feeling that the upside gradually started to take hold.'

Seema had paused in her circulation of the wine bottle. 'Who was it who first proposed it? Going along I mean.'

Michael smiled up at her and gave a mock sigh of relief. 'Well, I have to tell you I had a little speech all prepared about why, just maybe, they ought to tentatively consider whether it might not be a possible option to, you know, make a virtue of necessity; remind them it was something the US had signed up to in principle anyway and that there were quite a few positives to be taken out of it. But, boy, was I praying I wouldn't need to make that speech. Came down to the wire but it was Warren Taylor who tabled it – expertly I have to say.'

Seema was the only one who instantly knew the name. 'The President's National Security Adviser?' She had perched on the edge of the Bikaner and forgotten all about pouring wine. Toby removed the bottle from her hand.

Michael told them a little more about the handling of the affair by the Chief of Staff. At half past eleven, Toby raised his glass to his friend.

'Your weekends are a lot more fun than mine, mate.'

It was almost one o'clock in the morning when Michael managed a word with Seema on the landing as the others were descending towards the street.

'You'd like those things out of the apartment, wouldn't you?'

She nodded happily, looking into his eyes, knowing that she would be silhouetted against the light of her own room.

'Will you have dinner with me tomorrow night?'

The abruptness took her by surprise. 'Yes, of course.'

'Bring the flasks with you. Just as they are in their plastic bags. They're safe. Then you can leave it to me.'

'You're sure that's okay?'

'A hundred per cent.'

'Okay.'

'Top of the Tower, Beekman? At, say, 6.30, and we'll have a drink first? I'll have worked out what to do by then.'

She rested a hand on his arm and continued to look up at him on the landing, sure that he would kiss her goodnight. He bent and brushed his lips against her cheek. 'See you tomorrow.'

48 | Finding cold air

Seema had given up any pretence of not being extra careful with her make-up. She had also taken the afternoon off in favour of a rare shopping expedition for the outfit she was now wearing. So far there had only been meetings. This, she had decided, was a date.

She checked herself in the mirror. Surely tonight, with the great shadow lifted, it would be possible to talk of other things. Of themselves. And perhaps of the future. If there was to be a future.

She took the soft leather shoulder bag from the back of the door and carried it over to the spiral staircase. Not since the day it was installed had she as much as touched the tiny fridge. Kneeling, she tugged at the chromium door handle. The rubber seal gave a little gasp as it opened. With exaggerated care she removed the first of the two plastic bags, semi-opaque now, its folds rimed with frost. She placed it gently on the floorboards, the plastic crackling slightly with cold. The second bag lay further back than she had remembered. Crouching lower, she reached deeper inside. Her fingers found only cold air.

Three minutes later, she was running along West 4th, raising a hand to the oncoming traffic.

'Beekman Tower, 49th and First.'

49 | To love you or hate you

The Beekman Tower, John Mead Howell's art-deco masterpiece, had originally been built to provide female-only accommodation for the increasing numbers of single sorority women flooding into New York City to find work in the inter-war years. The single woman now entering the black marble lobby was making an effort to remain calm as she waited by the doors of the express elevator, holding a shoulder bag in her arms.

Two minutes later she was stepping out into the 26th-floor lobby, forcing herself to take the few remaining stairs at a pace suitable for someone heading towards a pre-dinner drink. It was slightly before 6.30 when she entered the Top of the Tower bar that looked out on one of the most spectacular views in Manhattan.

Michael was already there, sitting at a table in the narrow, glassed-in conservatory running around the parapet under the spotlit crown of the tower itself. He rose to meet her, signalling to the waiter before she could stop him.

'Mineral water, please.' Her voice sounded utterly unlike her own.

Michael took his time looking down the list of wines as the waiter placed menus before them. She glanced over the low wall to see First Avenue, three hundred feet below, as Michael

331

ordered a glass of Chablis.

He was about to say something as the inner glass door closed behind the waiter but was halted by the look on Seema's face.

'Michael, one of the jars is missing. Stephen has it. He's the only person who's been alone in the apartment. I left him for a few minutes when he came to tell me the news.'

Michael looked up towards the astonishing view, the lights beginning to come on all over Midtown. 'I wonder why he didn't take them both.'

Seema looked at him in disbelief. 'Michael, his metre's turned so high there's no telling what he might be planning. We've got to go to … to the authorities. It doesn't matter now what happens to us.'

The glass door opened again and the waiter reappeared to apply a cigarette lighter to the candle. The evening was becoming cool, spring only just beginning to lay the lightest of hands on the city. Without asking, Michael ordered another glass of the Chablis for Seema. When they were alone again, he looked up from the table, seeing the tears of worry in her eyes against the backdrop of a million lights.

'You've got the other jar?'

'Yes.' She touched the strap of her shoulder bag, now hanging from the back of the chair.

The waiter reappeared with the second glass and two small bowls of salted crackers. Taking an age, he refilled both water glasses. 'Little cool out here tonight, folks – sure you and the lady wouldn't prefer inside? Table for two by the window on the west side?'

'Hold it for us? We're good here for another fifteen.'

When the waiter had gone back into the restaurant, Michael stood, removing his jacket and circling the little table to place it around her shoulders. Returning to his seat, he lifted her bag from the back of the chair. Unzipping it, he reached inside for the plastic food bag. It was now clear of frost. Seema stared as he tore open the damp plastic and took out the thermos. In the candlelight, the hammered metal shimmered slightly as he unscrewed the cup. Other tables, other candles, were reflected in the glass behind, along with the lights of the city, as he took hold of the inner stopper and began to twist.

'Michael!'

Picking up the newly refilled glass of iced water, he poured a little into the now-open neck of the food jar. A half-melted ice cube and a slice of lime slipped over the rim with a splash. Seema closed her eyes for a second to shut out the scene. When she opened them again Michael had lifted the jar to his lips and was drinking from the thermos. She stared at him, thoughts racing with nowhere to go as he returned the food jar to the table between them and reached again for the stopper.

'What's in there, Michael?'

He held his breath for just a moment. 'Nothing. Same as the one Stephen has in his minibar in his room at the Chelsea Hotel. I'd better call him. Save him getting himself into trouble.'

Seema looked away towards the Citicorp building, its aircraft warning lights steadily flashing red over the city. After a few seconds, she pulled Michael's jacket closer around her shoulders. 'Can we stop this game now, Michael, and just tell me what's happening?'

Michael looked at her, as if not knowing where to start. 'Seema—'

'Tell me first of all – if only one of those jars had the virus, how on earth did Stephen know which one? He was the one who got to pick the one to leave at Grand Central.'

It was Michael's turn to look away, oblivious in his shirt

sleeves to the temperature as night fell over Manhattan. 'Do you remember me telling you about Paul Lewis?'

'Your colleague at the CDC? Yes, of course. We all assumed that was how you got hold of it.'

'Paul Lewis is dying of cancer.' Michael was clearly struggling. 'I didn't know if it was right to ask. I still don't know if it was right. But in the end I just told him the whole story. We were outside, on a park bench in the snow somewhere quite near the White House. When I'd finished he was quiet for maybe a couple of minutes. Then he said he couldn't think of anything better to do with his last few weeks.'

Seema saw that there were tears in Michael's own eyes now. When he remained silent she said softly, 'I knew you were close.'

Michael took a deep breath. 'In the end I think he was glad. Ever since med school the only thing Paul's ever wanted to do is make a contribution. And he did. He did. Both over all the years and at the end.'

Seema waited for a moment before pressing. 'You still haven't told me how you knew, how Stephen knew, which of the containers it was.'

Michael picked up the jar from the table and slowly screwed on the metal cup. 'I'm sure you can work it out.'

Seema took a first sip of wine, her thoughts returning to the morning that Stephen had picked up the thermos from the apartment. To her left, Manhattan's universe of lights retreated to the south where the Pan-Am building rose above Grand Central. Way below, the northbound traffic made a slow-moving river of lights on First Avenue.

After a minute, her lips parted slightly, her eyes widening as she returned the wine glass to the table. She looked up into his eyes.

'I'm being slow. All the thermos flasks were empty, weren't they?'

Michael gave her a half-apologetic smile, picking up his own glass. 'Especially the one left at Grand Central.'

Seema straightened her back, her shoulders still only half-filling his suit jacket. 'And the only thing you asked your friend for was to say it was smallpox. That was the favour you asked, wasn't it?'

Michael said nothing, watching every movement of her face as she continued. 'But it can't have been just Paul Lewis. You said they would have two or three experts look at it?'

Michael turned the jar round in his hands, as if checking it had come to no harm. 'And I'm sure they did. But what were they looking at? Fact is, I don't know myself. Either it was the real thing, put there by Paul and given to a couple of other virologists to examine. Or, as I suspect, it was just a set of slides, culture reports, electron microscopy images of a strain of variola major, a strain called "Harvey".'

Seema was still holding the collar of the jacket closed with one hand. 'And of course the slides would have been prepared by ... Paul Lewis.'

Michael zipped the thermos into the shoulder bag and hung it over the back of his own chair. 'You're right, of course. What Paul agreed to was to make sure that whatever was brought in that night from Grand Central was identified as smallpox.'

Seema shook her head, as if to throw off all past misconceptions. 'I have to get this right. You're telling me there never was any virus? Never any risk at all?'

'None at all.'

It took several more seconds for Seema to readjust every frame in the movie that had been the last month of her life. Finally she stood, slipping off the jacket and handing it back.

'I don't know whether to love you or hate you, Michael Lowell.'

He too stood, handing back the shoulder bag as she led him into the restaurant.

It was still only a few minutes after seven and there were few other diners in the candlelit interior. When the waiter had presented them with menus, Seema stared out at the city from a different angle, looking past the Empire State and Chrysler buildings to the more distant towers of the financial district. There were other restaurants with spectacular views of Manhattan, but not with this intimate atmosphere. Of all the fifty thousand restaurants in the city Michael had chosen the most romantic, and for a few moments she opened herself to the astonishing spectacle, thoughts suspended, letting the tensions fall away, rejoicing that an evening that had begun with such a weight of dread might now be so full of light and promise.

Aware that he was looking at her, and that he was still uncertain of her reactions, she punished him by continuing to look out of the window as if absorbed by the view. 'You chose a romantic place to tell me all this, Michael.'

He looked slightly embarrassed, and turned to look in the other direction towards the East River. 'There's also a very good view of the old smallpox quarantine building just down there on the tip of Roosevelt Island.'

Only for a moment did she think he might be serious, then they were both laughing, hands almost touching across the table.

'So friend Stephen is running around out there plotting to strike a blow against global capitalism when in fact what he's got is … ' – she paused and looked into Michael's eyes – '… zilch. Nothing at all.'

336

Before he could answer the waiter reappeared. Once they had ordered, Seema assumed a more determined look. 'There are still some things I don't get.'

'Seema, I'm sorry ... '

'And the first is, why didn't you tell us all the whole story?'

Michael looked down, twisting the wine glass around by its stem. 'I didn't tell you because keeping quiet about it was the one thing that Paul asked me to promise. And then he asked me not to promise because there might come a time and a place ... like here and now. '

Seema was not sure of the significance of the last words but determined to press on. 'I still don't get it. Why was that so important to him?'

'Because he was really the one in the firing line. It wasn't just that he wanted to be sure that none of us was taking the decision to do this ... too lightly, I suppose. If the secret came out ... well, that particular strain of the virus could have come from anywhere ... but if the deeper secret was ever known, that there never was a virus at all, then a positive ID could only have been down to Paul. No one else could have done what he did.'

'But you said he doesn't have long to live.'

'It wasn't himself he was afraid for. It was his family, Anne and their two boys. If he'd been exposed as some kind of bio-terrorist or whatever, how would that have been for them? And he couldn't really trust anybody but me, you can see that? He doesn't even know any of you.'

They sat in silence for a while as the plates of pasta arrived, followed by an ice bucket in a stand. Two more diners appeared, but were shown to a table at the far end of the gallery restaurant.

'There's an even bigger question though, isn't there? Why

337

involve the rest of us at all? You and Paul could have managed the whole thing between you.'

He replaced the glass on the table, shaking his head for emphasis. 'There was a good reason. More than one.'

'I really don't mind if you count them off on your fingers, Michael.'

Michael smiled at his food. 'Hélène was the one who really began it all. In Oxford. And Stephen too, in his own way. And it needed Toby. Boy, did it need Toby. What he did made all the difference. Up at that Mountain House place you could see the impact the statement made. The President read it. The Chief of Staff read it. The National Security Adviser read it. And none of them was in any doubt about the effect it would have. Plus which, even for themselves, I don't believe they weren't moved by it.'

'I wish I could have seen it.'

'It wasn't only that. It was Toby's idea to include the wording that had to be used in the announcement. Otherwise we might have gotten some half-hearted commitment that might not have attracted all that much attention. Something too easy to let slide as time went by. What Toby did was create something that didn't leave them any wriggle room. A Kennedy Moment is what they were calling it at Mohonk. Because they could all see how powerful it would be, how difficult to go back on.'

Seema pictured Toby's face; his bemused smile, his regrets over Hélène, his sense of his own weakness, his steady regard for Michael. And, now she thought of it, his mumbled comment, ignored at the time, that if anyone was likely to go off like a frog in a sock it was Stephen Walsh.

'Good old Tobe. So you think some of them might even have been with us in their hearts?'

'Maybe. It was difficult to read the statement without

something inside rising up to meet it. That was Toby's genius.'

'Michael, Hélène has to see everything that Toby wrote. Isn't there any way of recreating it, even if it's not exactly word for word?'

Michael almost blushed. 'I broke the rules. Made a coded copy.' He produced the small note book from the Gladstone bag at his feet. Opening it at the back, he flicked through the pages of numbers. 'Unbreakable. I made it for Hélène, and for you.'

Seema restrained herself from taking his hand, picking up her wine instead. 'You've still only used one finger. What about the rest of us? We didn't do anything you couldn't have done yourself.'

Michael again shook his head. 'Stephen had to be included. What he said was true. He did come to me that last morning in Oxford and make a kind of an academic argument along the same lines. Only he was talking about a real virus, a real threat.'

Seema considered for a moment. 'And what about Hélène and me? Hélène had already played her part. And I guess you needed someone with a fridge in Manhattan.'

'That wasn't the only reason.' He continued winding pasta on to the fork without attempting to pick it up. 'When I was first wrestling with all this, way back before Christmas, I came to a decision I can't really explain too well, even to myself.'

Seema watched him struggling for a second or two. 'And the decision was?'

'I decided I wouldn't take it any further if I couldn't persuade you.'

'Why me?'

'Hélène's an insider, seen so much. Stephen's judgement I

didn't trust. Toby I was pretty sure would go with it if Hélène and I were both in.' He tried to look at her but ended up staring down at the table. 'You were my touchstone, Seema. The one I had to convince. There's no one I'd trust with my own mind … no one more sane, not really what I meant, more human …'

Seema smiled to ease his embarrassment, feeling again the surge of tenderness at his sudden clumsiness with words. 'And that was the only reason? I was your … what shall we call it? … your test of your own sanity?'

Michael gave her the rueful smile, but knew there was no way out. 'Maybe there might have been something else.'

'Which was, Michael?'

'I guess, maybe …' He looked down again at his plate. 'I guess maybe I wanted to do something that would surprise you.'

When he looked up again her eyes were filled with tears and their hands reached out to touch across the table.

After a few seconds, she took out a tissue from the bag on her chair. 'I know I was an idiot twenty years ago, Michael.'

He took the tissue from her hand and gently dabbed her face. She took it from him and tucked it into her sleeve, then took his hand again.

He stared down at their interlocked fingers on the white tablecloth. 'I've also been giving quite a lot of thought to your sabbatical.'

She looked up in surprise, seeing in his eyes more irresolution than she had seen in all the hours of planning they had done. 'My sabbatical?'

'Yes, I've been wondering how you might feel about taking it on the shores of Lake Geneva?'

Epilogue

by Thomas Keeley

I do not know whether it was my good or ill fortune to have been the one member of the original group who was unable to attend those two college reunions in the early 1980s. Nor do I know for certain what happened there. More than thirty years later, none of the principal characters has ever referred publicly to the events described in these pages.

It is possible, of course, that this may change in the years to come if one or more of their diaries are published, perhaps posthumously. In the meantime, the reader may like to know something of what became of the five and of how I eventually came to suspect what really happened in that now-long-ago winter of 1980/81.

As the *Times'* chief medical correspondent, I had covered the story of immunization's astonishing rise, finding it a welcome change from my main beat of the 1980s – the progress of the HIV/AIDS crisis. All that need be said about it here is that the decade following 'The Kennedy Moment' saw extraordinary progress towards immunizing the world's children. Across the developing world, the proportion of children vaccinated against major diseases rose from below twenty per cent to almost eighty per cent, saving many millions of young lives every year.

It was of course an achievement to be celebrated. But it also raised an obvious question. The vaccines themselves had been cheaply available since at least the mid-1960s; what, then, was the cause of this sudden, dramatic surge in the 1980s?

The standard explanation says that it came about because of the commitment made by the Government of the United States on March 6th, 1981. The President's speech that day – his 'Kennedy Moment' as it became known – was a ringing declaration that the US would lead a worldwide effort to save the lives of millions of the world's children. It was, as several papers, including my own, could not resist punning, 'the shot felt round the world'.

I never bought it. Not for a minute. Coming out of a clear blue sky, the President's speech that day was totally out of tune with an administration that was preoccupied by the Cold War and known for its almost visceral abhorrence of major government initiatives. And I was far from being alone in my suspicions.

Those suspicions lay dormant for many years. And it was only after my retirement that something happened to cause me to speculate about an alternative explanation.

And it was, of course, Toby who gave it to me.

In retirement, Toby Jenks had become something of a sad character. His marriage to our mutual college friend, the distinguished Canadian paediatrician Hélène Hevré, had begun in bliss and ended in tragedy. Less than two years after returning to Canada to take up an appointment as Director of International Health with the Canadian International Development Agency, Hélène Hevré died in McGill Medical Hospital, Montreal.

Caroline and I visited her the week before her death. She was skeletal, and unable to breathe without an oxygen mask. Words were limited, and from her doctors I learned that the exhaustion had eventually reached the point where even breathing had become difficult. No amount of tests had been able to identify the cause, either of the bodily weakness or of the yeast infections that covered the inside of her mouth or of the lack of T cells that had left her immune system in tatters. All they could tell me was that she had a progressive disease of unknown cause, her lungs filling up with millions of the organisms known as *pneumocystis carinii* that were slowly suffocating this gentle, brave and dedicated woman. But, as Hélène herself told me between gasps of oxygen, 'No one dies of pneumocystis'.

Soon afterwards, I covered the controversial October 1982 New York University Symposium on AIDS. By that time, 691 Americans had been documented as having contracted the virus and 278 had already died. At the Symposium, French researchers presented data to show that many of the earliest confirmed cases had occurred among Africans and Europeans who had spent time in Central Africa immediately before becoming ill. Even earlier than this, Dr Ib Bygbjerg – friend and colleague of Dr Grethe Rask, who had died in circumstances not dissimilar to Hélène's – had also made the link between AIDS and infectious tropical diseases.

The mystery of Hélène Hevré's death was solved. Like Grethe Rask, she had been one of the first non-Africans to fall victim to what became known as HIV/AIDS. And, again like Grethe Rask, the virus had almost certainly been contracted through contact with blood in one of the over-populated and under-equipped hospital wards in which both of them had served with such devotion.

After the funeral, a shattered Toby kept his head above water for some years doing good work for Dick Manoff's social-marketing agency, which at that time was pioneering the use of professional advertising skills to communicate public-health messages. But eventually he succumbed to periodic mild depression and drifted south from Montreal to New York where he picked up sporadic work for one or two of the Madison Avenue agencies where he was still known and loved. But he had also drifted into spending the hours from six until late in the White Horse Tavern in the West Village where he now lived in a two-room apartment above a tattoo parlour.

I had seen Toby from time to time over the years. Following my own wife's death three years ago, he was more supportive than I could have believed. He was also unfailingly excellent company, kind and clever when you got below the surface performance. And so I was pleased when he called to say he had read about my retirement in the *Times* and invited me for a celebratory drink.

We met one Friday evening at Charlio's, just around the corner from the old Radio City Music Hall. After a couple of drinks (in his case I suspected it was a couple more drinks) he sat back in the booth and looked at me in a rheumy-eyed, wistful way, mumbling something whimsical about reaching a point when you realize that the meat and potatoes of your life are in the past and most of the puddings are off the menu. He also said some nice things about my own career and added that he wished he had done more with his own life. I demurred, but he waved my protests away and said 'And I wish, I wish, Tom, I wish you had been at that reunion, in Oxford, and that weekend here in New York of course, all those years ago.'

I had almost forgotten the college reunions that I had been unable to attend and asked him why, after all this time, he was wishing I had been there. 'No reason,' he said, checking himself. 'No reason. It was just a whole lot of intellectualiz-ing when all the time what was really happening was mostly hormonal.'

'So why should I have been there?' I persisted.

'Because then I could tell you what really happened,' he said, almost tearfully. 'But now I can't. Because, you see, you weren't there.' He was swaying very slightly on the bar stool, but I could see that there was something behind his words; something important, at least to him.

'You know, don't you, Tom, what Marshall McLuhan said? I'll tell you – he said "advertisements are the real history of our times". In a way, you see, I was the real historian. So, anyway, what was I saying? Yes, no, really, after that I did do something with my life. I did, you know. Did something, Tom. Something quite significant. With my life, I mean. Just the once. Didn't make a habit of it. Wouldn't want anyone to think I had a serious side.'

I was intrigued. 'So go on, Tobe, what was it?'

Toby stared into the bottom of his glass, clearly struggling to take hold of himself.

'Not saying. Can't say. Will one day. From the grave, shouldn't wonder.' He looked around the bar, clearly intending to find another topic of conversation. But by now my journalistic instincts were engaged.

'So something happened at those reunions that had to be kept secret – that the size of it?'

Toby stared again into his now almost empty glass. 'Trouble with keeping a secret is…no one knows you're keeping it. Wit and wisdom of Toby Jenks.'

'Well, it was obviously some kind of deal if it still has to be a secret after all this time.'

'It was some kind of deal. It was, Tom, really some kind of deal. Specially for me. Truth is, Tom, I only ever really did one do-goody thing. In my life, I mean. But here's the thing, it probably did more good than all the other do-gooders in the world rolled into one big, fat do-gooder, if you see what I mean. Going to write it all down before I dissolve entirely in this stuff. Be a great little book. Can you help me think of a decent title? No, of course you can't. Silly question.'

Toby staggered off to the washroom and it was there, sitting on a bar stool in Charlio's, with Manhattan's 'happy hour' getting under way around me, that the pieces first began to drift towards each other. Something had happened at those reunions. Something important enough for Toby Jenks to be clinging to it like a moral life raft more than thirty years later. Something that he believed had done some significant good in the world. Something that had to be kept secret even after all this time. And in one of those connections that the brain makes without any particular effort, I recalled something long forgotten – the lunch with Seema all those years ago, soon after I had arrived in New York. At the time, the fact that she had reacted so nervously to my asking what happened at the reunion had been just another of life's little unexplained oddities. But now, all these years later, her strange behaviour came back to me.

The noise in the bar was building up as I waited for Toby to return, but by this point I was in a world of my own and about to make the big leap. Michael Lowell had been at both those reunions. And it was Michael who had been in charge of WHO's global immunization programme through the 1980s – a programme that had succeeded largely because of the President's out-of-the-blue announcement that day. What if Michael hadn't merely responded to 'The Kennedy Moment'? What if he had somehow engineered it? And what if this was connected to the 'something significant' that Toby had done with his life?

Toby was making his way back through the bar now, bald head glowing and fading as he passed under the orange globe lights. It was an absurd notion. What could the connection possibly have been?

Toby hoisted himself back on to his stool, mumbled something about 'the booze talking', and turned the conversation back to my retirement plans. I postponed my speculations for a quieter moment and for the next half hour we talked of 'the things one has never had time to do'.

That quieter moment came as soon as I left Charlio's that night and began to walk back to my soon-to-be vacated apartment on the Upper East Side.

No sooner was I out in the fresh air than the preposterousness of the thought gained the upper hand. All I had was a few passing straws in the wind that a slightly inebriated imagination had snatched at and twisted into a fantasy. But I could not leave it alone. If Toby's great thirty-year secret was somehow linked to The Kennedy Moment, then some kind of leverage had to be involved, some kind of threat. And it had to have been something powerful enough to force the government into that totally out-of-character announcement.

Many unanswered questions litter a correspondent's life, and most of them have no connection with each other. But as I walked up 5th Avenue that night, some of those questions began to stretch out hands from the past. Around that time, in the early 1980s, there had been a big simulation exercise to test plans for coping with a bio-terrorist attack on a major US city. This had been public knowledge, not least because the New York City Health Commissioner at the time had invited journalists to participate on the grounds that an informed public response would be vital. But had it been just an exercise? Vague rumours had circulated at the time that the simulation might have been in response to an actual rather than a theoretical threat.

My thoughts continued to scurry around the possibilities, running into improbable channels and more than one dead end. But as I crossed to Madison and waited for the lights to change opposite Williams-Sonoma, I remembered the bomb scare that had shut down Grand Central station at around that time – and the unmarked van with the Dekalb County licence plates. One buried chamber of memory leading into another, I also dimly recalled my lunch with Stephen Walsh who, like Seema, had clearly been running scared at the very mention of that little reunion.

As I neared my apartment building on 89th, my speculative rollercoaster took another dip. It was surely all impossible. The CDC connection meant some kind of virus would have had to have been involved. And there were only two real candidates: the two that the US government itself had identified as Category A biological threats – anthrax and smallpox. Michael had been – still was – one of the world's leading experts on smallpox, and for a moment my imagination ran wild. But there was surely no way that someone as buttoned-down as Michael Lowell would ever have gotten himself involved in anything so off the wall. Not to mention the fact that not even he could have gotten his hands on the virus. As I well knew from the pieces I had written to mark the various anniversaries of smallpox eradication, the remaining stocks were held under about the same level of security as the nation's supply of enriched uranium. Absurd to think that it could have been stolen. I told myself to forget about the whole crazy notion. But, as I continued on up Madison Avenue, my thoughts kept returning to those deep-phase freezers in the Level 4 bio-containment facility down in Atlanta.

And to Paul Lewis.

Paul, who had died of pancreatic cancer at around the same time as the events I was struggling to recall; Paul, who had been Principal Deputy Director of the CDC and the country's top virologist; Paul, who had been the close friend of Michael Lowell; Paul, who would have been one of the very few people in the world with access to the pass codes for those freezers.

Totally preoccupied, I walked straight past my own building, only turning back when I had almost reached Mount Sinai Hospital. But, by the time I was nearing my apartment again, I was taking another reality check. No two men would have known better than Michael Lowell and Paul Lewis that smallpox had brought more suffering and death to this world than any other virus in history. Bar none. Neither of them would have taken the slightest risk with it. Neither would have done anything so mad, so evil.

And, even then, the penny did not drop.

I was thinking, more idly now, about my own years at the CDC when, apropos of nothing, inspiration dropped out of the night sky. Paul would have been the obvious go-to man if there had been any reason to suspect that an ampoule left somewhere – in a baggage locker at Grand Central Terminal for example – contained the smallpox virus. He would have been in a position to confirm that whatever had been brought in from New York that night was indeed variola. And no one would have dreamt of questioning his conclusion. Sure, it was unthinkable that the two of them would have stolen the virus. But what if they hadn't needed to?

I stepped out of the elevator on the 35th floor, key in hand, lingering for a while on the landing, not even wanting to enter my own apartment in case the vision of what might have happened all those years ago were to vanish on contact with the mundane and familiar surroundings of my life. Eventually I let myself in and sank into a chair, looking out across the East River and the lights of Jackson Heights and wishing I hadn't been too preoccupied to pick up something to eat.

And Toby Jenks? Dear old Toby, who had started me on this mad chase less than two hours ago in Charlio's. What might his involvement have been? The only possible connection I could think of was the powerful wording of the President's speech that day – the moving, Sorensen-like quality that had been much commented on at the time. Among the many writers I have known and worked with, very few would have been capable of writing a speech like that. And one of them was Toby Jenks.

As I sipped a beer, my estimate of whether any of this was even remotely likely veered first one way and then the other. Even if such a threat had been made, it was surely inconceivable that the government would have given in to it? On the other hand, it could have been argued that going down in history as the President who immunized the world's children was better than being known as the President who had presided over panic and been unable to protect the American people.

I eventually went to bed telling myself I had drunk more than usual and the thing to do was to sleep on it and see whether any of this still seemed plausible in what I was trying not to call the cold light of day. It was all speculation; but already it rang more true in my own ears than the President's 'Kennedy Moment' had ever done.

A few days after the evening at Charlio's, I called Toby and talked him into coming up to my home in Connecticut for the weekend. He had sounded dubious, mumbling something about the countryside being a dangerous place and asking if the Constitution State had gotten electricity yet. But he had eventually came around to the idea and arrived one Saturday evening in time for dinner at our local seafood restaurant.

It would be quite untrue to say that I plied him with drink. Toby could do the plying all by himself. But I confess to waiting until after he had drunk most of a bottle of Vinho Verde before raising the issue. We were talking, somewhat inevitably, about the pleasures and pitfalls of retirement when I mentioned that I had in mind to write a little book about smallpox. Toby looked doubtful and asked whether the subject hadn't already been done to death, if I'd forgive the expression. Pouring melted butter over a lobster tail, he mentioned not only D A Henderson's account but also the books by Donald Hopkins and Bill Foege. I said I was thinking more along the lines of the long-running controversy as to whether or not the remaining stocks of the virus should be destroyed. Toby wiped his chin on a napkin and said it would be nice to think it had gone for good but that it would surely be foolish for the US to destroy its stocks if we couldn't be sure that 'the little bugger wasn't still alive and well and living in Siberia'. Soon after that I let him steer the conversation away to some other topic. I had found out what I wanted to know: Toby Jenks knew more about smallpox than he could reasonably be expected to have picked up on Madison Avenue.

I telephoned Michael a few days later to suggest getting together. As I had half expected, he invited me up for a weekend.

And so it was that on Saturday, June 6th – as fair a spring day as New England has to offer – I made an early start from New Canaan with the intention of taking the slow route up through the Berkshires, crossing Massachusetts by the back roads. I had always loved the drive through this part of New

England, drawn to its clapboard houses and white-spired churches as if to a more solidly based world, and did not in the least mind the slow progress.

Many times over the years I had spent weekends with my old friends. Both were still much in demand: Seema as a guest speaker at every conference touching on the history of slavery; Michael as an Emeritus Professor at Harvard Medical School and still an occasional consultant to the WHO. Both were keen hikers and had completed most of the Maine, New Hampshire and Vermont sections of the Appalachian Trail. Neither had put on a pound over the years.

For much of the way on 202, picking up I90 after Springfield, I speculated on how they might respond when confronted with my suspicions. For it surely all fitted together. And surely it had all begun at those reunions I had missed.

I had no thought of alarming my hosts. I knew that Seema, who had always been self-possessed, and Michael, chess player that he still was, would have thought it all through a long time ago; would have known there was nothing to link the five of them to what had happened. Not then. Not now. But if it were true, then it would surely be impossible for them to remain entirely unmoved when confronted with my little hypothesis.

Shortly before noon, I turned off the highway onto Old Mill Road, heading up past the former rifle range to Caterina Heights and the loop road of lovely old New England homes. The azaleas were in full bloom on the lawns and the shingled gables and white-painted porches were a picture of modest, domestic elegance against a backdrop of birch, red oak and maple.

'Toby sends his love. Had a drink with him the other week.'

We had decided it was warm enough to have lunch on the terrace, a raised and paved area overlooking the yard with its lawns and lily pond. Wine was poured, news exchanged, home-made cookies made a fuss of. I helped re-lay the table outdoors and admired the garden, at its best on a fine June day.

Michael inquired about the route I had taken. I described the drive up and commented on the lovely part of the world they had chosen for their retirement. Seema said something about becoming President of the Concord Historical Society. Michael had heard from Stephen, now almost a recluse on his country estate in England and apparently crippled by arthritis. When Hélène was mentioned, the three of us sat in silence for a moment or two. I asked Michael if he still played chess in Washington Square.

'Haven't played there in years. Seems like another era.'

It was opening enough.

'I've been thinking about the past myself quite a bit. And there's something I want to ask you both. Do you remember those college reunions in the Eighties, the ones I wasn't able to get to?'

I had turned from Michael to Seema at the critical moment. The look of alarm in those still-lovely eyes was quite unmistakable.

Michael himself seemed unperturbed. 'We still think about Hélène, too. Still wonder if there's anything we might have done.'

'There was nothing anybody could have done. There wasn't even a diagnosis.'

With this, Michael steered the conversation to what had for many years been my own journalistic beat – those years of the early 1980s when prejudice and politics had made for such a disastrous delay in responding to the AIDS crisis. I was in no hurry, and for five minutes or so we talked about whether lessons had been learnt, and whether the health establishment would do any better if anything similar came along again.

But I had no intention of being deflected. 'Just to get back to those reunions, I've been wondering if they might have been a lot more significant than I thought.'

The two of them looked at each other again. It was clear that Seema was going to leave it to Michael. He turned to me, frowning pleasantly. 'Significant?'

'In view of what happened directly afterwards, I mean. I'm thinking of the US commitment to the global immunization effort. You were running the WHO immunization programme at the time, as I remember?'

'Yeah, and that commitment sure opened up the way.'

'And I've been wondering recently what opened up the way to the commitment?'

Silence for a few seconds. Then Michael put his head on one side and looked at me with half-closed eyes.

'Where are you going with this, Tom?'

I suppose it must have taken me all of three or four minutes to set my little narrative before them. Some of the pieces were missing, I admitted, but there were more than enough to suggest what had really happened in those early months of 1981. As I spoke, Seema looked out over the garden, her hands very deliberately relaxed in her lap but the strain showing on her face. Michael sipped his wine occasionally, paying close attention, as if listening to a complicated exposition of something he found new and interesting.

Finishing my account, in which I skipped lightly over Toby's indiscretion in Charlio's, I looked up at Michael as he reached over to fill my glass. 'And, you know, I didn't really believe any of it myself until it finally dawned on me that it could all have been done without you ever having the virus. That's when the penny dropped. It was a bluff, a gamble. And it worked, didn't it, Michael?'

'Fascinating.' Michael returned the bottle to the table. Seema would not look at me. Neither said anything, as if some impasse had been reached.

I sighed with elaborate forbearance at having to ask the question outright. 'So, what I would like to know, my friends, is … is that how it happened?'

Seema's look appealed to Michael, who allowed himself a smile. And. though the smile was more assured these days, it was still the same slow smile of the seventeen-year-old I had known at Amherst more than fifty years ago.

'If I may paraphrase, Tom, never has so much been built on so little.' He looked out, still smiling, over the yard towards the Musketaquid Pond and the distant hills. 'But, then again, you only have to go to Europe and see all those medieval cathedrals like we did last fall to realize how much can be built on very shallow foundations.'

I smiled back indulgently. But of course I would not be satisfied. 'But my little story is plausible, on the whole, wouldn't you say, Michael? Seema?'

A breeze stirred the lavender, bringing its perfume on the warm air. Over the pond, an emerald dragonfly held itself motionless. Michael took Seema's hand and raised his glass towards me. 'It's a great story, Tom. Wish I'd thought of it myself.'

Thomas Keeley
New Canaan, Connecticut
2017

POSTSCRIPT

The real story

The dramatic rise in immunization across the poor world during the 1980s is a matter of public record. Many millions of children's lives were – and continue to be – saved by a decade-long effort which saw immunization coverage climb from below twenty per cent to almost eighty per cent across the developing world. Many more millions of children were also protected from lifelong disability.

The Kennedy Moment *gives an entirely fictional account of how and why this great advance came about.*

The real story is perhaps more extraordinary.

Mission impossible

In 1977, smallpox was declared eradicated following a ten-year effort led by a small World Health Organization team under the leadership of the American epidemiologist Donald 'DA' Henderson. The strategy which made it possible – the 'surround and contain' technique described in the pages of *The Kennedy Moment* – was developed by William Foege, subsequently director of the US Centers for Disease Control.

Following this achievement, WHO established the Expanded Programme of Immunization (EPI) with the aim of protecting children against measles, diphtheria, whooping cough, neonatal tetanus and poliomyelitis. Together, these five vaccine-preventable diseases were claiming an estimated five million young lives a year and condemning hundreds of thousands more to a lifetime of disability.

To many at the time, the task seemed hopeless. Bringing such diseases under control would require much more than a one-off campaign to 'surround and contain'. It would require the routine, annual vaccination of all newborn children and pregnant women in all countries, most of which would need help with sourcing vaccines, disease surveillance, training immunization teams, developing infrastructure and logistical systems, and deploying cold-chain technologies. To lead such a massive undertaking, the EPI team in Geneva under another American epidemiologist, Ralph 'Rafe' Henderson, numbered eight professionals and four support staff with a budget of one million dollars a year.

At that same time, at the beginning of the 1980s, something was about to happen on the other side of the Atlantic that would transform the chances of success.

The scarcest resource

In one of his last acts as US President, Jimmy Carter nominated James P Grant, the head of the Washington-based Overseas Development Council, to be the new Executive Director of UNICEF. Within months, Grant announced that UNICEF would be devoting most of its efforts and resources, including several thousand staff in offices throughout the developing world, to the task of bringing about a 'child survival revolution'. Its main engine would be a campaign to lift immunization coverage from twenty per cent to forty per cent of the world's children within five years, and to eighty per cent by the end of the decade.

The audacity of such an announcement is, today, difficult to recapture. At the time, projects being run by UN agencies and NGOs would typically reach out to a few hundred, or at most a few thousand, children in villages and neighbourhoods here and there in the developing world. Grant's plan would require reaching out to all children – over 100 million newborns every year – with the right vaccines at the right times in the right hands and at the right temperatures.

No one doubted that this was technically possible; improved and more heat-stable vaccines had become available at a cost of a few cents per child. The problem was one of *scale* – of putting a known solution into action on the same scale as the known problem. And no matter how many partners could be enlisted, and no matter how many individual projects could be launched, sustained action on the scale required was impossible without the commitment of national governments. In other words, what was required was 'political will'.

Grant's response was to switch UNICEF's emphasis from programmes to advocacy. 'If the problem is political will,' he argued, 'then the job is to create the political will.'

Backed by UNICEF staff in country offices throughout the world, he set about the task of meeting personally with presidents, prime ministers and other influential figures in a great majority of the world's countries. At each meeting, he would ask if he or she knew the country's current immunization rate, or the number of children dying from vaccine-preventable disease, or the relatively low cost of preventing death and disability on this scale. Shamelessly, he would inform them that neighbouring countries were racing ahead with immunization, or point out that the country's child death rate was much higher than in other nations, or appeal to a head of government to set an example to the world. At the same time, he also met with the political leaders of most of the world's developed nations, hammering home the message that five million children a year were dying unnecessarily from diseases that five cents' worth of vaccines could prevent.

Gradually, the funds available for the immunization effort began to rise.

There were many critics. Some were shocked by the narrowness of the approach. And many were alarmed that Grant risked lending UNICEF's good name to leaders with appalling human rights records just because they had been persuaded to make a public commitment to immunization. Grant's answer was always the same: *You think we should wait to immunize children until all governments are respectable?*

No hiding place

Reaching out to entire populations – not only to ensure supply but to create demand – was often too big a task for health services alone. Grant's answer was 'social mobilization'. In practice this meant attempting to enlist every possible outreach resource in the society – the media, the teachers, the religious leaders, the business community, the trades unions, the non-governmental organizations, the youth movements and the women's groups – in a 'grand alliance' for immunizing children.

The strain of all this on UNICEF offices and their counterparts across the world was enormous. And there was no hiding place. Grant demanded regular reports detailing the progress of immunization coverage in each country. If the rate was not rising, or not rising fast enough, he wanted to know what the bottlenecks were and what outside help was needed to bypass them. On one memorable occasion, he refused to accept civil war as an excuse for El Salvador's low-performing immunization programme: flying to San Salvador, he enlisted the help of the Catholic Church, met with both government and guerrilla leaders, and negotiated a series of 'days of tranquillity' – suspending the war for three days every year so that the nation's children could be immunized.

UNICEF provided most of the vaccines. Meanwhile the World Health Organization (WHO), other UN agencies and national health services were working to translate high-level political commitments into action on the ground. WHO, in particular, trained thousands of immunization managers and advised on every aspect of immunization programmes from quality control to cold-chain technologies and the use of improved syringes, needles and sterilizing equipment. In many countries, non-governmental organizations also took up the cause: Rotary International, for example, raised over three hundred million dollars and mobilized its membership in more than one hundred countries in support of the immunization effort.

Endgame

Few believed that the intensity of all this could be sustained over a decade. Yet, as the immunization numbers began to climb in country after country, Grant used news of the progress being made to add to the momentum. As the forty per cent mark was passed, more governments and organizations were persuaded to believe that the eighty-per-cent target could be achieved.

By the end of the 1980s, when it was clear that the eighty per cent target was going to be reached in the great majority of countries, Grant proposed a World Summit for Children, bringing together the world's Heads of Government to consider what more could done. His aim was to set new targets for the deployment of other low-cost methods for saving the lives and protecting the normal health and growth of millions of the world's poorest children. And, by the time the World Summit convened in September 1990, he was able to confirm that the eighty per cent immunization target had indeed been achieved in almost all countries and to use this announcement to give credibility to new targets being set for the mid-1990s.

But as the new decade got under way, Grant himself was diagnosed with cancer. Operations, radiotherapy and chemotherapy followed. Yet in his last year of life, though visibly failing, he travelled tens of thousands of miles and held face-to-face meetings with over forty presidents and prime ministers, urging them to commit to the new targets for protecting their nations' children. By 1995, many of those targets had also been achieved.

Each and every child

James Grant died in a small hospital in upstate New York towards the end of February 1995. Around him were letters and cards from almost every country in the world, including many from the political leaders he had pushed so hard and for so long.

A card from President Clinton read: '*I am writing to thank you from the bottom of my heart for your service to America, to UNICEF, and most of all to the children of the world.*' Chinese Premier Li Peng wrote that Grant's death '*was an irretrievable loss to the children of the world*'. Nelson Mandela commented that '*his death is a great loss to each and every needy child in this world*'. Former President Carter said that his nomination of Jim Grant to head UNICEF was '*one of the greatest and most lasting achievements of my Presidency*'. And the *New York Times* mourned the passing of '*one of the great Americans of this century*'.

The 'real story' continues to inspire. '*Jim Grant's achievement,*' said Microsoft founder Bill Gates in committing the Gates Foundation to the eradication of polio, '*is the greatest miracle of saving children's lives ever*'.

The progress that Grant inspired in his sixteen years as head of UNICEF went beyond the expansion of immunization coverage. Other low-cost, life- and health-saving interventions, from oral rehydration salts to Vitamin A and iron supplements, were subjected to the same 'going to scale' treatment. Over and above the successes in reaching individual targets, the whole notion of promoting progress by means of measurable, internationally agreed goals was rescued from disrepute, contributing directly to the setting of the Millennium Development Goals that guided the international development effort into the twenty-first century. And behind all of the achievements of the Jim Grant years was the message that he had repeated endlessly to world leaders throughout his tenure as head of UNICEF – '*morality must march with capacity*'.

The Kennedy Moment is dedicated to the memory of James P Grant, with whom I had the privilege of working for his sixteen years as Executive Director of UNICEF. The full story of Jim Grant and the child-survival revolution is told in Adam Fifield's magnificent 2015 biography – *A Mighty Purpose: How UNICEF's James P Grant Sold the World on Saving Its Children* (Other Press, New York, 2015).

Peter Adamson

ENDNOTES

2 | I would know her by heart

30   *yard of ale* A trumpet-shaped beer glass, about a yard long
       (0.9 metres) with a closed bulb at one end and a wide opening
       at the other. The 'yard' contains about two and a half pints
       (1.4 litres) of beer. The future Prime Minister of Australia, Bob
       Hawke (who, like the future US President Bill Clinton, was a
       Rhodes Scholar at Oxford), broke the then record by drinking
       his yard of ale in approximately eleven seconds. Hawke later
       admitted that this feat had probably done more to advance his
       political career than any speech he ever made.

3 | Life and times

35   *two years at the International Centre for Diarrhoeal Disease
       Research in Bangladesh* The ICDDRB played a major
       role in the discovery and development of oral rehydration
       therapy (ORT) for the treatment of diarrhoea and cholera (see
       Postscript).

37   *Wasn't there a rumour about Jefferson* In 1980, the allegation
       of a long-term sexual relationship between Thomas Jefferson
       and Sarah ('Sally') Hemings, one of his slaves at Monticello,
       was still unproven. In 1998 DNA tests established beyond
       reasonable doubt that Thomas Jefferson was the father of all six
       of Sally Hemings' children.

5 | Not really cricket

49   *It's been rumoured the North Koreans might have hung on to
       it, and maybe even the French, the Iraqis, the Israelis* This
       was certainly the suspicion of Lev Sandakhchiev, long-time
       Director of Vector, the Soviet Union's State Research Center
       of Virology and Biotechnology in Koltsovo, Siberia. In the
       1970s and 1980s, Vector carried out secret research leading to
       the development of biological weapons. When the programme
       was later dismantled, in the late 1980s, Sandakhchiev helped to
       engineer the peaceful transformation of the Soviet germ-warfare
       programme.

6 | Next year in New York

53   *Just heard he might be going to the New School* The New
       School for Social Research was founded in Greenwich Village,
       New York, in 1919 by a group of university professors whose

vision was of a modern, progressive, free school where adult students could 'seek an unbiased understanding of the existing order, its genesis, growth and present working'. In 1933, it established the University in Exile as a graduate school for scholars fleeing fascism in Italy and Germany. Today's Graduate Faculty remains a home for left-leaning American political analysis.

55   *not even basic EOC*   Emergency Obstetric Care, the availability of which is the key to steep and sustained reductions in maternal death rates.

56   *follow-up to Alma Ata*   Alma Ata, in the former USSR (now Almaty, Kazakhstan), hosted the first International Conference on Primary Health Care (PHC) in September 1978.

10 | *Filer à l'anglaise*

88   *Les amis*   In French-speaking West Africa, '*les amis*' was used as compound slang for 'friends' and 'Americans'.

11 | Can we take a walk?

97   *interview with Shriver*   Sargent Shriver, brother-in-law of President John F Kennedy, was the first Director of the US Peace Corps.

97   *Some very odd PCP clusters*   Pneumocystis pneumonia, a severe infection of one or both lungs, is most often seen in people who have a very weak immune system and is a common opportunistic infection for people living with HIV/AIDS.

98   *Not even going to be in the MMWR*   The *Morbidity and Mortality Weekly Report* has been published by the US Centers for Disease Control since 1952 and is the official source of US public-health information, including current recommendations.

99   *a 'Welcome Home' banner across the street*   On January 20th, 1981, fifty two US hostages were released from Iran after 444 days in captivity. Five days later, they arrived home aboard 'Freedom One.'

99   *AMRIID will for sure have the final say*   The U.S. Army Medical Research Institute of Infectious Diseases is based at Fort Detrick, Maryland and was responsible for U.S. bio-weapons research.

13 | Flies on a summer day

110 *Billy's Bar on First Avenue at 52nd Street*   Long an East Side institution, Billy's Bar closed its doors in 2004 after a hundred and thirty years of serving Manhattanites. Located on First Avenue at 52nd Street, a cause of its demise was the 'social depression' that hit many New York businesses in the months following the September 2001 attack on the twin towers of the World Trade Center.

15 | Forget it ever happened

128 *The FBI break-in*   On March 8th, 1971, while much of America was preoccupied by the 'fight of the century' between Muhammad Ali and Joe Frazier in Madison Square Garden, two members of a citizen-activist group broke into an FBI office in a suburb of Philadelphia. The documents stolen revealed an extensive FBI 'dirty tricks' programme of illegal surveillance, entrapment and intimidation directed towards dissident groups, civil-rights activists and anti-war protesters. Copies were mailed anonymously to several newspapers, leading to the setting up of the Church Committee and the eventual reining in of the FBI. The burglars were never traced despite the deployment of more than two hundred agents by FBI Director J Edgar Hoover. The hunt lasted five years before finally being called off in March 1976. More than forty years later, in January 2014, the burglars revealed themselves in an interview for a book by Betty Medsger, a *Washington Post* reporter who had been one of the first to receive copies of the stolen papers. One of the conspirators, John Raines, is quoted as saying 'It looks like we're terribly reckless people. But there was absolutely no one in Washington – senators, congressmen, even the President – who dared hold J Edgar Hoover to accountability.' After the break-in, the eight seldom communicated with each other and never met again as a group.

132 *the Jacqueline Kennedy-Onassis Reservoir*   The Central Park Reservoir was renamed the Jacqueline Kennedy-Onassis Reservoir in 1994 in recognition of the former First Lady's contributions to the city. Jacqueline Kennedy-Onassis could often be seen jogging the Bridle Path around the lake.

19 | For the rest of our lives

159 *Drink ORS like Toby drinks Scotch* Oral Rehydration Salts is the term used for an inexpensive mixture of salts and sugar that, dissolved in water, can prevent the dehydration caused by diarrhoeal disease. In the early 1980s, diarrhoeal dehydration was responsible for approximately five million child deaths a year. ORS, along with immunization, was a key component of the child survival revolution inspired by UNICEF Executive Director James P Grant in the 1980s and early 1990s (see Postscript).

24 | The sender of this letter

184 *pull-out list of random numbers* A means of selecting a random sample of a given population is a critical tool in epidemiology. Various methods have been improvised in the field. For example, spinning a bottle in the centre of a village or neighbourhood is a way of deciding on a random direction for survey workers. Following this line (tossing a coin should a crossroads be encountered), households must then also be chosen at random – perhaps by using the serial numbers from a banknote. Whatever the method, the golden rule is that every household in the community being surveyed must have an equal chance of being selected.

25 | The presence in the shadows

188 *UNICEF's headquarters in the old ALCOA building* The former New York offices of the Aluminum Company of America.

26 | Let's do it

196 *crowded with Amtrak commuters* Amtrak carried its New York passengers in and out of Grand Central Terminal until the late 1980s when it switched operations to Penn Station.

29 | Take this cup from me

208 *HEPA filters* High Efficiency Particulate Air filters used to help ensure the safe recirculation of air.

30 | The girl next door

213 *can-do generation of global public-health pioneers that has become legendary* A group of international public-health

pioneers who made an enormous contribution to global health in the 1970s and 1980s. Their characteristic 'can-do' attitude was commented on by former US Surgeon-General Julius B Richmond who said, for example, that 'the reason the global smallpox eradication programme worked at all, at a time when not even WHO fully believed in it, was that the people involved were "too young to know that it couldn't work".' Another example of the 'can-do' mentality of those times is the effort mounted by the much-maligned bureaucrats of the Indian Civil Service who in 1974 organized a smallpox search that reached into every house in India (over a hundred million homes) in the space of just six days and succeeded in repeating this feat every three months.

31 | That can't happen

220 *We'll need a HazMat team* Abbreviation of Hazardous Materials, commonly used by emergency services.

221 *misdiagnosed as chickenpox or EM* Erythema Multiforme, a skin condition producing lesions.

223 *We don't have enough vaccine* Until 2001, US reserves of smallpox vaccine totalled no more than fifteen million shots. In November 2001, the US Department of Health and Human Services contracted biotech firm Acambis to bring the stockpile up to two hundred and eighty-six million doses.

32 | Ours not to reason why

231 *We'll need to get someone from Detrick to take a look at it and maybe someone from NIH* Fort Detrick, Maryland, is the home of the US Army Medical Research Institute of Infectious Diseases (AMRIID). NIH is the US National Institutes of Health, based in Bethesda, Maryland.

34 | To satisfy our masters

235 *a DVE under an electron microscope* Direct Viral Examination.

35 | Common ground

241 *Onesimus* Onesimus was a slave owned by the New England Puritan preacher Cotton Mather. He eventually bought his freedom and earned a living of sorts sweeping the streets of Boston. His name may be translated as 'useful'.

242 *Thomas Jefferson's letters to Jenner*   In 1806, President Thomas Jefferson wrote Edward Jenner, 'Future nations will know by history only that the loathsome smallpox has existed and by you has been extirpated.'

36 | It's Harvey

243 *It's Harvey*   Harvey is the name that was given to the strain of variola major, originally from India, that was first isolated by Professor Allan Downie of Liverpool University in the United Kingdom. It was distributed by the World Health Organization to registered smallpox research centres around the world so that all collaborating research laboratories could work on the same reference material. 'Harvey' was also the strain of variola major that escaped from the Birmingham Medical School laboratory in 1978, leading to the death of Janet Parker, a medical photographer in the same building.

243 *CAM results*   Chorio-allantoic membranes from developing chicken eggs are used to culture viruses.

246 *certify destruction of stocks*   World Health Assembly resolution 29.54 (1976) requested all institutions no longer involved in smallpox research to destroy any remaining stocks of variola.

246 *came in from California about a year ago*   In 1979, health officials in California found twelve unrecorded vials which turned out to contain smallpox virus. This led to all laboratories being asked to conduct new checks. In July 2014, six more glass vials of smallpox virus were found in an unlocked storeroom on the campus of the National Institutes for Health in Bethesda, Maryland.

40 | The words he knew by heart

275 *mutually verified destruction of stocks*   The Biological Weapons Convention of 1972 agreed on the destruction of any existing biological weapons and cessation of further research. Through the 1970s and 1980s, suspicions grew that the Soviet Union was continuing research into the weaponizing of smallpox and other pathogens. Following the collapse of the Soviet Union in 1990/91, a series of defectors confirmed the existence of Biopreparat, a large-scale programme for the development of biological weapons with smallpox as a top priority. One such defector, former Biopreparat chief scientist Dr Kanatjan

Alibekov, revealed that the Soviet Vector programme, based in Koltsovo, Western Siberia, had been attempting to produce weaponized liquid smallpox in quantities of between fifty and one hundred tons a year. Vector had also been attempting to develop a more lethal and more easily transmissible version of smallpox by combining it with a haemorrhagic virus. Kanatjan Alibekov became Ken Alibek after his defection to the United States in 1992.

41 | The cards face up

282 *Universal Childhood Immunization* One hundred per cent immunization is rarely achievable, and the term 'universal immunization' is used by the World Health Organization to indicate a coverage level of eighty per cent of children under the age of one – the level at which 'herd immunity' offers a significant level of protection even to unimmunized children.

43 | A little bit of your heart

299 *a group of citizens decided to employ distinctly illegal means* See first note on Chapter 15.

44 | Competing with James Dean

309 *that underarm delivery at the MCG* On February 1st, 1981, at the end of a One Day International between Australia and New Zealand at the Melbourne Cricket Ground, the Australian captain Greg Chappell instructed his brother, Trevor, to bowl the last ball of the game underarm, rolling it down the pitch to the batsman. This ensured victory by preventing a six being struck (because the ball could not be hit over the boundary without touching the ground). Though technically not illegal, bowling underarm is considered a violation of the spirit of cricket and the incident has since lived in infamy among lovers of the game.

Epilogue

348 *in response to an actual rather than a theoretical threat* In March 1988 a role-playing exercise conducted in California found that senior officials in the Clinton administration would almost certainly not be capable of an adequate response to a sophisticated smallpox attack.

Acknowledgements

The Kennedy Moment is dedicated to the memory of UNICEF Executive Director James P Grant, who led the campaign to immunize the vast majority of the world's children in the 1980s and 1990s (*see* Postscript: The real story).

This book also owes a very special debt to two other great names in the field of international public health – Dr Stephen Joseph and Dr Jon Rohde. Steve Joseph's encouragement and expertise have been invaluable throughout, and I have also drawn freely on his brilliant memoir *River of Stone, River of Sand: A Story of Medicine and Adventure* (available on Amazon Kindle). Jon Rohde, who first proposed a 'child survival revolution' and convinced Jim Grant that it was possible, has also been an inspirational collaborator in this as in many other ventures.

I would also like to thank my editor, Chris Brazier of New Internationalist Publications, and Candida Lacey, Linda McQueen and all at Myriad Editions for the professionalism, talent and enthusiasm they have brought to publishing *The Kennedy Moment* – and for being a pleasure to work with.

As always, no thanks are enough for my partner Lesley Adamson who has been colleague, enthusiast, critic and tolerator-in-chief of all that goes into writing a novel. My children, Naomi and Daniel, have also given the unstinting praise and encouragement I have always demanded of them. Naomi's suggested title for the book – *Say it with smallpox* – did not make the final cut.

Many former UNICEF colleagues have also contributed, knowingly or not, but I would especially like to thank two outstanding servants of that organization – Mehr Khan and John Williams – not only for their help and encouragement with *The Kennedy Moment* but also for their support and friendship with almost everything else I have undertaken in my career.

Adam Fifield's advice and support has also been very much appreciated and I would again like to recommend his exceptional biography of James P Grant – *A Mighty Purpose: How UNICEF's James P Grant Sold the World on Saving Its Children* (Other Press, New York, October 2015).

Special thanks are also due to the group of writers and friends in Oxford who share comments on each other's work-in-progress: John Marzillier, Anne MacFarlane, Jenny Stanton and Gabrielle Townsend. For their suggestions and encouragement I would also like to thank Tariq Ali, Peter Cotton, Alastair Hay, Rafe Henderson, Tony Hewett, Gareth Jones, Eve Leckey, Richard Lee, Sandy Loffler, Neil MacFarlane, Sarah Metcalf and Jean Wood.